KRISTAN HIGGINS

the
perfect match

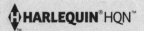

HARLEQUIN® HQN™

Recycling programs
for this product may
not exist in your area.

ISBN-13: 978-0-373-77819-5

THE PERFECT MATCH

Copyright © 2013 by Kristan Higgins

Printed in U.S.A.

This book is dedicated to Maria Carvainis,
my wonderful friend and agent.
Thank you from the bottom of my heart, Madame.

PROLOGUE

THE DAY Honor Grace Holland turned thirty-five, she did what she always did on her birthday.

She got a Pap smear.

Sure, sure, Honor was aware that gynecology was pretty low on the totem pole of celebrations. It was just easier to schedule the dreaded appointment if it was on a memorable date. Practical, that was all, and she was nothing if not practical. Faith and Prudence, her sisters, and Dana Hoffman, her closest friend, had planned to take her out, but there'd been a snowstorm last weekend, and they'd had to cancel. The family would gather this weekend for cake, so it wasn't like the Pap smear was the only celebration she'd be having.

She assumed the position on the exam table while her doctor kindly averted his eyes, and practiced the deep breathing the irritatingly flexible yoga instructor had demonstrated with such vigor until she and Dana had giggled like two little kids in church. Didn't work then, didn't work now. She stared at the Jackson Pollock print on the ceiling and tried to think happy thoughts. She really needed to update the website. Design a label for the new pinot gris Blue Heron Vineyard was launching. Check the month's orders.

It occurred to her that work should not be her happy thoughts. She tried to think of something not work-related. She had some Lindt truffles at home. That was good.

"So how are things, Honor?" Jeremy asked from between her legs.

"Working a lot. You know me." And he did. Jeremy Lyon was an old family friend as well as her sister's ex-fiancé. He was also gay, which didn't seem to make his palpation of her ovaries any less yucky.

Jeremy snapped off his gloves and smiled. "All done," he said.

Honor sat up fast, despite the fact that Jeremy was terribly nice and had famously gentle hands. The good doctor handed her a prewarmed blanket—he was thoughtful that way. He never made eye contact during the breast exam, and the speculum was always placed on a heating pad. Small wonder half the women in Manningsport were in love with him, no matter that he liked men.

"How's Patrick?" she asked, crossing her arms.

"He's great," Jeremy said. "Thanks for asking. Speaking of that, are you seeing anyone, Honor?"

The question made her blush, not just because Jeremy's famous hands had been Down Under, but also because…well. She was private. "Why do you ask?" Did he want to fix her up? Should she say yes? Maybe she should. Brogan was never—

"Just need to ask a few questions about your, um, certain personal aspects of your life."

Honor smiled. Jeremy, despite being a doctor, was still the cute boy who'd dated Faith all through college, and couldn't quite forget that Honor was a few years older. "If it's covered by HIPPA, then the answer is—" Yes, indeed, what *was* the answer? "The answer is yes. Sort of. And if you tell anyone in my family, I will kill you."

"No, no, of course not," he said, smiling back at her. "But I'm glad to hear it. Because, um…"

She sat up a little straighter. "Because why, Jer?"

He gave a half smile, half grimace. "It's just…you're thirty-five now."

"Yes, I know. What does that have to do with—oh." Her stomach sank abruptly, as if she was in a fast-moving elevator.

"Nothing to worry about, of course," he said, blushing again. "But the years are precious. Egg-wise."

"What? What are you talking about?" She pulled her hairband out and shoved it back on her head. Nervous habit. "Is there a problem?"

"No, no. It's just that thirty-five is considered advanced maternal age."

She frowned, then tried to stop. The mirror had shown a permanent line between her eyebrows just this morning (damn you, natural light!). She'd have sworn it wasn't there last week. "Really? Already?"

"Right." Jeremy winced. "I'm sorry. It's just the quality of your eggs starts to decline about now. Medically speaking, the best time to have a kid is around twenty-two, twenty-four. That's the sweet spot."

"Twenty-four?" That was more than a *decade* earlier. All of a sudden, Honor felt ancient. She had a wrinkle between her eyes, and her eggs were aging! She shifted on the examination table. Her hip creaked. God, she *was* ancient! "Should I be worried?"

"Oh, no! No. But it might be time to think about these things." Jeremy paused. "What I mean is, I'm sure it won't be an issue. But yes, the chances of birth defects and infertility do start to increase about now. They're still small, and infertility treatments are amazing these days. This doctor in New Hampshire just had success with a fifty-four-year-old woman—"

"I'm not planning to have a baby in my fifties, Jer!"

Jeremy took her limp hand and patted it. "I'm sure it won't come to that. I'm required to tell you as your doctor, that's all. Same as telling you to eat right. Your BP is just a tiny bit high, but that's probably white-coat anxiety."

She wasn't anxious. At least, she hadn't been when she'd first come in. *Fungus.* So now she had high blood pressure, in addition to leathery skin and hardening ovaries.

"You look fantastic," Jeremy went on, "so there's probably no cause for worry—" *Probably?* It was never good when a doctor said *probably!* "—but if you're seeing someone, it might be time to start thinking about the future. I mean, not that you need a man. There's a really good sperm bank—"

She yanked her hand back. "Okay, Jeremy, you can stop now."

He smiled. "Sorry."

Another attempt at a calming breath. "So think about babies sooner rather than later, is that what you're saying?"

"Exactly," Jeremy said. "And I'm sure you don't have anything to worry about."

"Except birth defects and infertility."

"Right." He smiled. "Any questions for me?"

SHE CALLED DANA from Jeremy's parking lot, safe within the womb of her Prius. Small wonder that everything was taking on obstetrical overtones.

"House of Hair," Dana answered, which made Honor mentally flinch every time.

"It's me," she said.

"Thank God. I just got done giving Phyllis Nebbins her monthly perm and blue rinse and I was this close to screaming. Like, do I really want to hear about her new hip? Anyway, what's up?"

"I just got out of Jeremy's. I'm old and need to have babies, quick."

"Do you?" Dana said. "I don't know if I can stand losing another friend to motherhood. All those stories of screaming and colic and precious, precious angels."

Honor laughed. Dana didn't want children—she said it was the main cause of her divorce—and often called to describe the brattiest behavior she saw at House of Hair in curdling detail.

But Honor loved kids. Even teenagers. Well, she loved her seventeen-year-old niece, Abby, and she loved her nephew, Ned, who still had the mental age of fourteen, even though he was twenty-two now.

"Other than that, what's up?" Dana asked. "Wanna go out tonight, grab a few drinks in honor of you being an old hag?"

Honor was quiet for a minute. Her heart started thudding. "I'm thinking that, given the news, maybe I should have a talk with Brogan."

"What talk?"

"*The* talk."

There was silence. "Really."

"Well…yeah."

Another pause. "Sure, I guess I can see your rationale. Aging ovaries, shriveling uterus."

"For the record, there was no mention of a shriveling uterus. But what do you think?"

"Um, yeah, go for it," Dana said with a decided lack of enthusiasm.

Honor adjusted her hairband. "You don't sound sure."

"Are *you* sure, Honor? I mean, if you're asking me, maybe you're not, even if you've been sleeping with the guy for the past however many years."

"Quietly, quietly, okay?" It's not like there were a dozen people named Honor in Manningsport, New York, population seven hundred and fifteen, and Dana and she had very different views on what could be talked about in public.

"Whatever. He's rich, he's gorgeous, you're hung up on him. Besides, you have everything already. Why not Brogan, too?"

There was a familiar edge to her voice. Honor knew her friend had a very rose-colored view of Honor's life, and yes, certain aspects of it were quite wonderful. But like everyone, Honor had her issues. Spinsterhood, for example. Aging eggs, for another.

Honor sighed, then saw her reflection in the mirror. There was that frown again. "I guess I'm just worried he'll say no," she admitted. "We've been friends for a long time. I wouldn't want to jeopardize that."

"Then don't ask."

The years are precious, egg-wise. She was going to have to talk to Jeremy about his delivery. Still, if there was a sign from God, it was probably those words. "Nothing ventured, nothing gained, I guess?" she suggested, hoping for some reinforcement.

Dana sighed, and Honor sensed her patience was coming to an end. Couldn't really blame her. "Honor, if you want to pop the question, do it. Just lay it on the line and he'll probably say, 'Hells yeah, I'll marry you! You're Honor Freakin' Holland!' And then you can go to Harts Jeweler's and pick out that rock you've been eyeing for the past year."

Okay. That was a nice thought. "Let's not get ahead of ourselves," she said. But yes. There was a ring in the window of the jewelry store on the green, and Honor had admitted—only to Dana—that if she ever *did* get engaged, that would be the ring she wanted. Just a simple, stunning, emerald-cut diamond set in platinum. Honor didn't think of herself as the type who loved jewelry (she only wore her mom's pearls) or clothes (gray or blue suits from Ann Taylor, tailored white shirt— sometimes pink, if she was feeling sentimental), but that ring *did* things to her.

"I gotta go," Dana said. "Laura Boothby's coming for a rinse. Rock his world, pop the question, see what he says. Or don't. Just don't be wishy-washy. Okay? Talk to you soon." She hung up.

Honor sat another minute. She could call one of her sisters, but…well, neither one knew about Brogan. They knew he and Honor were friends, of course, but they didn't know about the romantic part. The *sex* part. Prudence, the oldest of the Holland clan, would be all for it, having recently become a sex kitten as some weird byproduct of menopause or whatnot. But Pru didn't have much in the way of filters and tended to announce inappropriate things at family dinners or at O'Rourke's, the local pub.

Faith, the youngest of the three Holland sisters… maybe. She and Honor had always scrapped a little, though things had been better since Faith had moved back from San Francisco (the only Holland to live out of New York State in eight generations). She'd love the idea…she loved anything romantic, being a newlywed and kind of a mushy, emotional person in general.

And then there was Jack, their brother. But he was a guy and hated nothing more than hearing stories that confirmed the suspicion that his sisters were indeed female and, worse still, had sex lives.

So no sympathetic ear other than Dana's. That was fine. It was time to get back to work, anyway. She started the car and headed through town.

Manningsport was the jewel of the Finger Lakes region of western New York, a famed wine-making area. The winter months were the quiet time of year here— the holidays were over, and the tourist season wouldn't kick in until April. The grapevines had been pruned, and snow blanketed the fields. Keuka Lake glittered black in the distance, too deep to ice over completely.

Blue Heron Vineyard was the oldest farm around, and the sight of their sign—a gold-painted heron against a blue background—never failed to cause a surge of pride. Set at the top of the area known as the Hill, the Hollands' land encompassed more than two hundred acres of field and forest.

Honor drove past the Old House, a saltbox colonial built in 1781, where her grandparents (almost as old) lived and fought, past the New House (1873), a big white Federal where she lived with dear old Dad and Mrs. Johnson, the longtime housekeeper and supreme ruler of the Holland family, and pulled into the vineyard parking lot. The only other car here belonged to Ned. Pru, who handled the farming end of the vineyard, was either in one of the equipment storage barns or out in the fields;

Dad and Jack, and possibly Pops, would be checking the huge steel casks of wine or playing poker. Honor was the only one who came to work in the office every day, though Ned was part-time.

Which was fine. She liked being in charge of the business end of the vineyard. And besides, given Jeremy's little bombshell, she needed to think. She needed to make lists. She needed to color-code.

She needed a plan, given that the years were precious.

Into the main building she went, through the beautiful tasting room, past the gift shop and into the suite of offices. Ned's door was open, but he wasn't here. That was good; she did her best thinking when she was alone.

Sitting behind her large, tidy desk, Honor opened a new document on her computer.

Men were a field in which Honor didn't have a lot of…panache. She did business with dozens of men, as the wine industry was still heavily skewed toward males. If they were talking distribution or media coverage or crop projections, she had no problem.

But on the romantic front, she didn't really have the knack. Faith, who was built like Marilyn Monroe and had red hair and blue eyes and a slightly Bambi-esque, innocent air about her, practically caused a stampede just by getting out of her car. Pru, despite her lifelong tomboy ways and propensity for wearing men's clothing, had had no trouble getting married; Carl was her high school sweetheart. The two were still quite (if far too publicly) happy in their marriage. Even Dana, who was extremely picky when it came to men, always had some date lined up who would inevitably irritate her.

But Honor didn't have the touch. She knew she wasn't

bad-looking; average height, average figure, maybe a little on the unendowed side. Brown eyes. Her hair was long and straight and blond, her one great beauty, she thought. She had dimples, like her mom. Hers was a pleasant face. But all in all…average.

Unlike Brogan Cain, who was essentially a Greek god come to life. Turquoise-blue eyes (really). Curling chestnut hair. Six foot two, lean and strong and graceful.

He'd been her friend since fourth grade, when they were put into the Mathlete program, the only two chosen by their teacher. At the time, the other kids had made fun of them a little, the two class brains, but it had been nice, too.

All through school, they'd had an easy friendship. They sat together at assemblies, said hi to each other in the halls, maintained a friendly competition with grades. They went trick-or-treating together until they got too old; after that, they stayed at the New House and watched scary movies.

It was on prom night that things had changed. Brogan asked her to be his date, said they'd have more fun than the actual couples, who placed so much importance on the event. A sound plan. But when she saw him standing there in his tuxedo, corsage box in hand, something happened. From that moment on, she felt shaky and slightly ill, and she flushed when he looked at her.

At the high school, they danced amiably, and when the DJ played a slow song, Brogan looped his arms around her. Kissed her forehead and smiled and said, "This is fun, isn't it?"

And boom, she was in love.

And that love grew—like a virus, Honor sometimes thought. Because Brogan didn't feel the same way.

Oh, he *liked* her plenty. He even loved her, sort of. But not the same way Honor loved him…not that he knew how she felt. Honor wasn't that dumb.

The first time they'd slept together was when they were home on spring break their freshmen year of college, and Brogan suggested they lose their virginities together "because it'll be better with a friend than with someone you love." Sort of the prom theory, but with higher stakes.

Granted, she hadn't quite believed he was a virgin, and he *was* someone she loved, and if it was a line to get her into bed, she wasn't about to bring it up. The very fact that he wanted to sleep with her was somewhat miraculous, given that he could've chosen just about anyone. So they'd done the deed, and as losses of virginity went, it was pretty great. A few nights later, they'd gone to the movies, and it had been the same as always—friendly and fun, though a blade of uncertainty kept slicing through her. Were they together? *Together* together?

No, apparently not. He kissed her on the cheek when he dropped her off, emailed her when they both went back to their respective colleges.

The second time they slept together was their sophomore year, when she visited him at NYU. He hugged her and said how much he missed her, and she felt herself melting from the inside out. Pizza, a few beers, a walk around the city, back to his place, sex. She went home in a glow of love and hope…but the next time he called, it was just to catch up. No mention of love or even sex.

Four times in college. Twice in grad school. Definitely a friends-with-benefits situation…but the benefits only happened once in a while.

And the friend part stayed constant.

Once she started working at Blue Heron as the director of operations, she'd occasionally call him if she were going to be in Manhattan for a meeting...or a pretend meeting, as the case might be, though her conscience always cringed at the lie. "Hey, I have a late lunch in SoHo," she might say, her stomach twisting, helpless to just come clean and say, *Hi, Brogan, I miss you, I'm dying to see you.* "Want to meet for a drink or dinner?" And he was always more than happy to shift his schedule around if he could, meet her and, maybe, sleep with her. Or not.

Honor would lecture herself. Remind herself that he wasn't the only one out there. That if she was hung up on Brogan, she'd be closed off to other possibilities. But very few could compare to Brogan Cain, and it wasn't like they were standing in line for the privilege of a date with her.

He became a photographer with *Sports Illustrated,* basically the wet dream job of all American men who couldn't be professional athletes or Hugh Hefner. He was like that: incredibly lucky, übercharming, the kind of person who'd go out for a beer, comment on a baseball game to the guy next to him, strike up an easy friendship and only half an hour later realize he was talking to Steven Spielberg (who would then invite him to a party in L.A.). Sports photography with *SI?* Perfect.

Brogan met the mighty Jeter, photographed the Manning brothers, who had roots right here in Manningsport (or so the town liked to claim). He had drinks with Kobe Bryant and Picabo Street and went on the Harry Potter ride with the gold-medal gymnasts at Universal Studios.

But somehow, he was unaffected by it all, which was

probably why he could claim people like Tom Brady and David Beckham as friends. He flew all over the world, went to the Olympic Games, the Stanley Cup, the Super Bowl. He even invited her—just her, no other friends—to come to Yankee Stadium and sit in the *SI* box and watch the World Series with him.

And that was the thing. Brogan Cain was an *awfully* nice guy. He came home to visit his parents, hung out at O'Rourke's, bought the family house when his parents retired to Florida. He asked after her family, and if he blew her off the night of her grandparents' sixty-fifth anniversary party because he plumb forgot, well… those things happened.

Every time she saw him, she blushed. Every time he kissed her, she felt like she was floating. Every time his name popped up in her email or on her phone, her uterus quivered. And recently, he'd told her he was hoping to cut back on his travel, be around more.

Maybe the time really was right. Her eggs, his settling down…marriage might be just the thing.

Yes. She needed a list. She opened her Mac and started typing.

> Shock and awe to get him to see you in different light (think of something memorable).
> Make marriage seem like a logical step in the friendship.
> Do it soon so you don't chicken out.

THREE HOURS LATER, Honor got out of her car, tightened the sash on her beige raincoat, swallowed and went up the steps to Brogan's house. Her mouth was dry, her hands clammy. If this didn't work…

The years are precious, egg-wise.

Sigh.

No. Not sigh. Go, team! That was more like it. *We want company!* she imagined her tiny, aging eggs demanding. In her mind, they were starting to thicken around the middle, wore reading glasses and were developing an affinity for pinochle. *Don't age,* she warned them. *Mommy's got company coming.*

For one quick second, she let herself indulge in a mental picture of the future. The New House once again filled with children (or at least one or two). Kids who would romp through the fields and woods with her dad; they'd be able to tell a Riesling grape from a Chablis before they started kindergarten. Children who'd have Brogan's amazing eyes and her own blond hair. Or maybe Brogan's thick, curly chestnut hair. Yeah. His was better.

With that picture firmly in mind, she knocked on Brogan's door. The smell of garlic was thick in the air, and her stomach rumbled all of a sudden. On top of everything else, Brogan was a good cook.

"Hey, On!"

Okay, so he did have a flaw (see? no rose-colored glasses for her), and that was to shorten her five-letter, two-syllable name. She always pictured it spelled *On,* because *Hon* would've been short for *honey,* and he never called her that.

"This is a nice surprise!" he said, leaning forward to kiss her cheek. "Come on in."

She went in, heart thudding. Remembered to smile. "How are you?" she asked, her voice sounding tight to her own ears.

"I'm great! Let me just stir this so it doesn't burn. I hope you can stay for dinner." He turned to the stove.

Now or never. Honor untied her sash, closed her eyes and opened the coat, and let it slide to the floor. Oh, crap, she was standing in front of the table, so his view would be blocked. Stepping around it, she waited. Buck naked. *Shock and awe, shock and awe...* It was chilly in here. She swallowed and waited some more.

Brogan's father poked his head into the kitchen. "Smells good—oh. Hello, Honor, dear."

Brogan's father.

Brogan's *father*.

Oh, *fungus*.

Honor dove under the table, knocking over a chair with a crash, crawled a few paces and grappled for the damn coat. Held it in front of her. Noticed the floor could use cleaning.

"Dear? Are you all right?" Mr. Cain asked.

"Did you say Honor's here?" Mrs. Cain.

God, please kill me, Honor thought, jerking the coat around her shoulders. "Um, one second," she said, her voice higher than usual.

Brogan bent down, his face puzzled. "On? What are you doing under—oh, man!"

"Hi," she said, trying to get an arm in her sleeve.

"Dad, Mom, get out for a sec, okay?" He was already wheezing with laughter.

Where was the damn sleeve? Brogan squatted next to her. "Come on out," he managed, wiping his eyes. "You're safe for the moment."

She crawled out, then stood, wrapping the coat around her. Tightly. "Surprise," she said, her face on fire. "Sorry. I'll try never to be spontaneous again."

He tipped her chin up, and there it was, that mischievous, slightly lecherous smile, dancing eyes. Her skin tightened, lust mingling with mortification. "Are you kidding? My father will like you even more than he already does."

The words gave her hope. Honor smiled—it wasn't too easy, but she did—and readjusted her hairband. Dang, she'd meant to leave that at home. Hairbands with a Scotty dog pattern and nudity didn't really go together. "So. Hello."

He laughed and gave her a one-armed hug, then turned toward the living room. "It's safe to come back, parents!" he called.

And back they came, Mrs. Cain's face in lines of disapproval, Mr. Cain grinning.

Bite the bullet, Honor. "Sorry about that," she said.

"Absolutely no need to apologize," Mr. Cain said, his breath leaving in an *ooph* as Mrs. Cain elbowed him in the ribs.

"My parents are visiting," Brogan said, his eyes dancing with laughter.

"So I see," Honor murmured. "How's Florida?"

"It's wonderful," Mr. Cain said warmly. "Stay for dinner, dear."

"Oh, no. You… I can't. But thanks."

Brogan gave her another squeeze. "Yes, you can. Just because they saw you naked is no reason to feel awkward. Right, Mom?"

"Laugh it up," Honor muttered.

Mrs. Cain was still in lemon-sucking mode. "I didn't realize you two were…together." She never had liked Honor. Or any female interested in her son, one imagined.

"Please stay, Honor," Brogan said. "We'll just talk about you if you leave." He winked, utterly unfazed by her little show.

He got her a pair of sweats and a T-shirt, and she changed in the downstairs bathroom, avoiding looking at her face in the mirror. Okay, one quick glance. Yes, she looked utterly humiliated. But if she was going to be his wife, she'd just have to get over this little debacle. It would become part of the Cain family lore. They could laugh at it. A lot, no doubt.

Brogan covered the awkwardness over dinner with shop talk, telling them about the upcoming baseball season and spring training, who was out with what injury, and Honor tried to forget that Mr. Cain had seen her naked.

The elder Cains were only here en route to Buffalo to see Mr. Cain's sister, thankfully. Maybe the night wouldn't be a total wash, after all.

Finally, they left. The second their car pulled out of the garage, Brogan turned to her.

"That was maybe the best moment of my life," he said.

"Yes. You're welcome," she said, blushing again. But smiling, too, because there it was, that nervous, tingling feeling. The—she hated to think it, but it was true—gratitude. Brogan Cain, the hottie sports photographer, had just complimented her.

"So let's pretend the night is just starting, shall we?" he said, pulling back to smile at her. "You go outside, I hear a faint knock, and who is it but the beautiful Honor Holland!" He led her to the door and gently pushed her outside, though the rain had turned to sleet.

And so Honor did it again, and this time, things went

a little more according to plan. Except the kitchen table was covered in dishes, so they went to Brogan's bedroom instead.

And when they were done, and when Honor's heart was racing, not just from exertion, but from terror, let's be honest, she tried to draw in a calming breath. *Settle down,* she told herself. *He's your friend.*

Yes. He was. Honor raised herself slowly—Brogan seemed to be sleeping. That was okay. This way, she could just look at him. He was *so* handsome. Black lashes worthy of a mascara commercial, straight nose, perfectly shaped mouth. A hint of five-o'clock shadow gave his almost-beautiful face just the right amount of machismo. Hard to believe she was in bed with him, even after all these…encounters.

She knew he'd had a few girlfriends here and there. During those times, they didn't sleep together, of course, and Honor would try to be neutral on the rare occasions that Brogan did talk about these other women. Inevitably, he'd break up with them (which was a great sign, she thought).

As for other men, well…there'd been four other relationships, lasting between five and twenty-three days. She'd only ever slept with one other guy, and let's face it. It hadn't compared with this.

Now or never, Honor.

"You asleep?" she whispered.

"Nope. Just letting you ogle me," he said, opening his eyes with a grin.

She smiled back. "And I appreciate it." She licked her lips, knees tingling with adrenaline. "So."

"So." He reached up and tucked a piece of hair behind her ear. It was all the encouragement she needed.

"You know what I thought the other day?" she asked. Her toes curled, but she kept her voice casual.

"What?"

"I was thinking we should get married."

There. She said it. Suddenly, it was hard to breathe normally.

"Yeah, right." Brogan snorted. He stretched, yawning. "Man, that flight is catching up with me." Then he looked back at her. "Oh. Uh, are you serious?"

Play it easy here, her brain advised. "Well, yeah. I mean, it's a thought."

He stared at her, then his eyebrows jumped in bewilderment. "Really?"

His voice did not indicate that he'd just heard a wonderful idea. It indicated…bafflement.

"It's just, you know, we're good friends. Good, good friends. Really good friends." *Oh, youch. Stop talking. You sound like an idiot.* "You know, we've been friends for ages now. Long time." Her tongue felt like a piece of old leather, and wasn't that an attractive image! *Would you like to kiss my shriveled, dry, leathery mouth, Brogan? Because the years are precious, you know. Eggwise.*

She forced out an awkward laugh, then wished she hadn't. "Just putting that out there. It's been, what? Seventeen years that we've been together?"

"Together?" he said, sitting up abruptly.

"Uh, sort of. We always, um, fall back on each other." She sat up, too, leaning against the leather-upholstered headboard. Tears stung her eyes, and she immediately ordered them back. She cleared her throat. "I mean, we're such good friends. And then there's this. Sex."

"Yeah! Right. No, we're great friends. Definitely. I

think of you as my best friend, really. But, um…" Brogan took a deep breath. "I never really saw us as *together* per se." He swallowed and, to his credit, looked at her.

Calm, calm. "No, you're right. I just thought, we're getting to a certain age, and you said you were cutting back on traveling." She paused. "And neither one of us has ever found someone…permanent. Maybe that says something."

Please say you agree. Please realize what a great idea this is.

He didn't answer, but his eyes were kind. Horribly so, and that was answer enough. Her heart stuttered, then shriveled like burned paper. To avoid looking at him, she traced the stitching in the comforter. Now that the initial rejection was done, she could keep it together. She was a rational, calm person. Except she might be having a heart attack. She kind of hoped she was.

Brogan was quiet for a minute. "You know how I think about you, On?" He turned to see her face. "I think of you like an old baseball glove."

She blinked. Was he kidding? A *sports* analogy? Granted, he was full of them, but now?

He nodded. "Like an old friend, something you turn to when you need it."

"A baseball glove." Could she smother him with the pillow, maybe, or did that only work in the movies? How about panty hose strangulation? Too bad she hadn't worn any.

He took her hand and squeezed it, and she let it lie there like a dead fish. "It's like Jeter once said. Or maybe it was Pujols. Yeah, because this was back when he played in Saint Louis. Wait, was it Joe Maurer? No, because he's a catcher, so that'd be a mitt. Anyway, whoever it was, he was talking about how when he's in a slump, or when he doesn't feel right about an upcoming game, he puts on his old glove. He's had it for years, right? And when he puts it on, it's like an old friend, and he knows he'll have a better day because of it." He turned to her, tipping her chin up, and she blinked, her eyes feeling like two hot, hard stones. "But you don't need that glove every day."

Surely this was the worst breakup speech in history.

He winced. "Okay, that was the worst comparison ever," he said, and she had to laugh then, because it was that or burst into tears. "What I'm trying to say, On, is—"

"You know what?" she said, and her voice was normal, thank you, God. "Forget it. I don't know where the idea came from. Maybe it was because your parents saw me naked."

He grinned.

"But you're right," she said more firmly. "Why ruin a good thing?"

"Exactly," he said. "Because we are a good thing. Don't you think?"

"Absolutely. No, no, getting married was just…just a thought. Never mind."

He kissed her then, and it nearly tore her heart in half. An old baseball glove? Holy *fungus*. Yet her head was cupped between his hands, and she was letting him kiss her, like nothing had changed at all.

"Feel up for round two?" he whispered.

Are you kidding? You just compared me to an old baseball glove. I'm leaving.

"Sure," she said. Because nothing *had* changed. She was the same old glove she'd always been.

If she left, he might realize she'd been dead serious, and if he knew that, then she wouldn't have any pride left. And since her heart had just been poleaxed, pride was suddenly very important.

SHE APPEARED AT Dana's door an hour later, and the second she knocked, tears made a rare appearance, sliding down her face in hot streaks.

Dana opened the door, took one look and blinked. An odd expression—half surprise, half something else—came over her face. "Well, I guess I can see how that turned out," she said after a beat. "I'm sorry, babe."

She got a clean pair of pajamas, and Honor changed, then washed her face in the sloppy, comforting bathroom.

"At least you know where you stand," Dana said, leaning against the doorway. "I think drinks are called for, don't you?"

She made very strong martinis and handed Honor a box of Kleenex. *Shark Week,* a shared passion of theirs, played in the background. Somehow, it was the perfect backdrop to spill everything.

"I feel like such an ass," Honor said when she'd finished recounting the wretched evening. "And the thing is, I didn't know how much I loved him till it was out there, you know? Does that make sense?"

"Sure, sure it does." Dana drained her drink. "Listen, I hate to be insensitive here, but tell me the part about the parents one more time, okay?" she said with a wicked grin, and Honor snorted and complied, making Dana swear she'd never tell anyone, because as a hairdresser, Dana saw everyone, and knew everyone's business, and was pretty liberal with sharing it.

"Comparing your vajay-jay to an old baseball glove… that's going a little far, isn't it?"

"It wasn't my… Never mind. Let's talk about something else. Oh, look at that guy's stitches. I'm never swimming again." She sat back, leaning against her raincoat. Stupid raincoat. Where was the shock and awe now, huh? Wadding it up, she tossed it on the floor.

"Hey, it's not the coat's fault. And that's Burberry," Dana said, retrieving it. "But no, I see your point. You hate it now, so I'm going to make the ultimate sacrifice and take it from you. I promise never to wear it in your presence." She opened a closet, shoved the coat in and slammed the door.

Dana could be prickly, but she certainly had her moments. "So what now?" she asked as the guy on TV described what it was like to see his severed arm in a great white shark's teeth.

Honor swallowed the sharp lump in her throat. "I don't know. But I guess I can't sleep with him anymore. I have a little pride, glove or no glove."

"Good. It's high time," Dana said. "Now sit there and watch this next attack, and I'll make us another round."

CHAPTER ONE

FOR A GUY who taught mechanical engineering at a fourth-rate college in the middle of nowhere, Tom Barlow was packing them in.

At the university where he'd last taught, there'd been an actual engineering school, and his students were genuinely interested in the subject matter. Here, though, at tiny Wickham College, four of the original six attendees had stumbled into class, having left registration until too late, only taking mechanical engineering because it still had open slots. Two had seemed genuinely interested, until one, the girl, transferred to Carnegie Mellon.

But then, by the end of the second week, he suddenly had thirty-six students jammed into the little classroom. Each one of these new students was female, ranging in age from eighteen to possibly fifty-five. Suddenly, an astonishing array of girls and women had decided that mechanical engineering (whatever that was) had become their new passion in life.

The clothes were a bit of a problem. Tight, trashy, low-cut, low-riding, inappropriate. Tom tended to teach to the wall in the back of the room, not wanting to make eye contact with the hungry gazes of seventy-eight percent of his class.

He tried not to leave time for questions, as the Barbarian Horde, as he thought of them, tended to be inappropriate. *Are you single? How old are you? Where'd you come from? Do you like foreign films/sushi/girls?*

Then again, he needed this job. "Any questions?" he asked. Dozens of hands shot up. "Yes, Mr. Kearns," he said gratefully to the one student in the class who was there out of interest in the subject.

According to his file, Jacob Kearns had been kicked out of MIT for doing drugs. He seemed on the straight and narrow now, at least, but Wickham College was a hundred steps down academically. Then again, Tom knew all about shooting himself in the foot, career-wise.

"Dr. Barlow, with the hovercraft project, I was wondering how you'd calculate the escape velocity?"

"Good question. The escape velocity is the speed at which the kinetic energy of your object, along with its gravitational potential energy, is zero. Make sense?" The Barbarian Horde (those who were listening) looked confused.

"Definitely," Jacob said. "Thanks."

Thirty seconds to the bell. "Listen up," he said. "Your homework is to read chapters six and seven in your texts and answer all the study questions at the end of both as well as pass in your term project proposals. Those of you who flunked the hovercraft estimates have to do them again." Hopefully, he could break the Horde with a ridiculous workload. "Anything else?"

A hand went up. One of the Barbarians, of course. "Yes?" he said briskly.

"Are you British?" she asked, getting a ripple of giggles from a third of the class, whose mental age appeared to be twelve.

"I've answered that in a previous class. Any other

questions that pertain to mechanical engineering, then? No? Great. Cheerio."

"Oh, my God, he said 'Cheerio,'" said a blonde dressed like a Cockney prostitute.

The bell rang, and the Barbarian Horde surged toward his desk. "Mr. Kearns, please stay a minute," Tom said.

Seven female students clustered around him. "So do you think I could, like, work for an architect or something?" one asked.

"I've no idea," he answered.

"I mean, after this class." She lowered her gaze to his mouth. Crikey. Made him want to shower.

"Pass the class first, then apply and see," he said.

"Do you want to hang out at the pub, Tom?" asked another of the BH. "I'd love to buy you a drink."

"That'd be inappropriate," he answered.

"I'm totally legal," she said with a leer.

"If you don't have any questions related to the lesson today, get out, please." He smiled to soften the words, and with a lot of pouty lips and hair tossing, the Barbarian Horde departed.

Tom waited till the other kids were out of earshot. "Jacob, would you be interested in interning for me?"

"Yeah! Sure! Um, doing what?"

"I customize airplanes here and there. Got a project coming up. It might be good on your CV."

"What's a CV?"

"A résumé."

"Sure!" Jacob said again. "That'd be great."

"You can't be using, of course. Will that be a problem?"

The kid flushed. "No. I'm in NA and all that. Clean

for thirteen months." He pushed his hands into his pockets. "I have to pee in a cup every month to come here. The health office has my records."

"Good. I'll give you a shout when I need you."

"Thanks, Dr. Barlow. Thanks a lot."

Tom nodded. The head of his department was standing in the doorway, frowning down the hallway, where a cacophony of giggles was coming from the twits. When Jacob left, the man came in and closed the door behind him.

This wouldn't be good news, Tom thought. Droog Dragul (not a shock that he was called Dracula, was it?) had the face of a medieval monk—tortured, pale and severe. He looked even more depressed than usual.

"Dee cheeldren of dis school," Droog said in his thick accent. He sighed. "Dey are so…" Tom winced, fearing the next phrase would be *well fed* or *iron-rich*. "Dey are so unfocused." Phew.

"Most of them, anyway," Tom said. "I've got one or two good students."

"Yes." His boss sighed. "And you heff such a vay vith the ladies, Tom. Perhaps we can heff beer and you can give pointers."

"It's the accent, mate," Tom said.

"Mine does not seem to heff same effect, for some reason. Eh heh heh heh heh!"

Tom winced, then smiled. Droog was a good guy. Strange, but nice enough. In the month since Tom had been teaching here, they'd had dinner once, gone out for beer and pool twice, and if the experience had been odd, it seemed that Droog had a good heart.

His boss sighed and sat down, tapping his long fingers on the desk. "Tom, I am afraid I heff bad news. Vee von't be able to renew your vork visa."

Tom inhaled sharply. The only reason he'd taken this job was for the work visa. "That was a condition of my employment."

"I em aware. But dee budget…it is too overtaxed for dee court fees."

"I thought you said it'd be no problem."

"I vas wrong. They heff reconsidered."

Tom felt his jaw locking. "I see."

"Vee value your teaching abilities and experience, Tom. Perhaps you vill find another way. Vee can give you till end of semester." He paused. "I em sorry. Very much so."

Tom nodded. "Thanks, mate." It wasn't Droog's fault. But shit.

Dr. Dragul left, and Tom sat at his desk another few minutes. Finding another job in February was unlikely. Wickham College had been the only place in western New York looking for an engineering professor, and Tom had been lucky to get the job as fast as he did. It wasn't a prestigious place, not by a long shot, but that wasn't really the point. This time around, it was all about location.

He couldn't keep his job without a work visa, though it wasn't like Immigration would be breathing down his neck; an employed professor was less of a concern than most of their cases. Still, the college wasn't going to keep him on illegally.

If he was going to stay, he needed a green card.

Fast.

But first to the rather shabby house he'd just rented,

and then to the much better bar down the street. A drink was definitely required.

A FEW NIGHTS later, Tom sat in the kitchen of his great-aunt Candace's kitchen, drinking tea. Only Brits could make decent tea, and though Candace had lived in the States for at least six decades, she hadn't lost the touch.

"That Melissa," Aunt Candace said darkly. "She messed everything up, didn't she?"

"Well. Let's not speak ill of the dead."

"But I'll miss you! And what about Charlie? How old is he now? Twelve?"

"Fourteen." His unofficial stepson had been ten when Tom met him. Hard to reconcile that talkative, happy little boy with the sullen teenager who barely spoke these days.

A fleeting pain lanced through his chest. Charlie wouldn't miss him, that seemed certain. One of those situations where Tom wasn't sure if he was doing any good whatsoever, or if, in fact, his presence made things worse. Melissa, Charlie's mother, was dead, and her brief engagement to Tom qualified him as nothing in the boy's life today, even though Charlie had been just a few months away from becoming Tom's stepson.

Whatever the case, Tom didn't have much choice about whether or not he was staying in the States. He'd emailed his old department head in England, who wrote right back saying they'd take Tom back in a heartbeat. There weren't any other colleges in western New York looking for someone with his credentials. And teaching was what he loved (when the students were actually interested in the subject matter, that was).

And so, Tom had decided to drive to Pennsylvania,

visit the only relative he had in this country and start
the goodbye process. He'd been in the States for four
years now, and Aunt Candace had been good to him.
Not to mention delirious with joy when he called after
his last class to see if she was free for dinner. He even
took her to the mall so she could buy a coat, proving a
fact Tom firmly believed—he was a bloody saint.

"Here. Have more pie, darling." She pushed the dish
across the table toward him, and Tom helped himself.

"Thanks," he said.

"Lovely town, Manningsport," she said. "I lived near
there as a child, did you know that?"

"So you told me," Tom said. His lovely old aunt could
bake, that was certain.

"Finish that pie, you might as well. I'm prediabetic
or some such nonsense. Then again, I'm also eighty-
two years old. Life without dessert is too horrible to
contemplate. I'll just overdose on caramel corn and die
with a smile on my face. What was I saying again?"

"You used to live near Manningsport."

"Yes, that's right! Just for a few years. My mother
was a widow, you see. My father died of pneumonia,
and so she packed my brother and me up and came to
America. Elsbeth, your grandmother, was already married, so she stayed in Manchester with her husband, of
course. Your grandfather. But I remember the crossing, seeing the Statue of Liberty. I was seven years old.
Oh, it was thrilling!" She smiled and took a sip of tea.

"So that's how you became a Yank?" Tom asked.

She nodded. "We lived in Corning, and she met my
stepfather, and he adopted Peter and me."

"I never knew that," Tom said.

"He was a lovely man. A farmer. Sometimes I'd go

with him to deliver milk." Candace smiled. "Anyway, we moved after my brother died in the war. I was fifteen then. But I still have a friend there. More of a pen pal, do you know what that is?"

Tom smiled. "I do."

"A pity you have to leave. It's beautiful there." Candy's gaze suddenly sharpened. "Tom, dear…if you really want to stay in the States, you can always marry an American."

"That's illegal, Auntie."

"Oh, pooh."

He laughed. "I can't see myself going that far," he said. "It might be different if—well. It's not an option."

It might be if Charlie actually wanted him to stay. Needed him. If Tom were anything but a thorn in Charlie's side, he might give it a whirl.

He had two thin job prospects with manufacturing firms, both requiring experience he didn't have. If those didn't work out (and he was almost positive they wouldn't), he'd be heading back to jolly old England, which wouldn't be awful. He'd be near his dad. Probably meet some nice girl someday. Charlie would barely remember him.

The pie suddenly tasted like ash. He pushed back his plate. "I'd better be off," he said. "Thanks for the visit."

She stood up and hugged him, her cheek soft against his. "Thank you for coming to see an old lady," she said. "I'm going to brag about this for days. My grandnephew adores me."

"You're right. Ta, Auntie. I'll call you and let you know what's happening."

"If I happen to know someone who might be interested, can I give her your number, dear?"

"Interested in what, Auntie?"

"In marrying you."

Tom laughed. The old lady's face was so hopeful, though. "Sure," he said, giving her another kiss on the cheek. Let the old bird feel useful, and that way, maybe she wouldn't feel so bad when he went back to England.

There was that pain in his chest again.

It took four hours to drive back to Manningsport. Four hours of wretched, icy rain and windshield wipers that smeared, rather than cleared. The weather thickened as he approached the Finger Lakes. Perhaps he wouldn't get in too late to grab a bite (and a whiskey) at the pub he was becoming too fond of. Chat up the pretty bartender and try not to think about the future.

CHAPTER TWO

SIX WEEKS AFTER her failed marriage proposal, Honor was starting to panic.

Online dating sites had offered her all of four matches: her brother Jack (pass); Carl, her brother-in-law (he and Pru had registered to see if eCommitment would say that they were compatible, then planned to meet and pretend to be strangers as part of their ongoing quest to keep things fresh; he was also a pass, obviously); Bobby McIntosh, who lived in his grandmother's basement and had strange, reptilian eyes; and a guy she didn't know who listed "reincarnation" under his hobbies.

So. Here she was again, staring down the weekend with only Spike, her recently acquired little mutt, for company, and while Spike was indeed excellent company, Honor had sort of hoped for the human variety. Ryan Gosling would've been preferred, but he had plans, apparently. Dana was busy, and had been busy a lot lately, which was getting a little frustrating, as winter in the Finger Lakes meant there already wasn't much to do. Take the best girlfriend out of the equation, and there was even less.

Faith was busy being a newlywed. Pru was busy pretending to be a newlywed. Jack had come over to watch the gruesome medical documentaries they both loved on Honor's fabulous new TV, and she had the feeling she'd tapped him out on the social front. Abby was a popular kid, and Honor couldn't bring herself to beg the teenager to hang out and watch movies. Ditto Ned, who already spent enough time with Honor at work.

This left Goggy and Pops, who were always happy to see her but fought constantly, and Dad, who was acting a little weird lately. Jumpy. Secretive.

Would Mrs. Johnson be up for something? Sometimes she'd go to a movie with Honor, though she clucked about the unsanitary nature of theaters, theater staff and humans in general. Hmm. Mrs. Johnson was probably her best bet. They could bring Spike, who loved movies as well as popcorn.

At that moment, her phone rang, startling her so much that she sloshed her coffee. Spike barked from her little doggy bed and began leaping up against Honor's leg, tearing her panty hose. Though she'd only had Spike for a month, the dog was very protective.

"I'll get it!" Honor yelled to Ned, the only other employee here at this hour.

"Of course you will," he yelled back from his office, where the sounds of Angry Birds could be heard.

"Blue Heron Vineyard, Honor Holland speaking," she said smoothly into the phone, scooping up her doggy.

"Hey, On, it's Brogan."

A burst of heat raced up her legs. "Hey! Hi! How are you? How's it going?" *Down, girl,* said the eggs. *He rejected us, remember?*

True. But they'd only emailed a few times since then, and damn if she didn't miss him.

"I'm really good," he said. "How are you?"

"I'm good! I'm great! I'm great, too, I mean." The eggs sighed.

"So listen," he continued, "I'm in town, and I was hoping you could find some time to see me."

Honor paused. The words *old baseball glove* leaped to mind. Then again, they'd always been friends. Still were. "What did you have in mind?"

I'm really sorry about saying no, Honor. These past few weeks have given me time to think and I love you and I want to marry you. Now.

"Drinks at O'Rourke's?" he asked.

"Sure! You bet."

"Fantastic," he said, and his voice was warm. There was a pause. "I have something important to tell you, and I want to do it in person. I think—I hope—it'll make you really happy."

The eggs sat up straighter. So did Honor.

"Okay," she said, pressing her fingers against her hot cheeks. "That sounds great."

"Seven o'clock?"

Seven! That was in ninety-two minutes. "That works. I'll see you then."

She sat there another minute, then sucked in an enormous breath, having forgotten how to breathe normally. Spike licked her chin in concern, and Honor patted her out of reflex. Turned to her computer and typed in Brogan's words. Studied them. Read them aloud, very softly so her nephew wouldn't hear.

"Hey," the same nephew said from her doorway, causing Honor to slap her laptop closed. Ned gave her a strange look. "Chill, Honor."

"What is it, Neddie dear?"

"You okay? You look all blotchy."

"Shush, child. What do you want?"

"I'm leaving. I have a date. And a life. You should try it some time."

"Very funny, Ned. Have fun. Drive carefully."

She waited till his footsteps had faded away, then opened her laptop and looked at those words again. *I have something important to tell you, and I think—I hope—it'll make you really happy.*

Could it be?

Could this be exactly what she wished for?

For one second, the scene flashed in front of her eyes. Herself, sitting at a little table at O'Rourke's. Brogan on bended knee, the ring shining from a black velvet box. His question, her answer, the applause of the pub patrons, and then, finally, the feeling of his arms around her as he kissed her in public for the first time ever.

Her heart was thudding. Could this really be about to happen to her? The most unsurprising of the Holland girls, the one who was steady as a rock, about to be the subject of such a romantic proposal, finally claimed by Brogan Cain?

It was almost hard to believe. *Yeah, about that,* said the eggs. *The years are precious, sure, but don't jump the gun.*

She ignored them. Adjusted her hairband (pink-and-green plaid). Read the words again.

It sure sounded like what she wanted it to sound like. Oh, yes, indeedy.

Legs trembling slightly, Honor settled Spike in her purse (why have a five-pound dog if you couldn't take her everywhere?), gave her an absentminded kiss on the head and walked across the lawn to the New House, where Mrs. Johnson was banging pots and pans in the kitchen. Dad was there as well, his face red, stuffing his hands into his faded jeans, a tear in the elbow of his flannel shirt.

"Hi, guys," Honor said.

"Hello, Petunia," Dad answered, taking off his baseball cap and running a hand through his hair. Mrs. Johnson growled, which was not uncommon.

"Everyone good here?" Honor asked.

"Of course! Why would you even ask such a question, Honor Grace Holland?" Mrs. J. demanded in her lilting accent. She slammed a pot on the stove. "Dinner will be ready in twenty minutes. How's your brother? Is he hungry, do you think?"

"I don't know, Mrs. J. Give him a call. And I, uh, I have plans," she said.

"Good," Dad said, his face flushing all the more. "I mean, good that you'll get out with friends, sweetheart."

"Yes. Mrs. J., will you watch Spike tonight?" *I may be getting a marriage proposal.*

The housekeeper's face melted into a smile. "Of course I will! Come here, you precious angel! Your fur is almost all grown back, isn't it? Oh, my beautiful princess, give us a kiss!"

Honor floated up to her little suite. Since she was the only Holland kid left at home, she'd appropriated Faith's old room last year and made it into a sitting room. She did a lot of work there, and also watched TV, most often with her laptop open, doing all the things that she hadn't gotten to during the workday.

Going into her bedroom, she opened her closet and frowned at the sea of navy blue and gray. Hmm. Her clothes were either neat-as-a-pin business attire, or jeans and a Blue Heron sweatshirt, and she didn't want to be wearing either if Brogan was about to...you know.

Her hands were sweating.

I have something important to tell you, and I want to do it in person. I hope—I think—it'll make you really happy.

What else could it be?

From the bookcase, her mother's image smiled out at her.

Twenty years gone, and Honor still missed her. They'd been so close, and so alike, both practical with a healthy dose of yearning thrown in: Honor for a family, which Mom had had right out of college; Mom for travel and possibly a career, which Honor had in spades. Funny, that. They both wanted what the other had.

Mom would've liked Brogan, Honor thought. Yes. She definitely would've.

She showered, shaved her legs, moisturized. If she went back to Brogan's house, she'd have to call, or Dad would call the chief of police, Levi Cooper, who happened to be married to Faith.

She'd cross that bridge later on. Put on a pink dress she'd worn to a wedding a few years ago, added a gray cardigan so she didn't look quite so dressed up, but still suitably feminine. Honor looked at her shoe options. Flats and a couple of pairs of basic pumps. She didn't own slutty shoes. Too much to swing by Faith's and borrow some? Probably.

Calling a goodbye to Dad and Mrs. J., Honor got into her car, shivering at the cold. Drove down the Hill into the tiny village. Tonight, it looked more beautiful than ever, a coating of snow on the ground, lights in the windows of the houses and storefronts that ringed the town green, Crooked Lake dark and vast behind. The sky was a swirl of stars. O'Rourke's was typically full, as the little pub was open year-round, the only place in town that was, and she could hear laughter and music from inside.

So…romantic. There was no other word for it, though *romantic* didn't figure a lot into Honor's life.

Tonight would be different.

Brogan's Porsche was already in the parking lot.

This is it, she told herself, wishing abruptly she'd told her sisters to come tonight. But maybe it was better this way. Or…maybe…Brogan had asked them to come tonight, so they could see him popping the question live and in person. That would be just like him. The guy had flare.

Proposing to him had been a bad move. Men liked to do the work, according to the nine books she'd read recently on understanding the male psyche.

She touched her pearls for luck, then opened the door to O'Rourke's. "Hey, Honor," said Colleen from behind the bar. "Wow, you look nice!"

"Check you out," said Connor at the same time.

"Thanks," she murmured, not really seeing the O'Rourke twins, who ran the bar.

Brogan was waiting for her, that knowing, incredibly sexy half smile on his face.

Oh, Lordy. Could it be true? That in just a few minutes, she'd be engaged to marry this guy? She smiled back, heart galloping. "Great to see you," he said, bending to kiss her cheek. He took her coat and hung it up, ever the gentleman, and, oh, man, she loved him more than ever, and that was saying a lot.

Somewhere far in the back reaches of her psyche,

the eggs were saying something about assumptions and whatever, sort of like an irritating storm warning running along the bottom of the television screen when you're watching a really good show. Whatever. It was hard to form rational thought at the moment, which was odd, since her trademark was being the sensible one, the dependable, calm member of the Holland family.

Not this night. This night, she was just a woman in love.

The thoughts came in disjointed flashes, the only thing registering solidly was Brogan's hand on her back, warm through her sweater.

When she saw Dana sitting alone at a table, her heart did a strange flop, and for a second, Honor felt a little surge of sympathy—Dana, who had no problem finding a guy, but had huge problems keeping one, would now have to see her and Brogan together. Dana often mocked happy couples. But Dana *was* her best friend, and she'd be happy for Honor. She would set aside her own issues.

In fact, maybe Brogan had invited her here for just that reason, to see the whole thing. You know what? That would explain why Dana had been a little hard to reach, a little distant lately. She'd been afraid to blow the surprise.

Then Brogan held a chair at the same table where Dana was sitting, and Dana looked up at Honor and gave her a tight smile that didn't reach her eyes.

Okay, that was…huh. That little warning that scrolled across the screen was now accompanied by the loud beeping of the emergency signal.

She sat down. So did Brogan.

Later, Honor would wish she'd brought her dog, who

could have attacked either Brogan or Dana, hopefully both, biting them with her tiny, needlelike teeth. She might have even peed on someone.

What happened next was a bit foggy. A poison, industrial-waste, evacuate-the-area kind of fog. Honor could hear her heartbeat crashing in her ears, caught Dana looking her up and down, immediately making her regret her choice of outfit. Dana herself wore a yellow wraparound shirt that showed her tiny waist and great boobage, making Honor feel overdressed and prim at the same time. Dana's dark hair was a little different than the last time she'd seen her—gosh, two weeks ago? Three? Well, Dana was a hairdresser. Her hair changed all the time. Not like Honor, who'd had hers all one length for years. Alice in Wonderland hair, Dana called it. She was always urging Honor to let her cut it.

Honor cleared her throat. Probably should be thinking about something other than hair. The other thought, the big one, was trying to shoulder its way in, but Honor wouldn't let it. Where was the happy, rosy glow? She missed it. Damn that glow! Come back! "Hi," she said, forcing a smile.

One of the O'Rourke cousins brought Honor a glass of wine she didn't remember ordering. Red. Pinot noir, Californian, a little too much pepper for her taste, better at first sip than upon finish, when it left a burning sensation in the back of her throat.

Over at the bar, Lorena Creech bellowed something about beddy-bye time. She heard Colleen O'Rourke's belly laugh. Someone said, "Thanks, mate," in an accent not usually heard around here, and all the while, Dana's dark eyes held a gleam of something, and she kept wrinkling her nose when she laughed. Brogan talked, shrugging, smiling. Little scraps of their words came to her, and Honor was aware that she'd tipped her head and was smiling. Or, at least her mouth was stretched so that her cheeks bunched. It might've been a grimace. She wasn't sure.

Then Dana held out her left hand, and on her fourth finger was Honor's engagement ring. An emerald-cut three-carat diamond set in platinum. And then the words, all those words she hadn't quite been hearing, slammed into Honor's heart, Dana's voice bright and sharp as a razor, slicing through the fog.

"So obviously, we didn't plan on it. In fact, it was so crazy! We didn't want to say anything to anyone until we were sure it was real, right, honey? But you know that saying. When it's right, it's right, and you don't have to spend years wondering about it."

Oh. That was meant for her. Gotcha.

Dana paused, squeezing Brogan's hand. "Anyway, Honor, I know it's a little weird, since you guys hooked up once in a while…" She smiled at Honor, a bright, movie-star smile. "But as you told me, that was done, and we hope you'll be happy for us."

All this first-person plural. Us. We. Our. What the hell was that about? No, seriously. What the ffffff—no, no, Honor wasn't the type to swear, but really, what the ffff-ungus was that about?

"Excuse me?" Honor said, and her heart beat so fast that she honestly felt like she might faint. "You're getting married?"

Brogan stopped talking. His face began to register something was off. "Uh, yeah."

Dana reached over and squeezed her hand. "Maid of honor? What do you say?"

Right. Because if she asked Honor to be in the wedding, then clearly Dana was a *wonderful* friend. Clearly it wasn't a case of swooping in and stealing—okay, not stealing, but definitely swooping—and taking Brogan. Brogan, of all people!

And why not? Brogan was handsome and nice and wealthy and glamorous, and Dana was a shark. Honor had seen it before, little flashes of those lethal rows of teeth, but man-oh-man-alive, she never thought Dana would turn on her.

Breathing. Right. Had to do that to stay alive. Honor sucked in a fast, hard breath, then another.

Brogan was now looking downright concerned. "On?"

She dragged her gaze from Dana's face to his. "It's Honor."

He blinked those ridiculous (now that she thought of it) turquoise eyes. "Uh, Honor, you're okay with this, right? I mean, we were never..." He winced. "I thought..."

"Honor? You're not upset, are you?" Dana asked. "I mean, you and Brogan were never more than a friendly fu—"

That was when the wine appeared on Dana's yellow shirt, right splat on her chest, some beads of red rolling into her exposed cleavage. Dana's mouth opened and closed like a trout pulled out of the water, and Honor realized her glass was empty.

"Holy crap, Honor!" Dana shrieked, jolting backward in her chair. "What the hell?"

Honor stood up, her legs shaking with shock and—and—and something she wasn't used to feeling, but it seemed to be fury.

Dana stood, too, mouth hanging open in outrage as she stared down at her shirt. She looked up. "You bitch!" she said.

Honor shoved her. Not hard, but still. She wasn't proud of it, didn't plan it, but there wasn't really much time to think, because Dana shoved back, much harder, and Honor staggered a little, bumping into her chair, and then Dana shoved her again, and she could smell the wine and "Sweet Home Alabama" was playing on the jukebox, and then they were falling, and there was some grappling, and Honor's head jerked and a sudden pain lanced through her scalp—for the love of God, Dana was pulling her hair and it *hurt,* and she grabbed some of Dana's adorable, silky hair (which smelled like coconut, very nice) and gave *that* a tug, and a chair fell on top of them, and time was weird, it was so slow and so fast at the same time, and then Brogan was hauling Dana off her. "Honor, what are you *doing?*" Brogan asked, and Honor scrabbled up, too (hopefully not flashing anyone), then there was a crack and Honor's face stung.

Her best friend had just slapped her.

Honor's breath came in short gasps. A cocktail napkin was stuck to her left breast. She pulled it off and set it on the table.

Oh, God.

The bar was silent.

"Honor." Jack, her big brother, and who said they were never around when you needed them? "Are you okay?" he asked.

She swallowed. "Peachy." Her face *hurt.* The spot Dana slapped throbbed.

Brogan looked absolutely bewildered. "Honor," he said. "I—I thought…I didn't realize…"

"No? Well, then, you're stupider than I thought." Her voice was cool, despite the fact that she was shaking violently.

"Let's get out of here," her brother said, and she loved him so much right then.

"I can't believe it!" someone barked from the bar, breaking the silence. Lorena Creech, the biggest mouth in town. "Honor Holland in a catfight! Wowzers!"

"Come on," Jack muttered. "I'll drive you home."

But Honor just stood there another minute, unable to take her eyes off of Dana. Her *friend*. The one who watched movies with her on Saturday nights when neither of them had a date, who confided in her, laughed with her, didn't seem to mind that she was maybe a little quiet, a little predictable. The one who'd told her to go for it, propose to Brogan…the one who'd handed her tissues after he said no.

The one who'd had a strange look on her face when she answered the door that night, and now Honor recognized what that expression had been: triumph.

The one who was wearing the same engagement ring Honor had admired.

In Dana's eyes was a dark gleam of satisfaction.

"I'll drive myself," Honor said, finally looking at her brother. "Thanks, anyway, Jack." She straightened her sweater, took her purse from the back of the chair.

Over the back of Dana's chair, she noted, was a Burberry raincoat. *Honor's* raincoat.

She turned and headed through the still-silent bar. It was an awfully long way.

A man she didn't know slid off a bar stool and went

to the door ahead of her, weaving a bit, she noted distantly. "Thanks for that," he said, the origin of the British accent she'd heard earlier. "You don't get to see enough girl fights these days."

"Shut up," she muttered, not looking him in the eye.

He toasted her with his glass and held the door open, and the cool, damp air soothed her burning face.

Two HOURS LATER, with Spike curled under her chin and snoring slightly, Honor made a resolution (and a list).

No more catfights in bars.
No more letting the old imagination fly away like a rabid bat, inventing scenarios that clearly weren't going to play out.
Work less and play more (find ways to play ASAP; maybe hire someone?).
A relationship, and pronto.
A baby. Soon.

Time to get a life, in other words.
Time to take action.

CHAPTER THREE

THERE WAS LITTLE Honor dreaded more than Family Meetings. In the past, subjects covered included Jack's divorce, the care and feeding of Goggy and Pops, Faith's wedding(s) and Dad's terrifying girlfriend of last year.

Tonight, for the first time ever, the Family Meeting was about her.

In the three days since the catfight, Honor had done a lot of thinking. She'd always been the good one, not that her siblings were bad people. No, they were just more colorful. She was like that other kid in the story of the Prodigal Son. The one who never screwed up, who did his job.

And look where that had gotten her. Thirty-five, aging eggs, no man in her life, totally gobsmacked by her best friend, not to mention completely idiotic where Brogan was concerned. She lived with her father in her childhood home and worked a bazillion hours a week. For fun, she watched shows about tumor removal or the guy who had a foot growing out of his rib cage, courtesy of a malformed twin.

Her entire family had heard about the fight. She'd told her dad and Mrs. Johnson the morning after, not wanting them to hear it from anywhere else, and Dad had looked like someone had just eaten a live kitten while Mrs. J. muttered darkly and slammed the fridge.

Faith came over and had been quite sympathetic, re-minding Honor of her own public scene a few years ago, and leaving two cartons of Ben & Jerry's in the freezer.

The family meeting would be more of the same.

Her in-box chimed.

To: Honor@BlueHeronVineyard.com
From: BroganCain@gmail.com
Subject: Hey
Hi, Honor. Don't know if you got my call the other day.

Oh, she had. She'd just opted not to return it.

You might be avoiding me.

Why, the man was a genius!

So here's the thing. I'm so, so sorry, Honor. I really never meant for you to feel bad in any way, honest to God. When we talked a couple of months ago about get-ting married, I was sure you were cool with that. And then this thing with Dana... We both weren't sure how to tell you about it, exactly, but we figured once you heard, you'd be happy about it.

She heard an unpleasant sound. Ah. Her teeth, grind-ing. Brogan. Was. Sostupid.

And obviously, that was really stupid.

Her jaw unlocked. Whatever else, Brogan always did have a way of reading her mind.

I feel like utter crap that I misread the situation so com-pletely. Your friendship is incredibly important to me.

You're the only one I've kept in touch with since elementary school, you know? I'd kill to know that you and I can still be friends. If not, I understand. I'd be really sad, but I'd understand.
Hope you're okay. Miss you.
Brogan

"Yeah, you should miss me," she said, but her voice was shaking. Because let's not fool ourselves here. She was going to forgive him. Even now, her heart felt floppy and huge in her chest.

Ah, dang it. That was the thing with Brogan. He never meant any harm. He wasn't the type. With a sigh that made Spike yawn in sympathy, she started typing. May as well get it over.

To: BroganCain@gmail.com
From: Honor@BlueHeronVineyard.com
Subject: Re: Hey
Hey, you! Of course we're still friends. Don't be silly. I'm really embarrassed at how I acted, that's all. But I'm fine. It was surprising, that's all, and I guess

—here her typing slowed—

I had more invested in the idea of us than I realized.

A horrible thought occurred to her. That since the catfight, Dana had told Brogan about how wretched she'd been after the failed proposal. That he knew how much she loved him. But no. Dana wouldn't do that. It would make Dana look bad if she admitted she knew how Honor felt.

But I do realize that "us" was just an idea and not anything more than two old friends hooking up once in a while.

Oh, hell, that wasn't true. It felt horrible to be throwing her heart under the bus this way.

Anyway, I'm mostly just embarrassed. Not sure if you know this about me, but I generally don't fight in bars. :)

Reduced to emoticons. She sighed, feeling her throat tighten.

You're special to me, too, Brogan, and I'm glad you're happy.

The eggs rolled their cataract-riddled eyes.

Please don't give my girls-gone-wild moment another thought. In fact, I'd really appreciate it if we never talked about it again. :) I've got a crammed schedule for the next two weeks

—lying—

but maybe we can get together after that, okay? Take care.
Honor

It was better than the truth. *I love you. I've spent two months trying to talk myself out of loving you. How could you not know? Even if you really didn't see how I felt, Brogan, because you're an obtuse male, Dana did, so now my best friend has stabbed me in the heart, and you're marrying her.*

Last night, Honor had stayed up till 3:00 a.m., looking up the the term *toxic friendship* on Google and reading every article she could find on it.

Dana had a whole lotta ex–best friends. Honor had been treated to many a story about them, from Dana's sister to her neighbor to her high school BFF. And while Honor recognized that Dana was temperamental and tended to see things in black-and-white, she always thought she could handle it. In the five years that they'd been friends, a few people had said something to Honor about Dana—Gerard Chartier from the firehouse commented once that he thought Honor could do better in the friend department than Dana, and Mrs. Johnson had said she didn't trust her (but then again, Mrs. J. didn't trust too many people).

Nope, Honor thought she could handle Dana's big personality. And why would Dana fall out with her, after all? She was a great friend—available, sympathetic, a great listener. *Their* friendship was different. Honor would be exempt from the dramatics Dana described with such gusto.

Stupid. Apparently, she had no clue about women. Or men, for that matter.

But you know what? The days of ignoring red flags and waiting around for stuff to happen…those days were over.

"Hi, sweetheart," Dad said at her door at six o'clock sharp. His gentle eyes were worried. "Everyone's here."

"Your father and I don't want you to feel self-conscious," Mrs. Johnson said, worming past Dad to administer simultaneous pats and scowls. "It's just that we're all very concerned about you, child. Very concerned. Deeply concerned."

"Thanks." Honor forced a smile and followed them to the tasting room. It was really the only comfortable place on the vineyard where everyone could sit. Downstairs, a long, U-shaped bar dominated the room, but upstairs, there was a private tasting room for special events—one of Honor's ideas. That area was like a giant living room, complete with leather couches, a stone fireplace and a smaller bar along one wall. The post-and-beam ceiling was exposed; an old Oriental carpet covered much of the wide-planked floor.

Everyone *was* there, and heck, there were just too many people in this family. There were times when being an orphan held great appeal. David Copperfield never had to go to a family meeting, did he? Nor did Oliver Twist.

"Thanks for coming," Honor said to the room at large.

"A catfight?" Goggy blurted. "In a bar? Over a man?"

"I just wish I'd been there," Pops said, winking at Honor. "You won, I hope."

"It's not funny!" huffed Goggy. "Since when do my grandchildren fight in bars? I mean, I'd expect that of you, Prudence, but Honor?"

"Why would you expect that of me?" Pru said. "Have I ever been in a fight? No. I haven't."

"Well, I could picture it," Goggy said. "Though with Carl, not another woman."

Honor suppressed a sigh. Pru was colorful, Faith had the looks, Jack was the perfect son...Honor was what, then?

The boring one.

Which was going to change. Yes.

"Honor definitely won," Jack said. "You'd all be proud."

"I never really warmed up to that woman," Pru said. "Though she does have great hair."

"Pass me the cheese," Pops ordered.

"No more cheese for you!" Goggy said. "You know what it does to your stomach."

"Okay, shut up, everyone," Honor said mildly. Not that she didn't love her family. But with four generations present, two brothers-in-law, Faith, Pru, a teenage niece, a nephew who couldn't make eye contact without laughing, her bickering grandparents, Dad and Mrs. Johnson exchanging worried looks…well, it was feeling a wee bit overwhelming. "Dad, get this over with, okay? I'd like to make a few changes around here."

"I have an announcement," Dad said. "We're making a few changes around here." He seemed to realize he'd just echoed Honor, because he looked at her in surprise.

"Go ahead," she said, pouring herself a hefty glass of wine. It would only help, and besides that, it had a lovely nose of fresh-cut grass, grapefruit and a hint of limestone.

Dad looked at Honor and put his leathery, grape-stained hand over hers. "For a long time, I think we've all taken Honor for granted."

Her mouth dropped open.

"She puts in way too many hours, travels all the time, takes care of a hundred different things," Dad went on. "Which is why I hired you an assistant today."

She blinked. "You did what? Don't I get a say in who works for me?"

"Great idea, Dad," Jack said.

"You can't just—" Honor began.

"No, sweetie," Dad went on, his voice quiet but firm. "Mrs. Johnson and I talked it over—" Uh-oh. If Mrs. Johnson was in on it, she was doomed. "And it's done. Also, I think it's appropriate that Ned—" Dad nodded at his grandson "—take over half of the sales calls."

"Half? Not half!" Okay, sure, she'd wanted a little change. Just not this much. "Look, just because—"

"Finally," Ned said. "Wish I'd known all I had to do was to get Honor to punch someone in a barroom brawl—"

"Shut up, son," Dad continued. "Honor, he's been tagging along with you for a year. Time to let him step up."

"Um, that's okay, sure. Neddie, you're great. But we don't need to reorganize the vineyard because I had one bad moment."

"Sweetheart, you were punching your best friend in O'Rourke's the other night."

Honor paused. "I didn't actually punch her."

"I heard in school that you tackled her," Abby said.

"I didn't."

"And threw wine in her face."

"Um, I did do that, yes. More on her chest, but…" She glanced at Levi, who was still in uniform. He raised an eyebrow but remained silent.

"What kind of wine?" Jack asked.

"A pinot noir from California. Flat body, too much pepper, high acidity."

"It'll be cool, Honor," Ned said. "You can be my boss."

"I'm already your boss," she pointed out.

"I'll just be more useful. It'll be good for me. I can mend my sinful ways."

"You'd better not be sinning, sonny," Pru said. "But yeah, Honor, he can help."

"Sure. Fine."

"I hired Jessica Dunn to be your assistant," Dad added.

"What?" Jessica Dunn? The waitress? "That's fine, Dad. No. Ned is more than enough. He's very helpful."

"She has a marketing degree and wants to get some experience. Figured she could do some of the media and whatnot."

"Dad, do you even know what media is?"

"No, not really, but she said she could handle it."

"Well, so can I! I don't need her. No offense, Levi." He and Jessica were childhood friends. Everyone knew that.

"None taken," he said, stroking Faith's neck.

"She starts tomorrow," Dad said.

"Dad—" Honor's jaw was locked again. She loved that aspect of her job—the press releases, articles, updating the website, running Twitter and the vineyard's Facebook page, schmoozing with the tourism bureaus, wooing reporters, travel writers and wine reviewers. "I don't need an assistant. Ned is more than enough."

"I don't mind," Ned said. "Jessica's wicked pretty."

"Not to you she's not," Pru said. "She's way too old for you. Got it?"

"Maybe she's a cougar," Ned said.

"Ned, you're so disgusting," Abby said, raising her head from her textbook to glare at her brother.

"Honor, child," said Mrs. Johnson, "whatever this media is, you do too much of it. You work constantly, you eat at your desk, you have no children for me to spoil, and it's a shameful and terrible way to live."

"No one was complaining last week," she protested.

"No one was rolling on a filthy tavern floor last week, either." Mrs. J. gave her an arch look.

"You have an assistant now, sweetheart," Dad said. "Enjoy it."

"But media is about half my job, and sales is the other half. What am I supposed to do?" Honor asked, not liking that edge of hysteria in her voice.

"Live a little," Dad said. "Get some hobbies."

"Watching *World's Biggest Tumor* doesn't count," Jack said.

"You're the one who called me last week to make sure I TiVoed *Cottage Cheese Man,* you hypocrite!"

"The Black and White Ball is coming pretty soon," Faith pointed out soothingly. "You're chairman this year. That'll be a lot of work."

"Jessica starts tomorrow," Dad said. "Family meeting adjourned. Who's hungry?"

"I'm starving," Prudence said.

"I made ham," Goggy announced, beating Mrs. Johnson to the punch. "If you feel like coming down, not that any of you visit anymore, but there's also a Walnut Glory cake if you do decide to drop by."

"We'll meet you there in a few minutes," Dad said. "Honor, stay here, honey."

They waited till everyone had tromped out. "About Ned and Jessica, sweetheart. I'm sorry I didn't talk to you first, but I felt like I had to do something definitive. And I didn't want it to take forever, so I did it." He paused, taking off his old baseball cap and running a hand through his thinning hair. "Mrs. Johnson and I are worried about you, Petunia."

Yes, she'd heard them talking late last night, which

was a shock in itself, as Mrs. J. usually retired to her apartment above the garage by eight, and Dad was usually in bed by nine-thirty. Farmer's hours and all that.

She folded her hands in front of her. "Dad, I'm embarrassed enough as it is. I don't need people thinking I had some kind of breakdown at O'Rourke's and have to hire all these people."

Dad was quiet for a minute. "Well, you *did* have a little breakdown, Petunia."

"I just lost my cool. It wasn't as big a deal as it sounds."

"And when have you ever lost your cool?" he asked.

Dang. She didn't answer.

"Honey, I know it doesn't seem like I pay too much attention," Dad said. "But I know a few things. When your mother died, you…" His voice grew soft. "You grew up fast. You did everything you were supposed to, and you never needed much from the rest of us. Cornell, Wharton, and then you came home and looked after me."

She swallowed against the lump in her throat. "I really wanted to, Daddy. I love my life."

"I believe that." He paused. "But I also know you've loved Brogan a long time."

It was so mortifying, hearing the words said aloud like that. She shrugged, not trusting her voice.

"And I always did hope things would work out for you two," he said. "I can only imagine how you must feel, hearing that your best friend is marrying him instead of you."

"It was just a surprise," she said, and her voice shook.

He covered her hand with his own. "So this is a turning point. Time for you to devote some thought to what you want in life, rather than just waiting around for that bozo to call you."

Well, hell. Dad did pay attention, after all.

"I'm not asking," Dad said. "I'm ordering. As your father and as the legal owner of Blue Heron."

"So bossy. You can't tie your shoes without me."

"I've actually gotten pretty good at that," Dad said, smiling so that his kind eyes crinkled in the corners. "Mrs. J.'s been teaching me. So here's the deal. Your hours have been cut. You start at nine, you leave at five, or I'm dragging you out myself."

"Right," Honor said. "Like anyone can get a full day's work done in that time."

"That's the magic of my plan," Dad said. "You won't get it done. You and Ned and Jessica will get it done. Now I'm going to the Old House before Mrs. J. and your grandmother get into a fight over how long to cook the potatoes, and you have to come, too."

Honor sighed. "All right. Give me a few minutes, okay?"

Dad kissed the top of her head and left. After a minute, she went outside. It was already dark, and the stars spread across the sky in an endless, creamy sweep. The air smelled like wood smoke.

She loved Blue Heron with all her heart. It was home, and it was her pride and joy, too. In the eleven years since grad school, a lot had changed around here. When she came on board as director of sales, the vineyard was a cute, family-run business. Rather than rest on those laurels, she came up with a business plan that enhanced everything good about the place and added ten times more—prestige, visibility, recognition—all without losing the homeyness of eight generations of the Holland family farm. She'd proposed the construction of the post-and-beam tasting room and gift shop ten years ago, overhauled the labeling and brand, created a marketing campaign that brought Blue Heron's name to the attention of every outlet that mattered, from the *New York Times* to *Wine Spectator*. Blue Heron was practically a required stop on any tour of the Finger Lakes wine region. Honor knew she had a lot to be proud of. She loved working with her family, loved—to be honest—being the one in charge of the business end. Delegating had never been her strong suit.

But she never thought she'd have to worry about aging eggs. Never really pictured living in the New House with her dad and Mrs. J. forever.

There was supposed to be more. A husband. A family of her own.

She wanted to be special to someone. She wanted a man's face to light up when he saw her. She wanted a man to kiss her like his heart would stop if he didn't.

Somehow, Dana had wrangled what Honor never had—Brogan's love. In just a few weeks, no less.

How the *hell* had she done that?

Suddenly it seemed like the sky was pressing her down with the same paralyzing loneliness felt when her mother died, leaving her alone.

And God, she was tired of being alone. She didn't know if the words were a prayer or an admission of defeat. She pulled her hair from the clip and ran her fingers through it, sighing in the cool night air.

You know what? She wasn't going to Goggy's. Instead, she went home, went up to her bathroom and took out a pair of scissors.

All her life, her hair had been the same, thick and

long, hanging to the middle of her back, a dark blond with lighter streaks from the sunshine…when she was out in the sunshine, that was. It had been a while. She wore it up about half of the time, down and with a hairband at others. In fact, her hairband collection was a little ridiculous. How many did she own? Twenty? Thirty? Until now, she liked her hair, liked the old-fashioned beauty of it.

Not anymore. It was time for a change.

The snick of the scissors was oddly satisfying.

ON THE FOURTH Thursday of every month, in an effort to earn her heavenly reward, Honor volunteered at Rushing Creek, the assisted living facility at the edge of Manningsport. This Thursday, Goggy had come with her.

In the past year, Goggy and Pops had aged a little, as one would expect with people in their eighties. They were both still strong as oxen, but Goggy seemed more forgetful these days, and Honor could swear Pops limped on rainy days. Any day now, she worried, one of them might tumble down the steep, narrow staircases of the Old House, which was something of a death trap, full of the twists and turns characteristic of colonials. They didn't use two-thirds of the rooms, and the house would never pass inspection, not with Pops having nailed the front door closed last winter "to help with the drafts."

It was Honor's hope that they'd willingly move to a brighter, smaller place before one of them had an accident.

"I'll kill myself before I come to a place like this," Goggy pronounced dramatically when she came through the doors. A resident in a wheelchair glared before zipping down the hall in speedy moral outrage. Rushing Creek was comparable to the nicest luxury apartments in Manhattan, but Goggy viewed it like a Dickensian asylum.

"Let's try to use our inside voices, okay?" Honor said. "I love it here. I'm counting the years before I can move in."

"I'd *kill* myself. Oh, hello, Mildred! How are you?"

"Hello, Elizabeth!" Mildred said. "And Honor! You cut your hair! Oh, no! Why, honey, why?"

"Thank you," Honor said. Okay, so the haircut was a bit radical. But that had been the point. And yes, she'd gone to Corning, to a stylish, somewhat frightening place where a professional had stared in horror before shaping up her cropped hair.

Now it was no longer than the nape of her neck. Relieved of its weight, little wisps sprang up here and there, and if it was a shock, Honor told herself she'd like it eventually. Dad pretended to after his initial chest-clutching; Mrs. Johnson growled; Goggy wept; Pops, Pru and Jack had yet to notice. Faith, at least, had seemed genuinely enthusiastic, clapping her hands. "It's so chic, Honor! And look at your cheekbones! You're gorgeous!" Which, of course, she wasn't, but she appreciated the support.

"So…different!" Mildred said. "Anyway, dear, congratulations on your sister getting married."

"Thanks. Levi's a great guy."

"I bet they'll have babies any day."

"I wouldn't be surprised."

Mildred gave her a conspiratorial look. "And you, dear? Anyone special for you?"

"No, not at the moment."

"Such a shame. Why are you here, then, darling? Elizabeth, are you and John thinking of moving here?"

Goggy jerked back. "Oh, my heavens, no! We're just fine in our house. I hope to God I never have to resort to this."

"Goggy." Honor sighed, then smiled at Mildred "We're showing *A Walk in the Clouds* today. Have you seen it? Very romantic."

"I haven't," Mildred said with a dirty look at Goggy. "The last time I saw a movie with these old people, half were gabbing through the whole thing and the other half couldn't hear. Good luck!"

Between Goggy and Mildred, Honor noted, it did seem to be a habit to want to distance oneself from the capriciousness of aging. *Look at Ellington, he still pretends he doesn't need glasses. Walked into a post last week.* Or, *Did you hear about Leona? Alzheimer's. Thank God I'm still as sharp as a...what was I saying again?*

Sort of like single women, Honor thought. Rather than admit they were all desperately seeking someone—like the cannibals chasing Viggo Mortensen in that dreadful movie she watched last night—there were all sorts of excuses. *I'm getting over a long-term relationship* was a good one. *I wish I had time for a relationship!* was another. And then the ultimate lie, *If the right guy came along, maybe. But I'm happy on my own.* Sure. Which was why those dating sites had half the planet registered.

No, honesty seemed frowned upon in Dating Life. Honor wondered what would happen if she said, *I really thought I'd have a family by now. I'm lonely. Also a little horny, and since the man I love is marrying my former best friend, I may have to invest in a superdeluxe vibrator.*

"Come on," Goggy said. "Let's get this movie over with before someone comes to lock me up. They use restraints, I hear."

"Honor! How *are* you?" asked Cathy Kennedy, who didn't live here but came in for the movies. "Honey, Louise and I happened to be at O'Rourke's the other night. Such a surprise."

Honor's face heated in a rush. "Well, you know. It's a little quiet in the winter here. I was just trying to liven things up." Mercifully, it was time for her to get the film going.

Honor had started the Watch and Wine club a couple of years ago: show a movie that had even a little bit of wine in it and pair it with a themed tasting. For *Uncorked,* they'd of course had the Chateau Montelena chardonnay. Pinot noir for *Sideways.* A full-bodied cab for *Twilight,* though the combination of wine and Taylor Lautner's torso had proved too much for some, and 9-1-1 had to be called when Mrs. Griggs fainted.

The monthly gathering had almost immediately been renamed Watch and Whine, given the propensity of the viewers to discuss their most recent health issues, peppering Honor with questions, which she (and her iPad) did their best to answer. Hey. It was a hobby, and one she'd listed on Match.com. *Visits the sick and imprisoned.*

As Honor set up the film in the projector in the gorgeous auditorium, Goggy sat on one of the plush seats, sighing dramatically. "Just put a pillow over my face if it ever comes to this," she said.

"Goggy, you told Faith you wouldn't mind a new place," Honor said. "Remember? When she was moving into the Opera House?"

"Oh, I meant a place without your grandfather. But the old fool wouldn't last a week without me. He'd starve to death. I honestly don't know if he could find the refrigerator on his own." She paused. "It's a thought." Goggy suddenly sat bolt upright. "Speaking of miserable marriages, I found someone for you!"

Honor gave her a wary look. "Uh, that's okay, Goggy." Goggy had recently suggested she marry Bobby McIntosh "before he ended up a serial killer."

"No, he's wonderful! You should meet him. Plus, it would help you get over you-know-who. And then you could get married and give me some more great-grandchildren."

The projector's lightbulb was out. Was there another one? She opened the drawer of the AV cart. Bingo. "Just for the sake of conversation, who is this future husband of mine?"

"You remember Candace, my old friend? She moved to Philadelphia in 1955? They drove that enormous Packard?"

Honor gave her grandmother a quizzical look. "I wasn't born then, Goggy. So no, I don't remember."

"Well, before I married your idiot grandfather—"

"You make it sound so romantic."

"Hush up and listen. Before I married your idiot grandfather, I was engaged to Candace's brother. He died in the war." She gave Honor a regal, suffering look, perfected from years of practice.

"I know, Goggy. It's such a sweet, sad story."

Goggy's face softened. "Thank you. Anyway, Candace also had a sister, but she was older and stayed in England."

"Uh-huh." What this had to do with matchmaking was anyone's guess, but such was the mind of Goggy. Honor unscrewed the burned-out lightbulb with some difficulty.

"So this sister had a son, and then that son had a son, and Candace just adores him, and anyway, the boy's been living here for a few years and he needs a green card."

Honor squinted, trying to filter through the bundle of facts.

"So you should marry him. Nothing wrong with an arranged marriage."

"As in, you and Pops worked out so well?" She opened the drawer on the cart and took out a replacement bulb.

The old lady chuffed. "Please. You want to be married, or you want to be happy?"

"Both?"

Goggy snorted. "You young people. So spoiled. Anyway, there's nothing wrong with this boy. He's very nice and extremely good-looking."

Honor screwed in the new lightbulb. "Have you ever met him?"

"No. But he is."

"Seen a picture?"

"No. Charming, too."

"So you've talked to him on the phone?"

"No."

"Facebook? Email?"

"No, Honor. You know I don't believe in computers."

"Hi there, Honor," called Mr. Christian from the back

of the auditorium. "Heard you were in a girl fight the other day."

"Thanks for bringing it up," Honor said. "Anyway, Goggy, it sounds like you really don't know this person at all."

"What's to know? He's British."

"That may or may not help his case. If he sounds like Prince Charles, there's no way in hell I'll marry him. Does he have those big teeth?"

"Don't be so superficial, honey! He's a professor," Goggy added. "Electrical engineering or math or something."

An image of Honor's own math teacher in college, a damp man with onion breath, came to mind.

"So he needs a green card," Goggy said, "you're single, and you two should get married."

"Okay, first of all, sure, I'd love to get married if I met someone great and fell in love, but if that doesn't happen, I'm fine on my own." Oh, the lies. "Secondly, I don't want to get married just to check it off a list. And thirdly, I'm pretty sure marrying for a green card is illegal." She paused. "Why doesn't he just go back to England?"

"There was a tragedy." Another triumphant look from Goggy.

"What kind?"

"I don't know. Does it matter, Honor? You're thirty-five. That's when the eggs start spoiling. That's when I started menopause." Oh, snap. "Besides, if I can stay married to your grandfather for sixty-five years and not have murdered him yet, why can't you do the same with this boy?"

"How old is this person? You keep calling him a boy."

"I don't know. Anyone under sixty is a boy to me."

"So he's a math teacher and distantly related to an old friend of yours, and that's all you've got on him?"

Goggy waved to Mrs. Lunqvist. "Young people," she called. "They're so fussy!" Mrs. Lunqvist, who used to terrorize the kids in Bible study with tales of fiery devastation of Biblical cities, nodded in agreement. "So you'll meet him?"

What have you got to lose? the eggs asked, looking up from their quilting. *Didn't you hear what she said about menopause?*

Honor sighed. "Sure," she said.

"I just thought it'd be nice," Goggy said. "I have a soft spot for his family, that's all. You'd be surprised at how many times I think of Peter and what my life would be like if he hadn't died in World War II. Protecting freedom and saving the world. So when I heard his grandnephew was in town, all by himself, lonely, depressed, British—"

Such a prize. "You can stop now, Goggy, I just said I'll meet the guy."

"You did?"

"Yes."

Goggy smiled triumphantly.

"Don't go planning any weddings," Honor warned. "I'm just doing it to be polite." An image of a balding man with large, horselike teeth and a love of sharing math theorems popped into her head. "What's his name?"

"Tom Barlow." A completely ordinary name. Not

like Brogan Cain, for example. "I told him you'd meet him tonight at O'Rourke's."

"What?"

"And put on lipstick, for heaven's sake. You're such a pretty girl. And be nice! It wouldn't kill you to smile. Oh, there's Henrietta Blanchette. I heard she got food poisoning from that slop they serve here. I'll go say hi."

Honor's mood was soft after the movie. First, the wine had been fantastic, this lovely Tempranillo with hints of strawberries, cherry jam and leather. Then the Rushing Creek residents, who loved Watch and Wine and always had something nice to say (once they'd gotten their kicks out of mentioning her catfight, that was). But in general, whatever barriers seemed to exist between Honor and her peers evaporated with old people, who called her *honey* and *dear* and told her about their kidney stones and varicose veins. Also, one couldn't rule out the movie itself. Keanu Reeves, amen, sister. The kiss in that movie—*the* kiss, the babymaker—had she ever been kissed like that?

Er, no.

Nope, no man had ever been desperate to kiss her. No man had ever kissed her like he'd die if he didn't. No sirree. Didn't happen. Didn't seem like it was *going* to happen, either, not when a middle-aged British math teacher was her only prospect.

That could change. She'd update her dating website profiles. Ask Faith to help her out with things like push-up bras and flirting. Maybe some of the men she did business with were single, and maybe they'd notice her. It could happen.

It's just that no one was like Brogan.

Nope, nope. No more thoughts like that. So over him. Almost. Well, getting there. Okay, not at all, really.

As she walked through Rushing Creek, she heard a familiar laugh.

Right. Dana cut hair every other Thursday at Rushing Creek's salon. Honor had recommended her for the gig, actually.

The sound made Honor stop in her tracks, her stomach suddenly flooded with a cold rush of emotion. Anger, embarrassment, jealousy, loneliness…

Yeah. Loneliness.

Don't let her see you.

Dana looked up and saw. "Honor!" she called. "Do you have a second?"

Fungus. Feeling her face flush, Honor nodded. She went into the salon, which, though small, was a lot nicer than House of Hair.

"Mrs. Jenkins, I just need to take out your hearing aid, okay?" Dana asked, slipping it out. "There," she said to Honor. "Now we can talk. The old bat's deaf as dirt."

An unexpected yearning swooped through Honor's chest. For five years, since Dana moved to Manningsport, they'd been friends, the type of friend Honor hadn't had since college. Hanging out, calling for no reason, commiserating over work, family, men. They'd had a lot of good times together. A lot of laughs.

Honor didn't say anything. Then again, she didn't leave, either.

"That's some haircut," Dana said. "Not bad. Where'd you get it done? Parisian's?"

Still, Honor didn't answer. They were *not* going to talk about hairstyles (but yes, it was Parisian's).

"Look, you gave it your best shot, Honor. Okay?" Dana went on. "He didn't love you. You're the one who said you were done with him, and he and I just ran into each other one night at O'Rourke's, and one thing led to another. It was a complete shock to us both."

"I'm actually surprised you had waited as long as you did, Dana."

Bitter Betty, table for one. But it had only been six weeks since she'd been…betrayed. No other word would do.

"Honor, I'm sorry, I really am. I know you wanted Brogan to love you, but it's not my fault he didn't."

"Could you lower your voice, please?" Honor said, her face burning.

"Oh, please. She hasn't heard anything since Clinton was president." Dana cut her a glance, her face softening. "How many times have you and I talked about just this exact thing? The guy you least expect to fall for and then boom, you've fallen. And he happened to fall for me, too. We were just chatting at the bar." She gave Honor a small, smug smile. "And all of a sudden, there was this charge in the air."

Dana was gloating. Brogan and she knew each other, of course. Sometimes, the three of them had gone out together. If there'd been any charge in the air, Honor hadn't noticed.

Dana was quiet for a minute. "I know you had a crush on him since the dawn of time."

"It was more than a crush, Dana. Don't minimize my feelings to make yourself feel less guilty."

"I *don't* feel guilty," she said, turning back to Mrs. Jenkins, her scissors flying in a sinister hiss. She got paid sixty-five dollars a haircut, Honor knew. Sixty-five bucks for taking a millimeter off someone's hair. "Look, I know you were surprised. But I still think you owe me an apology."

The noise that came out of Honor's mouth was somewhere between a sputter, a choke and a laugh. "An apology?"

"Just a little trim around the ears," Mrs. Jenkins said. "Not too short, dear."

"Got it, Mrs. Jenkins," Dana barked. "Not too short." Her voice lowered, and she looked at Honor. "Yeah, an apology. I don't appreciate having wine thrown in my face, not to mention being shoved in a restaurant in front of the guy I love."

Honor's mouth opened and closed a few times. "You have got to be kidding me."

"Listen. I'm sorry it didn't work out for you, but does that mean that both Brogan and I are supposed to ignore what we feel for each other?" Her words might've had more impact if her tone hadn't been as sharp as her scissors. The horrible, beautiful engagement ring flashed as her hands moved over Mrs. Jenkins's head. "Seriously, we didn't plan it. It just happened."

Oh, that infuriating phrase! Nothing *just* happened. Vaginas didn't just happen to fall on penises. Unspoken words bubbled up like lava. *Do I look that stupid? You were supposed to be my friend. You made me a martini that night. I cried on your couch! We watched* Shark Week! *And a few weeks later, you were sleeping with the guy who broke my heart. For crying out loud, you told me in a bar. Two against one, in a bar.*

Yes, she could say those things, and denigrate her pride even further. Remind Dana just how pathetic she'd been…and give Dana more chance to gloat. Because wasn't that what she was doing?

"I guess we have different ideas of what it means to be friends," she said tightly.

"Yeah. Friends don't throw wine in their friends' faces."

"Fine. I was very surprised, and I reacted badly. But I seem to remember you reacting just as badly in return."

"Someone throws wine into my face, yeah, I do react badly." She gave Honor a little smile. "So. Are we good?"

In the mirror, Honor saw her own mouth fall open. She closed it. "I don't know that we're ever going to be good, Dana."

"Why? Water under the bridge, right? It was dramatic, you feel embarrassed, so do I, a little." She shrugged, still smiling. "Let's get past it. I mean, what else are we gonna do? Hate each other forever? Okay. I have to put this hearing aid back in or the old bag will start to suspect something." Unexpectedly, she gave Honor a quick hug. "I'm glad we talked. I mean, yeah, things'll be weird for a while, but we're still best friends, right? And hell's bells, girl, I have a wedding to plan!"

"Oh, I love weddings," Mrs. Jenkins said, adjusting her hearing aid.

"Come by the salon, and I'll shape up your bangs," Dana said. "See you soon!"

And, because she didn't know what else to say, and really, really wanted to get out of there, Honor left.

CHAPTER FOUR

HAVING TWO GLASSES of whiskey probably wasn't the most brilliant idea before a fix-up, Tom thought. But he wasn't driving. And also, though he hated to point out the obvious, even to himself, it was too late. One could not undrink whiskey, unless one vomited, which Tom was not going to do.

"Off to meet the future Mrs. Barlow," he told his reflection. "Excited, mate?"

This did not have a good feeling to it. First of all, the whole criminal aspect of the night cast a bit of a pall, didn't it? And secondly, his great-aunt was fixing him up. He still had a tiny shred of pride left after Melissa, but this would probably kill it. But for whatever reason, when Candace had called, clucking in excitement, he'd said he'd love to meet her pen pal's granddaughter.

He walked the three blocks to the town green. There was another thing. If he did manage to stay in this godforsaken town, he'd have to stay in this godforsaken town, and bloody hell! The weather! Made England look like paradise, and that was saying a lot.

But Charlie was here. Not that the boy wanted Tom around. Yesterday, Tom had gone the tried and true route and attempted to bribe his way into Charlie's affection with an iPhone. When Tom tried to show him a few of the new features, the boy went limp with disgust, rolled his eyes and then stared straight ahead, arms crossed, silently counting the seconds till Tom left.

So marrying just to stay here…it felt a bit like buying a house on Isle of the Damned. Not that he'd actually do it. But for some reason, here he was, trudging through the slush to meet some middle-aged woman Aunt Candy had said could keep her mouth shut. Someone who was desperate enough to consider marrying a stranger. Someone whose "clock is ticking." Fantastic. He could only imagine what she looked like. Dame Judi Dench came to mind. Talented, sure. Did he want to bang Dame Judi Dench? No, he did not.

Then again, he hadn't done so well on his own, had he? Melissa, though quite the looker, hadn't turned out to be such a prize.

The warmth of the pub was welcome. At least the little town had this, a little tavern at which to drown one's sorrows.

"Hello, Colleen," he said, because yeah, befriending the bartender was never a bad idea.

"Hallo, Tom," she said in a fair imitation of his accent. "Bass ale tonight?"

"I'll have a whiskey, love," he said.

"Not your first, I'm guessing."

"You're astute *and* beautiful. A bit terrifying."

"You driving?"

"No, miss." He smiled. She cocked an eyebrow and poured him his drink.

"I'm meeting Honor Holland," he said. "Do you know her?"

"I know everyone," Colleen answered. "I'll send her over when she gets here."

Tom made his way to a booth at the back of the bar

where they could talk about illegal matters privately. There was a uniformed policeman there, but he was occupied with a pretty redhead, so the fact that Tom was perhaps a bit drunk already might go unnoticed. And let's not forget. He was also planning to commit a crime.

He took a sip of whiskey and tried to relax. Yesterday after Candace called, he'd looked up green card fraud on dear old Google. Not encouraging. Jail time. Whopping fines. Deportation with no possibility of ever living in the States again.

He could go back to England. Visit Charlie once or twice a year. And then—Tom could see it already— the visits would become less frequent. He'd get weary of trying to carve out a friendship with some kid who bloody well hated him. Charlie would turn to drugs and terrible music—or even worse music, as the case might be. Tom would marry some nice English girl who'd resent the time and money it took to cross the Pond, and the memory of that small, lovely boy who'd once flown kites with him would fade into obscurity.

Fuck-all.

"Are you Tom?"

He looked up and there was Catfight Woman Number One standing right in front of him. "Hello! It's you!"

"Um, have we met?"

"Not officially," he said. "Though I have fond memories of you."

He could do worse, he noted. She was…all right. She was sort of pretty. Also, she was here, which was nice of her. Unfortunately, he seemed a bit knackered. This would be a case of subliminally shooting himself in the foot, he might say, if he were an aficionado of Dr.

Freud. Yep. Pissed. His vocabulary and accent tended to mushroom exponentially when under the influence.

She frowned. "I'm Honor Holland."

Something moved in her handbag, and Tom jumped. "Shit, darling, I hate to tell you this, but there seems to be a rat in your bag."

"Very funny. It's my dog."

"Is it? If you say so. Well, Honor Holland. Lovely to meet you."

"You, too." Her expression contradicted that statement, but she sat down. The rat peeked out of the bag and bared its teeth. Ah. It *was* a dog, he was almost positive.

"So." She folded her hands—pretty hands, very tidy with clear polish on her short nails—and looked at him. "I gather you're the Brit who was in the bar the night of my little...meltdown."

"Darling, that wasn't little," he said warmly. "It was bloody magnificent."

"Can we skip over that?"

"Absolutely! Though if you'd like to reminisce, I'm all ears. Your hair's quite different, isn't it? Looks better. That sister-wife thing was a bit off-putting. Also, there's less for people to grab if you get into another fight. Very practical of you. So. Shall we get married?"

His charm seemed to be lost on her. "Okay, I'm leaving. I don't think we need to waste any more time here, do you?"

"Oh, come now, darling. Give us a chance, won't you? I'm a bit nervous." He smiled. When he smiled in class, most of the females (and a couple of the lads as well) got a bit swoony.

She blushed. Brilliant. She covered by looking into

her purse, where the little rat dog was still baring its teeth at him. Tom tried smiling at the dog. Didn't have quite the same effect as it had on the wee beastie's owner.

The server appeared. "Hi, Monica," Honor said. "Got anything special tonight?"

"We've got two bottles of the McGregor Black Russian Red."

"I'll have a glass of that, then."

So Miss Holland wasn't leaving yet. "And I'll have another of these," Tom said, holding up his empty glass.

"No, he won't," Honor said.

"Taking care of me already, love?" he asked.

"You got it," the serving wench said, giving Tom the eye. He winked at her, and off she went.

"Are you drunk?" Honor asked.

"Please," he said. "I'm British. The proper word is *pissed.*"

"Great," she muttered.

"So, Miss Holland. Thanks for coming to meet me."

She didn't answer. Just looked at him, expressionless.

She wasn't bad. Nothing wrong with her. Blondish hair. Brown eyes. Normal build, though he wished the shirt was a bit more revealing so he could take a look. Those pearls weren't doing much for her sex appeal.

Take them off, and yeah, he could imagine her in bed. Quite vividly, in fact. On second thought, leave the pearls on and take off everything else.

Oh, shit. He rubbed the back of his neck. The server brought Honor her wine and Tom's whiskey.

His date didn't touch her glass.

"Right," he said. "Why don't I summarize what I

know about you, and you can fill in the gaps—how's that?"

"Fine," she said.

"As I understand it, you were in love with a bloke who was clearly using you for sex and is now marrying your best mate."

She closed her eyes.

"Don't forget, darling, I had a front-row seat that night. So now you've realized your knight in shining armor is, in fact, a faithless whore of a man—"

"You know what? It wasn't like that. So shut up."

Tom leaned back in his seat and squinted at her. "Funny, that. How women always rush to defend the men who've scraped them off their shoes. Interesting." Now was the time he should stop talking. "Anyway, you backed the wrong pony and now you're a bit desperate. Want to get married, prove you're over the wanker, pop out a couple kids while there's still time."

She sputtered. His mouth kept doing its thing. "That's all fine. As for me, I need a green card. Not sure about kids just yet, but I say let's get married and figure that out later. You're female, you're not old, you're not ugly. Sold."

God. He was such a bunghole.

She stared him down. Had to give her credit for that. "I'll let you get the check," she said.

The relief he felt was mixed with regret. "Cheerio, then. Lovely to meet you."

"Wish I could say the same," she said, sliding out of the booth.

"Don't forget the vermin," he said, nodding to her bag. She grabbed it and left without looking back.

"Well done, mate," he said to himself, a familiar

feeling of disgust in his stomach. He pressed his fingers against his forehead for a second, resisting the urge to follow Miss Holland and apologize for being such a prick.

It was just that using someone was easier in theory than in reality. Even for Charlie's sake.

Besides, he'd been with a woman who was in love with someone else. Been there, done that, had those scars.

And realizing she was the woman who'd been so… passionate that night…he rather liked that wine-tossing, hair-pulling woman. Someone like her deserved better than a marriage of convenience, whatever her reasons for coming here tonight.

CHAPTER FIVE

"I DON'T KNOW if I'm the red-lipstick type," Honor said two nights later. "I feel a little like Pennywise the Clown."

"God, remember Jack made us watch that?" Faith exclaimed from where she was smooching Spike on the bed. "I practically wet myself, I was so scared. Not that you look like him, Honor," she added. "Not even close."

Colleen O'Rourke, self-proclaimed expert on all things male, squinted critically at Honor. "Yeah, okay," she said. "A little like Pennywise. We had to try. But we're on the right path, don't worry." She plucked a pink-and-green hairband from the basket where they still resided. "And can I just say how glad I am to see that those hairbands have gone the way of the dinosaur?" She tossed it on the floor, where Spike immediately pounced and began gnawing. Blue, Faith's gargantuan Golden retriever, whined from his hiding place under the bed, as he was a big baby where Spike the Ferocious was concerned.

Honor frowned, then remembered not to (time for Botox?). She still wasn't used to her hair, kept trying to swoop it off her shoulders, only to realize it was gone. That, combined with more makeup than she'd worn in the past twenty years, made her reflection quite unfamiliar.

"You look great," Faith, the bringer of all this stuff, said reassuringly. Until her sister had arrived a half hour ago, Honor's dressing table had only contained a hairbrush and a jar of Oil of Olay moisturizer (the same brand Goggy used, Faith pointed out). Now, the table surface was awash in girlie stuff—blush, eye shadow, seven different types of moisturizer, brushes and wands and tubes and pots.

Yes. Honor had agreed to a makeover. Things were feeling a little desperate. Could new eye shadow change her life? She was about to find out at the ripe old age of *the years are precious, egg-wise.*

But doing things differently...that was the whole point, wasn't it? Even if she did look slutty. Then again, slutty might be good.

"I hear there's a makeover," came a voice, and Prudence banged into the room, clad in work boots and flannel and holding a glass of wine. "Why wasn't I invited?"

"You can be next," Colleen said. "I've been dying to get my hands on you for years."

"To tell you the truth, I *have* been wearing some makeup lately," Pru said. "Carl and I did a little *Avatar* the other night, and I'm still washing blue off the sheets."

"Thanks for sharing," Faith said. "Another movie dead to me."

"Why? What else have I ruined?"

"Last of the Mohicans, Les Mis, Star Wars," Faith began.

"Don't forget *Lincoln,*" Honor added.

"And *The Big Bang Theory,*" Colleen said.

"Hey, we didn't know that wasn't porn," Pru said,

grinning. "And go ahead, make fun of me. I've been happily married for almost twenty-five years." She took another sip of wine. "Honor, you look a little like Pennywise the Clown. Go easy on that foundation."

Honor gave Colleen a significant look, and Coll sighed and handed her a tissue.

"Is the mascara supposed to look this clumpy?" Honor said, leaning forward. "It's getting hard to open my eyes."

"Put on another coat. It'll smooth out," Colleen ordered.

Blue whined again from under the bed. "Man-up, Blue," Faith said. "Little Spike here only weighs four pounds."

"She's up to five. And she has the heart of a lion," Honor said. Blue remained where he was.

"So why were you meeting Tom Barlow the other night, Honor?" Colleen asked.

Honor looked away from her reflection and pulled on her earlobe, then made herself stop. Cartilage started to break down when you were over thirty-five, she'd just read. Didn't want droopy earlobes to match her AARP eggs. "He's the nephew of a friend of Goggy's or something. I was just being polite."

"He's cute, don't you think?"

"I did until he opened his mouth." She rubbed her lips with the tissue. Still more red. This stuff never came off, apparently.

"Really? He seems nice enough. Single. Keeps to himself most of the time. Too bad he's not older, or I'd totally go for him. It's the accent. I practically come when he orders a beer."

"You should hear Carl speak German," Pru said. "*Très* sexy."

Honor flinched at the image, and Colleen handed her another tube. "Here, try this shade."

She obeyed as Faith and Colleen doled out tips. *Press your lips together. Keep your lips apart. Blot. Rub. Dot. Smear.* Who knew lipstick was so hard? Now on to blush and bronzer, both women chattering away like blackbirds. They were being awfully nice, Honor thought, helping her become more appealing to men.

The only trouble was that men were hard to find in a town of seven hundred and fifteen.

You know, it was funny. When Honor had seen Goggy's friend's nephew in the bar the other night, she… *felt* something. Her heart did this weird twist, and hope rose so quickly and so hard that she literally stopped in her tracks.

Tom Barlow wasn't middle-aged or odd-looking. He was…he was…well, not quite handsome. Straight brown hair cut very short. Normal enough features. But there was something about him—maybe it was just the surprise that he was actually age-appropriate and not a balding, big-toothed math teacher who smelled like mothballs—but no, even past that, Honor *liked* that face. It wasn't a perfect, beautiful face, like Brogan's, but she had the feeling she could look at that face for a long, long time and not get bored.

His eyes were dark, though she couldn't exactly tell the color, and a scar cut through one eyebrow, and even though she realized she shouldn't be aroused by the mark of some past injury, she kinda was. His mouth was full and—holy ChapStick, Batman, suddenly, she could *see* things happening between the two of them;

she could *feel* a strong squeeze not just in her chest, but also from Down Under, the killer combination, and suddenly the eggs were primping in front of a mirror.

In a flash, Honor had imagined laughing with Tom Barlow about their fix-up and strange circumstances, and he'd be so grateful she came to meet him, and heck, what was this? A spark. A *connection*. He'd walk her to her car, then lean in and kiss her, and she'd bet both thumbs and a forefinger it'd be fantastic.

Tom Barlow had looked up. Smiled. His front tooth was just slightly crooked. For some reason, it made her knees go soft and weak, and those bridge-playing eggs of hers made a rush for the door.

And then he spoke, and thus died the fantasy.

Colleen leaned over her with what had to be the seventeenth makeup item.

"Okay, no sparkles," Honor said. "I think we're good, don't you? I feel like I could write my name in this."

"You look gorgeous," Faith said. "Years younger."

Ouch.

"Not that you need to, of course," Faith added with a grimace. "Thirty-five is the new, uh, eighteen."

"So a date, this is exciting," Pru said, rubbing her hands together. "What's his name again?"

"Um, it's Slavic. Droog."

"Oh, dear," Colleen said. "Can you imagine calling that out at the big moment? 'Droog, Droog, don't stop!'"

Honor grimaced. "It's something to overcome, I'll admit."

"What's in a name, though?" Faith said. "If he's cute, the name won't matter. You'll probably love it after ten minutes."

"I hate dating," Honor admitted. "I'm so bad with men."

"Yeah, that's true," Prudence said thoughtfully at the same instant Faith said, "No, you're not!"

"Oh, sure I am," she said. "But I'm really good at accounting. We all have our gifts."

"Girls!" Dad bellowed up from downstairs. "Levi and Connor are here!"

"John Holland!" yelled Mrs. J. "Stop yelling like your daughters are a team of mules!"

The bedroom door opened. "Ladies," Levi said. His eyes stopped on Faith, and Honor suppressed the familiar envy. Her sister and Levi had known each other for ages, but only recently started getting along. As in, the air was thick with pheromones of the newlyweds.

"Blick. Young love. I'm so over them, aren't you?" Colleen asked Honor.

"Nah. I like them. Hi, Connor."

"Hello, Holland women, hello, twin sister," Connor O'Rourke said. "Wow, your hair, Honor. I keep forgetting."

"I found him wandering the streets," Levi said. "Figured we'd come see what you girls were up to."

"Go have a drink with my dad," Faith said. "This is a girl thing."

"No, you know what?" Colleen said. "This is great. Boys, what do you think? How hot is Honor? Not historically, but right here and now."

"Please don't answer," Honor said.

The two men exchanged a relieved glance.

Hang on. Why wouldn't they want to talk about how hot she was, huh? "Actually, do answer. How hot am I, guys?"

"I'll go see about that drink," Levi said. "Connor?"

"Don't you move," Honor ordered. "You owe me, Levi Cooper. Okay, I realize this is awkward, you being my brother-in-law and all, but Colleen's right. I could use a male opinion."

"Is invoking my right to the Fifth Amendment a good enough answer?" Levi asked.

"No," said Faith. "You have to answer."

"No, I don't."

"Then I'm cutting you off," she said.

Levi gave her a sleepy look. "You'd climb me like a tree after one day."

"I would, too," Pru said. "You're a good-looking guy, Levi."

Honor turned away from the mirror and trapped both men with her gaze. because yeah, she was good at that. Authoritative. "Boys, you don't want to be on my bad side, do you?"

"I know I don't," Connor said.

"Smart of you. Relax. I'm just looking for some insight." Hey, why not? She'd already lost all dignity with the catfight. Plus, these guys knew her. "Why don't men think dirty thoughts about me?"

"We do," Connor said. "Not to worry."

"No, you don't."

"No, we do. We're guys. We automatically assess any woman for sex. Right, Levi?"

Levi scowled in response.

"Is that true?" Honor asked. Men were such aliens. "Really? You look at a woman, every woman, and imagine having sex with her?"

"I don't," Levi said.

"He's lying," Connor answered. "We're guys. We think about sex with every woman."

"Really. Every woman?" she asked. Connor nodded. "So someone like Lorena Creech," she continued, naming the scariest woman she could think of. Lorena, age sixtysomething, fifty pounds overweight, a penchant for see-through animal-print clothing. "You've thought about having sex with her?"

"Well, yeah, same as you think about being eaten by a shark or getting your testicles caught in a bear trap," Connor said. "If you're a guy and a woman walks past, you look at her, imagine sex, then you either shudder in horror or make a play."

Honor pursed her lips. "So I got the shudder of horror?"

Connor looked stricken.

"Busted, jerk," his twin said.

"Um, no. I… You're not *horrifying,* Honor. You're quite…"

"Quite what? That's what I'm trying to figure out."

Connor appeared to be sweating. "Um, it's hard to put a finger on it. You're very, uh, attractive."

"You're an idiot, Connor," Prudence said.

Honor sighed. "Levi? Got anything? I'm your sister-in-law. Help me. As a man, what do you think when you look at me?"

"My wife's sister."

"Before you married her, dummy."

He cocked an eyebrow. "See, there you go. You're a little…"

"Be careful," Faith warned. "I'll have to kill you if you hurt her feelings. Is your life insurance paid up? If I have to be a widow, I want to be rich."

"No, just be honest, Levi. Go ahead." Honor folded her arms and waited.

Levi paused. Sighed. "I guess Connor's right. It probably crossed my mind once or twice." He glanced at his wife. "But just as a fleeting thought, and way before we hooked up, babe."

"Because I'm not pretty enough?" Honor guessed. It was to be expected. Faith got the looks.

"You're pretty enough."

"Don't blow smoke."

"Okay, you're not pretty. I thought you were, but you must be right."

Huh. That was kind of nice, and Levi *was* rather known for being blunt. "Sorry. And thanks. But if I'm pretty, why didn't you ever want to sleep with me?"

"This is very uncomfortable."

"Just theoretically."

"Yes, Levi. Theoretically," Faith said.

"Better you than me, pal," Connor muttered.

Levi closed his eyes briefly. "It's not your looks. You're a little…unapproachable."

Honor's mouth dropped open. "What?" She was not! She was very pleasant! *Very* approachable. *Extremely* polite. Like…finishing-school polite. First Lady's social secretary polite and pleasant. That was basically her life, being nice to people all the livelong day, no matter how much she occasionally wanted to strangle them.

"Exactly," Connor agreed. "You're—what do you girls call it? Walled off. Shut down. You have armor."

"I don't have armor!" Honor barked. "I don't! What armor? There's no armor!" Spike barked in agreement.

"You want to go out for dinner?" Levi asked Faith.

"Maybe you're just unaware of the vibe you give

off," Colleen said. "The hairbands, for example. Do they scream sex? No."

"I'm not unapproachable," Honor said to her brother-in-law.

"Okay, you're not. I apologize. Faith, save me."

"I have an idea," Faith said. "Honor, pretend you're meeting Connor for the first time. Like you guys are on a first date, you've been chatting online, but this is the first time you've laid eyes on each other."

"Great idea," Honor said. "Sit, Connor."

Unapproachable. Armor. Please. Spike came over and whined to be picked up. She obliged, kissing the dog on the head. So approachable. Even animals thought so.

"That dog will have to go," Colleen said. "It's worse than a cat."

"How dare you," Honor murmured, giving Colleen a look. "Come on, Connor. Get in character."

"Yeah, Conn, get to it," said Colleen. "We have a bar to run. Who's opening tonight, anyway?"

"Monica." Connor sighed and sat obediently across from Honor at the foot of the bed. "Hi, are you Honor? I'm Connor."

"Oh, Connor and Honor! That rhymes!" Colleen said. "Sorry. Back to you two."

"Hi, Connor. Nice to meet you." Totally approachable. She shot Levi an icy glare. He was busy giving Faith a steamy, *let's-get-it-on* look.

"You're even prettier than your picture," Connor said.

"Thanks." She smiled brightly.

"Eesh, you look like a wolverine when you smile like that," Colleen said. "Easy, girl."

Honor sighed, then tried again, baring only a few teeth this time.

"Now you look feeble. Don't worry about it, we'll work on that later. Just keep going."

Connor was Faith's age. A nice guy. Good-looking. An excellent bartender. Otherwise, she didn't know him too well. "So tell me about yourself," she said.

"Good line," Faith murmured, swatting at Levi's hand.

"I'm a bartender who likes the smell of crisp autumn leaves and Johnson's baby shampoo."

Honor paused. "That's kind of creepy."

"See? You're gutting me already. I feel emasculated."

"Well, then, you need to sac up a little, don't you?"

"And we're done," Connor said. "Levi, how about that beer, pal?"

Pru went off with the guys, but Faith and Colleen spent another half hour giving her advice on how to talk to men, which was not something Honor would've suspected she needed to be taught. With Brogan, she'd just been herself.

Okay, not a great example. Thinking his name still made her brain cringe.

The troops finally left, and Honor got dressed in the outfit Faith had picked out. Jeans (Colleen's, and they stopped a good four inches below the belly button and felt freakishly uncomfortable), purple suede ankle boots with three-inch heels (Faith's, obviously), a pale green shirt (Colleen's), pearls (Mom's), four silver bracelets (Faith's) and long, dangling silver earrings (Faith's again).

Clearly, Honor had no idea how to dress herself.

Then again, that was the point. Short hair, better clothes, makeup. She'd be married in no time.

"Droog. This is my husband, Droog." Okay, it lacked a certain élan.

Spike was sleeping on Honor's pillow, worn out from emasculating Blue, who wanted very much to love Spike but which Spike wouldn't allow. Her doggy had been a rescue, so Honor wasn't sure what her history was with other dogs. Bossy, obviously, which Honor admired.

At any rate, Mrs. J. would take her into her apartment for the night and watch whatever violent TV show she was into this week. The housekeeper loved Spike more than she loved most humans.

She tiptoed down the stairs, terrified of falling in the high-heeled boots and breaking a femur or rupturing her spleen, and went into the kitchen.

"Oh, God!" she blurted. She leaped back into the hallway, pressing her back against the wall. Holy. Fungus. "Sorry, sorry!"

"We weren't doing anything!" her dad yelled as a kitchen chair crashed to the floor. "It's not what you think!"

"Honor Grace Holland, why are you sneaking around this house, creeping up on people?" Mrs. Johnson said.

"We were just kissing!" Dad said.

"Is it safe to come back in?" she asked, feeling a laugh start to wriggle around in her stomach.

"Yes! We weren't…we were just… Oh, jeesh. Is that the phone?"

"Don't you move, John Holland. We were *not* kissing, Honor," Mrs. Johnson said darkly. "Your father, the ridiculous man, asked if he could kiss me just the one time. And just the one time it will be, John Holland, if you can't keep track of which of your many children is skulking around corners."

"Okay, okay," Honor said, going back into the kitchen. Dad's face was bright red, and Mrs. Johnson looked like she was about to kick a baby dolphin, she was so mad. "I'm sorry I didn't make more noise. I didn't know there was a romance unfolding here. I'll tie a bell around my neck next time."

"There are no bells required! There is no romance!" Mrs. J. thundered. "It was an experiment only, and one of complete failure, given your intrusion, Honor. We thought you had left with the others. Your father *said* we were alone."

"Mrs. J., I'm sorry, okay? Don't murder my dad." He sent her a grateful look.

The clock ticked on the wall.

"So," she said. "Dad and Mrs. J. I like it."

"There's nothing to like, you wretched child," the housekeeper muttered.

"Oh, stop. Your guilty secret is safe with me. But let me tell you, if I'd been Faith, you'd be packed into the back of her car, on your way to a justice of the peace this very minute. And Jack would be dead on the floor of a heart attack."

"My poor Jackie," Mrs. J. said. Honor rolled her eyes.

"Anyway, more power to you," she said. "I'm going on a date. Mrs. J., would you watch Spike?"

"Of course. Where is the little baby now? And why did you name her Spike? She should have a delicate name. A girl's name. Princess or Sugar-Paws."

"Or Hyacinth," Dad said. It was Mrs. Johnson's first name, and he was gazing at the housekeeper with a dopey smile.

Well, well, well. Honor said good-night and walked out to her car.

Last fall, Dad had decided to start dating…sort of… but after a few failed attempts, he seemed to give up. Mrs. Johnson was single (they all thought; she was a mystery wrapped in an enigma), and she'd been with the family since Mom died.

But a romance between the two of them, huh? If there'd been handwriting on that wall, Honor had missed it completely.

It could work, though. Certainly, Mrs. Johnson was a wonderful (if terrifying) person. She took good care of Dad and all his kids. Certainly, she knew all of them inside out and out.

It was nice to picture her father with someone. Not so alone anymore. He'd always had her, of course, which was a little pathetic when she put it like that. But still. They'd always been two single people alone together.

A surprisingly strong band of loneliness tightened around Honor's chest. If Dad and Mrs. Johnson became a couple, where would that leave her? She'd have to move. She couldn't be the spinster daughter, living with the newlyweds, sneaking Bugles into her room and misery-eating as she watched *I Didn't Know I Had a Parasite.*

All the more reason to put the pedal to the metal and get going, the eggs said. *We want to be fertilized.*

"You have a point," Honor muttered, starting her car. If Dad could find a honey, surely she could, too. eCommitment had recently come up with two matches for her. One was married, a Google search had revealed (thank you, Faith). So Droog it was.

See? She was trying. Really hard. She did need to

get a life, and not just because Dad might beat her to the altar.

Three days ago, Dana emailed, asking if she was ready to hang out. Honor had been out of town on a sales trip to Poughkeepsie and had only responded to say so. Then yesterday, Brogan left a message, saying he was back from Tampa and would love to see her for dinner.

And last night, Honor had a panic attack, abruptly terrified that she'd die in this bed where she'd slept most of her life, and Dad, not the most observant man in the world, would think she was traveling, and Spike would chew off the tip of her nose for food, which would mean closed casket, definitely. This pleasant little fantasy had led her to visiting OnYourOwn.com and cruising through profiles of sperm donors, and then panicking a little further. She'd soothed herself by making a list of things she needed to do for the Black and White Ball, which was only a month and a half away, and ended up working until 3:00 a.m.

"Mom?" she said as she drove out of town. "I could use a little help finding a man. Okay? Be my wingman."

Please God, Droog Dragul would be nice.

"Honor?"

Honor's head snapped around. Oh. Oh, dear. "Droog?"

"Yes. How luffly you look," he said. He grabbed her by the shoulders and leaned in to kiss her (eep!). She leaned back as far as possible, which caused his lips fall on her chin, where they stayed for a horribly long moment before she wrenched away.

"Um, hi. Hi, Droog. Nice to meet you."

Don't judge on first impressions had been the advice from Faith and Colleen. Droog was lucky, in other words.

They were in the middle of the student center at Wickham College, where Droog headed up the Science and Engineering department. The Droog in front of her bore little resemblance to the Droog in the eCommitment photo (she should really stop thinking his name, which was not improving with repetition). No, his photo had apparently involved Glamour Shots, a spray tan and many dedicated hours with Photoshop. The actual live Droog (there it was again) looked ten years older and was considerably whiter. Also, he carried a purse. Not a cool, battered leather satchel, but a purse that Honor had been eyeing last week at Macy's.

"Come. Vee vill go in my car. I heff Dodge Omni. It is old, but very good gas mileage."

"You know, I think I'll drive myself," she said, wiping sweat from her forehead. "It's, uh…it'll be easier for me to get home."

"As you vish."

It was possible, Honor thought as she followed him outside, that Droog Dragul's accent would grow on her. After all, hadn't she loved the Count on *Sesame Street?* Perhaps his narrow face would be more attractive in a softer light. And she herself was no supermodel.

She wondered if he could see himself in a mirror. If he sparkled. *Stop judging,* she told herself. He couldn't help being Transylvanian or Romanian or Hungarian or whatever it was.

She smiled firmly (though hopefully not like a wolverine) as he led the way to the parking lot. If nothing else, this date would be practice. It had been several years since she'd been on a first date. Years.

The sound of feminine laughter, and lots of it, made her turn her head. A gaggle of girls clustered around a man. He turned her way.

Oh, fungus. It was Tom Barlow.

Without thinking, she ducked, pretending she dropped her keys. Hey, why not actually drop them for authenticity purposes? She did. Kicked them under the car a little so she could have more time. Hopefully, Tom and the gaggle would move on.

"Heff you lost something?" Droog asked, bending to help. He was very tall.

"Um, no, no. I just dropped my keys." Right. So she should pick them up and not just stand here, hunched over like Quasimodo. She squatted down and reached under the car, feeling only gritty pavement. Took a peek. Great. She'd effectively kicked them out of reach.

"I vould help you, but dee cartilage in my knees has torn and shredded, and I can no longer kneel. Eh heh heh heh."

One! One beeg mistake! Two! Two bad knees!

"Hallo, Droog. Hallo, woman on the pavement."

She sighed. Busted.

"Tom, Tom, how are you, my friend?" Droog asked. "I vould like you to meet my date, Mees Honor Holland."

She looked up. Tom raised an eyebrow, a small smile playing around that mouth. "Oh," she said flatly. "Hi."

"Lovely to see you again," he said.

"Heff you met before?" Droog's eyebrows rose way, way up on his giant forehead.

Tom just kept looking down at her. "We both live in Manningsport," he said after a beat, and his accent was *so* much more appealing than the Count's. "Met at the pub one night, had a bit of a chat. Small town and all. Have you dropped something, Honor?"

"Um, my car keys," she said.

He knelt down next to her, and she caught a whiff of his soap. He hadn't shaved recently, and his jaw was bristly with stubble. Or maybe it wasn't bristly. Maybe it was soft. Those *lips* would be soft, that was for sure.

Give us five minutes and we can be ready, the eggs said.

Tom leaned over, and something surged inside her. For one nanosecond, she thought he was going to kiss her, and yes! That would *fine!* Her eyes fluttered; the left one got stuck, thanks to the clumpy mascara. But no. Of course he wasn't going to kiss her here on the pavement (or ever). He was reaching for her keys.

Which put his head very close to her, um, special places. Her uterus wobbled, and she pictured the eggs taking up a battering ram.

"Everything all right with your eye?" Tom asked with a knowing grin.

"Everything's fine."

She could probably hate this guy, if they spent much more time together. With superhuman eyelid effort, Honor managed to unstick her lashes as Tom groped under the car, then straightened up and handed her the keys. "There you are," he said, his eyes filled with laughter. Gray eyes.

Kind of a gorgeous color, really. The lake in November, dark and deep.

"So you're on a date with Droog, are you?" he asked. "Great guy."

"Yes," she said briskly. She'd almost forgotten about

the Count. "Droog, sorry about that. Let's get going, shall we?"

"Have fun," Tom said.

"Tom, I veel see you tomorrow," Droog said, opening the door of his rusting, maroon-colored Dodge Omni.

"Thank you," she said to Tom. He smiled over his shoulder as he headed for his car, and damn. That was a Mack truck of a smile. And by the way, he was not built like Ye Typical Math Teacher, no sir. Broad shoulders. Rather perfect ass.

Then he glanced back again, and Honor was abruptly aware that she was still staring after him. He cocked his eyebrow as if knowing she was ogling him. He was probably used to it, she thought as a young (and beautiful) woman cantered to his side. Why didn't he marry that one, huh? Why meet Honor if women were throwing themselves at him?

The man was not particularly likable. Droog, on the other hand, thought she was luffly. It didn't make sense to let Down Under start getting all tingly and warm when the man causing those feelings had been such a boor.

"Do you like bowling?" Droog asked a half hour later as they sat in the little restaurant. "I luff eet. Dee crash of dee pins, dee joy on the dee faces of dee cheeldren." He smiled. "Perhaps we may try it sometime."

There would be no bowling.

Honor had definitely ruled out marriage and children with Droog Dragul. In addition to the faint fear that he was going to throw his head back and start howling, or start counting things. (*One...one pointy knife! Two! Two major blood vessels in dee neck!*) Droog had wiped down everything at their table with antibacterial wipes he produced from his purse, including their chairs and the floor around them. "Now I heff created clean space," he said, smiling.

Dexter the serial killer leaped to mind.

Then Droog ordered water and took a sandwich from his purse. Baloney on white bread.

It was a long eighty-three minutes.

To his credit, when he asked her for a second date, Droog took her rejection well. "Ah, yes, I understand," he said. "Vee don't have the cleek."

"The cleek?" she asked.

He snapped his fingers. "The cleek."

"Oh. Right. The click." Honor forced a smile. "But it was very nice meeting you, Droog."

"And you, as vell, Honor. Good night."

So. No potential husband. Maybe she'd call Jeremy and ask about sperm banks.

It's just that she *wanted* a husband. A nice man would be enough. He didn't have to be Brogan—all that and turquoise eyes, too—he just had to be…decent. And normal. Not someone who brought his own food to a restaurant.

Too bad Tom Barlow had been such a twit.

CHAPTER SIX

"Oh, Tom. It's you. Hello. Take off your shoes, don't forget."

He obeyed. "Janice. How are you?"

"Fine, fine. Come on in." She held the door open, and Tom entered, ignoring the sinking feeling he always had when he was in the home of Charlie's grandparents. The living room was a pinkish color, making him feel as if he were sitting inside a salmon. His feet sank into the plush pink carpet as dozens of sightless eyes stared at him. Creepy, those dolls. Janice collected them—hundreds of them, all the same size, dressed in everything from a frilly bikini to a wedding dress, sat in specially made glass cupboards like a tiny, evil army, ready to break out of their bondage and attack anything male.

Poor Charlie, having to live with all these dolls. Tom could only imagine what the boy would say to his friends. Not that he had friends who came over. Or any friends, for all Tom could tell.

"And where's Walter today?" Tom asked, rubbing the back of his neck. "Is he about?"

"No, he's down at the barber shop. Hiding, and I can't blame him." Janice eyed his crotch, as was her habit. Uncomfortable, to say the least. He was always a bit afraid to turn his back on her. "You're good to come,

Tom," she said. "You don't have to do this, you know. You're not obligated."

"No, no, I love spending time with him." Janice raised her eyes from his groin long enough to give him a dubious look. Right, so that might be pushing it a bit. "And he can always visit me any time, stay over."

"You're a saint," she said. "Sit."

Tom obeyed, the plastic furniture cover squeaking as he sat.

"He's so sullen. He barely speaks to us, and why, I have no idea, after all we've done for him."

"Yes, you've been wonderful," Tom lied.

She gave a martyred smile. "It's what Jesus would do. Well, you must want to be on your way. Charlie!" Tom jumped at the abrupt shift in volume. "Tom's here!"

There was no answer.

"I'll get him." Janice sighed. "He's locked in that room of his and never answers." With that, she tromped up the stairs, leaving Tom alone with the doll army.

It was impossible not to look at them. Today, the doll dressed in the flamenco outfit seemed especially hostile. "Piss off," Tom whispered. No wonder Charlie was in a bad mood all the time.

And speaking of, here was the boy himself. "Hallo, mate!" Tom said, standing up. "How are you?"

It was almost a shock to the eyes, the black of Charlie—clothing, hair, nails and mood. At some point last year during what seemed to be a particularly horrifying puberty, Charlie had turned punk, or Goth, or whatever they were calling it these days. Baggy black clothes, black eyeliner, black fingernail polish. There were a few of that type at Wickham, shuffling around campus, their chains rattling, but they seemed like happy enough kids.

Charlie, on the other hand…

He didn't look at Tom, just walked past, out the front door, as cheery as if he were on his way to get a lethal injection.

"Right," Tom said to Janice. "I'll bring him back around seven, then?"

"If you can stand him for that long," she said, staring at his junk.

"You, um, enjoy your time."

He walked out to the car, where Charlie was already seated, earbuds in place, starting ahead with the long-suffering expression only a fourteen-year-old boy could manage—*Look at me, surrounded by these wankers, counting the minutes till I can get away.*

"How've you been?" Tom asked, getting in and starting the car. No answer from his companion, though Tom could hear the tinny sound of…well, calling it music wasn't really fair. "School going all right?" No answer. "Buckle up, mate, be a good lad." And no answer still. "Charlie, come on."

Charlie said nothing, just buckled up, rolling his eyes as he did so.

"So I thought I'd take you into town, do something fun, then back to my place for dinner—how's that sound?"

No answer.

And he had the kid for four more hours.

There seemed to be a new piercing through the cartilage of Charlie's left ear. Looked infected from here, the skin angry and red from the safety pin stuck through it. "Make sure you clean that properly," Tom couldn't stop himself from saying.

He doggedly kept up the chatter: the weather, the town, the lake, the Buffalo Bills (he had no idea if Charlie was interested in football, and he himself wasn't, but you never knew) until they pulled into the parking lot. And finally, the boy spoke.

"What are we doing here?" His voice, once so angelic, had changed over the past few months to a respectable baritone. Still a bit hard to get used to, that voice. Like when the little girl starts speaking with the demon voice in *The Exorcist*.

"It's a gym," Tom answered.

Charlie cut him a glance so filled with disgust it was hard to recognize the boy who'd once jumped into his arms.

"Right, right, the sign does tell you that, doesn't it?" Tom cleared his throat. "Thought we could check it out."

The truth was, Tom had no idea what to do with Charlie, whose only interests seemed to be terrifying music sung by Satan and body-piercing. The days of kites, bike-riding and make-your-own sundaes were over.

But Tom had boxed for years, gone through university on a scholarship, in fact, and made it through several regional championship matches. It had been a bit of a surprise that Manningsport had its very own boxing gym, an old-school type of place filled with the smell of sweat and leather and the rhythmic smacks of men and women punching the bags or jumping rope. He'd joined the first week he moved here.

"I'm not going in there," Charlie muttered, looking out the window.

"I can't leave you in the car."

"Yes, you can."

"It's cold. Besides, I've got you till seven, so we've got to find something to do."

He waited, and after a second, Charlie opened the door and shuffled inside the gym. Tom followed, gym bag in hand.

"It stinks in here," Charlie pronounced, the earbuds still in place.

"It smells like a gym, that's all. Come on, mate, give it a try."

"I'm not your mate. That sounds so gay." His voice was loud.

Tom tried not to clench his teeth. "Where I'm from, it means *friend*."

"You're not my friend, either. And you're not my father, or my stepfather, and I hate it when you call me your stepson."

"Right. At any rate, I thought we'd give boxing a shot. No harm, is there? It wouldn't hurt for you to have some life skills. I got you some trunks, a helmet, a pair of gloves—it'll be fun."

"It's not *fun!*"

"And keep your voice down, all right?" He pulled out one of Charlie's earbuds, and the kid reacted like Tom had slapped him.

"Don't touch me! I don't have to do what you say!"

Oh, fantastic, someone was coming over. Someone with impressive muscles, a military-looking tattoo, no less, and a badass look on his face.

"Problem here?" the guy said.

"Not unless you count moody teenagers as problems," Tom said, forcing a smile.

The smile was not returned. Nor did the man look sympathetic to Tom's plight. "Everything all right?" he asked.

"No," Charlie said, rolling his eyes. Tom almost wished they'd get stuck, the way his own father had always promised.

"I'm Police Chief Cooper," the man said to Charlie. Bloody wonderful. "How do you know this man?"

Soon, Tom imagined, he'd be in a cell for attempted child abduction, or worse. Though now that he thought of it, being sent back to England—or prison—didn't actually seem so bad, when compared with dealing with the kid.

Charlie didn't answer.

"I'm a friend of the family," Tom said.

The chief didn't seem impressed. "Is that true?" he asked.

"I don't know," muttered Charlie.

"Would you like me to take you home?" the chief offered.

"No." Charlie said it in the way he said everything these days: with thinly veiled disgust.

"And what's your name, sir?" the cop asked, and Tom found himself giving his name, address, Janice's phone number and waiting as Chief Cooper verified the information and then called the police station to run a check of his criminal records, of which there were none. Finally, he put away his phone, then offered Tom his hand. "Sorry," he said. "Can't be too careful."

"No worries. Thanks for checking up." *Perhaps you can do a cavity search next time, mate. Cheerio.*

The chief nodded and walked back to the bag from which he'd come, and began throwing some jabs.

"I'm not *boxing*," Charlie said. "It's so stupid."

"Fine," Tom said. "Then sit here and watch. And don't walk out, or I'll have to call the nice officer over and report you as a missing child."

Tom went into the locker room, changed out his teacher's clothes and into boxing trunks and a faded Manchester United T-shirt. Sighed at his reflection in the mirror, then went out again.

He'd reserved the ring for an hour, naively thinking that Charlie might welcome a little instruction in self-defense. Back in the day, they used to pretend to spar. Back in the day when Charlie loved him. "Into the ring, mate," he said, keeping his voice cheerful.

Charlie obeyed, his baggy pants making it difficult for him to get between the ropes. "All right, now, I thought I'd show you a few basic jabs and punches," Tom said. "First thing, fighting stance. Relaxed, yeah?" He demonstrated, holding his hands up by his head, feet apart. "Keep your weight on the balls of your feet, because you want to be able to move. This is your space, and you own it."

His unofficial stepson slumped to the floor of the mat and took out his phone, which began emitting irritating little burps and beeps. Tom went over and squatted in front of him. "Charlie? Pay attention, mate."

"Why?"

"You might learn something."

"It's stupid," Charlie muttered, going back to his game.

It was hard not to slap the stupid thing out of his hand. "Right," Tom said. "So you move like this, always keeping your feet going. In, out, in, out. Just a little movement, very controlled, hands up by your temples, weight forward."

Charlie wasn't listening. And it was bloody embarrassing, talking to a kid who was clearly ignoring him, the eyes of the cop on them more than once. But they were here, and a boxing ring was one of the few places Tom knew what he was doing. "Jab, turning your hand, put your shoulder into it, and then, snap, back again to protect yourself."

The computer game continued to chirp and beep.

Bollocks.

The clock slowed to a crawl, but that was the thing with kids, right? You couldn't let them dictate everything. Or something.

After a lifetime, the endless hour passed, and Tom pulled on his sweatshirt.

"Let me know if you want a sparring partner sometime," the cop called.

"Will do," Tom said, raising a hand. "Thanks. Come on, Charlie. Off we go."

The boy remained barely conscious, for all that he interacted with Tom, as they drove the short distance to Tom's place. He unlocked the door and stood back as the kid went in.

"So I decorated a bit, tried to make it a little more homey than the last time you were here," Tom said. "I bought some things for your room." Was that a mistake, to call it Charlie's room? He'd wanted him to feel like he had an option to Janice and Walter's, that any time he wanted a place to go, he could come here.

Hadn't happened yet. Despite the Tuesday afternoons, when Janice forced the lad to spend time with him more for her sake than his, Charlie hadn't taken him up on the offer.

But now, to his surprise, the boy went upstairs, his feet thudding heavily on the stairs. Tom followed. Charlie glanced in at Tom's room, which was bare bones at best, then went into the room across from it. This was the room Tom had worked to make appealing, and he said a silent prayer that Charlie would like it.

The walls were white; the bed was covered in a black comforter (Charlie's favorite color, after all). A bureau from IKEA, which had taken seven hours to assemble, and him a mechanical engineer.

On one wall hung a Manchester United poster; once upon a time, Charlie had watched matches with him on the rare occasions that American television carried British football. On the bureau was the Stearman PT-17, the last model airplane he and Charlie had worked on together, still waiting to be finished. A bookcase filled with half of the young adult and science fiction novels the small bookstore in town had stocked, because Tom didn't know what Charlie was reading these days. A collector's edition of *Lord of the Rings,* just in case. The complete *Harry Potter* series, once beloved by the boy.

And then there were the photos. A shot of Charlie— his school picture from last year, one of those ghastly photos set against a gray background, Charlie's face unsmiling and hard. Another of a younger Charlie, standing in front of a stream. Tom had taken him fishing—they'd caught nothing, but had a fantastic time throwing rocks into the water.

And on the nightstand, a photo of Charlie and Melissa, both of them smiling.

She'd had her flaws, absolutely, but she had certainly loved her son.

Charlie stared at the photo.

Then he turned and shut the door in Tom's face without a word.

LATER THAT NIGHT, after the agonizing visit had ended and Charlie had been returned to his grandparents', Tom was considering a trip to O'Rourke's, which had a magnificently stocked collection of single malt whiskey and Scotch in addition to eighteen types of beer. Perhaps Droog was up for a drink and some darts.

Then again, it was past ten.

Perhaps Tom should get a dog. Or a cat. Or a fish.

But chances were he'd be leaving America soon. He'd had emails from both of the companies he'd applied to, informing him they'd hired another candidate, as Tom had expected they would. No work visa meant he'd have to go home.

It would be all right, he told himself, ignoring that flash of pain in his chest. It wasn't like he was doing any good here, anyway.

The bleat of his cell phone startled him. He looked at the screen. "Charlie?" It was a first, the boy calling him.

"Can you come get me?" The words were muttered, barely audible over the background din.

Tom paused. "Yeah. Of course. Where are you?"

Charlie mumbled an address and hung up.

Twenty minutes later, Tom turned onto a grungy street in Bryer, two towns over from Manningsport. His heart pulled the second he saw Charlie, a small, dark smudge sitting on the curb.

"Hey," Tom said, rolling down the window. "Hop in."

Charlie did, walking faster than his usual shuffle. He slumped in the seat.

"Buckle up, m—"

"Just get out of here," Charlie said, pulling the seat belt across him.

Tom obeyed. It was hard to tell in the dark, but by Charlie's careful breathing, he thought the boy might be crying. A block down from where Charlie had been waiting, people streamed and yelled from the porch of a dilapidated two-family house. Most were wearing similar clothes to Charlie's—black, torn, adorned with chains and metal. A thunking bass rhythm slammed into the car, making it reverberate.

Charlie sat low in the seat, looking at his lap.

When they left the neighborhood, Tom glanced over. "Bad time?"

Charlie shrugged. There was a trickle of blood coming from his ear, where the safety pin pierced the cartilage, and for a second, Tom's vision flashed red. He turned his eyes back to the road and loosened his death grip on the steering wheel.

"Did someone hurt you, mate?" he asked softly.

"No."

"Your ear's bleeding."

Charlie reached up and touched it. "It got caught."

Bullshit. Someone had roughed up his little boy. Again, he had to force his hands to relax. "Want to stay at my place tonight?" he asked, trying to keep his voice casual.

"Okay." Charlie looked out his window, his face away from Tom. "Don't tell my grandparents the party was so...whatever. They'll freak."

"Right. I'll call them when we get home and let them know you're with me."

When they got to Tom's, Charlie headed straight upstairs. "Do you need anything?" Tom asked.

"No."

"Make sure you clean that cut, all right? There's hydrogen peroxide in the cabinet." He nodded toward the loo.

"Okay." Much to his surprise, Charlie turned and almost managed to make eye contact. "Thanks," he mumbled to the region of Tom's collarbone.

Despite the black eye makeup and piercings, Charlie's face was still that of a little boy, his skin unroughened by beard, his jawline still soft, reminding Tom of the kid who'd never run out of things to talk about at bedtime.

"You're welcome," he said, then cleared his throat. "Any time."

Then Charlie closed the door, and Tom felt a rush of love so deep and fast and helpless that it felt like he'd been punched in the chest.

What kind of a gobshite picked on a kid who still didn't weigh a hundred pounds? And just who would Charlie have called tonight if Tom went back to England?

No matter what it took, he was staying.

CHAPTER SEVEN

AT 4:45 ON Friday afternoon, Honor was contemplating another cruise through eCommitment or OnYourOwn.com and wondering if four was too many times to see the latest Bond movie. But Dad and Mrs. Johnson had an in-house date, since Mrs. J. thought it was too soon to go out in public, so Honor wanted to make herself scarce. Because, my God! What if an in-house date meant she had to overhear something? Then she and Spike would have to kill themselves.

However, once again making the trek to the theater and power-eating popcorn and Sour Patch Kids (the ugly face of addiction…or the ugly hips, as the case may be) held little appeal, even if she could look at Bond, James Bond, for two hours. Plus, the low-bellied clouds looked like they were about to birth some snow. The lake was black from here, and the grapevines were dark and twisted. The air was raw with cold.

Maybe she'd just stay here and work, despite her pledge to be different. The Black and White Ball wasn't far off, and it was Honor's pet project of all the charity events Blue Heron participated in or hosted. The ball raised money for the parks and recreation services in town. In years past, the ball proceeds had funded a new playground, replacing the rusting equipment Honor herself had played on, a skateboard park and the municipal pool.

This year, the funds would go toward making a hiking and bike trail through some of Ellis Farm. Everyone could use it, of course, not just kids, but it was special to Honor's heart. Manningsport, while as beautiful a town as America made, had pockets of need. Kids who grew up in the squat brick houses at the edge of town, or the trailer park, didn't have what Honor had growing up—woods and fields to romp in. Orchards and sledding hills, a shallow pond for skating. In her mind's eye, she envisioned buying a small herd of Scottish cattle for the 4-H program, a flock of chickens, maybe a few rescued horses. The land would be for those kids, so that they could enjoy the riches of the area, get away from their televisions and Nintendos and feel the connection to the land the way she did.

The ball would be held in the Barn at Blue Heron, the space that Faith had converted last fall—once a crumbling stone barn, now a stunning, bright space overlooking the rest of the vineyard. Her sister had quite a talent. And red hair. And the cutie cop.

Okay, none of that. She ran her hand over her own hair. She had good hair now, too. The rude Brit had been right: it had been a little sister-wife.

So yes. While Jessica Dunn and Ned were doing just fine, the Black and White Ball was Honor's. And lists needed to be made. Or remade. Or color-coded.

Just then, her phone rang, making Spike leap up from her beauty rest and bark four times. Honor lunged for the phone before Jessica could answer it. "Honor Holland," she said, using her smooth, Blue Heron voice.

"It's your father speaking," Dad said. "Reminding you that you have a life and need to leave the office."

"Dad, no one leaves work at five."

"Get out. Go to O'Rourke's with one of your friends."

Honor winced. Unluckily, no one in town had died since the catfight...no one had even been arrested or had sex in a public place (except maybe Pru and Carl, though they hadn't been caught). In other words, she was still the hot gossip. O'Rourke's was out.

"And, um, don't be home before ten," Dad added, his voice sheepish.

"Why? Wait, scratch that, I don't want to know." Honor sighed. "Okay. Maybe I'll swing by Pru's and stay over."

"Oh, honey, that'd be *great*."

"Dad, please."

"I'm sorry," he said. "It's just...well, you do what you want, Petunia. Just give me a call if you do decide to come home. Let the phone ring twice. That'll be our code."

"Got it. Code, as in don't you dare be doing anything in the living room that would cause emotional scars for your spinster daughter."

"You're not a spinster. Go out. Have fun. Meet some young people."

"I hate young people." She paused. "Can I at least come home to change and feed my dog?"

"Of course. Just, um, make it quick, okay? Oops, I have to go. Mrs. Johnson's glaring at me. Love you!"

"You should probably start calling her by her first name," Honor said, but her father had already hung up. She sighed. It'd be nice to be able to tell her sisters about this (it might be fatal to Jack), but Mrs. Johnson had made her swear not to tell yet.

Honor scooped up Spike and kissed the dog's little head, getting a joyful snuzzle in return. "Let's run away, just us two," she said. Spike wagged in agreement.

Young people and friends. Outside of her relatives, no one leaped to mind. Maybe Jack would want to watch *Top Ten Tumors,* a show dear to both their hearts. She could go to Rushing Creek and talk about artificial hips, or she could go to her grandparents' house and do the same thing. Maybe get rid of some of their stuff. Help Goggy clean out the pantry, which held canned goods from the 1980s.

A knock came on her door frame. "Hey. Sorry to interrupt," Jessica Dunn said. "I took a whack at the press release for the tourism magazine."

"Great! Let's take a look." Delegation, delegation. It was supposed to be a good thing.

Jessica handed her the paper. "I also posted a picture of the cask room on Facebook and Twitter and asked everyone what wine was in their fridge. And I made a list of some potential blog topics for you, too. Oh, and here's your calendar for next week."

"Thanks," Honor said, her heart sinking a little.

Jessica had worked here for two weeks now, and Honor was a little intimidated by how terrifyingly efficient she was. Didn't smile much, did everything from empty the trash to bring Honor coffee to write copy (pretty damn well, too).

Jess stood there a minute as Honor read what she'd done. It was friendly, informative and seemed to be missing all of one comma. Honor looked up. Jess was frowning.

Honor knew this was her first job outside of waitressing; the girl (woman) had acknowledged that on her first day. So far, she'd been quiet, hardworking and a little tense, almost as if she was worried she'd be fired. It was kind of endearing. Faith had mentioned that she'd always been a little scared of Jessica Dunn; Honor didn't see why.

"This is great," she said. "I almost can't remember what I did before you came." *You worked sixteen hours a day,* the eggs told her.

Jessica smiled a little. "Thank you."

"Hey, Jess, do you want to get a drink? Since it's time to go?"

"Shoot, I can't. I have to work. I'm on at Hugo's."

"Right." Crap. "Another time, I hope."

"I'd really like to. I just…I still need the other job. Student loans, you know?"

"No, no, it's fine." Maybe she shouldn't have asked. Maybe that was inappropriate. Maybe Jessica didn't want to have a drink with her boss.

"I could do Tuesday," Jess offered.

The relief was a little pathetic. "Great. Sure, Tuesday, then."

Just then the phone rang; they both lunged, but Honor won again. "Blue Heron, Honor Holland speaking."

"Hey, On, it's Brogan."

She felt the blood drain to her feet. Since the catfight (cringe), she hadn't actually spoken to him, aside from a few very superficial and cheery emails. "Hi there, Brogan!" she said. Her voice sounded weird. "How are you?" Better.

"I'm good, I'm good. How about yourself?"

"I'm really great. So good. Truly. I'm excellent!" Oh,

Lordy. Jess gave her a sympathetic look and slipped away to her desk. "So, what's up?"

Brogan paused. "You think you could meet me for dinner tonight? Or a drink?" he asked. Honor grimaced hugely. "Just you and me," he added.

I'd rather swallow a live eel, Brogan. "Oh, shoot, hang on a second, I have another call," she lied. She pushed the hold button. "Jess? You still there?"

Her assistant reappeared. "Yes?"

"I'm sure you heard about my brawl a few weeks ago." Jessica nodded. "Brogan wants to get together for drinks."

"Yick." Jess pulled a face.

"Thank you. Do you think I should go?"

"Have you seen him since the fight?"

"Nope. Do I have to go?"

Jessica leaned in the doorway, then shrugged. "Yeah, you kind of do. Sorry. You don't want him to think you're sulking."

"That's what I thought, too. Crap. Thanks."

"Come to Hugo's. I'll spit in his drink for you."

"Really?"

"No. But I'll want to." Jessica smiled.

"I appreciate that." Honor pushed the button back. "Sorry, Brogan," she said. "Sure, I can meet you for a bit. How's Hugo's?" Jess gave her the thumbs-up and disappeared again.

Brogan let out a breath. "Oh, that's fantastic. Can you be there in an hour?" His voice still made her stomach pull.

"Okay. Um, Brogan, I can only stay for a little while," she added. God forbid they were together long enough for him to...*get* to her again. "I, um, I'm meeting someone. Later. After I see you. It's a date. I mean, I'll have a date later tonight. I *do* have a date."

Spike stared at her, hypnotized by the lies.

"Awesome," Brogan said happily.

"Yes, yes. Okay, I have to go. I'll see you at six o'clock at Hugo's. Great. Bye. Take care."

She hung up and let her head fall backward. Her armpits were damp with sweat. Plus, the clouds were releasing their burden, and fat snowflakes filled the air. Beautiful, except it was March. Just when you thought spring was really going to come through, Mother Nature bitch-slapped you with a storm.

Spike scrabbled at her leg, and Honor lifted her into her lap. "You get to stay home," she told the dog. "And you better TiVo *Top Ten Tumors* for me."

AND SO IT was that an hour and twenty-three minutes later, Honor was fake-laughing at Hugo's, sitting across from the only man she'd ever loved, slightly sweaty, stomach churning with acid and vodka from the perfectly chilled, slightly sweet Saint Germaine martini Jessica had brought her.

This was…what was the word for it? *Hell.* Yes. This was hell, and she was pretending to have a wonderful time. *Oh, Satan, you're so droll! Hahahahaha!*

Because yes, Honor's stupid heart had done that squishy, painful thing when she saw him. At the moment, Brogan was telling a story about an athlete who did a sport that involved running, and you know, at least she could stop storing away this kind of information so as to be the Most Perfect Companion Ever. At least there was that.

Your attitude could use adjusting, said her aging

eggs, fanning themselves. *Yowza! Here comes another hot flash!*

"You're kidding. That's just crazy," Honor said out loud. Hopefully her comment made sense, since she clearly wasn't paying a lot of attention.

It wasn't fair.

She still felt for him. You don't love a guy for seventeen bleeping years and then just stop. At least, Honor didn't. Unfortunately.

Brogan had now moved on to a story about his parents, whom he'd just seen in Florida. Kind of surreal that just over two months ago, Honor had been having dinner chez Cain, had flashed Brogan's parents, had imagined them as her in-laws.

Now, she just hoped her sweat wasn't showing and was counting the seconds till she could leave for her pretend date. At least the restaurant was practically empty, given the raw weather and the fact that Hugo's had just opened for the season last week.

You know, she was so good at her job. For the past eleven years, she hadn't made one major misstep at work. All her decisions had been sound, had proved to be good investments, smart moves.

On the personal front, a fail. She'd chosen the wrong friend, the wrong guy.

Next time she had an instinct about someone, she was going to do the opposite thing.

Nodding all the while, Honor stared at Brogan. Why were his eyelashes so long? Why had God seen fit to give him that perfect, curling, chestnut hair? Hmm? Anyone? Bueller?

They'd been here for twenty-seven minutes. About twenty-eight minutes too long, in other words. Did Dana know he was meeting her? Was Dana at Brogan's right now, in the same bed where Honor had—

Oh. The sports story was over. Brogan was looking at her, his face concerned. "Honor, are we okay?" he asked gently, and her face burned with heat.

"Yes! Yes, we're fine. It's fine. I've practically forgotten about it." She forced a laugh, making her sound like a dying seal. Faking. Not her area of expertise. Jessica, who was taking an order at a nearby table, shot her a look.

"It's just that we've been friends for so long," he said. Damn those blue eyes. The concern in them seemed genuine. It probably was. Brogan was not a faker, either.

"Look, Brogan," she said, keeping her voice low. "I was surprised, I overreacted and I'd love it if we could just drop the subject. Okay?"

He nodded. "Of course. It's just…I hate thinking that I led you on," he said. "I always thought we felt the same way about each other."

She took a large swallow of her drink. "No, we did. We do. Um, I care for you. As a friend. When I asked you if you wanted to get married, it was an ill-formed thought." One she'd spent roughly six years thinking. "I'm over it. Really."

He smiled a little. "Good. I'm glad. You mean so much to me."

God. This night was endless.

"Can I get you guys anything else?" Bless her, Jessica was here with a pitcher of water.

"We're good, I think," he said. "Do you want another martini, On?"

"Oh, no! No. Nope. Thanks. I have to get going pretty soon," Honor added.

Brogan's face lit up. "Right! Your date. We'll take the check, then, Jess."

Thank you, baby Jesus! This interminable evening would finally end, and then she *was* going home to watch *Top Ten Tumors,* and she didn't care if Dad and Mrs. J. were doing it on the hallway floor. On second thought, maybe she would call Pru and see if she could crash. She and Abby could watch the tumor show together.

Jess went off, and Honor forced a smile and looked at Brogan. Three more minutes, and she'd be free.

He was staring at his glass. "I'm so glad we can still be friends," he said. "And I hope you and Dana can be patch things up, too."

Two and a half minutes. "Oh, you know. I'm...it's..."

"She said you guys talked a little. Told me you cut your hair. It looks really nice, by the way. Kind of shocking, but really nice."

"Thanks."

He shifted in his chair. "Um, did I tell you I'm gonna join the volunteer fire department here? I thought it'd be good."

"That's great," she said. Two minutes and twenty-four seconds.

"So you're seeing someone?" Brogan asked.

"Excuse me? Oh, yes. Yes, I am. Mmm-hmm."

"What's he like?"

"Uh, he's so..." An image of Droog mopping the floor with Wet Ones popped into her head. "He's, uh, European. Very funny. Cute accent." *One! One terrible lie! Two! Two minutes till you can leave!*

"Think it's something special?" Brogan asked.

"Possibly. It's a little early to tell. Maybe." She

smiled, hopefully not like a wolverine. A bead of sweat trickled down her back, irritating as a housefly.

"That's good. I'm really glad to hear it." He took a breath, then another. "Honor, I have to tell you something, because I don't want you to hear it from anyone else." He hesitated. "Dana's pregnant."

Honor was fairly sure her expression didn't flicker. Her eyes, though…something was wrong with them. *Blink,* the eggs advised. Right. "Pregnant?"

"Yeah. We just found out. It was a surprise, but we're really, really happy."

He was. She could see it in his ridiculous-colored eyes.

He was going to be a father.

Dana never wanted kids. She'd mock the obsession of new mothers, saying, "Another friend gone." And when a patron would ask if she wanted to hold a baby, Dana would pass, then later say, "Why would I want to hold that little petri dish, right? And the smell, Honor! Can you imagine wiping someone's butt eight times a day?"

The thing was, yes. She could. She'd *love* to wipe someone's butt eight times a day. To cuddle a baby against her cheek, breathe in the smell of a sweet little head, hold a tiny hand in hers.

"Are you okay?" Brogan asked.

"Yes," she said faintly. Oh, crap. There were tears in her eyes. She looked down, then forced a smile. "I'm happy for you, Brogan. I am. This is great. Babies are… they're so…magnificent. This is great news! Good for you guys!"

"Honor? Hey, sorry to interrupt." It was Jessica, angels bless her. The woman was getting a raise. "Your date's here."

Honor blinked. "He is?"

"Yeah." Jessica gazed down at her, her expression calm. Okay. Right. She must've heard the lie from before and was throwing her a rope.

Brogan looked at her expectantly.

He was going to be a *dad*. She could picture it so clearly—tall, handsome Brogan Cain cradling a little bundle in his arms, looking at the tiny face with wonder.

She took a deep breath. "I have to go. Brogan, congratulations on the…on the baby." Her voice wobbled. "I mean it. Best wishes." Tears wrapped around her throat and squeezed.

"Thanks, On." Brogan stood up. If he hugged her, she would lose it.

He hugged her. Her heart folded in on itself like a dying bug as she breathed in his familiar cologne. Chanel for Men. It always got to her.

"So," Brogan said, releasing her. "Where is this guy? Can I say hi?"

Oh, fungus. Honor stood up, grabbed her coat. "We're meeting in the parking lot." If she didn't get out of here, she was going to cry. In public. And wouldn't that suck.

"No, he came in," Jessica said. "He's at the bar."

He was? They all looked, Honor half expecting to see Droog Dragul. But Jess had never met Droog, and if Droog was actually here, it would be the universe's biggest coincidence. Nope, no Droog.

Brogan took out his wallet (and yes, by all means, let him pay). Mercifully, his phone began playing the theme song to *Monday Night Football,* and he picked up. "Hey. How's it going?" he said, turning slightly away.

"Who are you talking about?" Honor whispered to Jess.

"What do you mean?"

"I don't have a date."

Jessica's eyes widened. "Oh, shit," she whispered. "I heard you say you were meeting someone, and he had a cute accent...."

"I was lying," Honor whispered back.

"But there's a European at the bar. He's British, I think." She pointed to someone's back. Manningsport wasn't exactly a microcosm of the world. Europeans were in short supply. Honor looked.

Oh, God. It was Tom Barlow. He seemed to feel her looking, because he glanced over, did a double take and waved.

In about four seconds, Brogan was going to stand up and want to meet her nonexistent boyfriend.

Honor was across the restaurant before she was aware she'd moved. "Hey," she said without preamble. "I'd be eternally grateful if you'd pretend to be my date for a second." *Please don't be an ass. And please be sober.*

His eyebrows raised. He glanced to where she'd been sitting. "Oh, right," he said. "There's the object of the catfight. You look like you might vomit. No puking, please, and if you cop a feel, it'll cost you extra." He put his arm around her. "There you are, darling," he said in a slightly louder voice, and before she knew it, he kissed her on the lips.

Instinctively, she tried to jerk away, but he held her a little closer. "Now, now," he murmured against her mouth. "We're deeply in love."

And he kissed her again.

And that mouth…oh, Mommy, it felt good. Soft and firm, and not too much, but just exactly the kind of kiss a woman would want if she were meeting her man, and something locked inside of Honor opened in a rush.

Then he stopped and smiled at her.

That was some kiss. That was a food-for-thought kiss and would require some serious analysis.

Analysis? the eggs said. *You gotta be kidding.*

Jessica was fixing a drink behind the bar, and here came Brogan, all tall, easy grace. "Hey, there. I'm Brogan Cain. An old friend of Honor's."

"Hallo. Tom Barlow. A new friend of Honor's."

"Where are you from?" Brogan asked.

"England."

"Awesome! I've been there a few times. The Olympics, a few soccer matches."

"Football, mate."

Brogan laughed easily. "True enough. It's football when you're over there."

Super. Brogan was about to make a new best friend.

Her eyes felt too wide. There was Jeremy the-years-are-precious-egg-wise Lyon, leaving with his boyfriend, Patrick. He waved and gave her a subtle thumbs-up, lest she forget that her breeding years were almost behind her. Emmaline Neal, who worked at the police station with Levi, also waved, holding the door for her mother.

Tom turned to her, and touched her earlobe with one finger. Her entire left side electrified. "Honor, darling, are you hungry?"

She swallowed. "I am. I'm starving. I'm really, really hungry. Let's eat."

"I love how she babbles when her blood sugar's low." Tom shook Brogan's hand. "Great meeting you."

"You, too. Have a good night." Brogan leaned in to kiss her—something he'd always done, on the cheek, in public, one of the ways he'd always made her feel special. But times were different now, and she took a little step closer to Tom. Brogan caught himself, and for the first time ever, he looked a little…awkward. "Well. See you soon, On."

They both watched him leave. "Smug bastard, I thought," Tom said.

"Thanks." She was suddenly aware that his arm, heavy and warm, was still around her shoulders. "I'm so sorry," she said, stepping back. "It was a rock-and-a-hard-place moment."

"Absolutely. I owe you for being such a prat when we met before." He took a sip of his whiskey. "Care for a drink?"

Honor started to shake her head automatically, but caught herself. Different. Doing different things, being different. That was the color-coded plan.

"I'd love one." She looked at Jessica. "I'll have a Grey Goose. Straight up, please." Jess obliged, and Honor took the drink and drained it.

"That bad, is it?" Tom asked.

"No, not at all. Why do you ask?"

That was some kiss.

"Why don't you guys grab a table?" Jessica suggested. She pointed them to a table in the corner of the bar, over by the fireplace.

They went over, the warmth of the fire at Honor's back, snow falling heavily out the window. Now that she had a moment, she took in her companion—a green river man's shirt, the top three buttons undone, giving her a glimpse of a silver chain. Dark jeans and sturdy leather shoes.

He looked utterly...male.

Jess brought her some seltzer water, which was her drink of choice at work. Sweet of her to remember. "Do you want another Grey Goose, Honor?" she asked. "Or anything to eat?"

"No, no. I'm all set."

"I thought you were starving," Tom said.

"Nope. Just one of the many lies I told tonight."

He smiled, and Jessica patted her shoulder before sliding away.

"Nice girl," Tom said.

"She is. She works for me," Honor said. "At the vineyard."

"Blue Heron, isn't it?"

"Mmm-hmm." The adrenaline rush was fading, leaving her feeling a little limp. "You should come on a tour sometime."

"Maybe I will."

"Every day at three, then four times a day after May 1."

Tom Barlow smiled a fast, sweet, crooked grin, and Down Under tightened in response.

No. She wasn't the type. She didn't pick men up in bars, not that he was interested. What had he said that night? *You're not ugly.* Talk about damning with faint praise. Nope. Not gonna get involved with a man looking to commit marital fraud.

That had been some kiss.

Do something about it, the eggs said. They were now sporting bifocals and quite irritable. *Can you please get a move on here? We're going to bed when* Dancing with the Stars *is over.*

Tom took another sip of his drink and looked at her. "Tell me again what you do, Honor. I was too busy being an idiot to ask the night we were set up."

Work. She could always talk about work. "I'm the director of operations for our vineyard. Media, sales, staffing, distribution. My dad and brother make the wine, my older sister handles the farming, my nephew helps out everywhere and runs the tasting room in the season. And my grandparents are semiretired. Can't forget them."

"Sounds idyllic." He seemed to mean it.

"The farm's been in the family for eight generations. We're all part of it in some way."

"What's it like, working with your family?" he asked.

"Oh, it's wonderful, except when it's horrible." He grinned again, that flashing, unexpectedly sweet smile, and again, Honor felt a little jolt of lust. His smile changed his face from rather somber to utterly adorable, like a mischievous little kid, and wow, yes. It worked.

"I always thought it'd be lovely to come from a big family," he said.

"It has its moments."

Maybe it was because he'd already seen her at her worst, or had already essentially rejected her, or simply because he'd been nice and pretended to be her boyfriend. Maybe it was the snow and the quiet of the evening; Jessica was reading a book at the bar, and all the other patrons had left. Maybe it was the Grey Goose on an empty stomach. Whatever the case, Honor felt herself relaxing. The armor (if there was armor, and she was pretty sure Levi was wrong on that front) was nowhere to be found.

Do something different.

"How about you, Tom? Do you have any brothers or sisters?"

"Sorry to say, I'm an only child. My dad lives in Manchester."

"Go United."

He winked and flashed that smile again. "I think I just fell in love with you."

Had she found him irritating? She couldn't seem to remember why. "Don't take it personally," she said. "It's my cocktail party brain."

"Say again?"

"My cocktail party brain," she said. "I can make small talk about anything."

"Anything?"

"Mmm-hmm."

His eyes narrowed, a smile playing at his full, gorgeous lips. "Is that right? Tell me something about developments in medicine."

"There's a new drug that stops the progression of Alzheimer's. FDA approval expected within three months."

"Is there? Of course, you can make stuff up, I'll be none the wiser. Music trivia?"

"Ray Charles had twelve children."

"Did he? Fancy that. All right, let's get to my side of the pond. Royal family?"

"Philip and Elizabeth, Margaret, Harry, Andrew, Kate, William, Beatrice, Pippa…you'll have to be more specific."

"Divorces in the royal family, then."

"Everyone except the old folks and the kids."

He laughed. "True enough. American foreign policy?"

"Speak softly and carry a big missile."

"Mechanical engineering."

She opened her mouth, then shut it. "I give. I don't know anything about that."

"I'm a mechanical engineer."

"I thought you taught math."

"No. Do you know what a mechanical engineer does?"

"Um… You can fix a lot of stuff?"

His smile grew. *Oh, sigh,* said the eggs. *Think of what we could do with his DNA.* "Yes," he said, "That's it exactly."

"You understand how things are built," she said. It sounded vaguely dirty.

"Yes."

"You know how to…get things going."

His eyes dropped to her mouth. "Mmm-hmm."

"You're good with your hands."

He leaned forward. "Are you flirting with me, Miss Holland?" he asked, his voice low.

Oh, crap. Well, she'd been trying to. Where was Colleen O'Rourke when you needed her? She practically had a master's degree in men. Honor straightened up and put her hands in her lap. "No."

"You don't need to stop," he said mildly. "It was quite nice." He leaned back in his chair. "For the record, a mechanical engineer is responsible for how just about anything is built. We make sure any type of structure or vehicle or roadway is strong, safe and will stay together."

Strong, safe, stay together.

Meow.

Flirt with him. Do it! the eggs demanded.

It was now impossible to flirt. She racked her brain for flirtiness. Tried to channel Colleen. Nope. Nothing. She shifted, her leg bumping his. *We can work with that,* said the eggs. *Almost there.*

Shut up, Honor said. *We're not getting pregnant tonight, okay? Just go back to* Dancing with the Stars.

"I saw you at the college that day," she said. "You seem to have a lot of female students."

"The Barbarian Horde, I call them, most of whom will flunk out before midterms. Speaking of that, how was your date with Droog?"

"Oh, he seems very nice."

"Did he swab down the table before sitting?"

She smiled. "Yes."

"He does that everywhere. Good chap, though." He paused. "Will you see him again?"

All of a sudden, Honor could hear her heart beating. "No."

They didn't say anything else for a minute. The fire hissed and snapped, and the snow was piling up, a lot more than the dusting the forecasters had predicted. It would be smart to head home, as conditions on the Hill tended to be worse than here in the Village, thanks to the difference in elevation.

She didn't move.

"So you and Prince Charming are still chums?" Tom asked. "Even though he chose your friend?"

She felt the start of a slow burn in her cheeks.

"Sorry," Tom said. "None of my business."

"No, it's fine," she said. "Brogan and I have known

each other since elementary school. Slept together on and off for years." Probably more than Tom Barlow wanted to know. "He wanted to tell me that he's going to be a father."

"Are you joking?" She shook her head. "Bloody hell." Tom rubbed a hand across the back of his neck. "And what does Brogan Cain do for a living?"

"He's a sports photographer. Baseball, football, basketball."

"I know what sports are, darling." He took a sip of his drink. "Brogan Cain," he said thoughtfully. "I hope they pick out a really shitty name for the kid. Candy Cain. Sugar Cain. Rain. Wayne. Jane. Hickory."

Honor smiled faintly. It was still almost too great a shock to process—Dana and Brogan, and now Baby Cain on the way. She'd like to laugh about it. It just didn't seem probable.

"I hope your friend gets really fat," Tom continued. "No glow for her. Heartburn. Acne. Swollen feet. A full-blown, Jessica Simpson Pop-Tarts and ice cream kind of fat."

It seemed like she was laughing, after all. "That's cute. Jessicker Simpson."

"I did not say that." He raised an eyebrow, the one with the scar running through it.

"You did. It was cute. You have a nice accent."

"I haven't any accent all, darling. It's the English language, remember? And I'm English. You're the one mucking things up, you ungrateful Yank."

Tom Barlow was growing on her.

And that had been *quite* a kiss.

"How's your green card situation?" she asked.

"It's fine. All set." He looked out the window. "Sorry

again for my behavior that night, by the way. It was a very odd meeting."

"Don't worry about it." His mood seemed to have changed. "So you just moved to Manningsport, but you've lived in America for a while?"

"Yes."

"Why'd you move?" she asked.

He paused. "A job," he said, and she sensed there was more to the story. Something tragic, Goggy had said.

"It's a nice town," she said. "You won't be lonely for long." And where had that come from?

Tom frowned. "Why do you think I'm lonely?"

She hesitated. Why had she said that, really? Somewhere in his eyes, behind the easy flirting he seemed so good at, she sensed a little bit of…sadness.

"You were here alone until I forced you to talk to me."

"Doesn't that make you lonely as well, then?"

"Nope. I'm just being nice. It's good for tourism."

"A shame. Think of the things two lonely people could get up to."

Good thing she was sitting, because her knees went hot and loose all of a sudden. *Why are you not unbuckling his belt at this very moment?* the eggs demanded, scowling over their bifocals.

"I'm not really the type," she said, her voice a little unsteady.

"Pity."

Her internal organs seemed to be melting.

Come on! said the eggs. *We're dying here! Literally!*

But doing something different did not mean picking up near-strangers in a bar. Honor wanted to get married, not just sleep with someone. She'd been sleeping with someone for fifteen years, and that had gotten her exactly nowhere. She wanted a courtship, not sex. Well, sex during courtship, that was, once a relationship had been established. Hey. She'd read all the books. Control the pace. Don't be slutty. Sex too early = abject disaster. Tom Barlow had the sexiest mouth ever.

He just looked at her, his gray eyes unreadable.

At that moment, Jessica came over. "Hey, guys. We're closing, sorry to say. It's really piling up out there."

"Right," Honor said, grabbing her purse. "I'll get this, Tom. Since you were so nice to cover for me."

He looked at Jessica. "I am rather nice," he said with a wink.

"That's not what it says on the bathroom wall," Jessica returned, deadpan.

Yes. Jessica was flipping beautiful. And Tom was *ridiculously* appealing, not to mention that accent. He'd flirted with Honor because she was there. Because he was nice, it seemed, and because it was a distraction. He'd probably flirted with Jessica and he flirted with Monica O'Rourke the night they'd met, and no doubt he flirted with Colleen. He was a flirt. Nothing wrong with that; she just shouldn't read into it.

Crap, said the eggs.

"Okay," she said, putting a twenty on the table. She'd call Pru from the car, see if she could crash there. "Thanks again, Tom. See you Monday, Jess."

"Have a great weekend," Jessica said.

"Thank you," she said to Tom, meaning it.

"A pleasure," he said. He stayed seated.

Outside, the wind gusted off the Crooked Lake, slapping wet snow against her face. She stopped for a minute, her car roughly fifty feet away. She wore suede shoes with a very modest heel because yes, she had dressed up for Brogan. Sort of. A little. She had her pride, after all. No treads, however. Hopefully she wouldn't fall.

"Honor." It was Tom, coming out of the restaurant as he pulled on his coat. "Are you wearing ridiculous shoes? You are. So impractical."

With that, he picked her up, eliciting a squeak of surprise. "You don't have to— Put me down."

"Oh, stop. You women love this sort of thing."

"Tom, really, I—"

"Stop flopping around, you're making it harder. Which car is yours? The Prius? How did I know?"

She slid her arm tentatively around his shoulders. He certainly was…solid. "It's the only car left."

"And here I was going to claim a relation to Arthur Conan Doyle."

Being carried…not quite as romantic as it seems, especially when one is not prepared. She felt a bit idiotic. His shoulders, on the other hand, were wide and solid and…and…rational thought was a little hard to summon at the moment.

He set her down next to her car. Honor's face was hot. "Well, thank you," she said. "It was nice talking to you."

He ran a hand through his hair, which was wet from the snow. "Same here."

Different.

With that, she stood on her tiptoes and kissed him, there in the soft light of the streetlamps and under the pink-hued sky. His mouth was soft and warm and utterly lovely, and he kissed her back, gently, slowly. A floating sensation filled Honor, deepening as his hand slipped to cup the back of her head.

Then he pulled back a little and tucked a bit of hair behind her ear. His eyes were soft and kind.

"Tom?" she whispered. "I think I'm that type, after all."

A corner of his mouth pulled in a smile. "The type who'll come home with me, then?"

Her hand, she noted, was resting over his heart, and she could feel it thudding solidly against her palm. "Yes," she heard herself say. "Hop in."

THIRTY-NINE SECONDS later, they were at Tom's house, which had once been the Eustaces' place, Honor remembered, a plain little house with a front porch and small yard. She opened the car door, but Tom was already out and around. He offered his hand, and she took it. That was a big hand. That was a *paw,* practically, swallowing hers.

"Change your mind?" he asked.

"Nope." Nevertheless, her heart was stuttering and racing, and a slight tremor shook her hands.

She was inside now, and Tom turned on a light that did little to brighten the gloom. She could make out an ordinary living room, ordinary furniture. A couch. Coffee table. Then he was unbuttoning her coat, and Honor swallowed. Slid her hands up his torso, feeling the hard muscles there, the contour of his ribs and shoulders under his shirt. His eyes met hers, and he gave her a small smile.

God, his mouth was…delicious. Aside from that feature, there was nothing particularly special about his face. Normal eyelashes. Normal nose. Normal everything, except put it all together, and he was incredibly delicious, and she was *pulsating* for him.

Then he led her to the couch. She'd never done it on a couch. Or anywhere but a bed, come to think of it. Was she actually going to have sex in a living room? What about the floor? The floor would be…well, she didn't know. Sex on the floor? Her? Honor Holland, the boring sister? Oh, Lordy, how did that even work? Would she get rug burn? Would he? What about—

"Sit. Your feet must be freezing."

She sat. He slid off her shoe and rubbed her foot in those mammoth hands. He was right. They were freezing, which she might not have noticed if his hands weren't so warm. He switched to her other foot, rubbing it briskly, then looked up and smiled, that lovely smile that changed his face from solemn to incredibly adorable.

She didn't realize she'd launched herself at him until she was kissing him, and hell, it'd been what, almost two minutes, possibly more, since he'd last kissed her, and she *missed* it. He landed on his back with an *ooph,* but she didn't really care.

"Hallo, what have we here?" he murmured, and she kissed him again, sliding her tongue against his, dying to kiss him, taste him, feel him. Her hands were in his hair, and he smelled like cold air and soap and tasted a little like whiskey, and my God, it was amazing, and look at her, practically straddling him, her legs tangled with his, kissing and kissing and kissing that generous, wonderful mouth, feeling a throb right down into her bone marrow.

Tom rolled over, pressing against her, cradling her face in his hands. "You sure you want to do this, love?"

he whispered, and even though it was just a Britishism, the word went straight into her.

She nodded.

"Enough said, then." He grinned again, and he lowered his mouth to hers, and suddenly, you know what, being that type was *fantastic*. The whole night was strange and surreal—Brogan and the baby and then Tom, the quiet bar, the snow, the kiss, this house where she'd never been, and good God, the kissing! Those full, soft lips, so unlike any other kiss she'd ever had, giving and tempting, making her want to do sweet, dirty things.

She wasn't the type, but hells yeah, she was doing a good impression. Her skirt slid up around her thighs as she wrapped her legs around him, bringing him closer, and Lordy, he felt so good, so solid and hard and male, completely unfamiliar, definitely a landscape worth exploring.

His hand slipped between them to unbutton her shirt, kissing the skin he exposed bit by bit, his mouth hot and gentle. Honor's vision flashed, her breath shuddering out of her. She tugged his shirt from his waistband and slid her hands up his back, feeling thick muscle and hot skin, and pulled his shirt over his head. Something metal brushed against her—a medallion, dangling from a silver chain around his neck.

He pulled back a bit, looking down at her. His own breath was ragged, and though his face had been gentle earlier, he now looked somewhat…fearsome. Down Under clenched at the word.

"You're lovely, you know," he said, smoothing the hair off her forehead, and damned if she didn't fall a little in love right then and there. Then he kissed her again, hot and deep and fierce, heavy on top of her, and she kissed him right back, her hands exploring the warm, hard expanse of his back, his heavy, corded arms.

"You're not built like a math teacher," she said raggedly.

"I'm not a math teacher," he muttered, and she felt him smile against her mouth. Then she licked his full bottom lip like she was some kind of sex goddess, like she knew exactly what she was doing and didn't have to think at all. Like she was the most beautiful woman in the world with his hands sliding into her hair, his mouth on her throat, lower now. His clever fingers unhooked her bra, and his mouth followed the path of his hands.

And Honor discovered she was most definitely that type, after all.

CHAPTER EIGHT

TOM WOKE UP in small pieces, little flashes of an unusually happy feeling bringing a smile to his face before his eyes were open.

Then his hand brushed something soft, and his eyes did open then.

Honor Holland was sleeping on her stomach, her face turned away from him. She was naked.

Right.

Last night had been…unexpected. Pretending to be her man in front of that wanker who'd broken her heart, hell, that was easy. He owed her for the night they'd met, when he'd made damn sure she wouldn't like him.

The problem had been…well, she was quite decent, Honor was. Seeing her sitting there, throbbing in pain once again because of Brolin or whatever his name was, Tom had wanted to make her feel better. Flirted with her a bit, because a talent was a talent, let's be honest.

And then something changed. When she said that thing about him being lonely, he felt like he'd been punched in the chest by Iron Mike Tyson. Funny, how a person could ignore something so effectively until someone pointed it out. Next thing he knew, he was carrying her to her car.

When she kissed him, he hadn't expected that electric current to slam through him like a thousand volts.

Hadn't really planned on asking her home. But she'd been right. He was lonely. And maybe, despite her big family, maybe she was, too.

Which was all fine and lovely, but now he had a naked woman in his bed, and aside from the obvious, he wasn't sure what to do about that. Or what to say when she woke.

Taking care not to disturb her, he got out of bed, grabbed some jeans and a pullover and closed the bedroom door behind him.

The kitchen was still a bit of a mess. Tom made coffee, then surveyed the contents of the fridge. Good. He could offer Miss Holland breakfast if she was so inclined. He'd have to clear off the table, though, because he'd set out the airplane model last night. The PT-17 Stearman, one of the great planes of World War II. Three years ago, he and Charlie had gone to an air show and seen one fly, and Tom had ordered the model the next day. Finished, it would've been the sixth model they'd done. He wondered what happened to the others.

At any rate, the Stearman was in pieces, the fuselage waiting for sides, the many pieces of balsa laying out in optimistic order. Charlie was supposed to have come around for dinner last night, and Tom thought that maybe if the airplane was right there on the table, it might garner the kid's interest. Granted, the odds of that were the same as being eaten by a giant squid, but he had nothing left in terms of new ideas on how to reach Charlie. And hope sprang eternal, or some such rubbish.

As it was, Janice called, saying Charlie had a stomachache (a lie, no doubt) and didn't want to come; hence Tom's foray to Hugo's, as the boisterous atmosphere of O'Rourke's had seemed a bit much.

Hence the hookup with Honor Holland. Probably ill-advised.

Still, a surprisingly fantastic shag was nothing to regret.

And speaking of, he heard footsteps on the stairs. She peeked into the kitchen, and he felt attraction slam into him. Hard.

"Morning," he said.

She blushed. Her clothes were rumpled, her hair disheveled. The classic walk of shame if ever he'd seen it. "Hi," she murmured.

"Coffee?"

"Sure. Thank you." He poured her a cup, and she took a sip. Her hands were shaking slightly. "How did you sleep?" she asked, and her cheeks grew pinker.

"Very well. And you?"

"Fine." She set the cup on the counter. "Listen, Tom, last night was…not my typical, um, modus operandi."

Latin, so early in the morning? "Yet you seemed quite the expert." He grinned.

The blush spread to her neck. "I'm not usually so, er, slutty. I don't want you to get the wrong impression."

"Nothing wrong with slutty. From my perspective, anyway."

"It's not that I— See, I don't generally…"

He patted her on the shoulder. "It was just a shag, Honor. You picked me up in a bar. Own it. Be proud."

She ran a hand through her hair and looked at the floor, and he felt a dart of regret sing through him. She wasn't the teasing type, was she?

"I had a nice time," he said more seriously. "I hope you did, as well."

Her cheeks practically gave off heat, they were so red. "Mmm-hmm."

"Have a seat. I can make you breakfast if you like."

"Oh, no, that's fine." She did sit at the table, however. "Model airplanes, huh?"

He sat across from her and picked up a piece of the PT-17. "I work on the real thing as well, if you're trying to impugn my masculinity. Bit of a side business. One of the many things a mechanical engineer can do, for your cocktail party brain to store away. Customize airplanes for the very rich."

She appeared to be hiding behind the coffee cup. "So this is your hobby?"

He paused. "I used to make these with my unofficial stepson," he heard himself say. "We started this one a few years ago."

"What's an unofficial stepson?"

He filed a piece of aluminum tongue, as the fit was a bit snug. "It's a surly teenager whose mother and I were once engaged." The cabane struts came next. He'd have to go slowly. Wouldn't want to finish it on his own, just in case hell froze over and Charlie decided he wanted to work on it.

"You were engaged?" Honor asked.

"Yes. She died."

He heard her quick intake of breath. "Oh, Tom, I'm so sorry."

He gathered up the rest of the wing pieces to put back in the box. "Don't worry about it." He glanced at her face. "It's been three years."

Honor nodded, still holding her coffee cup like a shield. "How old is this unofficial stepson?"

"Fourteen."

"Are you close?"

Tom rubbed the back of his neck. "We used to be, when I lived with them. Not so much anymore."

"Does he live with his dad?"

"No." As ever, the thought of Mitchell DeLuca made Tom's eye throb. "He lives with his grandparents. Janice and Walter Kellogg? Perhaps you know them. They moved here a few months ago, and I followed."

She shook her head. Took a sip of her coffee. Didn't say anything, and blessed be, because a woman who thought before speaking…that was a nice change. "How long have you lived in America?"

"Four years. I met Melissa when I was here on holiday and ended up staying. We got engaged a few months later, and she died a few months after that."

"How did it happen?" Honor's voice was soft.

"She was hit by a car crossing the street." An utterly stupid and completely preventable incident. With great care, he put the Stearman back in the box.

"I'm so sorry," Honor said again. "My mom died in a car accident, too. It's an awful way to lose someone. Not that there's a good way."

"True enough." He stood up. "I've got eggs and toast, and I'd be more than happy to make you breakfast."

"No, I'm fine, thank you."

"More coffee, then?"

"That'd be great. Thanks."

He got up and poured her a cup.

"So why aren't you close, you and Charlie?" she asked as he handed her the coffee, and some coffee sloshed over the rim, onto her skirt.

"Shit. Sorry," Tom said, grabbing a dish towel and blotting at the stain.

"It's okay. Don't worry about it." She looked at him, straight in the eye, as he was kneeling at her side.

Brown eyes. Lovely, really, dark and quiet. And at the moment, she was giving him a no-nonsense look, a tolerates-no-shit look combined with something else.

Kindness.

He looked back at her skirt and blotted some more.

"He blames me for her dying. She was…away when it happened. With Charlie's dad, who apparently liked to pop in and out just enough to fuck with everyone's head. So off they went for a weekend, and I was watching Charlie like an absolute wanker, really, taking care of my fiancée's kid while she was screwing around. Then she decided to text me while crossing the street against the light, and that was that."

"Oh, God."

"Right. When the dust settled, Charlie's dad didn't want to take custody." The familiar red haze flared, then faded. "I wanted to adopt Charlie, but I didn't have any claim on him."

The clock over the door ticked. Honor was still looking at him. "So this whole green card is so you can be around Charlie."

"Yes."

"And you didn't get one, did you?"

He rubbed the back of his neck and sighed. "No, I didn't." He stood up and took his coffee cup to the sink, dumped it. Outside, the snow fell from the branches in clots, the temperature having jumped overnight.

The chair scraped as she stood up. She came over to the counter and leaned against it, folding her arms over her chest. "What other options do you have?"

"Not many. I've been looking for another job in the

area, but I haven't had much luck. The truth is, I imagine Charlie'll be relieved to be rid of me. He barely
speaks to me."

Honor nodded. Took a slow breath and released it.
"So let's get married."

He glanced at her sharply. "Oh, no. That plan is off
the table. Thank you, but it's not…necessary."

"Of course it is," she said briskly. "You love this
boy, you need to be around for him. I'll marry you and
you can stay. You should've said this up front and not
been such an ass."

He gave her a quick smile. "Right. Sorry about that.
But you're not going to marry me. Marrying a stranger
isn't going to cure your own issues with Brighton—"

"Brogan."

"Whatever. And you want rug rats, sure, but you
barely know me. You strike me more as the sperm
donor type. That way you can get the whole list of as-
sets—blond hair, green eyes, Harvard education—and
boom. A happy single mum with an adorable tot. Possibly twins, given that you're getting up there in age.
Am I right? You're more likely to pop out a duo when
you're past forty?"

"I'm thirty-five. And don't pull that idiot act again."

Busted. "Sorry."

"The grandparents…is he close with them?"

"They do their best."

"I'll take that as a no." She pursed her lips. "Look.
I'm not going to let some poor kid who's already riddled
with abandonment issues watch his unofficial stepfather get deported. You need a green card. I'm offering."

The image of Charlie's bloody ear flashed. The
sound of the boy trying desperately not to cry in the

car. "You're right. I want to stay near him. But there are other ways."

"Which you've already tried."

He took a slow breath. "Honor, you're being a real champ here, and I appreciate it. But oddly enough, I like you, and I don't want you to marry me because you feel bad for some kid you've never met. I mean, what do you get in the bargain? It's a bit drastic, isn't it?"

"Sometimes drastic measures are called for." She looked at him steadily for a moment. "You want to get married or not?"

CHAPTER NINE

HONOR MANAGED TO sneak back into the house without running into Dad or Mrs. J. *Why* neither was around was a question best left unexplored, but still, at least Honor wouldn't be caught in her walk of shame.

It had been *years* since she spent the night in a man's bed. The entire night, that was. With Brogan, she'd yearned to stay…but he was usually in town only for a day or so, often flying out early the next morning. And despite her advanced age, she did live with her father, who would need to be informed just why his baby girl wouldn't be coming home that night.

But back to the issue at hand. She'd just proposed to Tom Barlow, whom she'd met exactly three times. Her second proposal in two months. They'd be meeting again this afternoon to talk it over.

Holy orgasm.

See what good sex could do? Check that. *Great* sex. Sex on the floor! And things were pretty fabulous down there! She had a little rug burn on one knee and one shoulder, but the rest of her had been all for it.

Tom hadn't seemed to mind, either.

No, indeed. The memory of his amazing mouth, and the way his face could change from so…intense to kind of goofy and sweet made her knees wobble as she climbed the stairs. The walk of shame, please. It was the walk of pride today.

"Hey there, Spikey-doodles," she said to her dog, who was curled on her pillow, snoring. "Want to go skating? Hmm?"

She took a shower, and it was funny. Before this morning, showers had been a way to get clean, and all of a sudden, she was lathering and daydreaming and thinking thoughts that rivaled the billows of steam.

Honor Holland: the type of woman who picks up British hotties in bars. Who went back to Hottie Tom Barlow's place and shagged him within an inch of death.

Who was maybe going to marry him.

A wave of icy panic slapped through the steamy water. Oh, God. What was she thinking?

She was meeting him later on, after the family wine tasting at four. A brisk skate at the pond would be just the thing. She got dressed, put Spike in a pink fleece doggy sweater, kissed the dog's little face four times, then tucked her into her jacket. In the mudroom, she grabbed her skates and headed out to Willow Pond, where the ice would still be thick enough.

Honor had skated all her life. She'd even done a little competing before Mom died. eCommitment had asked her to list her hobbies, and Honor was relieved to see that she still had one, at least, not counting *watching documentaries on bizarre medical conditions*.

She didn't skate too often—a few times a winter with Abby, and on Christmas Day, which was a family tradition. The Finger Lakes were too deep to freeze in the winter, but Blue Heron had a much shallower pond, a beautiful little secret, down near Tom's Woods, ringed in hemlocks and Douglas fir trees. The wind had scoured the snow from the ice, and if there was a more beautiful spot on earth, Honor didn't know what it was.

Honor sat down on her usual rock, strapped on her skates, checked that Spike was secure into her coat and pushed off. The wind whisked through her short hair and brought tears to her eyes as she glided around the pond. A cardinal flashed across the snow; Spike gave a little bark and wriggled in delight. Push and glide, push and glide. She flipped around and skated backward now, protecting her little dog from the wind.

Tom Barlow.
Reasons for:
Good in bed. (Shallow but *so* true.)
Noble reason for staying.
Likes kids.
Obviously able to commit.
Seems nice. (Okay, that was pretty weak. She could only imagine telling her father that one.)

Reasons against:
Basically a total stranger.
Doing this is illegal.
Isn't in love with me.

"Then again," Honor said aloud, her breath coming harder now, "that's not uncommon. No one's *ever* been in love with me before."

Spike barked.

"Except you," she corrected.

There was no reason to think Tom was any worse of a choice than the men on eCommitment. And then there were Goggy and Pops. Theirs had been an arranged marriage. Okay, bad example.

If I land this jump, Honor thought, *it's a sign I should go for it.*

She did the easiest jump she knew, just a little leap. Fell on her ass.

"If I land this second jump," she told Spike, "it's a sign I should go for it."

She fell on that one, too.

HONOR SPENT THE rest of Saturday in her office, researching marital fraud and immigration and giving herself an ulcer. Good God. To soothe herself, she forced herself away from YouTube and checked some orders from her distributors, ran a quick inventory, designed a new label and made sure the Black and White Ball link was live. Jessica was great, but it came as almost a relief that Honor still had things to do. Then, exactly at four, she left her office, Spike under her arm, and went into the tasting room.

This was, understandably, her favorite part of the wine business. The family gathered several times a year at least to pour the newest vintage, discuss its flavors and selling points. If it was a new variety, they'd pick a name—Half Moon Chardonnay, for example, because the harvest had gone on into the night one October and the moon had been so clear.

The rest of the family was already there. Pru, with Carl, who was making a rare appearance, and Ned. Faith and Levi, holding hands. Jack and Dad, both of them in faded work shirts and Blue Heron baseball caps. Mrs. Johnson was setting out wineglasses. Goggy and Pops sat at opposite ends of the tasting bar where, even so, they managed to annoy each other. Abby was curled into a chair, reading. "Hi, honey," Honor said, giving her niece's head a kiss.

Then Goggy spotted her and pounced, surprisingly lithe for a woman in her eighties. "Whatever happened with you-know-who?" she asked, dragging Honor a few yards away. "Who needed the you-know-what?"

"Um, let's talk later," Honor whispered.

"He's nice, isn't he? And handsome?"

And great in bed, Goggy. "Very nice," Honor admitted.

"See? I told you." Her grandmother gave her a triumphant smile, fluffed her hair and walked back to her seat.

Honor put thoughts of Tom aside. She'd deal with him soon enough, and besides, she had work to do.

When she'd graduated from Wharton, her first order of business was to overhaul the tasting room, and it was her pride and joy. A long, curved bar made by a Mennonite craftsman from wood harvested here on Holland land. A blue slate floor below, arching beams above, a stone fireplace in the corner and, best of all, the windows, which looked out over the vineyard and woods, all the way down to the Crooked Lake.

It never failed to thrill her.

As the boss of everything, she now turned to the rest of the family. "Everyone ready to taste some excellent wine?"

She poured the first, a pinot gris, and held the glass to her nose. Green apple was her first thought, then some vanilla and clove. Very nice.

"Anyone getting apple?" Dad asked.

"I am," Goggy said. "Green apple. Tart."

"I'm getting red apple. A new red apple. McIntosh," Pops said.

"It's definitely green apple," Goggy said with a glare.

"I get red," Pops said blithely. "An unripe red apple."

"Which is a green apple," Goggy growled.

"Isn't it time for one of them to go to a nice farm?" Ned whispered.

"I heard that, young man," Pops said. "Respect your elders."

"I wish I could," he said.

"A little limestone, maybe?" Faith said, and Honor nodded encouragingly. Faith hadn't been around too much in the past few years. It was nice to have her back.

"I'm getting nesberry," Mrs. Johnson said.

"Oh, yes, nesberry," Dad agreed, smiling at Mrs. J., who didn't seem able to meet his eyes.

"What's a nesberry?" Jack asked.

"I don't know. But I bet it's wonderful," Dad murmured.

"Anyone else picking up some hay?" Pru asked.

"Definitely," Ned said. "Wet hay."

"I'm getting overtones of fog and unicorn tears," Abby said from the couch, "with just a hint of baby's laughter."

Honor smiled at her niece and typed up the other comments. The nose of the wine, the taste, the finish. The texture, the overtones, the legs. Wine was like a living thing, striking everyone a little bit differently, changing with air and age, dependent on the life that happened before.

This was the culmination of the family's work. From the care of the soil and vines to the harvest to the winemaking itself, every one of them had a hand in it, big or small. The whole family, taking care of family business. Sort of like the Mob, but a little bit nicer. No murders, though you could never rule it out with Goggy and Pops, who were still fixated on the green-versus-unripe apple debate.

How strange, to picture Tom here, too. She might be married. Soon.

The thought of it made her knees zing with nervousness.

An hour later, they'd tried all four of the new varietals. In a few weeks, Honor would do another tasting with the staff and sales reps and get their input, too.

"While I've got you all here," Dad said as Goggy and Mrs. J. wrestled glasses from each other in the battle for who worked harder, "I have, um, an announcement. Of sorts. Something to tell you kids." He swallowed. Blushed. Stuffed his hands in his pockets. "Mom? Mrs. J.? Would you mind?"

"Fine," Goggy said. "I'll wash up later."

"*I'll* wash up later," Mrs. Johnson growled.

"Mrs. John—uh, Hyacinth? Would you come over?" Dad asked.

Honor's breath caught. She looked at Mrs. Johnson, who studiously avoided her gaze.

Well, well, well. Her throat was suddenly tight. She glanced at Faith, whose mouth was slightly open, and at Jack, who was eating some cheese with Pops.

"What's the matter?" Goggy asked suspiciously. "Is someone dying?"

"No, no," Dad said, wiping his forehead with a napkin, "you all remember how I started dating again last fall."

"That woman. Lorena Creech. And those clothes! I

saw her at the market last week, and she was wearing nothing but a—"

"Hush, woman, your son is trying to talk," Pops interrupted, then paused. "Nothing but a what?"

"I'm not telling you now, old man," Goggy said. "Not when you just told me to be quiet."

"Go on, Dad," Jack said. "If you must."

"It's kind of funny—no, not funny, really. Uh, why don't you tell it, Mrs.—um, Hyacinth."

"You have a first name?" Abby asked Mrs. Johnson.

"Shush, child." Mrs. Johnson crossed her arms. "Faith, this is your fault, of course. You and Honor, on a mission to marry off your poor father."

"I was also on the mission!" Pru said. "But I never get credit for that kind of thing. Is it because I wear men's clothes?"

"Fine. All three of you girls are responsible, then."

"Responsible for what?" Abby asked.

"Holy shit," Jack muttered.

"Don't curse, Jackie, my darling," Mrs. Johnson said. "But yes. After several weeks of your father irritating me and getting in my way, I relented."

"I don't understand," said Pops. "Are you quitting, Mrs. Johnson?"

Dad didn't answer, but his eyes were bright with tears, and he was smiling. He looked at her and gave a small nod.

"No, Pops," Honor said, still looking at her father, and feeling her own eyes well. "I think what they're trying to say is, Dad and Mrs. J. are getting married."

She couldn't help thinking that Mom would be awfully happy.

TOM'S CAR, AN unassuming gray Toyota, pulled into the parking lot in front of Blue Heron's tank room. The man himself got out, looking somber. Honor swallowed. What had seemed easy to say in his kitchen this morning was now a little trickier. This was their fourth meeting, for crying out loud. And that was counting the parking lot where he'd retrieved her keys.

"Hallo," he said. That accent was really unfair.

"Hi. Nice to see you again," she answered, clearing her throat.

"You, as well." He looked around. "So this is it, then? The family farm?"

"Right, yes," she said. "Um, want a tour?"

He looked at her oddly. They were here, after all, to discuss marriage, not wine. "Absolutely," he said. Maybe she wasn't the only one who was nervous.

"Okay," she said. "We grow seven different kinds of grape here. Down there is the cabernet franc and pinot noir, to the west is the gewürztraminer and merlot. On the eastern side, we've got chardonnay and pinot gris. And up on the hill is the Riesling, which this area is known for. We have some of the best Rieslings in the world, in case you didn't know."

"Yes, I've read the brochures," he said.

"It's the soil. It's magic," she said. "I mean, not literally magic, but the weather, combined with the lakes and the hills…anyway, we harvest in October or so. There's the grape harvester there. Those fingers agitate the vines, and the ripe grapes fall on the conveyer belt."

"Fascinating," Tom said.

"It is," Honor said sharply.

"No, I meant it. I love machines," he said. "Mechanical engineer, remember?"

"Right. Sorry."

"Go on, then," he said.

She led him around the barn to the juicer, explaining how the grapes were loaded and gently compressed so as not to crush the seeds and make the wine bitter, showed him how the juice ran through the tubes to the fermenting tanks.

"About ninety percent of our wine is aged in here, the tank room," she said, leading him into the barn that held the giant steel containers where the grape juice fermented. "Mostly what you need is time, but we add things like yeast, egg whites, sugar, that kind of thing."

"It's very scientific, isn't it?" he said, assessing one of the tanks.

"Yes. Jack likes to say that wine-making is ninety percent science, ten percent luck."

"And who's Jack?" he asked.

"Oh. Um, my brother. He's three years older than I am. He and my father are the winemakers, and my grandfather, too. My sister Pru runs the farming end, and I handle the business stuff."

"I see." He looked around the tank room. "Do you use wooden barrels anymore?"

"We do, though we use the tanks more," Honor said. "Come on, here's the bottling room."

"Oh, more machines," Tom said, flashing that crooked smile. "Lovely."

She started to explain how the bottling machine and labeler worked, but it was clear Tom had already figured it out. He knelt down to look at something under the conveyer belt. Nice to have someone who was genuinely interested in the process. Most people on the tours were itchy to hit the tasting room.

"And then we have the cask room down these stairs. That's where the barrels are. Watch your step. It's kind of old-school, but it's pretty, and the tourists like it."

"I can see why."

The cask room was a vast, dark room, formerly a root cellar, a stone storage area for potatoes and onions and the like. Now it held several dozen wooden barrels, a long, battered oak table surrounded by leather-upholstered chairs, some low lighting and *voilà*. People felt like they were in the Old Country.

"We use different kinds of wood for each wine. Hungarian oak gives off a nice spicy flavor, French is very mellow, American is fresh and clean."

"Interesting." He rapped one barrel. "Feel a bit like I'm in an Edgar Allan Poe story."

"It's very private here. I figured we can talk without being overheard." Her heart was rabbiting already.

"Absolutely." He sat down and folded his hands. "I don't suppose we can drink any of this?"

"Oh, sure." She poured him a glass of the cabernet franc they kept down here for just that purpose, then watched as he gulped it down.

He was nervous, too.

"Okay," she said. "I've done some research."

"Why am I not surprised?"

"Well, obviously, I have to know what I'm getting into."

"Of course. Go on, then."

Honor opened her bag and took out the outline she'd worked up today (and then deleted from her computer, just in case the Feds came looking). "Okay. So INS, which is now called something else—"

"USCIS," Tom said.

"Right." Yes, of course he'd know that. "The regulations state that we have to stay married for two years, minimum, or you get deported, and you can never get a green card or be a citizen."

"I know."

"And if we get caught and convicted of marital fraud, you get deported, and I could get ten years of jail time. And fined a quarter of a million dollars."

"That's a bit stiff, isn't it? Murderers get off with less."

"Yes. But that's what it says." She folded her hands and tried to put on her business face. "Look, Tom, here's what I hope. Instead of viewing this as marital fraud, I'd like to think of it as an arranged marriage, sort of. I'd like to go into it with a good attitude."

"What do you mean?"

She looked over his shoulder. "Just…with the thought that maybe it could work out permanently."

"You mean, we'd stay married and grow old together."

"Um, yes."

He raised one eyebrow. "Are you madly in love with me, Honor? Already?"

"No." Hell. Time to be brutally honest. She'd pussyfooted around Brogan for years, and where had that gotten her? Nowhere. "Look. I'm thirty-five. I haven't met anyone—"

"Except Braedon."

"Brogan."

"Whatever."

"Yes, except Brogan. And my views on marriage have changed from when I was a dopey teenager. I'd like to be married. I won't lie. I'd like to have a baby."

"Just one? How about two?"

"Um, sure. Two would be nice."

"Possibly three?"

"Well, I'm thirty-five."

"So we'd have to bang them out, then, all in a row. Or have triplets, maybe? How about quints?" He grinned, flashing that crooked tooth.

She waited a beat. "Can you be serious? I'm trying to work this out for both of us."

"Sorry. How have your views on marriage changed, Honor dear?"

She took a slow breath. "I think people expect too much, maybe. Maybe that's why it's so hard to find the perfect person. Because no one is perfect, of course. You're nice, sort of. You're smart. You seem like a decent guy."

"Don't forget fantastic in bed."

"You know, sure. Fine. Yes. Last night was…fun." She was sweating. It wasn't hot in here, but she was sweating. "I'd marry you, Tom. But I'd like to think that you'd give it a try. Not just…tolerate me for two years."

Suddenly his face grew serious, wiping away the ridiculous appeal. "What if you meet someone, Honor? Someone real, that is? And fall in love, just like on the Hallmark channel?"

"I'd still give you the two years. I understand what's at stake." She cleared her throat and wiped her hands on her pants. "As for the baby thing, I figured we'd give it some time, see if we're really compatible."

He glanced away and rubbed his thumb across his bottom lip. "So you're willing to give up two years of your life to me, just so I can be near Charlie?"

Honor looked at her hands. "Yes."

"That's incredibly noble of you. Why else?"

"Quite honestly, you're my best prospect in years."

The smile flashed and was gone. "You don't have very high criteria, do you?" There was something in his gray eyes...pity, maybe.

"I don't know about that," she said tightly. "But I can tell you that I'd try to make things work, I'm an honest person, I'd never cheat on you and...and that's it. If you can say the same, then let's give it a try."

"Is there anything else you'd like to say?" he asked.

Aside from Brogan, you're the first guy to kiss me in six years. I'd rather have something with a stranger than nothing with no one. "Nope."

"What else is on your list there, love?"

Her toes curled in her shoes at the endearment. "We should have a timetable."

"Very well."

"Do you think INS will be investigating you?"

"I've no idea."

"In any case, I think we should move in together, the sooner, the better. Your place, by the way. My father's getting married, and I don't want to hang around and be underfoot."

"You live with your dad?"

"Yes. So we should move in, start getting to know each other, then I can meet Charlie, and we can look like the real thing if INS does check up on you."

"And possibly become the real thing."

She looked up from her notes. Her heart felt suddenly too big for her chest. "Maybe."

He didn't say anything. Just looked at her.

Damn. She already liked that face way too much.

He still said nothing. "So here's my basic information," she said, handing over a piece of paper. "You should memorize this—"

"And then burn it?"

"Yes. Oh, okay, you're making a joke. Very funny, but yes, get rid of it."

"Honor Grace Holland. Pretty name, by the way. Birthday, January 4. Cornell, Wharton, very impressive, darling."

"Thanks. We should also make up a story about how we met and, um, fell in love. And we have to make sure your aunt and my grandmother don't say anything."

"Right. Aunt Candy won't, I'm sure. Can your grandmother keep a secret?"

"Goggy?"

"Dear God, you don't call her that to her face, do you?"

"Yes. She can keep quiet. I hope." It would be a first.

"Fingers crossed, then."

"So what should our story be?" Honor asked. Her cheeks warmed again. Everyone in the *universe* had a better story than this. Even the people who met online had cute stories about how their emails had sparked something, or how they met for the first time, smiled and bada-bing, they were in love. eCommitment was much more romantic than a contract negotiated in a stone basement, like some illicit agreement between two shady government agencies.

"Why don't we just stick as close to the truth as possible?" Tom asked. "You picked me up in a bar, we shagged, you're getting older, we figured what the hell? Let's do it."

She stiffened. "You know what I did this afternoon? I watched YouTube interviews about convincing INS that you're actually in love. That's the *only* reason you can marry someone seeking a green card. It has to be a love match."

He smiled again. "Sorry. I love you, Honor. Will you marry me?"

Her jaw clenched. "This is your ass on the line, Tom. And your relationship with Charlie. So try to be serious, okay? What do you love about me?"

"It's not your sense of humor."

Had she thought he was charming? Lonely? Adorable? When was that again?

"Sorry," he said. "I appreciate this. It's just...I'm nervous. Not just about getting caught, but about what you're offering." He looked away and rubbed the back of his neck, then looked back at her. "No one's ever done anything like this for me before."

Oh, yeah, that's what it was.

Sincerity.

"Well," she said, and her voice was a little husky. "Let's give it a shot." She paused. "But, um, I don't think we should sleep together. Again. I mean, you know. Until we get a sense of whether or not this is going to work."

Now why'd you say that, dummy? her eggs asked. *We just opened that special anti-sag moisturizer.*

Because. She was already risking an awful lot. She'd be lying to her family, linking her life with a virtual stranger, committing a felony.

She wasn't going to risk her heart, too. Not yet. And if last night was any indication, her heart would be following her body and opening right up to him.

"That sounds wise," Tom said, and yes, she was a little disappointed.

"I'll need some information on you. Your family and where you went to school."

"Very well."

"And you need to meet my family. I thought Wednesday would be good. I can tell them we've been seeing each other for about a month. I don't think I can stretch it further than that."

"You're a bit terrifying, you know that?" She gave him a pointed look. "Fine. Wednesday works for me, I'm sure."

"And then we'll move in together."

"And then we'll move in together."

They looked at each other from across the table. Then Tom reached out, and they shook on it.

CHAPTER TEN

TOM WAITED UNTIL the last school bus had gone before he went into the school. Much brighter and bigger than his own high school. Smelled better, too, as there was no tire factory down the block.

"Can I help you?" asked the secretary in the front office.

"Yes, thank you. I need a word with the principal."

"Are you a parent here?" the woman asked.

"No. But I think there may be a bullying problem with one of your students."

She gave him a dead-eyed stare and, without looking away, picked up her phone and pushed a button. "Bullying complaint," she said. A second later, another woman came into the office. She was short and squat with graying hair and an ill-fitting suit.

"Hey," she said. "I know you, dude. You box at my gym."

"Hello," he said. "Tom Barlow."

"Dr. Didier. Call me Ellen. I was gonna ask you to spot me the other day. I lift weights. Tournaments, stuff like that. I'm a little old to go pro at this point, but I love it. I can press about two-fifty at this point. How about you?"

"Uh, I'm not sure."

"We should be spotting partners!" She flashed him

a broad smile. "So what can I do for you? You said bullying? Come into my office."

She certainly seemed cheerful, he had to give her that. Her office was typically crowded, and she whipped off her suit jacket, revealing massive shoulders. Flexed her biceps. "Not bad, right?"

"Very impressive," he said. "Anyway, I'm here because I'm concerned about Charlie Kellogg."

Dr. Didier sat down and tapped a few keys on her computer, then frowned. "I don't see you listed here under contacts. What's your relationship to Charlie?" she asked.

"I was engaged to his mother. She died several years ago."

Dr. Didier gave a nod, then stretched her hands over her head, cracking her knuckles. "I'm sorry to tell you this, but I won't be able to discuss anything with you."

"I realize that. I'm a professor over at Wickham."

"Cool beans!"

"But I did want you to be aware of the fact that I think Charlie's being bullied."

Dr. Didier sighed. "So you're still in touch with this kid?" she asked. "Even though his mom died, what… three years ago?"

"Yes."

"And do his guardians know you're still involved? Because when an adult not related to a child expresses an interest, you know…the bells, they go a little crazy."

Tom blinked. "Excuse me?"

"Are you a pedophile, in other words?"

"Christ! No!"

"I'm just gonna put in a request with the police to check you out, okay? It's routine."

"I'm not a child molester! Besides, the police have already talked to the Kelloggs about me." And didn't that sound damning. "Look," he said more calmly, "I lived with the boy and his mum. His grandparents are… distracted, and his dad is barely in the picture. I'm just trying to look after the kid."

"And by look after, what do you mean?" Dr. Didier asked. "Because it sounds creepy, Mr. Barlow."

Oh, now he was Mr. Barlow? He was Tom when he was going to be her weight-lifting partner. "What I mean is, I think I should report it to his fucking school when I think he's getting roughed up!"

"All right, all right, settle down," the principal said, holding up her hands. "I appreciate your concern, and I'd ask that you appreciate mine. You can't be too careful these days. I will be calling Charlie's grandparents to tell them that you came by, for the record."

"Fine." Great. Janice would tell Charlie, and Charlie would be furious.

But still.

"So why do you think Charlie's been bullied?" Dr. Didier asked.

"I picked him up from a party a couple of weeks ago, and his ear was bleeding. He says he's fine, but he's not very talkative."

"Did he tell you why his ear was bleeding?"

"No. He said he got it caught. It's a piercing. Nasty thing." Tom swallowed.

"So it could've been that."

"It could've been, yes. It also could've been some prat who smacked him or yanked his earring or—"

"Look, Tom, our school has a no-tolerance policy on bullying. If it was witnessed, our students have been told since they were in kindergarten that they are not to stand for such behavior, and saying nothing is akin to bullying itself." She rolled her eyes. "And we all know how well that works. Kids still get bullied. It's just more subtle these days."

"So what will you do?"

She pulled a face. "We'll do everything we can. If you have a name, if Charlie would like to talk to a staff member or the guidance office, if anyone comes forward, or if there's a witnessed event, we'll aggressively investigate. We don't tolerate bullying. But we also can't control what those little shits do on their own time, forgive the language. And frankly, I can't do anything with some vague complaint from a person who's not even involved in Charlie's custody. I'm sorry. I'll keep an eye out, and I'll tell the teachers to do the same thing, but that's all I can do."

Shit.

"Is he doing all right here?" Tom asked, unable to help himself.

She gave him a small, sympathetic smile. "I'm sorry. I can't discuss it." She sighed. "Do you talk to Charlie's grandparents?"

"Yes." And they'd been as receptive as two fat bricks—Janice staring at his crotch, Walter nursing a drink, both of them feeling sorry for themselves for having to deal with their recalcitrant grandson.

"Wish I could do more."

"Right. Thanks for your time, Dr. Didier," he said, standing up and shaking her hand.

"You're welcome. See you at the gym." She held up a fist for a knuckle-bump, and he complied.

Walking out into the rain, Tom remembered how,

back in the day, fights were held in the schoolyard or on the streets in his run-down neighborhood. At least it was out in the open and done with. Now, in this day and age, when kids seemed smarter and crueler, where half the parents didn't pay attention or wouldn't believe that their precious little Sam or Taylor could possibly be anything other than a perfect angel, because to admit such would be to have to spend more than ten minutes a day with the creature. No, today, bullying was a casual sport, and if a kid killed himself over it, ah, well, he must've been really fucked up, and little Sam or Taylor wouldn't lose any sleep over it.

In other words, Charlie was on his own.

But he had Tom. And, whether he liked it or not, soon Charlie would have the Holland family, as well. Honor's dossier included a niece and a nephew, the girl in high school. And, please God, that might help.

AN HOUR LATER, Tom had managed to get Charlie out of his room at the Kelloggs' and into the car.

The kid looked like a vampire, with his dark hair and eyes, white skin and Goth clothing and general exhaustion. "You eating all right these days?" Tom asked as they drove to the lake.

Charlie grunted.

"I thought a bit of fresh air would do us both some good. We could take a hike if you want."

"I don't."

Of course. "Okay, we can just sit and breathe, then."

Tom pulled into a parking area at the edge of an abandoned train track, and they got out. He'd read about the town's plans to develop a bike trail along here, and wouldn't that be splendid, being able to cycle through the farmlands and forests? Across the way and up the hill a bit, he could see a red kite against the gray sky. "Look there," he said, pointing.

Charlie barely glanced. If the kite reminded him of what they used to do together, he said nothing, and though Tom was used to such reactions these past three years, he nonetheless felt his throat tighten.

"So, Charlie, it's been a while since your mum died. I was wondering how things are for you."

Charlie shrugged and made a trisyllabic grunt, which Tom took to mean, *I don't know.*

"Right. Well, if you ever want to talk about things, I'm always here."

An eye roll. Charlie looked exhausted from having to deal with the idiocy of adults; Tom half worried he was about to pass out from boredom.

"Listen, I've got some news." He rubbed the back of his neck. "I'm seeing someone."

Charlie, who was not moving to begin with, seemed to freeze nonetheless.

"She's really nice."

No reaction.

"She's looking forward to meeting you."

And still nothing. There was maybe a quiver around his mouth.

"Her name's Honor Holland. She's Abby Vander-beek's aunt. Do you know Abby?"

No answer.

"She's a couple years ahead of you. A junior this year."

Nothing.

"I wanted to let you know. And it's not like I'll for-get your mum—"

"I have homework. Can we go?" Without waiting for an answer, Charlie pushed himself up and trudged to the car, his mood as black as his clothes, a stark contrast to the dancing kite across the hill.

CHAPTER ELEVEN

"I TOLD YOU he was perfect," Goggy crowed. "Finally, someone listened to me!"

"You can't go around bragging about it, Goggy," Honor warned. "I'm only telling you because...you know...you mentioned the green card issue, and I don't want anyone to have the wrong impression. Because that would be illegal, Goggy. And I'd be in big trouble."

"Of course I won't tell! You think I can't keep a secret? I can keep a secret. Your grandfather lost ten thousand dollars in the stock market last year, and did I tell anyone? No. I didn't. When I walked in on Prudence and Carl doing it on their kitchen table, did I mention it to anyone? Not a soul!"

Honor rubbed her forehead. "Wow. Okay. So this time, you really, really can't tell. And we're, um, we're in love. It was fast, but we, uh, we love each other." Four more hours on YouTube had stressed that little nugget to the thousandth degree. *The only reason to marry a non–U.S. citizen is for love,* attorney after attorney had warned. *And here are some of the questions you might be asked. Who made dinner last night? What did you do last weekend? What is your spouse's favorite dessert?*

"I knew it! I knew you'd love him! He's wonderful. And so handsome."

"You still haven't met him."

"I don't need to." Goggy folded her arms and smiled. "Oh, you're getting married! I want more great-grandchildren, pronto."

"Okay," she said. "Thank you, Goggy. I have to go tell Dad now, so don't call him, okay?" She glanced around her grandparents' cluttered living room. Like so many colonials, it had several doors—to the kitchen, the front stairs, the dining room. "Your heating bill will be a lot less if you close those doors." She paused. "I sure would love to see you in a new place. Or, at least, on one floor, Goggy. I hate having you go up and down those stairs all day long."

"Oh, pooh. That's my exercise. Go. Get out of here. You want some cookies? I baked today."

She wanted them, all right. Any fortification for her talk with Dad, because she sensed this wasn't going to go well.

SHE WAS RIGHT. Dad was in the living room, nursing a glass of dry Riesling and waiting for Mrs. Johnson to allow him into the kitchen to eat.

"Petunia!" he said as if it had been weeks since they'd seen each other and not two hours. "How's my girl?"

"I'm great, Dad. Um, how are you? Excited about the wedding?"

Dad and Mrs. J. wanted to get married fast "in case either of us dies first," Mrs. J. had said, and so the wedding would be in six weeks, just after the Black and White Ball.

"Very," he said. "What's new with you, baby?"

"Um, well, funny that you asked." She cleared her throat, trying to remember a time when she'd lied to her dad. It had been a few decades. Possibly never. "You know that guy I've been seeing?" *Sorry, Daddy.*

"No. What guy?" He frowned.

"Um, the guy I told you about?"

The kitchen door banged open. "Jackie!" Mrs. Johnson said from her domain. "Are you hungry, dear boy?"

"Mrs. Johnson, you get more beautiful every week." Honor rolled her eyes, but sure enough, her brother came into the living room a second later, holding a piece of the lemon pound cake Honor had been told she couldn't touch. "Hey, Dad. What's up, sis?"

Right. Well, better to have an ally (sort of) in the form of her big brother. "I was telling Dad about a guy I've been seeing." She fixed Jack with a stern gaze.

"Really? I thought you were headed for the convent."

"Oh, Jack. Don't make me hurt you again."

Dad put down his newspaper. "Getting back to this person…what's his name, anyway?"

"Tom. Tom Barlow. The mechanical engineer, remember?" Best to feed Dad information as if he already knew it.

Dad frowned. "Huh. I guess I wasn't paying attention. Anyway, what about him? You want to have him up for dinner?"

"Oh, sure. But, uh, the bigger news is, um, we're moving in together."

For a second, Honor thought her father might clutch his chest and drop stone-cold dead. Silence filled the room, thick and ominous. The mantel clock ticked loudly.

"No, you're not," Dad said loudly. "I don't even know this Tom person. Who's Tom? You're not moving in with a stranger I've never even met. Why on earth would you do that? Is this about Mrs. Johnson and me?"

"Shouldn't you be allowed to call her by her first name, Dad?" Jack asked around a mouthful of cake. "Since you're sleeping with her?"

"Jackie! Don't you dare discuss this!" Mrs. Johnson banged a pot down in the kitchen, then stomped out to the living room. "This is your fault, John Holland," she declared. "You and this silly marriage idea. Honor, you're not going anywhere. John, I refuse to come between you and your children."

"Now look what you've done, sis," Jack said. "Can I have another piece of cake, Mrs. J.?"

"Jack, shut up. And Mrs. J., please," Honor said. "You are so going to marry Dad. Just calm down. I'm thirty-five years old."

"That is getting up there," Jack murmured.

Honor shot him a murderous glance. "I can move in with someone if I want to, and I do. I'd like to live somewhere other than the house where I was born."

"You were born in the hospital," Dad said sharply.

"You can't move in with some stranger," Mrs. Johnson said. "I don't condone living in sin."

"Well, then, you should stop shtupping Dad, shouldn't you?"

Dad looked like he was indeed considering that heart attack, and Mrs. Johnson gave her a regal, icy look.

"Sorry, Mrs. J.," she said. "But I am going to move in with Tom. He has a very cute place in town, and I want to do it. It's not because of you two. It's because of...him." She felt her face get hot. "He's really great."

"No, he's not!" Dad yelped. "He's not great. If he's

so great, how come I've never met him? How long has this been going on?"

"Not long, John Holland, not long," Mrs. Johnson intoned. "But you weren't paying attention, were you? No, you were chasing after some woman—"

"Aren't you the woman in question, Mrs. J.?" Jack asked.

"—and your daughter is going to live with a stranger who could be a serial killer."

"And then there's that," Jack said.

"He's a math teacher. I mean, mechanical engineering. He's a professor at Wickham. And he's very nice. British, too."

"What does that have to do with anything?" Dad asked. "Don't they make serial killers in England? Haven't you ever heard of Jack the Ripper?" He looked at his only son for solidarity. "Tell her, Jack. This is ridiculous. You can date him, Honor, but moving in? It's rash."

As her father, Mrs. J. and Jack all weighed in, Honor couldn't help noting how vastly different the standards were for the four grown Holland children. Faith was never questioned, as she was the delicate flower of the bunch, her occasional seizure giving her an opt-out clause for everything. Honor knew it wasn't by choice, but she couldn't help thinking Faith was pretty damn clever, being born with epilepsy. Prudence had sown her wild oats when the rest of them were still little, and those oats had largely gone unnoticed as Mom and Dad had diapers to change and toddlers to chase. Plus, Pru had married Carl at age twenty-three, spawned two lovely kids and now served more as entertainment than a cause for concern. Jack was the son and heir and little prince, and therefore beyond reproach.

But it always seemed to Honor that a higher standard had been applied to her. She was the one who'd brought no surprises, who'd done exactly what was expected, who never caused her parents a moment's worry. Good old Honor. The boring one.

Time for that to change. And oddly enough, it felt good.

"Okay, you guys, that's enough," she said. "I'm moving in with Tom. Sorry you don't approve, but I'm not a kid anymore."

"You live under my roof, don't you? My roof, my rules."

"I just told you, I'm moving out."

"Why would a guy want to move in with you, Honor? You're so mean." Jack grinned.

"Jackie, for shame!" Mrs. J. said in a rare reproach.

"She's not mean," Dad said. "She's my angel."

Honor smiled sweetly at her brother. "An angel," she murmured, scratching her cheek with her middle finger.

"An angel who should know better," Dad added.

Jack grinned. "Let her go, Dad," he said. "If she doesn't jump on this, she'll just end up here, changing your diapers and owning more and more cats."

"I'm more of a dog person."

"Really? I thought you had a cat."

"Spike is a dog."

"You sure?"

"Bite me. Anyway, I would love for everyone to meet Tom, so he's coming here, and so are a few other people. Wednesday night, okay? Okay. Mrs. Johnson? Would you like me to have this catered, or would you—"

"How dare you, Honor! Has my cooking become so abhorrent to you that—"

"Oh, heck, look at the time. I have things to do. Talk among yourselves."

THREE DAYS LATER, Honor opened the door and smiled at the boy in front of her.

Eesh.

"Hi!" she said. "You must be Charlie. It's really nice to meet you. I'm Honor."

He lifted his black-lined eyes to hers as if each eyeball weighed three hundred pounds, then shuffled past.

"You're the woman, then?" said an older lady.

"Uh, yes! Hi! I'm Honor Holland. Nice to meet you, Mrs. Kellogg."

"Mmm."

Mr. Kellogg came in next. "Hello," he said. "Do I smell mold? I'm allergic to mold. And cheese. I hope we're not having any cheese tonight. I'm lactose intolerant. But I'll have a Scotch. Thanks, dear."

My kingdom for a Xanax, Honor thought.

In the interest of killing all family members with one stone (the literal idea of which held greater and greater appeal), Honor had decided that the Kelloggs and the Hollands should meet at once. And the next time such a brainchild occurred to her, she hoped someone would hit her with a crowbar, because it couldn't be any less uncomfortable than this.

"I *love* him," Faith said. "I mean, wow. He's really cute!" Her sister flashed a huge smile. "Where did you find him?"

"Are we talking about how hot your guy is?" Prudence said, coming over to join them. "Love the accent.

I missed about thirty percent of what he was saying, but I was too busy looking at his neck. I would lick that if I was single. Hey, Carl, get me some more wine, okay, pal?"

"Darling, your family utterly terrifies me." Tom came up behind her and put his arms around her. "Give us a kiss, what do you say? Oh, hallo, girls, didn't see you there." Honor watched her sisters visibly sag with swooniness.

She herself, not so much. First of all, she wasn't sure how much Tom had had to drink. He was being very jolly, and it was making her nervous. And secondly, he was playing the part of doting boyfriend/fiancé a little too forcefully. Which was nice. Except it was uncomfortable, since it was fake. But it was also nice. Which meant she was pathetic, to be lapping up this attention, when she knew quite well that Tom was in this for fraud purposes only. Which didn't make the feeling of his arms any less incredible. No. He wasn't built like a math teacher at all. Or a mechanical engineer.

"I bet you're great in bed," Prudence said.

"I've heard that," Tom said. "Though Honor is more of the expert on my abilities, aren't you, darling?"

"I hear Mrs. Johnson calling me," she said, extracting herself from Tom's brawny arms.

An eternity later, they were crammed around the dining room table. Mrs. Kellogg couldn't seem to stop eyeing Tom and licking her lips, which made Honor's skin crawl, given that a) Tom had been engaged to Mrs. Kellogg's daughter, b) he was now about to be engaged to Honor and c) Mrs. Kellogg was a good thirty years older than Tom. There were cougars, and then there was disgusting.

Mr. Kellogg, meanwhile, sniffed each piece of food before putting it in his mouth. Abby was secretly (or not) texting; Charlie was staring at her, then at his plate. Her siblings, Ned, Goggy and Pops, Dad and Mrs. Johnson all talked at once, it seemed. Carl ate without pausing between bites, and Levi seemed content to bristle with testosterone and occasionally stroke Faith's neck.

Tom sat next to Honor, his shoulder solid and warm against hers.

Any minute now, someone was going to start the interrogation. The theme song from *Jaws* began playing in her brain. *Da-dun. Da-dun. Dadundadundadundadun...doo doo loo, doo doo loo...*

"So how did you meet my daughter?" Dad asked sternly.

Tom swallowed a third of a glass of wine. "At O'Rourke's, actually. Lovely place. Nice people, those twins."

"When was this?" Dad asked.

Tom looked at her and frowned. "When was it, darling?" He looked back at her father. "She was slugging another woman, and I said to myself, 'Tommy old chap, I think you've met the woman of your dreams.'"

Carl laughed, then took another huge bite of salt potatoes. The rest of the table was silent. Honor gave Tom a gentle nudge to the ribs.

"I found out who she was, pestered her to go out with me and it was...what's the phrase, love? Meant to be?"

"That's beautiful," Goggy said loudly, giving Honor an arch look. "I can tell how deeply in love you are. Both of you. It's a love match." Apparently Goggy had been watching some of those YouTube videos, as well.

"As opposed to what, Goggy? Like, do people get

married these days because they hate each other?" Abby asked, earning a snort from Charlie, his first sign of life.

"At any rate," Tom said, "I understand ours isn't the only wedding being planned. Congratulations, Mr. Holland, Mrs. Johnson."

There was a rare silence.

Oh, fungus.

"Honor, you're getting married?" Abby shrieked, and there was yelling and wine sloshing and exclamations and Mrs. Kellogg burst into tears (not the happy kind), and Charlie left the table.

"We were gonna keep that to ourselves for a little while," Honor said tightly, turning to Tom.

"Oops," he said. "Cat's out of the bag now, isn't it?" He rubbed his forehead. "I'll go talk to Charlie."

"You can't marry him!" Dad barked. "You just started dating!"

"Do I need to point out your hypocrisy, Dad?" Honor asked as Faith hugged her.

"I've known Mrs. Johnson for twenty years," he grumbled.

"Yet you still can't call her by her first name," Jack said.

"And we're old, Honor dear," Mrs. J. said. "I have to agree with your father. Take some time."

"I disagree," Goggy said, giving Mrs. J. a dirty look. "They should get married. Right away. Otherwise, Tom might—"

"You know what? We're both adults. We'll get married when the time is right," Honor said, watching as Mrs. Kellogg poured ten ounces of wine into a water glass and chugged it.

"I call maid of honor," Faith said.

"What? I don't think so," Pru countered.

"Pick me," Abby said. "That way, you don't have to choose between sisters."

"Or me," Jack said, giving her a one-armed hug and pouring himself some wine with the other hand. "Man of honor. It's very hip."

"We'll talk about this later," Dad said. "You can't be engaged to a man you just met."

"I can and am, Dad," she said. He glowered. She glowered back.

Family. Headaches. Heartburn.

"Is there any more cheese?" Pops asked.

If Honor made it through this meal, it'd be a miracle.

"CHARLIE? OPEN THE door, mate." At least it wasn't freezing today, though the wind could cut a foreskin, it was so sharp. "Charlie, come on, don't be a prat."

You know, he was just not good at this. Once, he'd thought he was good with kids. That's why he'd become a teacher. He loved it. Kids like Jacob Kearns, who visibly drank in learning, whose eyes lit up with excitement when they got a new theory; there was nothing better.

But in these three long years since Melissa had died, Tom had really lost his touch. Especially with her son. And yeah, drinking a bit much had been a stupid idea.

The boy stared straight ahead. His eyeliner was smeared. Not a sign of good cheer, wasn't it?

"Look," Tom said, bending so he was at eye level. "She's really nice. I think you'll like her after you get to know her."

"Who says I'm gonna get to know her?" he said. Good. At least he was talking.

"I think you will. I mean, nothing will change with you and me."

"Except you'll have a wife."

"Yeah. That. But I still want you to come over, and I want to teach you to box, and come to your school events and all that." Charlie hadn't invited him to a school event in years. "Whatever you want, mate."

No answer.

"Her family are nice, don't you think? Abby and you must see each other in school."

That got a flicker of a glance.

"And maybe it'll be good, knowing some more people from around here. Having more family."

"They won't be my family. *You're* not even my family."

The kid knew where to aim, Tom would give him that. "I feel like I am."

"You're not."

"All right, Charlie. I'll leave you here." Tom started to go back inside, then turned around and bent down again. "I'll always love your mum, you know. That won't ever change."

"Why? She didn't love you."

Another direct hit, right in the testicles this time. It was a second before he found his voice. "Come in if you get cold."

Honor met him at the door of the big white house. "Is he okay?" she asked as he came into the hall.

"Oh, he's wonderful."

"Well, everyone in there is freaking out."

"Right."

"Tom," she said, dropping her voice to a whisper, "you have to take this more seriously. We have to be convincing, or we're going to get caught. Levi's the chief of police. If he gets a sense that we're not really a couple—"

He grabbed her and kissed her hard, not trying to be gentle, a fierce, primal kiss that had nothing to do with seduction or tenderness, and everything to do with frustration.

Then her mouth opened, and her hands went to his chest, and he pushed her against the door, pressing against her softness, gentling the kiss, cradling her head in his hands, her short hair soft and silky, the taste of her making him forget everything else, and there was only the softness of her mouth, the sweetness of her.

Then he released her abruptly and took a step back. "How's that? Good enough?"

Her eyes were wide.

"Sorry." With that, and his frustration far from spent, he went back into the din of the mob.

CHAPTER TWELVE

TOM HAD FORGOTTEN about the little rat-dog.

Spike. That was it. The little rodent had already bitten him today. Twice. Granted, its teeth were the size of staples, but it was the principle of the thing.

Honor sure had a lot of stuff. Boxes and boxes of things. Books. A bloody giant computer. Pictures to hang on the wall. Two enormous suitcases.

She was serious about this thing.

"Okay," she said when he'd brought in the last thing in her car. "I guess I'll unpack."

He couldn't seem to drag his eyes off all those boxes. "Right."

"Which bedroom should I take?"

"Oh, right. Whichever one you like."

Her cheeks grew pink. "If Immigration does a house check, our stuff should be together. In the same bedroom, I mean."

He looked up. "Oh. Sure, then. Mine's on the right."

"Okay. I'll put my things in there and, um, sleep in the other room?"

"Great."

"We should also take some pictures of the two of us, looking happy. Different settings. Courtship photos."

"Sure. Whenever you want."

She gave a nod. "Then I'll go settle in."

"Need any help?"

"Nope! I'm fine. I'm good. It's all good." She went, obviously eager to nest, or get away from him, or both.

The little dog squatted and peed on the rug. Lovely thing, really. Then it followed her up the stairs, so tiny it had to leap up each step.

Tom glanced at the clock on the stove. Four o'clock. Too early for a drink, unfortunately. Very well. He could correct the midterm debacles, and then take a look at the plans for the little Piper Cub he was supposed to modify. And give Jacob a call to set up a meeting so the lad could get a little glimpse of what a mechanical engineer could do.

But a drink would be nice, seeing that Tom was now engaged to one Honor Grace Holland, who wanted very much to have this all work out.

And if it hadn't worked out with Melissa, how in bloody hell was it going to work out here?

FOUR YEARS AGO, Tom had come to Manhattan for the summer, as he hadn't been to the States before. Had never left England, for that matter, always too busy working or boxing or in school. Figured he'd start in the legendary city and possibly head to some of the national parks the Yanks were so proud of.

After a few days in Manhattan, he went to see his great-aunt Candace, who lived in Philadelphia—The Birthplace of Freedom, the sign announced, rather cheekily. Honestly, the Americans thought they invented air. Tom barely knew Aunt Candy, but she was his late grandmother's baby sister. His dad had fond memories of her and asked him to make a point to see her. So Tom rented a car and made the obligatory trek, and Aunt Candy embraced him like he was her long-lost son. She showed him the sights, the cracked bell, Independence Hall. When she brought him to the art museum, he ran up the steps (along with three or four other tourists), and danced around at the top near the statue of Rocky Balboa, making his great-auntie laugh. He treated her to dinner, and when she asked him if he'd stay one more day so she could show him off to her friends, he agreed. She was quite the lovely old bird.

He went to her church picnic the next day, where her friends cooed over his accent and told him he was adorable, clucking that he wasn't married yet at the ripe old age of twenty-eight.

"Will you help me fix this?" came a voice, and Tom looked down. A smallish boy with a mouthful of teeth too big for him held up a cheap plastic kite. One of the plastic braces was broken.

"That's Janice Kellogg's grandson," Candy said. "Charlie, this is my grandnephew, Tom."

"Let's have a look, then, mate," Tom had said. He took out his pocket knife, cut a stick from a nearby bush, bent it so the wind resistance would be greater, whittled the ends, sliced off a long strip of plastic tablecloth and replaced the tail. A few minutes later, Charlie's kite took off, higher and faster than any other in the park. Who better to fix a kite than a mechanical engineer with a minor in aeronautics? The look of delight on the kid's face…it was lovely. He knelt down next to the lad and showed him how to make the kite do a figure-eight, getting a yelp of joy as reward.

"Thanks for helping my son," came a voice. Tom looked up, and fell hard.

Melissa Kellogg was beautiful, all long black hair

and blue eyes. Twenty when she had Charlie, thirty now, single. "His father is a rat-bastard," she confided in a whisper, "but I try not to let Charlie know." She worked as a paralegal, loved her kid, had a flowery tattoo on her neck that flirted with the edge of her blouse.

By the end of the picnic, she'd asked Tom if he wanted to have dinner with the two of them.

He did.

He had dinner with them on Monday as well, and Wednesday, and Thursday, and on Friday, the elder Kelloggs took Charlie for the night, and Tom took Melissa to bed.

He never did get to those national parks.

By September, Tom had a work visa and a TA position at a small college, a step down from his post at University of Manchester, but it seemed like a small price to pay. He moved in with Melissa and Charlie in their duplex in a worn but respectable part of Philadelphia, totally smitten with both of them.

The kid never shut up; he was interested in everything, made obscure references to Jedis and Dr. Who—right up Tom's alley, in other words. Melissa often used to comment that they were the same mental age. Charlie asked if Tom would build him a tree house, sought his advice on making a car for the soapbox derby and made so many paper airplanes that Melissa complained about not even being able to find a piece of paper for a grocery list.

For a while, it was perfect. A beautiful woman, a great kid, a not-bad job. Incredible sex. His teaching career, which had started off with him beating out thirty-seven other candidates for a fast-track tenure position back in England, didn't matter so much anymore. For extra money, Tom did a bit of consulting for a guy who made custom airplanes for the wealthy, so it was all good. No, it seemed like Tom had walked straight into a perfect little family.

He'd been in love quite a few times before, starting out with Emily Anne Cartright, his next-door neighbor who broke up with him when they were six. But Melissa...she was special. Amazing in bed—no man would underrate that. Fiery and funny, too. She seemed to like to fight over little things, but given what happened after those spats, Tom grew to love fighting.

And she was a good mum, even if she relied a bit too much on the orange macaroni and cheese that came from a box, even if she let Charlie watch too much television and play violent video games. But she loved him, it was obvious. Fussed over his hair, cooed over his Lego creations, laughed with him at bedtime.

At first, Tom couldn't quite believe his luck. Why this beautiful woman would be so available was a mystery. She seemed to be the entire package. She seemed... perfect.

She wasn't, of course.

After the initial blush wore off, Tom started to see that Melissa was a bit of a malcontent. She didn't like their house, though Tom thought it was pleasant enough. She wanted a different job. Hated her coworkers, felt the company's policies on sick time, lunch hour and vacation were unfair. In seven years, she'd held eleven jobs, everything from a waitress to a shampooer at a posh salon to a medical assistant. When he suggested she look into something else, she'd snap that she didn't know what she wanted, then go on to name rather ridiculous ideas, Tom thought—veterinarian or restaurant owner or architect…jobs for which she had no skills or schooling, and no willingness to get them.

And then, after a few months, he felt her discontent latch on to him. It was a terrifying spotlight to be in. She had a way of looking at him, as if calculating just when she'd ask him to move out. If he talked about kids in his classes, she often sighed or started doodling, her boredom clear. Whereas Tom loved the normalcy of their lives, of watching movies with Charlie on Friday nights and taking a bike ride through the city on Sundays, Melissa wanted to go out, hear a band, *party,* that American word for *get pissed*. Their first big fight came when her parents couldn't babysit, and she wanted to leave Charlie home alone.

"We can't do that," Tom had said. "He's too young."

"I think I can make up my own mind about my son," she said icily. "He's almost eleven."

"It's the law," Tom answered.

"Fine. Stay home, then. You like him better than me, anyway. I'm not just gonna sit around and grow mold." And she had gone out, and hadn't come back till 4:00 a.m., when Tom had been debating whether to call the police. But she'd been apologetic and sweet, took him to bed, then said she was sorry about staying out so late; she'd just had a lot of stress lately and needed to blow off steam.

Which, it became apparent, she had to do quite often.

By Christmas, Tom was aware that he probably should've taken things a bit more slowly with Melissa. The problem was, he was crazy about her kid, and Charlie adored him right back. And that, it seemed, was becoming a reason for Melissa to break up with him.

She was jealous.

One day, when Melissa had called out sick from work (again), Charlie burst through the door after school, yelling, "Tom! Tom! Tomtomtom!" a paper clutched in his hand.

"Don't you mean, Mom, Mom, Mommommom?" Melissa said in a nasty voice. "Or is Tom your mommy now?" It didn't register to her that Tom, with his teacher's schedule, had been the adult who'd greeted him at home for months now. Nor did she ask about the paper, which had been Charlie's spelling test: an A+, the first time he'd gotten all his words right, thanks in large part to Tom helping him study.

Another time, she said, "Charlie, honey, let's go out for ice cream, just you and me." She cut Tom a glance. "Just family." But that night, when they got back, and Charlie was sticky with marshmallow, she'd given Tom a kiss and handed him a half-melted hot-fudge sundae, the ice cream oozing down the sides of the Styrofoam container.

And that was the problem. If she'd been beastly all the time, he would've left…probably. But those moments, he wanted very much to believe, showed the true Melissa, the one who didn't complain, trash-talk her co-workers and parents, didn't flare up in temper for no apparent reason. She'd been a single mother since twenty, lived at home with her parents until just two years ago… she was still adjusting, maybe. She was smart. Sharply funny. When she was nice, she was utterly fantastic.

When she wasn't, she went for days without speaking to him, bending over backward to be supersweet to Charlie, almost as if proving who the real parent was.

So, being a man, and therefore idiotic about matters of the heart, Tom figured he should propose.

Right.

That went right up there in the Great Decisions of Tom's Life along with the time he'd tried to skateboard down a metal railing, ending up with a bruised scrotum that hurt for three weeks.

But propose he did. He bought a ring, got a dozen red roses, dressed in his one and only suit and went to her workplace, figuring she'd like a big fuss. Got down on one knee and asked the big question, and when she said, "Holy shit, Tom," he took that as a yes. So did everyone else, because they laughed and cheered and congratulated her, and she did seem happy, blushing and looking at the ring.

And that worked, for a while. She liked going dress shopping and tasting cakes and crossing people off the guest list when they irritated her, then putting them back on later (or not).

But, Tom noticed, she was also growing more distant. They had sex less often. She went out more with the girls, and stayed out later. And then came the phone calls, when she'd leap to answer and then say, "Hold on a minute," before dashing to the loo to talk, always locking the door behind her.

By the time April rolled around, Tom was fairly positive she was having an affair. "Melissa, are you sure you want to marry me?" he said one night as they lay in the dark, not touching.

"Oh, great." She sighed. "Yes, Tom, I want to marry you. I said I did, didn't I? Can you not be an old woman about this?"

He almost broke up with her a dozen times. But who was he fooling? If he ended things, he'd lose Charlie, and that was an intolerable thought. Maybe it was why she stayed with him as well—she might make snide references to the boys' club, but her son adored Tom, and for the first time, Charlie had a steady male influence in his life, and Melissa, in one of her nicer moments, acknowledged that Tom was good for her boy.

But those moments were becoming more and more rare.

Then came the Friday that Tom came home to find her throwing some clothes into an overnight bag. "I'm going away for the weekend with a friend," she said with a quick glance. "You'll be around, right? Charlie hates staying with my parents."

"Where are you going?" he asked. "Which friend?"

"Can you not interrogate me, please?" she snapped.

"Melissa," he began, "I think I have a right to know where you're going."

She sighed. Stopped folding her clothes. He couldn't help notice that her trashiest underwear was in the suitcase. "Look, Tom," she said slowly. "I need a little thinking time. Okay? So don't ask too many questions, because I just need some space, and I'll see you Sunday."

"Can I come, Mom?" asked Charlie from the doorway.

"Not this time, baby," she said, hefting her bag off the bed. "I'll bring you a present, though, okay? Now smooch me." Charlie obliged, and the two of them went out on the porch to watch her leave.

"Go back inside," she ordered. "It's chilly out here. Bye! See you Sunday."

They obeyed. "What should we do tonight?" Charlie asked. "Can we go to the movies?"

"Yeah, sure, mate," Tom said. "Let me, uh, let me just get the paper to check the times, all right?"

He went outside, into the little yard, scrubbing his hand across the back of his neck.

There she was, four houses down, pulling her suitcase behind her. At the intersection sat a blue muscle car, one of those growling Detroit monsters. A man got out, opened the door for her, tossed her bag in the back, then got in the driver's seat, and they were gone.

Tom closed his mouth, tasting bile.

So she *was* having an affair. He'd known it in his heart, but seeing it was the equivalent to a left hook to the kidneys.

"He didn't even come in," came Charlie's voice. Tom turned. The boy's face was pale, his funny little eyebrows knit together.

"Who, mate?" he asked, his voice hollow.

"My dad."

MELISSA DIDN'T ANSWER her phone, though Tom left eleven messages, telling her Charlie had seen them and wanted to know very badly why his parents hadn't taken him along. The bitterness in Tom's own voice was shocking. One thing to be a bit of a whore, right? Another to be whoring around with your son's father and not even bother having the man come in and say hello to the lad. Oh, and let's not forget, asking your fiancé to babysit your kid while you were busy shagging someone else.

But when she didn't come home on Sunday, he waited till Charlie was watching the telly, then bit the bullet and called Janice Kellogg.

"Oh, for God's sake," she said when he told her what Charlie had said. "Will she ever learn?"

Ever since she'd first met Mitchell DeLuca, Janice said, he'd been like crack. On again, off again, on again, off again, the man waltzing into Charlie's life, then disappearing for another year, sometimes more. Just enough to really screw the kid up.

"Any idea where she might be? Charlie's worried. Not eating, either."

"I have no idea," Janice said, sounding irritated rather than concerned. "Tom, if I could tell you how often this happens… We almost said something to you, Walter and I. I'm sure she'll come back, though. She's never left for more than a few days before those two have another huge fight and decide they hate each other again. Until they decide they can't live without each other, that is."

Bloody great. "Thanks." He hung up and glanced in the living room, where some show with a loud laugh track was playing. Charlie was staring straight ahead. The little guy hadn't said much since he'd seen his parents together. Tom started pushing in the numbers of Melissa's friends, bleeding a little more dignity with every call.

Melissa never did come back.

According to Mitchell DeLuca, and the police report, they'd had a big fight, yelling loudly enough for the people in the next motel room to hear. Melissa had a few drinks. Took a walk. Decided to send Tom a text.

Tom, you won't be

That was when the car hit her, killing her instantly. Awkward, being the cuckolded fiancé at the wake, standing next to the casket of the woman you thought you'd marry, right next to her parents and lover/ex-husband. Going home to her white-faced child, feeling like your throat was clenched in God's fist. Utterly fucking helpless.

Mitchell DeLuca came over after the funeral. "I'd like to talk to my son," he told Tom amiably.

And Tom, who had once knocked out Great Britain's top-ranked middle-weight fighter with one punch, stood aside and let him come in.

Charlie seemed to have shrunk since his mother left, but his face lit up at the sight of his father, and Tom's heart lost another healthy chunk. "I'll, um, I'll start supper," he said, going into the kitchen. That way he could eavesdrop from amid the casseroles left by the nice women from Aunt Candy's church.

"Am I gonna live with you now, Dad?" Charlie asked, and damn it all if tears didn't come to Tom's eyes. *Say yes, you bastard,* he ordered Mitchell.

"Buddy, I wish you could," and Tom could practically feel the boy's heart break for the second time that week.

His lifestyle, Mitchell told his son, wasn't right for a kid. He traveled too much. He was sorry, though. Told Charlie to study hard in school, then ruffled his hair, stood up and simply left.

Tom gave it two seconds, then went into the living room. "You all right, mate?"

"He's really sad he can't take me," Charlie whispered, and Tom had to fight not to run after the guy and beat him to a bloody pulp.

"Absolutely," he said instead. "You can tell he loves you a lot, though."

"I *know,*" Charlie said, and it was the first time Tom heard the hatred in the little sweet voice he'd come to love.

Tom asked the Kelloggs if he could adopt Charlie. They said no. After all, Tom hadn't even known Charlie a year. What would a twenty-nine-year-old man want with a ten-year-old boy, anyway? He could come visit, if he wanted to.

So Charlie moved in with his grandparents, and as they walked out of the little duplex for the last time, Charlie turned to him. For a second, Tom thought the boy might hug him.

He was wrong. "Why were you so mean to her?" he screamed, throwing himself on Tom, punching him, scratching his face. "You made her leave! I hate you! I hate you! I hate you!"

Charlie got grief counseling. It didn't seem to work. Living in a different part of town meant he went to a different school, which didn't make matters easier—a dead mum, an idiot father and now separated from his classmates. Tom kept visiting doggedly, watching as the little boy he loved became more and more withdrawn. Charlie seemed to be disappearing, not to mention aging overnight. No longer did he want to watch sci-fi movies or make model airplanes or kick around a soccer ball. His mother was dead, his father didn't want him, his grandparents were doing only their duty and Tom... Tom was the reason for this whole mess.

CHAPTER THIRTEEN

A WEEK AFTER she'd moved into Tom Barlow's house, Honor was thinking that she must've been insane (possible), drunk (improbable) or really, really pathetic (bingo) to have agreed to the whole idea.

For seven days now, she and Tom had spent evenings together. Mostly silent evenings. She came home from work, he came home from work. They exchanged the politest of pleasantries. They took turns making dinner. She would have a glass of wine. Tom would have a beer...or a glass of whiskey. Sometimes more than one (she tried not to count). They'd eat. Conversation was sparse; Tom seemed tense, and Honor definitely was. Then they'd go hide in opposite corners, Honor working on the details for the Black and White Ball, Tom correcting papers or making up lesson plans.

Household chores were shared, and Honor was pleased to find that Tom was tidy, even if he made his bed crookedly (hers looked like a magazine photo, thank you very much). He rinsed the sink out after shaving and owned a vacuum cleaner.

They watched a movie one night, but each of them appeared to be the polite type who didn't talk during movies, so it hadn't exactly been a bonding experience. "Good film" had been Tom's comment, and Honor had agreed with "Yes. It was."

On Tuesday, Charlie came over, and Tom had been manically cheerful, ignoring the fact that Charlie didn't answer questions, eat dinner or make eye contact. "How's school going?" Honor asked. He grunted in response. "Do you have Mrs. Parrish for English?" He sighed and nodded once. "She was my teacher, too." Charlie dragged his eyes to her face as if to say, *And why would I care?* "Does she still smell like menthol?" A shrug.

"Charlie. Answer, mate," Tom said.

"Yes. Mrs. Parrish still smells."

"How about some grape pie?" she offered. She'd baked it in honor of this painful evening, hoping it would go better than it had thus far.

"He hasn't finished his dinner," said Tom.

She looked at the kid. "Well, it's a special occasion. Your first dinner with us. So maybe we can bend the rules, Tom."

He hesitated. "All right. Would you like some pie, Charlie?"

He shrugged. But, Honor was pleased to note, he also ate three pieces. In silence, mind you, but still. When Tom got back from driving him home, he went for a run. A long run.

So communication didn't seem to be their strong suit.

Things were strained, to say the least. On the one hand, this was a business arrangement, more or less, so the typical romantic pressure off. On the other, she *had* already slept with the guy, and late at night, as she listened to the unfamiliar sounds of Manningsport Village and the occasional car passing, Honor wondered if she'd been stupid to tell Tom they should stay apart. Maybe sex would've made this seem a little more natural.

But then again, if things didn't work out, sex might have just complicated the already unusual situation.

Didn't keep her from stealing looks at him, that was for sure. Unfortunately, he didn't seem similarly affected…or if he was, he covered it well.

On Thursday evening, Faith called, asking her if the two of them could have dinner. Honor said yes, albeit reluctantly. Feigning the role of smitten bride-to-be—or any role, really—wasn't going to be easy, especially given the fact that Faith *was* an actual smitten bride. Faith offered to drive and asked to meet at Cabrera's Boxing Gym first, because Levi had a "thing," and so Honor walked the three blocks, Spike's cute little black-and-tan head popping out of Honor's purse, alert for danger.

Honor had never been to Cabrera's, which was unusual, as she'd been in every other business in Manningsport. It was a circle of Dante's Inferno, as far as she was concerned—cold, dark and poorly lit, with all sorts of smacking, thudding, punitive sounds coming from various areas. There was Faith, easy to spot in her yellow dress, staring into a dimly lit ring.

Honor went over, pausing as she passed a teenager sitting on a metal chair. It was Charlie Kellogg, dressed in gray sweatpants and a T-shirt with a picture of a horned goat on it. Maybe he was in a club that met after school or something. He was clutching a phone, earbuds firmly in place.

"Hi, Charlie," she said.

He glanced at her, but didn't answer.

"Nice to see you again," Honor murmured, moving over to her sister.

Faith's eyes were glued on the two men in the ring;

apparently, Levi's *thing* was to be ogled by his wife as he boxed with someone. Really not Honor's cup of tea, two sweaty men bludgeoning each other, but whoever it was seemed to be giving Levi a pretty good time of it. The other guy was tattooed on both shoulders, muscled, glistening with sweat, and you know, maybe there *was* something to be said for boxing, after all. Both men wore helmets, but she could see Levi smile as he jabbed (or whatever). The other boxer answered with a left-right-left combination, and Levi staggered back, then recovered, saying something unintelligible to the other guy.

"Who's putting the smackdown on Levi?" Honor whispered.

Faith gave her a strange look. "Your fiancé," she answered.

Honor jerked in surprise. "Oh, sure. It's just with the helmets, and the funky lighting, it looked a little… like, uh, Gerard. Gerard Chartier. From the firehouse."

Gerard was six foot five and rather resembled Mr. Clean. Tom was a good five inches shorter, maybe a hundred pounds lighter and had a Union Jack tattooed on his shoulder. Might've been a clue. Then again, the one time she'd seen him without his shirt, he'd been on top of her (oh, happy memory), and she'd been too busy shoving her tongue in his mouth to examine him for identifying marks.

The bell rang, and both men hit each other's gloves and exited the ring. Levi wrapped his squealy wife in his arms and kissed her, and then Tom leaned in and kissed Honor, as one would expect a young(ish) couple to do.

It was a quick kiss, but it took Honor by surprise,

anyway, sending an electric pulse through her so hard and fast that she swore the lights flickered. That mouth of his, so…excellent, and the masculine smell of sweat and soap. His hair was spiked from his exertion, and his abs were sinfully magnificent, and a bead of sweat sliced down toward his—

"Hallo, darling. Here to cheer me on as I beat up your relatives?" He seemed completely unaffected, and Honor tried to snap out of it, dragging her eyes off his torso to his face.

"Well, technically, Levi's not related to me, but, uh, what was the question?"

"What are you doing here, sweetheart?"

"I'm meeting Faith. Um, you looked good, uh, Pooky."

"Oh, man. That's not really what you call him, is it?"

Honor turned as her niece appeared at her side, Helena Meering, her best friend, in tow. "Hey, sweetheart," she said.

"Hi, Auntie," Abby said, then turned to Levi, her hands on her hips. "Are you already done? I thought you were supposed to teach us to protect ourselves, Levi. That's why we're here."

Right. Prudence had mentioned that she wanted Abby to know a little self-defense before entering the world of dating.

"You're an hour late," Levi said, cocking an eyebrow. "I told you four o'clock. It's now 5:07."

"You look incredibly hot, Chief Cooper," Helena said.

"Inappropriate, young lady."

"And so do you, mister," the girl added, ogling Tom,

who was taking off his boxing gloves. With his teeth. She had a point.

"That's Dr. Barlow to you," Levi said. He paused. "Hey, Tom, I don't suppose you'd be interested in doing a self-defense class with me, would you?"

"OMG, do it," Helena said. "There'd be, like, a hundred girls signed up in minutes."

From several yards away, Charlie sat up straighter and took out one earbud.

Tom glanced at Honor. She gave a little nod in Charlie's direction, and Tom looked over. A hint of a smile flashed in his eyes, and that tingle of electricity sliced through Honor again. "Sure, I'll help out," he said. "I'd love to."

"You're *British?*" Helena squealed. "Hi. I'm Helena. I'll be eighteen in seven more months."

"He's taken, okay?" Abby said. "Remember? He's gonna be my uncle. He and Honor are engaged."

Helena turned to Honor, her mouth hanging open most unattractively. "You? Seriously?"

Irritating. "Yes, Helena. We…we're getting married." Man. Hard to say that out loud, especially with an officer of the law watching. Her legs felt sweaty. From the corner of her eye, she saw Charlie approach.

"Tom Barlow. A pleasure," Tom said. "And this is my unofficial stepson, Charlie Kellogg," Tom said. "He's a bit of a boxer, as well."

"Cool," Helena said.

"Hey, Charlie," Abby said.

"Hey, Abby," he returned. A flush crept up his still-boyish cheeks.

"All right, we're off," Faith said, kissing Levi once

more. "I plan on getting all the juicy details on you, Tom, so consider yourself forewarned."

"Thanks for the heads-up," he said. He put a heavy arm around Honor. "Don't tell her all my secrets, darling."

Heat flared in Honor's face, making her blotchy, no doubt. Tom was *much* better at this…this faking than she was. "Right," she said, her voice too loud. "Okay. Off we go."

And for the next few hours, she lied. To her younger sister.

Well, not lied, not exactly. She just didn't tell her the full truth. Yes, it had been fast. Yes, his accent was adorable. Yes, he was quite attractive, wasn't he? Yes, yes, yes.

The secret wriggled around inside her. But while she and Faith had been getting closer since the youngest Holland had come back home, Honor couldn't ask her sister to keep something from her police chief husband. She couldn't tell Pru, either, as Pru tended to blurt out information like a bleating goat. Jack, forget about it. She might've considered Jessica Dunn, but Honor was Jess's boss, and it didn't seem fair to put her in a position where she'd have to conceal fraud.

Not so long ago, she would've told Dana. It was an odd thought.

ON WEDNESDAY EVENING, Blue Heron hosted Kites and Flights, one of the off-season events designed to keep people coming to the vineyard all year-round. It was a singles event; a couple of weeks ago, Honor had seen some people flying kites and came up with the idea—

kite flying, then a flight of wine in the cask room afterward.

As she finalized some tasting notes, she remembered what Tom had said—what if she met someone while she was with him? Someone single and age-appropriate and straight, someone employed. This imaginary man would be good-looking, but not too pretty, and he'd be smart and well read and…and…he'd talk to her, as Tom did precious little of that. No. Only when they were in public did he turn on the charm.

Her imagination (and eggs) had told her that she and Tom would move in together and start growing closer immediately. They'd laugh and have a good time. The chemistry would be undeniable. Before long, it'd be the real thing.

Yeah. Not yet. Not even close.

Spike licked her thumb, and Honor stroked her head with one finger. The dog had come a long way from when Honor had first met her. "Look at you," she said. "Love has changed you, am I right? It's time to go herd the singletons. Are you ready?"

If there was a more perfect afternoon for kite-flying, Honor couldn't imagine it. The early April sky was achingly, perfectly blue, the sun was warm—it was fifty-two degrees, in fact, though she knew quite well it would snow again before spring decided to stay. A brisk breeze gusted from the west, and the sweet smell of the vineyard permeated the air as she walked up to Rose Ridge, where the single kite flyers milled around.

It was a pretty sight, the bright kites and clothes. At least six heads of gray hair and three baldies caught the light…. Why did singles events always attract the elderly? *Hey. Glass houses, okay?* the eggs said. Oh, gosh,

Pops was here, too…hopefully not flirting too much, or Goggy might beat him with a stick later on. But there were a few younger people, too. Lorelei from the bakery, Julie from the library. The perfect man she'd just been imagining was missing. He always was.

There was one couple already hitting it off, their backs to her. Then the guy turned, and Honor froze midstep.

It was Brogan. And Dana.

Pregnant Dana.

She remembered to keep walking. Told her face to smile.

"Hey, Honor!" Brogan said, taking a few steps toward her. "How are you? Great idea, this! I was home, I said, 'Dane, we should go!' And, of course, that way we could see you."

He was trying. A little too hard, but he was trying to keep their friendship, and Honor's heart gave an unwilling tug.

"It's good to see you guys," she lied. "I just didn't expect you."

"How could we resist? Superfun," Dana chirped, smiling so brightly her nose crinkled. "How are you, pal? Long time no see."

"Yeah. Um, congratulations again, by the way!" She'd sent an email, of course. "It's really big news."

"Thanks. We're so happy." Dana's hand went to her stomach—a little high, Honor thought, as if she had heartburn. She *hoped* Dana had heartburn. Really bad heartburn. And the pukes. *Now, now,* said the eggs. *Don't be catty. After all, it could be your turn soon! Because we know* we're *ready!*

She gave herself a mental shake. "I didn't expect you two because it's a singles' event."

"It is?" Dana said. "That's not what the newspaper said."

At that instant, Jessica came running over, her face set in a frown. "Honor, I'm so sorry. The newspaper cut the line about this being for singles only, and half the people here are—oh. Hi, you guys."

"Hey, Jess, how's it going?" Brogan said. God, he was so *nice* to everyone. Then he reached for Dana's hand, the gesture so familiar and lovely, such a statement. He'd never held *her* hand. Never.

Aren't we over him yet? the eggs asked.

"It's fine," she told Jessica. "They always get something wrong. We'll clarify for next week, but for today, everyone can just have fun and drink wine." She paused. "Except you, of course," she added for Dana's benefit.

"Why me?" Dana asked. "Oh, right! I keep forgetting. Wouldn't want to do anything to hurt our little bambino," she said, leaning back against Brogan.

On second thought, we're with you on the heartburn, the eggs said.

"Honor!" called Carol Robinson, one of the married people. "When do we get to the eating part? I'm starving."

"Easy, girl. First we're going to do a little meet-and-greet," Honor said. "Folks, unfortunately, there was a line missing in the newspaper write-up. This is actually a singles' event, but don't worry. We're very glad you're here today. Next month, though, will just be for singles, okay?"

"Isn't that discrimination?" Brogan murmured, surprisingly close to her ear. Honor jumped. He was smiling, that killer grin.

"Shush, you," she said, feeling a traitorous tingle. "Okay, so if you *are* single, please group over to the left with Jessica, and you can start getting to know one another. And if you're not, let's get those kites in the air, all right?" She held one up—special ordered, dark blue with the gold heron logo emblazoned on it. "It's a beautiful day here at Blue Heron, and Carol's right. After this, we get to eat some lovely food and drink some incredible wines."

It was the PR side of her. Always smiling, always focused on presenting the best possible front of the family business, always looking for ways to bring people in and remind them of the family mantra: life was too short to drink bad wine.

The kites went up, Pops getting his line tangled with Carol Robinson's (probably on purpose; Carol was adorable). Lorelei from the bakery, who was always so cheerful, listened intently as Elvis Byrd, a pale, scrawny computer programmer a few years younger than Honor, explained why fracking would cause massive earthquakes, ending life as they knew it. Suzette Minor was flirting with Ned (Honor would have to put the smackdown on that, because Suzette was far too old and trashy for Ned, though Ned would disagree). Jessica snapped photos, and the kites soared and ducked against the pale blue sky.

And Dana and Brogan were certainly having a good time. They made a very attractive couple, she'd give them that. Very Hallmark card-ish, Dana standing in front of him, giggling like a fifth grader, Brogan tall and manly behind her, making the kite swoop and circle.

Dana glanced over, and Honor quickly averted her eyes. Went over to her grandfather and kissed his grizzled cheek. "Hey, Pops. How are you?"

"I'm good, sweetheart. See any ladies for me? I'm thinking of divorcing your grandmother."

"You couldn't find the front door without my grandmother," she said.

"So? The front door's nailed shut," he said. "But you're probably right," he admitted. "And I suppose one person is as good as another."

"Such a romantic," she said, adjusting his collar.

"You'll see," he said, cuffing her fondly.

When the sun began to set in shades of peach and lavender, the group adjourned to the cask room, where cheese and hors d'oeuvres had been set up. Honor went through her paces, talking about wine pairings and flavors, the bouquet of each wine, the body, the texture and finish. Spike stared adoringly at Lorelei, who gave out doggy treats at the bakery, and Pops and Carol flirted.

Dana and Brogan always seemed to be touching.

In all the years she'd known Brogan, she never remembered him being in love. He certainly seemed to be now.

By the time Jessica had herded the participants upstairs to the shop, where they would hopefully buy vast quantities of the wines they'd just tasted, it was almost eight and nearly dark. Honor picked up Spike and snuggled the dog under her chin, then stood on tiptoe to peek out of the narrow windows that ran along the top of the stone wall.

The cobalt sky still held streaks of red and purple at the horizon. Lights were on in both the Old and New Houses, and a wave of homesickness washed over

Honor. She missed home, the big, comfortable living room and aging kitchen, her gorgeous bedroom with its pale blue walls and soft white rug. Her sitting room, where she had spent so many happy hours watching *Bizarre Tales from the E.R.* and *Diagnose This!* with Jack or Mrs. Johnson.

Maybe she and Tom would move into the New House someday if they decided to get married (and stay married). But not yet. She couldn't see living there under false pretenses. Home was too precious to sully with a fake relationship.

A *real* relationship—with Tom, anyway—seemed a bit impossible. In ten days of living together, she had yet to see him smile. And you know…it was his smile that had done her in. A smile like that hinted at all sorts of wonderful things. Where was that smile now? Because his somber face wasn't nearly as appealing as his goofy, sweet, smiling face. In fact, Tom sometimes looked a little intimidating.

"So I hear you're getting married," came a voice. Dana stood in the other entryway, her arms folded.

"Yes," Honor said. Spike, whose brain was about the size of a cashew, barked and wagged, the faithless cur.

Dana didn't bother looking at the little dog. "Yeah, it's all over town. Weird that I had to hear about it from Laura Boothby. And you haven't even said if you'd be my maid of honor yet."

Seriously? Granted, Dana had always been the type who seemed only to tolerate another person's stories, just waiting for the chance to bring the conversation back to her. God forbid that anyone else have something going on. Had that always been the way? Kind of, yeah. Dana's life was full of drama, fights, betrayals, triumphs. Honor's life, on the other hand, had always been pretty normal. And happy.

"Well, it's been a busy time," she said, setting Spike in her purse, where the dog immediately curled up in a ball.

"Kind of a coincidence, don't you think?" Dana asked, studying her engagement ring. "I mean, I didn't even realize you were seeing someone."

"It just happened," Honor replied. *Same as you and Brogan,* she didn't say.

Her former friend looked up. "Interesting, the timing and everything. I mean, if you were really in love with Brogan, enough to throw wine in my face, I'd think you wouldn't be engaged all of a sudden."

Honor raised an eyebrow. "*Was* I in love, though? I mean, you told me it was just a crush, remember?"

"Whatever," Dana said. "Look, if you don't want to be my maid of honor, that's probably best. My sister—Carla, not Penny—really wants to. By the way, I'm thinking of booking the Barn for the wedding."

There was no way in hell Dana Hoffman and Brogan Cain were going to get married on Blue Heron land. Nuh-uh. "Give Jessica a call. She handles that now. We're pretty heavily booked, though." That was true. Faith's renovation had made quite an impression on event planners throughout western New York.

"Then again, the Barn might not be big enough. You know how his parents are, right? We're trying to keep the number under five hundred. Anyway, with all the sports celebrities who'll be coming, we need to have something really fabulous. I mean, the Barn is cute and all, but…we're going for elegant. Because if we're going to have, like, Derek Jeter and Jeremy Lin, it has to be amazing. And we'd like to do it before the baby comes, of course."

"Uh-huh."

Well played, the eggs said from behind their quilting frames. They had a point. Lack of interest was always the thing that infuriated Dana the most.

"Anyway, I guess we were really surprised when you turned up engaged."

"Well, as you said yourself, Dana, when it's right, you just know it."

Dana crossed her arms and raised an eyebrow. "So me and Brogan getting engaged, that had nothing to do with it."

Brogan and I, for the love of God. "Can't see why you'd think that."

"Oh, please!" Dana threw her hands in the air. "You expect me to believe that you're not getting married out of *jealousy?* Brogan and I get engaged, and then look at this! A *month* later, Honor's engaged, too! I mean, I have to wonder where you dug this guy up, because it sure feels like some kind of stunt to me."

Which, of course, it was. But more than that, more upsetting, was this side of Dana, a side Honor has seen unleashed on other people more than once. Honor had always thought she was exempt. Irrationally, tears burned behind her eyes. Once, Dana and she had laughed and drank and commiserated together, watched movies and suffered through yoga class.

"That's what it is, isn't it?" Dana said, hands on her hips. "You just can't *stand* that Brogan and I have something *special,* so you go out and somehow find some *loser* to—"

"Hallo, darling."

Tom stood in the doorway, his eyes on her. "Jessica said you'd be down here. Didn't mean to interrupt."

"Not at all," Honor said, clearing her throat.

Dana's face had grown very red.

Spike awoke and, realizing that her nemesis was here, pounced on Tom's shoe, snarling.

"Come now, Ratty, haven't we had this talk?" He picked up the dog and handed her to Honor. "I'm Tom Barlow," he said, offering Dana his hand. "Honor's man. I don't think I've had the pleasure."

Honor would bet her left pinky that Tom remembered exactly who Dana was. He'd remembered *her,* after all. Men loved catfights, for some reason.

"Dana Hoffman," Dana muttered.

Tom came over to Honor and kissed her on the temple, then took her damp hand and squeezed it. "Well, I just wanted to stop by and have a peek at you, love."

"Hi," she said, squeezing back. She kind of loved him at the moment.

"And the kite-flying went well?"

No *kind of* about it. She'd mentioned this to him last night, but she hadn't been quite sure he'd been paying full attention, as he'd had some airplane plans up on the computer. "Yes. Thanks."

"Lovely. Dana, what do you do for work?" Tom asked.

"I'm a hairdresser."

"Very nice." Tom smiled. "Right-o. I didn't mean to intrude on your chat, ladies. Honor, I'll see you at home, then. Unless you want me to stay and help clean up?"

"No, that's... I have some things to take care of first. But yes, I'll see you at, um, home."

He leaned in, cupped her cheek with one (big) hand

and kissed her, and she kissed him back. Would've probably done him on the floor in gratitude had Dana not been standing there, one eyebrow arched.

Tom looked at her, his gray eyes unreadable, smile gone. Then he turned to Dana. "Lovely to meet you."

"We should have dinner sometime," Dana said unexpectedly. "The four of us."

"Absolutely," Tom said. "And, sorry, who would make the fourth?"

Oh, yes. Honor would name their firstborn Tom, boy or girl.

Dana snorted (unattractively, Honor was pleased to see). "Um, Brogan?" she said.

"And who is Brogan?"

If she had twins, Honor would name them *both* Tom.

"Really?" Dana said. "I'm surprised Honor's never mentioned him. Since she used to sleep with him not that long ago."

Tom turned to her. "Oh, yes, that friend of yours I met at Hugo's. Right. I didn't realize he was your old boyfriend, Honor," he lied, his voice warm and delicious. "We absolutely must have dinner now. Any other old lovers you have stashed around town?"

"Oh, I—you—Ryan Gosling?" Honor said, her voice odd. "No one. It's…yeah."

Tom grinned. "I'll let you girls alone, then." With that, he kissed her quickly once more, and she practically staggered after him.

When his footsteps had faded away, Dana turned to her and pursed her lips. "I'm having a hard time believing that guy just fell out of the sky with a marriage proposal."

Honor cleared her throat. "As I said, it just happened. Took us both by surprise."

Another line borrowed from Dana herself. She didn't seem to recognize it.

Dana fake-smiled. "We'll be looking forward to that dinner."

TOM HAD ALREADY had one glass of whiskey and was working on the second when the front door opened, and his fiancée came in. That suit didn't do anything for her perfectly acceptable figure (which was quite nice, now that he thought of it). Plain navy blue skirt and jacket, white shirt, distressingly sensible shoes. The little rat-dog's head was visible in her purse.

"Hi," Honor said, setting the little creature on the floor, where it snarled at him. "Thank you for saving me there."

"With Dana, you mean?" He kept his eyes on the dog. Ratty had peed on his gym bag yesterday.

"Yes. I owe you."

"Do you?" He could think of a few ways she could repay him, starting with getting out of those boring clothes. Hopefully, she had slutty underwear.

Not the line of thinking that was going to help.

The only reason Tom had any hope of this working, this marriage, was because he and Honor were a business arrangement. Love hadn't worked out for either of them, had it?

But when he'd heard that nasty little baggage laying into her, he'd wanted to…help. Laid on the British charm, played the part of the devoted fiancé, pretended not to know about either Dana or Brighton.

And when he kissed her, it felt like a current jolted

right through him. Not good. He wasn't up for having his heart skewered again. Melissa had done that so well, and her son was keeping up the tradition. But Honor was *nice*. Honor was pleasant. Nice and pleasant were about all he could handle these days, so electric jolts and the urge to pull a little white-knight action…not smart.

Honor was looking at him. Right. Because he was staring at her.

"Well," he said now. "I'm getting good at acting. As are you."

Something shut down in her eyes. "Yes. You are." She sat on the couch and slipped off her completely un-imaginative shoes.

"By the way," he said. "I got you this today." He picked up the small velvet box and handed it to her.

It had taken a surprisingly long time to pick out a ring. He'd figured he'd go into the first store he saw, ask for a ring in his price range and wham-bam-thank-you-ma'am, he'd be done. Instead, he'd looked at every damn ring in the store before settling on this one.

Honor opened the box. "Oh," she breathed.

"Like it? If not, I'll return it, and you can pick out something more to your taste." Tom realized belatedly that he was holding his breath.

"No, no. This is…it's beautiful."

"It's an antique."

"Yes." She raised her eyes, and Tom glanced away from the soft, sweet emotion there and looked out the window instead. "Thank you," she said softly. "It wasn't necessary."

"Of course it was. If we're madly in love and getting married, you should have a ring." He finished his whiskey and stood up. "Glad you like it. I've got to correct papers. And I should call Charlie and listen to him breathe at me."

"Okay. Thank you again. For...you know. For everything."

Bollocks. *You'd best be careful, mate,* his conscience warned him. *Wouldn't want to hurt a nice girl like her.* But she wasn't a girl. She knew what they were about. At least, she should.

With that, he went upstairs, leaving her sitting on the couch, looking at her ring.

CHAPTER FOURTEEN

"IT'S NOT MY stuff that's cluttering up the house. It's his." Goggy folded her arms and glared.

Grandparenticide. It held more and more appeal these days. Honor sighed. Theoretically, she had better things to do on a Saturday morning than try to declutter her grandparents' house. She could get another Pap smear, for example. It would be more fun than this. "Goggy, the two of you are this close to being hoarders."

"Oh, we are not. You kids. I have laundry to fold."

"I'll fold it! Goggy, you can't be going up and down the stairs so much. They're a death trap."

"How else will I get my exercise? Jeremy told me I should exercise. So I exercise." She gave Honor a triumphant look.

"Speaking of that, there's a gorgeous pool at Rushing Creek."

"Where people drown," Goggy said.

"No one has ever drowned there."

"It's just a matter of time." Goggy turned her back and clumped up the narrow, dark, terrifying stairs of the Old House, one hand on the railing, one hand on the wall.

Faith had tried to help the cause last weekend, managing to sneak one of Goggy's more hideous cardigans out of the house, which, considering that Goggy could give Pharaoh a run for his money in the stubborn department, was pretty good. Prudence had been less successful; she'd pointed out that they really didn't need four rusty flour sifters, which had led to Goggy calling Williams-Sonoma, ordering two more and still refusing to part with the other four.

Maybe her grandfather would be more agreeable. He'd been sitting at the kitchen table, ignoring both females in favor of doing the crossword puzzle. "Okay, Pops, let's take a look and see what we can get rid of, okay?" She tugged on a kitchen drawer, which was stuffed full of crap. Pointless crap, she thought, groping around inside to clear the logjam. Took care not to catch her ring.

And what a ring it was.

Funny, how she thought she loved the stark simplicity of Dana's ring, that unadorned diamond flashing for all to see. The ring Tom had chosen was an Art Deco style (original, she thought). A square diamond surrounded by two triangular diamonds, encased in engraved platinum…ornate and unusual and utterly, hypnotically beautiful.

The drawer jerked open with a clatter. "Good God."

"I need those," Pops said, not looking up from the paper.

"Pops. Come on. How many corkscrews do you need?"

"I'm a winemaker! I need a lot!"

"There are…what…two dozen corkscrews in here? Come on." She paused for a second, counting. "You don't need twenty-seven corkscrews."

"I know how many there are." The old man scowled at her.

"And you really need every single one?"

"Yes."

She squeezed the bridge of her nose. "Pops, wouldn't it be nice to live in a clean, sunny, organized place where you had more than one outlet per floor? Where you could use all the doors because you didn't have to nail one shut to cut down on drafts? Where you didn't have to worry about falling down the stairs and breaking your neck?"

"Your grandmother's the one who runs up and down those stairs fifty times a day. I never go up there."

"What if Goggy fell and broke her hip? How'd you feel then? Oh, stop. You'd be devastated." Surreptitiously, she slipped a corkscrew out of the drawer. If she couldn't get Pops to agree to purge, she'd just steal all his crap and bring it to Goodwill. Not that there was a booming market for used corkscrews. "Seriously, Pops. You can't be up on the ladder cleaning out gutters anymore. It's not safe, and it's not smart."

He groaned. "When you're my age, you won't want anyone telling you what to do, either, sweetheart. If I can't clean the gutters, what's next? I can't dress myself? I can't feed myself? This is my home. These are my things. Don't make me a helpless old man who sits around in diapers."

She felt a tug of sympathy. "No, Pops, that's not the point. But you have to be realistic. Your balance isn't great anymore, and it's way too easy to trip in here. Let alone fall off the ladder like you did last year."

"You might have a point. Probably not, but maybe. Now put that corkscrew back. That's my favorite one."

A knock came on the kitchen door, and Honor looked up.

It was Tom. And Charlie.

"Hallo," her fiancé said. "Thought we'd lend a hand."

"Oh! That's…that's really nice of you." She'd mentioned where she was going this morning over breakfast. Hadn't expected him to turn up.

"Mr. Holland," Tom said to Pops. "You remember my stepson, don't you?" The boy sighed with gusto and rolled his eyes, apparently unable to summon the energy to correct Tom on the title. "Charlie, say hello."

"Hi," Charlie said, shaking her grandfather's hand.

"Hello, young man!" Pops said, clapping him on the shoulder. "Maybe you can be on my side and keep these marauding invaders out of my things."

Charlie's lips tugged, and Honor glanced at Tom.

His face was full of…yearning, like a dog at the pound who's been passed over too many times but can't help pricking up his ears at the sound of footsteps just the same.

Then he saw her looking, and gave her a quick smile that covered up any hint of loneliness.

He was a tough one, Tom Barlow. She felt like she knew him less now instead of more.

"When are you two getting married, anyway?" Pops said.

"Um, soon," Honor said.

"We should take care of that, shouldn't we?" Tom murmured.

They should. Once they filed for a marriage license, they had sixty days to get married, or Tom would be deported. Which was exactly why she hadn't filed yet. What had seemed like a good plan now seemed as thin as March ice, and as sharply dangerous.

"Pops," she said, "Let's go down to the cellar. I know there's stuff we should throw out down there."

"I have to check the vines," Pops said.

"Don't run off, you coward. You said you'd tell me what I could throw away."

"Nothing. There. I made it easy for you."

Goggy reappeared in the kitchen, wearing a different dress and a little scarf, indicating that she was going out. "Hello, boys! Give me a kiss! I never know when I'll get to kiss a handsome man, and here I have two!"

Tom obliged. Charlie did, too, and Goggy patted his cheek. Sweet, how she didn't berate him for his black eyeliner and earrings. If he was a Holland, he'd never hear the end of it.

"I have a church meeting," Goggy said. "There's a huge debate over whether or not to replace the altar cloth. That Cathy Kennedy gets downright vicious sometimes! See you later, dears! Don't touch anything upstairs, but by all means, get rid of some of your grandfather's junk."

"It's not junk, old woman," Pops retorted. She ignored him and left in a cloud of Jean Naté.

"I'm here," came a weary voice. "As ordered. Like I don't have better things to do on a Saturday." Abby came in the back door. "Hi, guys," she said. "Oh, hey, Charlie. I didn't know you'd be here. Another slave for my aunt to boss around?"

Charlie's face flamed. "I guess," he mumbled. Ah, adolescence. Honor had been just as awkward around Brogan, come to think of it. Sigh.

"Let's get to work," Honor said. "Rubber gloves are under the sink, and I have plenty of trash bags, and stop glaring at me, Pops."

"This would be a great place to hide a body," Abby announced as they went down the warped cellar stairs. "Charlie, this place was built in—what, Pops?—1781?"

"That's right, sweetheart," he said. "The first Holland got this land as a reward for fighting against your people, Tom."

"Is that right?" Tom said. "Seems more of a punishment with this weather we've been having."

He had a point. The temperature had dropped to twenty last night.

"Okay," Honor said. "We can definitely get rid of some of this stuff." She reached for a likely candidate.

"Put that down," her grandfather said. "I need that."

"Pops, it's a moldy piece of cushion foam. And it's torn."

"So? I can wash it and use it for something."

"Like what? When would you need moldy torn cushion foam?"

"It's gross, Pops," Abby said.

"I'm not going to stand here and watch you make fun of my things," Pops said. "I have vines to check. Nice to see you, young man," he said to Charlie. "And you," he added to Tom. "Marry my granddaughter and make an honest woman out of her."

"Yes, sir." Tom shook his hand, and Pops clumped up the old wooden steps.

"He's gone. Maybe we can just burn the place down," Abby said.

For the next hour, they stuffed bags with Pops's precious belongings, which included a bent golf club, a broken mirror and newspapers from the 1960s. Abby talked almost nonstop, bless her, and Charlie answered, shyly at first, then with more confidence as their talk turned to music.

"And what have we here?" Tom asked from the far end of the basement, bending down to examine something. "Hallo. These might be worth something." He looked up at Honor and grinned.

It was a pile of magazines. Men's magazines, to be specific.

Tom opened one up. "Miss September, 1972. Not bad." He straightened up. "Think we should check eBay and see what these are going for?"

"Oh, ick."

"Nothing ick about her. She's lovely."

"Shush. Just toss them." Man! There were dozens.

"Hopefully we don't read about a priceless collection of *Playboy*s found at the dump later this week." He glanced across the cellar at Charlie. "You're right, though. Best get rid of these before the lad sees them. Hard enough being a pubescent boy without this kind of stimulation."

They shoveled the magazines into a black trash bag, and amid the smell of stone and old paper, Honor caught a hint of Tom's soap.

It felt like years since they'd slept together.

When the *Playboy*s were bagged, Tom stood up and pulled off his gloves. "Honor, do you still want to get married?" he asked, his voice quiet.

She jerked her gaze to his. "Sure. Yes."

"Because if you don't, I need to make another plan."

"No. I do." She took a deep breath. "Do you?"

"Yes." His face was solemn.

"Are you sure?"

"Yeah. Seeing naked women has only lit a fire to

get it done." He grinned, and Honor's knees practically buckled. On the one hand, it'd be awfully nice to have a serious conversation with him for more than one or two seconds; on the other, that smile went straight to Down Under.

"Guys! Look what we found!" Abby said, and the two teenagers came over.

Tom looked away. "Is it alive?" he asked.

"Yeah!" Charlie said, holding up his find.

It was a snake.

"Snake!" Honor shrieked, leaping behind Tom. "Snake! Snake!"

Charlie jerked back, and, oh, *fungus,* he dropped it, the snake was on the floor, wriggling and black and evil. Then it was gone in a hideous, lithe movement, and Honor was climbing onto the garbage bag full of *Playboy*s and crawling onto Tom, clutching his head and awkwardly heaving herself onto him.

"Bit of a phobia, darling?" he asked gamely, boosting her a bit.

"Where is it? Where is it?" she said, already sticky with sweat. If that thing went over her foot—or in her pants—oh, God! The idea of its hideous, cold, twisting body against her skin made her dry-heave in terror.

"I forgot you were scared of snakes," Abby said.

"Well, it's gone now," Charlie muttered, squatting down.

Tom hoisted her so she was basically piggyback on him. "Settle down, love, you've scared it."

"*I've* scared *it?* Who in their right mind picks up a snake and holds it! What if it's poisonous?"

"It was a garter snake," Charlie said.

"What if was a poisonous garter snake?"

"No such thing, darling." Tom shifted.

"Don't put me down! Please! Get me out of here." She tightened her grip around his throat, earning a choking sound. Couldn't be helped.

"Here it is," Charlie said.

"No! Stop it, Charlie! Please!" She gripped Tom with her legs so hard he wheezed.

He loosened her chokehold around his neck. "Charlie, get rid of it, mate."

"Do you want to hold it, Honor?" Charlie asked sweetly.

Honor burst into tears.

"Oh, man, I'm sorry!" the boy said, looking stricken.

"No, no, she's got a phobia. Obviously," Abby said, putting her hand on Charlie's shoulder. "Let's get it out of here, okay?"

"I'm *sorry,*" Charlie said, and already resentment was darkening his face.

"Me, too. Sorry," Honor said, tears still streaking down her face. "I'm afraid of snakes."

"Yeah. I got that."

Oh, God, this was so embarrassing. She was wrapped awkwardly around Tom and shaking with revulsion, but she wasn't about to set foot on the floor, either. Not when the place was riddled with nests of vipers, no sir.

Tom started to put her down.

"No!" she barked, making him flinch, as her mouth was right next to his ear. "What if there are more? Don't put me down! Don't move! Don't drop me!"

"All right, settle down. But here, slide around so I can see you," he said, and he pulled at her, Honor still gripping him like a jockey, her arms locked around his neck. "Christ, you're not making this easy, are you?"

"I can't! I'm afraid, okay? Sue me."

His shoulders shook. He may have been laughing, the wretch. A few more tries, and he tugged her so that she was facing him. Well, she would be facing him if she could bring herself to, um, face him. Instead, she buried her face in his shoulder, shuddering.

"There, there, sweetheart," he whispered. "It's gone."

He smelled so good. An hour of working in a damp and filthy cellar, and he smelled like soap and rain, and he was warm, and solid, and safe.

After a minute or two, her breathing returned to normal, and the involuntary tears stopped leaking out of her eyes.

"Can I put you down now?" he asked.

She couldn't stay like this forever. And it was rather, ah, intimate, her legs wrapped around his waist.

She lowered her feet and stood on his, still afraid to touch the floor. Tom pulled back a little. He cupped her face in his hands and slid his thumbs under her eyes, wiping away the tears. "Better?"

She nodded.

He nodded, too, a small smile flashing.

Then he kissed her forehead. Then her nose. Then her lips.

And this time, it wasn't for anyone's benefit. Just the two of them in this damp old cellar, his mouth so perfect against hers. He tilted her head, his arms like a fortress around her, the best feeling in the entire world. His hair was baby-soft. She'd forgotten that. And he tasted, so, so good.

"Guys. Gross." Honor jumped back at the sound of her niece's voice. "I mean, sorry you were freaked out, but please. I have to see enough of this at home."

Tom cleared his throat. "Back to work, shall we?" he asked.

There was no way in hell she was going to stay down here. One snake probably meant a thousand, possibly a million. She shuddered again. "I'll go upstairs and start on the kitchen," she said.

And yet, even with the threat of snakes, she wanted to stay.

BY THE TIME Tom left to take Charlie to the gym and Prudence arrived with her sturdy truck for the dump run, fifteen garbage bags had been filled. Horrifyingly, both cellar and kitchen looked exactly the same. "See you at the wedding dress place?" Pru said.

"Sounds good." Today, the three Holland girls were going with Mrs. Johnson to pick out a wedding dress. Against Mrs. Johnson's will, it should be noted.

"We should buy yours while we're at it," her sister said.

"Oh, no. This is Mrs. J.'s day."

"What are we gonna call her now?" Pru asked. "*Mom* doesn't seem right. I swear, I didn't even know she had a first name till a few weeks ago."

"I have no idea. Listen, I have to run back and shower," Honor said. "I'll see you there."

Four hours later, Honor, Faith and Prudence sat in Happily Ever After's waiting area as the now disheveled and sweaty Gwen, who owned the store, brought Mrs. Johnson the sixteenth dress to try on. The girls had been shown zero, as Mrs. Johnson kept declaring the dresses *foolish, hideous* or, for some reason, *arrogant.* Her requirements were many: nothing that made her look whorish (strapless, in her world view), nothing that made her look cheap (which meant no beading or sparkle) and nothing that made her look doddering (no lace). No ball gowns would be tolerated (pretentious). No sheath dresses (nightgowns). Nothing shorter than floor-length (disrepectful), and nothing with a train (pompous).

"Does anyone have alcohol?" Faith asked. "I could really use a drink right now."

"Or Valium," Pru added.

"What are you and Tom planning for your wedding?" Faith asked.

Honor jumped. "Oh, I figured it would just be a city hall thing."

"What? No! You have to get married at the Barn," Faith said.

Honor cleared her throat. "It won't be at the Barn. We, uh, we might just elope."

"And kill your father, Honor Holland?" came Mrs. Johnson's voice. The woman had batlike hearing.

"Huh. I hadn't thought of that."

Faith turned to her. "So. Let's get to the good stuff. What was it like, your first kiss with Tom?"

"Oh, uh, it was great." A lame answer. "Um, how was yours with Levi?"

"Amazing. He kissed me after a seizure."

"Isn't that against the law?" Pru asked.

"Not in this state. It was the morning after. Actually, our first kiss was in high school. That was hot, too. He's the best kisser in the history of the earth."

"I don't know about that," Pru said.

Honor didn't, either. Tom was gifted in the kissing department. The memory of the kiss in the cellar made her feel downright…swoony.

"You're blushing," Faith said.

"Hey, you'd blush, too, if you know where Carl and I did it this morning," Prudence said. "Oh. You were talking to her. Yeah, Tom's a hottie, that's for sure. That accent is incredible, even if I can barely understand him."

"What kind of accent is that, anyway? Cockney?" Faith asked.

"Nope. Manchester. Just a basic blue-collar accent, I guess." But yes, it had a certain pull to it.

Gwen darted past again, fear on her face and rightfully so, then returned a second later with another dress, brave girl. They could hear some murmuring and a respondent growl from Mrs. J.

Prudence sighed. "I can't believe we of all people didn't bring wine to this. Mrs. J., come on! Show us one, for the love of God!"

"Fine, you rude girls," Mrs. Johnson called. "But I look ridiculous."

She came out of the dressing room, and all three girls leaned forward. "Oh, Mrs. J.," Honor breathed. "You're beautiful."

The dress was simple—a mermaid-style gown with ruching and the requisite, nonwhorish straps. It hugged Mrs. Johnson's rather stunning figure. Her dark skin glowed against the white fabric, and her close-cropped hair made her neck look long and lovely.

"Sold," Prudence said.

"I love it," Faith murmured.

Mrs. Johnson frowned down at the dress and gave the bodice a tug. "This would look nice on you, Honor. Not me. I'm an old woman."

"How old are you, anyway?" Pru asked.

"None of your business, you impudent child."

"Hey," Faith said. "You're going to be our stepmother. Be nice."

"This *is* my nice." She gave them a regal scowl.

Honor got up and stood next to Mrs. Johnson. "Dad will love this dress," she said, bending to kiss Mrs. J.'s cheek. "Come on. Take a look at yourself."

She slid her arm around Mrs. J., and the two of them looked at the mirror.

"Shall we put on a veil and get the whole idea?" Gwen asked.

"Do I look like the type to wear a veil?" Mrs. Johnson said, though her voice was dreamier now. She couldn't seem to take her eyes off her reflection.

"Get a veil. Here, I'll come with you," Pru instructed. "Faith, come with me. I don't know a thing about this girlie stuff." Indeed, Pru was still in her farming clothes, not that she got out of them much.

The three other women to the accessory room, and Honor just looked at Mrs. J. "I think this is the dress," she murmured. "Don't you?"

"I think you may be right," Mrs. Johnson said. A smile gentled her face.

"I'm so glad you and Dad found each other," Honor said.

"I've loved him for years," Mrs. J. said. "Oh, dear, don't tell anyone I said that. My reputation will suffer greatly." She gave Honor a squeeze. "But it's true."

"You hid it well."

Mrs. J. gave her a pointed look. "And you're hiding something, too, aren't you, Honor?"

Guilt over lying flashed hot and sharp. "Um, no."

Mrs. Johnson huffed. "Please. You can't fool me any better than when you were a little girl."

"I was sixteen when you met me."

"Exactly. And you're a terrible liar. Why are you marrying this man you just met?"

"Shh! Mrs. Johnson, come on!" Honor's face was brick red in the mirror.

"Is it for a green card?"

"Shh! That would be fraud! And I'm not exactly the law-breaking, Jesse James, Tony Soprano kind of person. Am I?"

"No. Which is why I'm so concerned."

"It's just...love."

"Bah."

"Mrs. Johnson..."

"Honor, my dear," she said gently, "I won't tell anyone. But do you think you should be marrying someone you don't love? Settling for a person because he's pleasant and needs a favor?"

Honor wiped her hands on her skirt. "Um, no. I shouldn't. But I—" She took a shaky breath. "You can't tell Dad," she whispered.

"I won't." The housekeeper's eyes were kind, even if her face was solemn.

Honor took a deep breath. "Not everyone gets a true love, Mrs. J.," she whispered. "Some of us make the best with what life offers."

"And you've done that ever since I've known you, Honor Grace! Don't be a martyr!"

"Martyrdom is our family motto," Honor said. "You should know that by now. And Tom's nice. He's a good person. I do have...feelings for him."

"Does he have feelings for you?"

"Yes. I think so. He could, at any rate. Maybe."

"Doesn't that sound heartening." Mrs. J. gave her a pointed look.

Honor sighed. "Faith and Pru are coming back."

"If you need someone to talk to, my dear, you can always come to me."

Her heart softened. "Thank you."

Pru and Faith approached, a long lacy veil trailing from the hands of the consultant. "Don't bother," Mrs. Johnson said. "I'm not wearing it. It looks impudent. The dress, however, I'll take."

As they were paying for the dress, Faith leaned over the counter. "Gwen," she said to the shop's owner, "so long as we're here, can we schedule an appointment for my sister?" She flashed a smile at Honor. "Is that okay? You can't really elope or just go to city hall."

Honor swallowed. "Sure. Why not?"

Because especially after that kiss in the cellar today, she wanted to marry Tom Barlow. Illegal or not.

CHAPTER FIFTEEN

"THAT'S IT, CHARLIE. Get that hand up, mate." Tom stood behind the heavy bag, trying not to wince. Charlie's jab was pathetic. "Put your shoulder into it, remember?"

"I'm *trying!*" He wasn't, that was the problem.

"Good! Now your hook. Side of the bag, come on. Get that hand up." Charlie flailed listlessly, his so-called hook weak and off-center. "Brilliant! So how's school these days?" *Anyone beat you up recently?*

No answer.

One would imagine that if Charlie were being bullied, he'd be interested in learning to fight. Perhaps it was a positive sign that he didn't seem to care about these lessons.

The gym door opened, and Charlie threw himself into the effort, punching like a little dervish, his voluminous T-shirt flopping around him like sweaty wings. The lad glanced at the door—not Abby Vanderbeek. His arms dropped to his sides.

"Hands up," Tom said, reaching out to tap the lad on the side of the head to demonstrate that an opponent could find an opening.

"Don't touch me," Charlie muttered, returning to his lethargic punches.

"There's a tournament coming up," Tom said, more to make conversation than because he thought Charlie would actually be interested. "Ages fourteen and up, division by weight. You could enter. You're getting really good." A lie, of course.

The bell rang, and without a word, Charlie slouched away. Lesson over, apparently.

Furthermore, the kid wouldn't shower at the gym, so he rather reeked on the short drive back to the Kellogg house, ignoring Tom completely, staring out the window.

It was bloody amazing, Tom thought as they pulled onto Apple Blossom Drive, how long the kid could hold a grudge. Even if Charlie was correct in blaming Tom for Melissa's death, when would Tom be forgiven? He wasn't the one behind the wheel of the car that'd struck Melissa. He wasn't the one who told Melissa to text and cross a busy intersection at the same time. He'd rewritten his life these past few years for Charlie, and the little bugger wouldn't give him the time of day.

He loved Charlie. He hated Charlie. He was afraid for Charlie. Every day, there was another tragic story of a teen suicide. Those faces on the news—so young, so doomed—made a cold sweat break out on Tom's back.

He pulled up in front of the Kelloggs' house. "See you soon, mate," he said.

Surprisingly, Charlie didn't move. "Is anyone else doing that tournament?" he asked, not looking at Tom.

"Um, no, not that I know of." *Anyone else* would probably mean Abby Vanderbeek. "I'll mention it on Tuesday at the self-defense class." He paused. "Are you interested?"

Charlie shrugged. "I dunno. Maybe."

"Great! That's brilliant." So maybe boxing *was* a

way to bond. Or impress girls. Hell. That's why Tom started. Either way, it was a step in the right direction.

"I can look into it for you," he said. "I'd need permission from your grandparents."

Another shrug.

"Right. Well, I'll walk you to the door and mention it, shall I?"

Janice greeted him with her usual once-over. "Hello there, Tom," she said to his crotch.

"Janice."

"How was he? Horrible?"

"No, he was great. See you, Charlie." Tom waved, but the gesture was not returned. Then again, Charlie didn't flip him off, either, so maybe that was progress. "Listen, Janice, Charlie might be interested in a boxing tournament for kids his age."

"Really? I can't imagine that he'd beat anyone."

"That's not a great attitude, is it?" Tom said. "If he's motivated—"

Janice snorted.

"He's got potential. I mean, perhaps he's not born to the sport, but if he's interested, let's encourage that."

"Fine. I suppose it'll cost more money."

"I'll cover it. Not to worry." She was staring at his neck, vampirelike, if there were middle-aged vampires who wore pink tracksuits, that was.

"I don't know why you bother," Janice said. "He's not exactly a joy to have around."

Tom gritted his teeth. "He is to me."

"Right." Derision painted her features, and for a second, it felt like Melissa was standing right there.

"I'll be in touch," Tom said.

"Suit yourself," she said. "But don't count on him following through. He's lazy, just like Melissa." One more look at Tom's junk, and she closed the door.

How was that for positive reinforcement?

Tom's jaw was clenched as he got back in the car. Add to this, it was allegedly spring but utterly beastly out. Freezing cold and damp.

How was it that Charlie was better off with those wretched grandparents instead of him? Maybe, Charlie would have a chance in life if the people he actually lived with liked him a bit more. Didn't call him lazy or horrible in front of him.

Tom needed a drink.

The little rat-dog went off in hysterics when Tom came in, yapping without stop. *Yark! Yark! Yark!* "Spike! Enough," he ordered. The dog ignored him.

Where was Honor? Had she told him she had plans? Was she still cleaning her grandparents' house? There was no note, and no message on his phone. He could call her, he supposed. Then again, what would he say? *Where are you? Get back here, I'm in a bloody horrible mood and I'd really like not to be alone.*

Yark! Yark! Yarkyarkyark! The little dog skittered into the room, then commenced growling. "Really impressive," he said, pouring two fingers of whiskey. "I'm bloody terrified."

He sat there, trying to ignore the little ankle-biter, who now had his pants in her tiny teeth. "Come on now," he said, reaching down and scooping up the dog. "Let's be friends, what do you say?"

Spike sank her teeth into his thumb. "Piss off, Ratty," he said. He set her on the floor and went to the sink to rinse off the blood. Ridiculous little dog. He should get a proper mutt who'd hopefully teach her some manners.

Picking the nasty little baggage up but keeping his hand on her neck so she couldn't twist around and bite him again, he carried her upstairs, opened Honor's bedroom door and set the dog on the bed, where the precious thing continued to snarl at him, sounding more like a rabid hedgehog than a real threat.

It smelled nice in here. Lemony. Neat as a pin, and looking very much as he'd had it, thanks to her paranoia about being discovered. While some of her clothes were in Tom's room, there wasn't room enough for all of them. He opened a drawer to find out.

Rather nice panties, he thought. Pink here, black-and-white polka dots there. Matching bras. Hello there. The woman who dressed like a modern-day Puritan had quite lovely knickers. Almost slutty, in fact, and wasn't that a plus in the marital column?

Yark! Yark!

Ratty was back, gnawing on his ankle. "You know, Ratty, for a squirrel, you're a right pain in the arse," he said. "Enjoy your solitude."

With that, he closed the door behind him, ignoring the scrabbling paws against the door. Back downstairs. No bleeding on the ankle, as the dog's teeth appeared to have gone straight into the bone marrow instead.

He finished his whiskey. Poured another one and drank half of that.

The door opened, and in came his bride-to-be. "Darling," he said. "Where've you been?"

"We were shopping for a wedding dress."

Bloody hell. "Do we really need to go all out?" he asked, turning to survey her. She looked…good. Irritatingly so.

"We should talk about that." She was blushing. "It

was pointed out to me that my family expects something a little bigger than just you and me and a justice of the peace."

"Are you becoming a bridezilla, Honor?"

"No. I'm just saying that I have a family to consider. And also, maybe it'd be more convincing if we had a real wedding. With a dress and flowers and all that. And by the way, the shopping wasn't for me. It was for Mrs. Johnson." She paused. "But I made an appointment for myself." Her face grew even redder.

"Shall we see if Pippa Middleton is free to be your bridesmaid, in case your sisters aren't enough?"

"Why are you in a mood?"

"Your dog bit me. Twice."

"Poor baby."

"Thanks."

"I meant her. Where is she, by the way?"

"I ate her." She waited. "She's in your room."

"What? I told you she has to have run of the house. She'll pee if she's locked up."

"She gets more appealing every minute, doesn't she?"

Honor went upstairs and returned with Ratty, who was pretending to be sweet and demure, her head tucked under Honor's chin. "She's a rescue, Tom. You can't shut her away. It makes her anxious."

"I just told you, she kept biting me."

"She weighs five pounds."

"And her teeth are like needles."

"Man-up."

He raised an eyebrow. She raised one, as well.

The phone rang. Tom took another sip of his drink and stared at his bride-to-be. She looked good. Better than good. Flushed and pretty and a little irritable, too, her eyes flashing. He felt the start of a smile, and the irritating dog growled.

The phone rang again, and Honor sighed and answered it. "Hello? Excuse me?" Her expression changed. "Oh! Hi, Mr. Barlow! How are you? It's Honor."

"Give it to me," Tom said, holding his hand out. "I'll take it."

She didn't obey, the cheeky thing. "Honor Holland? Your son's fiancée?" she said. "Oh, he didn't?" She leveled a glare at him. "Shoot, I'm sorry. I thought you knew."

"Great," Tom said. His father would be over the bloody moon about this. Rather a pathetic romantic, Dad was.

"No, it was pretty sudden…. Oh, sure. He's so, so wonderful."

"Give me the phone," Tom ordered again. Again, she didn't listen. Was that still a part of wedding vows? Love, honor and obey?

"What made me fall in love with him?" She rolled her eyes. "Gosh, that's really hard to say."

"Just tell him the truth," Tom said, taking a step closer. "I'm great in the sack. Give me the phone, Honor."

"It was probably his love of animals," she said.

"All right, that's enough," he said, pinning her against the counter and prying the phone from her hand. God, she smelled good. The dog snarled and bit his sleeve, but Tom stayed put, rather enjoying having Honor trapped against him. "Hello, Dad."

"Son! You sly devil!" Hugh Barlow's voice was filled with joy. "When did this all happen?"

"Dad, I wanted to be the one to tell you, but Honor's so delighted, she can't keep the news to herself," Tom said. "She's crazy about me."

"Oh, indeed," Honor muttered.

"Of course she is, my boy," Hugh said. "What's she like?"

"She's lovely," Tom said, staring at his intended. "Bossy. Very affectionate. Always with the kissing and the grabbing and the like."

She gave him the finger. He smiled in return, and a flush colored her face.

"Wonderful," Dad said. "When's the happy day, then? I want to come see my boy get married."

Tom sobered and took a step away, releasing Honor. "Not sure yet, Dad, but we were thinking a quick ceremony, just us two."

"A big wedding," she said loudly. "Very soon, Mr. B."

"Just the two of us," Tom repeated. "But then we can fly you over and have a lovely long visit." He shifted the phone away. "You'll make my dad some blood pudding, won't you, darling? It's his favorite."

"Whatever you kids want!" Dad said. "This is wonderful news, Tommy. Just great."

Guilt rose up hard in Tom's stomach. "Thanks."

"I hope it'll work out better this time for you."

"Me, too."

"Can I talk to her again?" Dad asked.

"Sure. Honor, darling, Dad's keen to get to know you. Dad, talk to you later, all right?" He passed the phone to Honor.

"Hi again, Mr. Barlow," she said. "Oh, okay. Hugh."

Tom finished his drink, watching Honor as she smiled into the phone.

This fraud they were committing…it wasn't just on the government. It was on all these people, the Hollands and all Honor's friends, and Charlie and the Kelloggs, and now Dad, too.

And lying to his father had never been a strong suit.

Honor hung up. "Nice guy," she said.

"Yes."

"Do you have any other family?"

"No."

She put the dog down, and Ratty dashed off to investigate a noise from the street. "What happened to your mother?"

"She left when I was little."

Honor nodded, looking at the floor. "Sorry."

"It's not your fault, is it?" He certainly made it sound that way. "Thanks, I mean. Listen, I've got to correct papers. Are you hungry?"

"No. My sisters and Mrs. J. and I went out after shopping."

"Right. Listen, buy whatever dress you want. I don't care." Ah, bollocks. That didn't come out the way he meant. Hurt flashed across her eyes.

But really, what did she expect? This was not a typical situation. He really *didn't* care what she wore, or if they got married with her family there and whatnot.

What he did care about was if she started to get caught up in all the wedding and happily-ever-after crap that women so loved. Had the world learned nothing from Charles and Diana? The only reason Tom had agreed to go along with this was because he couldn't figure out another way to stay in the States, and because she was coming into this with her eyes wide open. She was a sensible person who didn't seem prone to…whatever women were prone to.

But he didn't like where this seemed to be heading. First that kiss in the grandparents' cellar earlier today. Now he was staring at her and wondering what she'd do if he kissed her again. And then banged her silly on the table there.

"I'm off, then," he said. "I left something at school yesterday."

And that, friends, was a lie. But it did get him out of the house.

WHEN TOM CAME home, it was much later than he'd planned. But he'd taken the shuttle bus to school, because only bungholes drove after drinking whiskey, and Tom was a bunghole in some ways, but not that way. Drunk driving, driving while texting, walking while texting…it would not be the way he died. So he'd done some work on a demonstration he'd be showing the students about wind sheer and torque and made good use of his time at school. Might as well.

Then, Droog had shown up, and he and Tom ended up getting a beer, and Tom told his boss the news that he was getting married.

"Ah!" Droog cried. "You and Mees Holland have dee cleek! Yes! I thought I smelled something in dee air that fateful night. Congratulations, my friend!"

"Right," Tom answered. "Thanks, mate. Um, we'd love for you to come to the wedding, of course."

Droog had offered a ride home, but Tom wasn't sure the man's car would make it and opted for the bus instead. He had, however, forgotten that the bus stopped running at ten, and found himself walking home. Five miles. Not too far. Just very bloody dark.

The house was quiet, as one would expect at 1:00 a.m. He put his coat away and rubbed his eyes. Took a seat and turned on the television set. The remote control was rough from Ratty's teeth marks. He'd have to remember to buy her some proper toys.

Not much was on. Infomercials. Basketball, not his sport. Ah. A special on the homes of good Queen Bess. Might as well see how his tax dollars were being spent.

"Hi."

He looked up. "Sorry. I didn't mean to wake you."

"That's okay."

She sat down beside him, her hair rumpled. She wore flannel pajamas with polka dots on them and bunny slippers.

Rather adorable.

Without thinking, he put his arm around her. Said nothing, just looked at the telly. Tiny Evil jumped up with only a slight snarl and settled onto her owner's lap, and Honor stroked the dog's rough fur, earning a little moan of pleasure from the beast. Tom almost felt jealous.

Actually, he *was* jealous.

"Are these your relatives?" Honor asked.

"Yes," he said, snapping out of it. "That's Auntie Liz right there. Cousin Chuck. The boys. Lovely lads."

They watched a few minutes in silence. "How was the rest of your day?" she asked.

"It was all right. Did Mrs. Johnson find a dress?"

"She did. It's beautiful."

"Good."

Honor looked back at the screen. "So you like documentaries?" she asked, nodding at the screen, and he was oddly grateful for the neutral question.

"Yes," he said. "Especially about how different things were made. Bridges, dams, subway systems. That sort of thing. What about you?"

"Medical shows. *The 149-Pound Tumor,* stuff like that."

"Ah. You romantic, you." He glanced at her, saw her smile. "Honor," he said, "I'm sorry we squabbled before. Just because ours isn't a typical arrangement doesn't mean I don't want it to work."

Her eyes softened. "Me, too."

"I just don't want to...disappoint you."

"You won't. And you're not."

"I'm not so sure about that." She didn't look away until Tom settled back against the couch. *Don't kiss her,* his brain warned. *That'd be dumb.*

Right, except they'd be getting married soon. Shagging again, as soon as she gave the green light. Which could be in about three minutes, he suspected, if he put the moves on her.

"Tom?"

Ah-ha. So she was feeling it, as well.

"Yes, love?"

"Do you think you might be drinking too much?"

All right, so she wasn't feeling it.

"Perhaps," he answered. "I am British, though."

"I just thought I'd mention it."

"Already nagging, darling?"

She didn't take the bait. "A little concerned."

He didn't speak for a minute, then sighed. "I suppose you're right. It doesn't help anything, does it?"

"No."

"One drink a day, then. Two if I deserve it, and no more than that. Scout's honor, as you Yanks like to say."

This time, she was the one to pull back and look at him. "You're a good guy."

Something tightened in his chest. "Glad you think so," he answered.

"Your dad thinks the world of you."

He smiled. "It's mutual."

"He's a butcher?"

"Yes. Don't get him started on great cuts of beef." He paused. "My mum left when I was six."

"I'm sorry."

"She wasn't a great mother. Wasn't bad, either, just not born to it." He paused. "She visited a bit for the first year or two, but that tapered off. My dad's been single ever since."

"Mine, too. Ever since my mom died. That's why we're all pretty thrilled about him and Mrs. Johnson."

"And your mum died in a car accident?"

"Mmm-hmm."

"Shit." The urge to kiss her was back. "I'm sorry."

"It was hard. We were really close." She paused. "I haven't had too many close relationships. You might've guessed that."

He tucked some hair behind her ear. "I wonder what she'd think of all this," he said softly.

Honor smiled. "Me, too." She glanced down at her dog, and her cheeks pinkened. "I guess we should get a marriage license."

At which point the clock would start ticking till their wedding…and his green card. "Yes."

"I'll get one Monday, then."

He took her hand and turned it palm up, stroking the

silky skin of her wrist. "Thank you," he murmured. He brought her hand to his mouth and kissed it.

Her eyes were soft and wide, her lips slightly parted. His eyes dropped to her mouth.

And then, just as he was about to kiss her, she stood up abruptly and picked up the sleeping dog, cuddling it against her chest. "I should—I should go to bed. Um… Good night."

With that, she padded upstairs, leaving him alone in the cold living room.

Which was not what he expected at all.

CHAPTER SIXTEEN

IT WAS ONE of those days. Not in the good sense.

First, Honor had woken up to the sounds of Tom in the shower. He was whistling slightly, and not very well, and the image of him, warm and wet and soapy, had the eggs tossing aside their dairy-free meals and stampeding for the door.

They were getting *married*. They were going ahead with it. She'd come home from work yesterday and stopped at city hall for a license, and once that was filed, they had sixty days. That meant that by June 10, she would be someone's wife.

Tom's wife.

The thought inspired equal parts of terror and disbelief, with a side of lust and a chaser of panic. They were going through with it. Committing fraud against the government of the United States of America.

And then again, there was that lust.

Last night, she sat at the kitchen table after dinner and filled out the paperwork. Learned a few things about Thomas Jude Barlow. First, he was younger than she was by three years. Just in case *the years are precious* wasn't enough. Secondly, he'd been born in the back of a cab.

Thirdly, well…she couldn't remember what thirdly

was, not with Tom in the shower just fourteen or so feet away.

He'd been about to kiss her the other night on the couch. And she stopped it. Why, she had no flippin' idea. Cowardice, probably. Because if he kissed her, she'd sleep with him, and if she slept with him, she was pretty sure she'd fall in love with him, and she was already a bit swoony, and he wasn't. Not at all.

Men didn't feel the same way women did about sex. They'd take it when offered, same as they wouldn't pass up a cookie warm from the oven. No, it was the women who counted calories and fell in love. Which was really not fair. Okay, Pru didn't count calories, not the way she and Carl were going through hot fudge these days. And Faith didn't, either, always looking like a porn star when she ate dessert, which was often.

The water turned off, and Honor resisted the urge to run into the hallway and get a glimpse of Tom in a towel. She got dressed instead, feeling clumsy and irritable with lust. Spent four minutes with Tom before he left for the Barbarian Horde at his college. She felt almost jealous. Maybe she'd take a mechanical engineering class, too.

Her work morning was filled with eight scheduled phone calls, a marketing meeting with Ned, Jack and Jessica to talk about wine club sales and writing an article for a tourism magazine. Then, she somehow acquired Goggy, who showed up at the office after lunch, when Honor was finishing up a conference call with the sales staff. "Who's this?" she asked, staring suspiciously at Jessica. "Honor, who is this?"

"It's Jessica, Goggy. Guys, my grandmother just came in," Honor said.

"Hi, Mrs. Holland!" came a chorus of voices from the phone.

"How do you *do* that?" Goggy asked, ever amazed that Edison's little invention had such diversity. "It sounds like there's a dozen people in there!"

"It's a conference call," Honor said.

"Amazing!" The old lady clucked in awe.

"Okay, call me with any questions. Thank you!"

There was a chorus of goodbyes, and Honor hung up. "This is Jessica Dunn, Goggy. You met her before." Was it her imagination, or was Goggy forgetting more these days?

"Have I?" Goggy pursed her lips. "I don't remember. You're very pretty, dear."

"Thank you, Mrs. Holland. Would you like some coffee?"

"Oh, no, thank you. It goes right through me. I used to be able to drink it all day long, but not anymore."

"Jess, will you email those talking points to the gang?" Honor asked. Now that she was used to it, it was pretty nice having an assistant.

"You bet. Nice to see you again, Mrs. Holland."

"I'm sorry if I interrupted, Honor. I didn't realize you were *on the phone,*" Goggy whispered. Better late than never.

"I've got a bunch of errands to do, Goggy. What can I do for you?"

Goggy sighed. "You young people. Always running around."

"I have to go to Rushing Creek. Want to come along?" It was all part of the sainthood campaign. Honor was fairly sure she was a shoe-in, but she did love her grandmother.

"Rushing Creek? That place? I'd rather be murdered in my own bed than live there," Goggy said happily. "But I'll come, sure! Thank you, sweetheart!"

It took Goggy fifteen minutes at the Old House to find a coat ("in case it rains"), apply more Blushing Peach lipstick ("you never know who you'll run into"), go to the bathroom ("I'd probably catch a disease at that horrible mental hospital") and trundle into the car.

Sainthood seemed assured.

"How's Tom?" Goggy asked on the car ride over.

"He's great."

"How did you meet again?"

Honor shot her grandmother a look. No, it seemed Goggy was completely serious. "Um, you fixed us up, remember?"

"I know that, dear," the old lady said. "I meant where did you meet him. I misspoke. Don't get that look on your face. I don't have Alzheimer's."

"We met at O'Rourke's."

"Right, right. I'm glad for you, honey. It's nice that one of us found happiness through an arranged marriage."

"It's not really an arranged marriage, Goggy," Honor said, hoping Goggy wouldn't inadvertently blow it. "You fixed us up. You have good instincts with people." Flattery would distract her, hopefully.

"That's true," Goggy said. "I always thought so, but it's nice to hear. How does this car work again? There's no key."

As they pulled into the Rushing Creek complex, Honor wished for the thousandth time that her grandparents would consider living here. So much safer, cleaner, brighter… "You sure you and Pops want to stay in the Old House forever?" Honor asked.

"It's our home, honey."

"I know, but didn't you ever want to live somewhere else?"

Goggy shrugged. "I've thought about it. I've never lived anywhere but on the Hill."

"Neither did I, until a few weeks ago. Don't you think it'd be fun to live somewhere different?"

"Oh, who knows? Maybe." Progress! That was a more positive answer than Goggy had ever given before. "What are we doing here, anyway?"

"I have to drop off some tickets for the Black and White Ball. You and Pops are coming, aren't you?"

"Of course, of course. Except I'll have to dress up." Goggy sighed heavily. "And probably dance with that old fool. He has two left feet, that one."

"I don't know. You guys looked pretty cute at Faith and Levi's wedding."

Goggy gave a little smile. "Oh, I don't know about that."

Honor took out her phone and sent a quick text to Margaret, the director of Rushing Creek. Any chance we could see a unit? I'm doing a soft sell on my grandmother.

Margaret came through.

"Plenty of closet space," she said, showing Goggy the master bedroom of a very pretty apartment, "and a spare room for visitors."

"No one visits me anymore," Goggy said with a significant look at Honor.

"Don't look at me. Look, Goggy, this kitchen has so much counter space! Much more than the Old House."

"Hmmph. What do I need with counter space?"

"Imagine baking Christmas cookies in here," Honor said. "So much easier than doing it all on the kitchen table."

"Have you ever had a bad cookie in my house?" Goggy asked.

Honor put her arm around her. "Never. You make the best everything, and don't tell Mrs. Johnson I said that, or she'll kill me. I'm just saying it'd be nice for you to have a place like this, new and clean and efficient. You deserve it."

"Well," Goggy said, mollified. "That's a nice thought, sweetheart."

Progress indeed.

After Rushing Creek, they drove into town to talk to Laura Boothby about the flowers for the ball. "I was thinking ivory centerpieces with black velvet ribbons tied around the vases," she said, turning the pages of Laura's photo album.

"Beautiful," Laura said. "Great idea."

"But it's the Black and White Ball," Goggy protested. "Not the Black and Ivory Ball."

"Right, but this will just be a little contrast. Remember when Lyons Den hosted two years ago? And they had pink flowers?"

"I thought that was tacky," Goggy said.

"Oh, no, it was wonderful," Laura said. "Jeremy has the best taste. And he's such a good doctor!"

"You don't have to tell me," Goggy said. "He's practically my grandson. And those hands? So gentle."

Which reminded Honor...she and Tom would need a blood test. Not that one was required, but she wanted one, anyway. Just to make sure there were no red flags for baby-making.

"Honor, while you're here, would you like to look at wedding bouquets?" Laura asked craftily.

"Um, no, that's okay. Not yet, anyway."

"Oh, come on. Just a little peek."

And somehow, an hour passed. First, visions of a wedding dress. Now, poring over pictures of roses and lilies and hydrangeas. Like a regular bride...which, of course, she wasn't.

But she was falling for him. She knew that. How could she not? First, the smile. The accent. The tattoos, which she'd never really liked before and now heartily adored.

And then there was his unflagging love of Charlie, who didn't give Tom so much as a crumb of affection, and for whom Tom was rewriting his life.

And then there was the kissing. That one night of moon-and-back sex, when Honor had acted like a stranger and felt right at home. One amazing night that seemed to be playing in a constant loop in her head, making her break off in midsentence weeks after the fact.

Hot diggety.

It was probably being around all this love... Dad and Mrs. Johnson snuggled up on the couch, arguing amiably about who should win *Top Chef.* Faith and Levi, who seemed like two magnets when they were in the same room, always near each other, always touching somehow. Even Pru and Carl, with their goofy grins and rock-solid knowledge that the other was simply there, still dependably in love.

She and Tom were a business arrangement. They

were both getting something out of this. He would have his green card, and she was saving face.

Yes. People were now looking at Honor with new respect these days. Tom Barlow, the hottie Brit with the killer smile, had chosen quiet, reliable, boring Honor Holland.

What Honor knew, and shouldn't forget, was that Tom Barlow was only with her because of his unofficial stepson.

Otherwise, there was no way she'd get a guy like that.

"Honor?"

She looked up abruptly. "Sorry, Goggy. What were you saying?"

"I think these are nice. I've always loved carnations."

"Very pretty. I'll think about it. Thanks, ladies. Goggy, we should go. I have to hit up some businesses for raffle donations."

They went to O'Rourke's, where Colleen once again complimented her on "shagging and bagging Tom"; to Lorelei's Sunrise Bakery, where the eternally cheerful baker offered to make their wedding cake for free in thanks for all the business Blue Heron had given them; to Mel's Candy Shoppe, where Mr. Stoakes told her she could eat as much candy as she wanted, now that she was off the market. To Hart's Jewelers, where Tom had apparently bought her ring, as she was welcomed in and fussed over like a soldier returning from war.

"You really like it, then?" Mrs. Hart asked.

"I love it," Honor said honestly. Every time she looked at the ring (which was often), she seemed to notice something new.

"He's adorable. Well done, dear," Mrs. Hart said, beaming.

"I fixed them up," Goggy announced. "I knew it was Meant to Be. They're perfect for each other. A perfect match. A grandmother knows about these things. We have a certain sense about us—"

"Okay, Goggy, we should go," Honor said. "Thanks for the donation, Mrs. Hart."

"See you soon!" the jeweler said. "For your wedding bands!"

"Right! Yes. Thanks again."

"I'm hungry," Goggy said. "Let's eat. Is it too early for dinner?" She glanced at the man's watch she wore. "Nope. Four-thirty. That works for me."

"One more stop, okay? The gym said they'd offer a six-month membership."

"Why do people go to gyms?" Goggy asked.

"I have no idea," Honor answered. "But people do."

And Tom's car was in the parking lot. Today was the self-defense class. Coincidence? Probably not.

They went into Cabrera's Gym, Goggy clutching her purse in both hands like she was about to encounter a gang of thugs in desperate need of coupons. It was dark (the less you saw, Honor supposed, the less grossed out you'd be). Music boomed over the loudspeakers. "Can I help you?" said a young man behind the desk.

"Is Carlos here?" Honor said.

"He's over there with the kids." The man pointed, and Honor peered ahead.

There they were—Charlie, Helena, Abby and quite a few other kids. The class seemed to have mushroomed.

Tom was there, as well. He wore black boxing shorts and a faded blue T-shirt that said Gulfstream. The bottom of the Union Jack was just visible, and his hair was sweaty. She could see the chain of his Saint Christopher's medal where it disappeared into his shirt, and the memory of that medal, hot against her own chest, made Down Under clench in a strong, hot surge.

She swallowed.

"Hallo, darling! And hallo, Honor." He came over to Goggy, giving her a kiss on the cheek. "Kids, for those of you who don't know, this is Honor Holland, my fiancée, and her lovely grandmother, Mrs. Holland."

"Call me Elizabeth," Goggy murmured, batting her sparse eyelashes.

"Hi, Auntie," Abby said.

"Hi, Honor," Charlie echoed.

Well, well. Charlie spoke to her. Voluntarily and everything.

"Honor, I didn't know you were engaged to Tom here! Congratulations!" Carlos said.

"Mmm-hmm," Honor said faintly, dragging her eyes off Tom's mouth.

"You want a gift certificate for the thing? The ball, right? I'll go take care of that. Back in a flash." Carlos smiled and trotted off to his office.

"Darling, will you help me here?" Tom asked, putting his arm around her shoulders. The smell of soap and sweat made her knees nearly buckle. Would it be wrong to lick his neck in front of the kids? Yes. Probably. Maybe not.

"Right, kids, so here's my lovely Honor, and as I was saying, boxing's a sport for everyone, isn't it, love?"

"It so is," she said.

"Honor herself adores it, though you can't tell from the look of her. But we've seen *Rocky* at least twenty times, isn't that right, love?" He grinned at her, and her knees did buckle then, but she managed to stay upright.

"Oh, yes. At least. And *Cinderella Man.*"

"Right." He gave her a squeeze. "Don't forget *Warrior.*"

"And *Raging Bull.*"

He leaned in close, his mouth almost touching her ear. "You have no idea how randy you're making me by knowing all these films," he whispered, and her breath was suddenly ragged. He turned back to the kids. "And Honor here weighs about how much, love?"

"Nice try," she said.

"Less than I do, at any rate. But if she knew where to hit—"

"The groin," she said. "Go right for the nuts, girls. Sorry, boys, but it's true." Goggy nodded in agreement.

Tom turned and looked at her. "Darling! I didn't know you had a violent streak. Yes, the groin is an excellent target. But say you can't do that. You still have a lot of options. If Honor knew where and how to hit, she could level me. Couldn't you, sweetheart?"

"Yes. I could." Gray eyes. So...unfair, somehow, the gentle color of a rainy sky on a winter morning, and wasn't someone feeling romantic? That mouth of his. She could do a lot with that mouth. Or rather, he could.

What are we waiting for? the eggs asked.

How about "not an audience of children"? Honor mentally answered.

Don't get testy with us, the eggs said. *We're just trying to get a little action here.*

"Into the ring with you, then," Tom said.

What? Her stomach lurched. "Oh, I don't think so. I'm not dressed for it." Indeed. A pencil skirt and blouse, the sturdy-heeled pumps that Faith had deemed "not too nunnish" on their last lunch date.

"She's not, is she?" Tom left her side, unbalancing her a bit, as she seemed to have leaned up against him. It was cold without him there. He bounded up the two stairs to the ring. "But that's the point. You have to know you could defend yourself whenever you needed to, no matter what you were wearing. Come on, Honor, let's show the kiddies how it's done."

Honor glanced at the teenagers, who waited expectantly. "Go for it," Abby said.

"Yes, honey, do it," Goggy said. "I want to see this."

Hesitantly, she climbed the steps. "How do I get in here?" she murmured to Tom, who held the ropes for her. It looked very complicated.

"Just scoot in."

"Right." She started with one foot, then the other, holding her skirt down. Tripped (of course), only to have Tom grab her arm.

"There you are." A slight smile flashed across his face.

"Hey, Honor! Look at you!"

Oh, fungus. A damning flush started prickling across her chest. "Hi, Brogan."

Her former...person...walked over, gym bag slung over his shoulder, the easy grace of a natural athlete evident. "And Tom, isn't it?" Brogan asked. "The lucky guy! We've met before. At Hugo's?"

"Of course," Tom said, reaching over the ropes to shake his hand. "Nice to see you again. Honor and I are just demonstrating a move for the kids."

"Fantastic. I'm just in time." Brogan set his bag down and folded his arms, winking at her.

After the little showdown in the cask room with Dana, Brogan had sent Honor an email, full of hearty congratulations and a few possible dates for dinner. Unsurprisingly, Honor hadn't had any free time. Not that she'd looked. But now, seeing Brogan's smiling face, she couldn't help missing him. As a friend.

Yes. For the first time, his presence didn't make her quiver. She smiled back at him, relieved.

"You ready, darling?" Tom asked.

She jerked her eyes to his face. His face was grim. "Ready for what?"

"To demonstrate a punch."

"Not really," she said. "Can someone else do this?"

"You'll be brilliant. Kiddies, an uppercut starts here," he said, holding his hands next to his temple. "You don't scoop up so much as bend your knees and turn, like so—" he swiveled, bringing his shoulder down "—and hit with your whole body." He demonstrated, touching her chin with his fist, his eyes on the assembled kids. "Bend your knees, turn so that it's not just your arm doing the work, it's the entire body, and extend that fist with the whole of you right behind it." He went through the move again, slow motion. "Your turn, Honor."

What looked like a fluid, easy motion was a lot harder when Honor tried it. It was hard not to feel self-conscious and awkward while everyone, including two-thirds of all the men she'd slept with, were watching. If there was anything less sexy than trying to channel Muhammad Ali while wearing a skirt and not-too-nunnish shoes, she didn't know what it was.

"That's it," Tom said. "Practice a bit, Honor. Kids, you, as well." He left her in the corner, bobbing like an idiot, and walked over to the other side of the ring to watch the kids' form. "Hands up, don't forget, you don't want to leave yourself open. Mrs. Holland—Elizabeth, rather—don't just stand there! Get moving, darling." Goggy giggled and cooed and put her hands up and began punching the air quite vigorously. Good Lord.

"This punch is brilliant if you're in close quarters," Tom continued, "because it's tight and brutal." He demonstrated the move again. "So if someone's got you against a wall or whatnot, this is your punch, and it's a knockout if you do it right. That's it, Molly, you've got it. Good job, Charlie. A little more pivot, Abby. Brilliant."

He had a way with kids, that was certain. And they seemed to like him, too. Even Charlie looked a little more cheerful than usual, which wasn't saying a lot, but still. The boy was supposed to come for dinner tonight. Hopefully, he'd speak.

"Looking good, On," Brogan said, grinning up at her. She rolled her eyes. "No, really. You remind me of Iron Mike."

"Thank you. He and I are very close."

"He's a good guy. I photographed him a few years ago out in Vegas." He paused. "How've you been?"

"Good. Busy. You know. Just…wedding stuff."

"I know. Dana's gone crazy with it. And, uh, we're kind of in a rush now." His expression was sheepish. "Want to get it done before the baby."

"Right." Tom was showing Helena how to turn her arm, and Helena was eating it up.

"Anyway. It's good to see you."

"You, too. Um, do you box?" she asked, rather than have to stand here alone, punching air.

"A little. Here and there. You know me."

Yes. He loved all things athletic, from rock climbing to rowing to football to sailing. Rather tiring to a person whose idea of outdoor activity was taking her book outside to read.

"All right, Honor?" Tom said, walking to her corner.

"For what?" she asked.

"To hit me, darling." The kids laughed. Brogan, too.

"Oh, uh, no. No, thanks. I don't want to hit you."

He towed back to the center of the ring. "Sorry," he said in a low voice. "Didn't mean to interrupt your chat with Brandon."

"Brogan."

"Right." His eyes were flat and neutral.

"We weren't chatting," she said. "We were just… It was nothing."

"Of course it was nothing. Since you're so in love with me and all." He turned to the kids. "Pay attention, kids. Honor, hands up."

"I'm not going to hit you." Just the idea made her feel a little sick. "No, thanks."

"Sure you are. I can take it."

"No, really. I'm not comfortable doing this."

"Exactly! Kids, did you hear that? She's not comfortable fighting. And she does have a point. Most girls don't grow up scrabbling in the schoolyard, do they? Maybe they've been conditioned not to hurt anyone, and yeah, it can go against the grain, which is all the more reason to learn this."

Honor didn't feel so good. Tom was right; her mother used to have a fit if they so much as wrestled. The one time fighting might've come in handy—aside from the catfight, of course—she'd been frozen in shock.

Crap. Not the time to remember that. Her heart

seemed to thud in fits and starts, and there was a roaring in her ears.

"Come on now," Tom said. "It's a good lesson for them." He raised the eyebrow with the scar running through it. "And you can look adorable in front of your boyfriend."

"He's not—"

"Ready, then?" He put his hands on her shoulders and turned toward the kids. "So say I've grabbed the *incredibly* beautiful Honor here." He wrapped her in an abrupt hug, pinning her arms at her sides, and adrenaline spurted into her limbs. Her breath left in a gasp. Was it hot in here? "And then I shove her against a wall. No way out." He pushed her gently against the corner post and leaned in. "Give me your money, or are you alone, sweetheart—you all get the idea, right?"

Why was she so nervous? Her legs were shaking, and gray spots were floating in front of her.

"She can't get away, she's totally helpless, she's just a soft little female, or so I think. Okay, love, on the count of three, a right uppercut, bend your knees, turn that gorgeous—"

Her left fist appeared out of nowhere, slamming into his eye. Tom staggered back, one hand covering his eye. The kids gasped, hands flying over their mouths. Honor's hand—her nonviolent hand—was over her mouth as well.

"Oh, my God, she hit him!" said one girl. "That's so mean!"

"Are you all right?" he asked her. She tried to answer and couldn't find her voice, nodded instead.

He was *bleeding*. Blood was pouring down his face. It seemed her engagement ring had cut him under the eye. Goggy clucked in concern and handed Tom a tissue, which instantly bloomed with red.

"I guess I was wrong about the soft helpless bit, yeah?" His voice was tight.

Her knuckles started to throb. Carlos Mendez was suddenly in the ring with a towel, and blood was dripping onto the mat. Brogan, too, came through the ropes. "You okay?" he asked, putting a warm hand on her shoulder.

"I'm so sorry," she said to Tom, her voice thin and shaky.

"I'm fine, gang," he said to the kids. "Honor here proved a good point. You're all quite strong enough if the situation demands it, yeah? Her engagement ring caught me. Nothing to worry about. Shows the importance of blocking, doesn't it."

"You're gonna need stiches, bro," Carlos said.

Tom glanced at her, his eye already beginning to swell. "Feel like a run to hospital?" he asked. "Kids, class is over for today. Good job all around. Abby, would you mind driving Charlie home?"

"Look, I told you I didn't want to do it," Honor snapped.

"And clearly you were sincere," Tom snapped back, lifting the gauze the nurse had given him when they came in. "Quite the hotshot, aren't you?"

"Yes! I am! The thing is, you were right," she said, looking away. "Most women don't fight for fun. I didn't want to do it, I was nervous. I told you not to make me do it, but you wouldn't listen."

"Blame the victim, that's it. Does 'on the count of three' mean nothing to you, darling, or was there another reason for that punch?"

"I was nervous! I'm sorry, okay? I'm really, really sorry."

He gave her a one-eyed glare, the flesh around his eye puffy and red. "You're welcome to make it up to me, darling. I can think of about ten things you can do for starters."

"Don't be a jerk," she said, even as a hot, tight nervousness grabbed her insides.

"Hello, hello!" The door to the exam room opened, and a tiny Asian girl came in, roughly five foot nothing, ninety pounds and perhaps twelve years old. Honor instantly felt like an Amazon. Not in the good way. "I'm Dr. Chu, and what have we here?"

"A bit of a cut," Tom said. "My girlfriend has a mean streak."

"There was a slight accident," Honor ground out.

"Dude, that's awful!" the doctor said. "Bummer."

"How old are you?" Honor asked.

"Um, twenty-three?" she answered. "I started college when I was, like, sixteen. A complete trip. But I'm totally a real doctor. Well, sort of. I'm an intern? And I've never done stitches before, so I'm totally psyched."

"Great," said Tom. "I have absolute faith in you."

"Cool!" she said, turning on the water. "Washing hands, check. Pleasant demeanor, supercheck. So what happened, Mr., um, Barlow?"

"My fiancée punched me," he said.

"OMG! That's horrible!" She turned to Honor. "Are you his mother?"

"No!" *Kill us now,* said the eggs. "I'm the fiancée."

Tom grinned. If she'd felt sorry about hitting him, it was fading. Fast.

"Really? Mr. Barlow, do you mind if she stays?"

Tom pondered the question. Honor sighed. "You'll protect me, won't you?" he asked, smiling at the tiny doctor.

"Totally! Yeah! Plus, I can always call Security?"

"Then I feel safe." He cocked his good eyebrow at Honor as Dr. Chu pulled on exam gloves. "So sixteen when you started college, eh? I bet you're really smart."

"Not to toot my own horn? But I did graduate first in my class at Stanford."

"Congratulations," he said. "That's incredible."

"Thanks! So let me get to work here. Um, she punched you? Is that all? Like, how did you get this cut?"

"From her engagement ring."

"Wow. *So* ironic," Dr. Chu said.

"You're telling me."

The two shared an adorable smile.

"He was teaching a boxing class and *asked* me to hit him," Honor said. Dr. Chu didn't so much as flicker a glance in her direction, too busy lifting the gauze off Tom's eye.

"Awesome! That's some cut! Plus I think you're gonna have a black eye! Kind of sexy, hopefully?"

"Whatever you say, Doctor." His crooked tooth flashed, making him look like an incredibly appealing, adult version of the Artful Dodger from *Oliver Twist.*

"Awesome! So, like, let me get stitching, okay?"

It was clearly the best day of Dr. Chu's brief life. "Suture kit, check. Sterilizing the field, check! This is fun."

"I love a woman who loves her job," Tom said.

"I *totally* love it! And what do you do, Mr. Barlow?"

"I'm a professor of mechanical engineering."

"That rocks! Okay, this is gonna sting. So sorry about that. Sympathetic attitude, check."

"Very sympathetic indeed."

"Supercheck, then!" Dr. Chu giggled, then raised a needle of painkiller to inject under the cut.

Guilt wasn't an emotion Honor was used to.

Honor looked at her hand. It was slightly swollen, which she supposed she deserved. It was also the first time she'd ever hit someone in her entire life.

Well, no. She'd smacked Dana, hadn't she? She was building quite the reputation.

"Do you have a regular doctor?" Dr. Chu asked. "He or she can take out your stitches in about a week. Or I can totally do it! You just have to come back here. I can give you my number if you want to see when I'm on duty."

Tom glanced at Honor. "You can go to Jeremy," she said. "He's a family friend."

"I'll do that, then," Tom said.

"Sure! Just look at these gorgeous sutures, right? Listen, it was so nice meeting you!" Dr. Chu said. "I'm just gonna ask my attending one thing, okay? I doubt we need X-rays, but I want to be supersure."

"Thank you," Tom said.

"You're totally welcome! Back in a flash!" She practically skipped out.

Honor forced herself to look at her fiancé. "Not bad," she said. Dr. Chu's stitches were small and neat, for all that she talked like a love-struck tween.

"Good. Such a pretty face, I'd hate for it to be ruined."

"I'm really sorry. As I believe I've said fifteen or twenty times."

"Don't worry about it. Sorry I put you in that situation." He rubbed the back of his neck and looked at the floor.

Out in the hall, they could hear the noise of the hospital, the clatter of gurneys and the hiss of the automatic doors. A baby was crying.

"Why were you so scared?" Tom asked unexpectedly.

She shrugged, her heart rate surging once more. "I don't know." She started to speak, then stopped. "I was mugged once. He, um, shoved me in a doorway. Just like your little scenario."

His eyebrows jolted upward. "Are you bloody joking?" he said. "That would've been *really* good to know."

"You didn't ask. And I didn't think to mention it."

"Why the hell not? I wouldn't have pretended to be *assaulting* you if I'd known that, Honor! Why didn't you say something?"

"I don't know! Don't yell at me. It was a long time ago, in Philly when I was in grad school. He grabbed me, asked for my purse, I gave it to him, he left. He had a gun, so I just did what he said. It wasn't a big deal."

"You were held up at *gunpoint,* but it wasn't a big deal?"

"You can stop yelling anytime, you know. I thought you Brits were all about keep calm and carry on. And don't tell anyone I was mugged," she added in a softer voice. "No one else knows."

He was staring at her, mouth slightly open. "Yes, God forbid you should let anyone know you're human."

"And what does that mean?" she snapped. "Are you an expert on me all of a sudden?"

There was a knock on the exam room door, and in came Levi, dressed in his police uniform. He jerked to a stop at the sight of them. "Oh. Hey, you two."

"Hi, Levi," Honor said, glad for a friendly face. "What are you doing here?"

He drew in a breath. "Uh, I have to ask Tom some questions."

"What for?" Tom asked.

"The doctor suspects domestic abuse," Levi answered. "And I did just hear yelling."

First a catfight, now this. "Do your thing," she said wearily.

"Mate, it was nothing," Tom said. "She was helping out at the self-defense class and caught me off guard."

"So really, this is kind of your fault," Honor said. "Since the class was your brainchild."

"I'd have to agree," Tom said. "It's certainly not Honor's."

Levi did not look amused. "Let me talk to Tom for a second. I have to follow procedure, even if you're Faith's sister. Especially because you're Faith's sister."

"You bet." She slipped out and stood in the hallway. So now her brother-in-law/supercop was investigating her. She sighed, then force-smiled at an old man with an oxygen mask over his face. He didn't smile back. Poor guy. Honor looked away.

Hospitals had always creeped her out, ever since Mom had died. That had been the worst day, of course. The worst day in her life. She'd been the one to answer the phone; Dad was in the fields, and she was waiting for Mom and Faith to return from Corning. They'd been late, and Honor was jealous, imagining them out to lunch somewhere, or bopping into the cute little shops on Market Street.

"Is your father there, sweetheart?" Chief Griggs had asked, and Honor knew in that second that something horrible had happened. "I need to talk to him."

"Why?" Honor asked.

"I just do, honey."

A white, icy fear flashed over her. Her knees buckled, then straightened. "Are they dead?" she whispered.

"Sit tight, okay? Is your dad home?"

"Yes."

"I'm on my way," the chief had said, and the terrible kindness in his voice had confirmed it. Death stood in the kitchen with her as she put the phone down on the counter next to her chemistry textbook. It followed her to the back door, out into the yard, and yet she was calm as she called to her father.

Faith and Mom, gone. Dead. So this is what people meant when they said they felt numb.

Dad was going to need her. As Chief Griggs pulled into the driveway, she wrapped her arms around her father's waist. Heard the words—Faith was okay, but Constance didn't make it.

Honor felt her dad sag, heard the horrible small sound that he made as the chief said the words. Held his brittle, dry hand all the way to the hospital where one ambulance had taken Faith, and one had taken Mom.

That ambulance would've gone more slowly, Honor thought, standing outside Faith's room as Daddy went in. No lights, no sirens. Somewhere below her, her mother's body was being slipped into a dark, cold cupboard.

Mommy.

The horrible magnitude of the loss threatened to swallow her whole and suck her down. The only one who really got her, who had made her feel so special, was *gone*. It was over. Life would never be the same, never as good, as whole, as happy.

The black grief had to be held off, though. Honor was her mother's daughter: calm, logical, pragmatic. No one else in the family was like them. She would keep her shit together, she would duct-tape her heart so it wouldn't shatter and she'd do what had to be done.

But those happy, perfect days of wholeness…they were done.

Only with Brogan—and only once in a great while, admittedly—did she ever get a little glimpse of that again. Not that she'd been miserable. Just that life hadn't been firing on all cylinders. She'd been waiting since she was sixteen years old to have that piece of her returned, and every once in a while, when she and Brogan were out to dinner together or when he forgot what time zone he was in and called her in the middle of the night had she ever glimpsed a sliver of what she'd been missing.

Which did make her wonder what she was doing with Tom. He was still mostly a stranger…a stranger who flirted with anything that sported breasts and a pulse. Who was occasionally so wonderful that she'd start to hope for that missing piece, only to have him withdraw seconds later.

The door opened, and the man in question appeared, Levi close behind him. "I've decided not to press charges," Tom said. "So long as you're on your best behavior from now on."

"Very funny," she said.

"You guys need anything?" Levi asked.

"We're all set," she said. "Thanks, Levi. Sorry you had to come out here."

"All in a day's work," he said. "See you soon." He started to walk away, then turned and looked at them, a frown creasing his forehead. "Are you guys sure you're okay?"

"We're fine, mate," Tom said, sliding an arm around her shoulders. "Right, darling?"

"Yes! Yeah, absolutely. It's just been a long day."

Levi looked at them another minute, and Honor's stomach cramped. She tipped her head against Tom's shoulder and smiled. "Thanks again. Tell Faith I'll call her later."

He nodded, then lifted a hand and walked away.

Tom took a breath, then released. "All right, then," he murmured, and with that, he went back in the exam room to wait for his release.

CHAPTER SEVENTEEN

PEOPLE HAD WARNED Tom that the weather in this area would be unpredictable, but this was bleeding ridiculous. Four days ago, he'd gone for a run at the college, and it had been sixty-five degrees. Buds on the trees, all that.

Today, it was snowing. And despite four years in this country, Tom still hated driving in the snow. He'd fishtailed on his way into the Village and nearly rear-ended Honor's little Prius, which was parked on the street, rather than in the driveway, for some reason that only women would fathom.

He got out of the car and headed inside, a clot of snow falling down his collar as he opened the door. "Get off me, Ratty," he said when the dog attacked.

"She's not a rat," Honor said. She was pouring herself a glass of wine, still in her incredibly uptight navy blue suit and ugly shoes. Why on earth Honor Holland wasn't slutting it up and showing off her wares was a mystery. There was absolutely nothing wrong with her. "How's your eye?"

"Fine." They hadn't talked too much since two days ago, aside from apologizing to each other repeatedly (and ineffectively, he thought), he for putting her in an uncomfortable situation, she for drawing blood.

Held up at *gunpoint*. Never told anyone. Christ.

Every time he thought of it, the red haze descended. He wanted to kill the bloke who'd done it, picking a woman with a complete lack of street smarts. Which, of course, was exactly what muggers looked for. Didn't change the red, though. And it didn't make Tom any more able to say the words that were stuck in his chest. *Don't ever get hurt again. Don't ever take chances. Don't get sick. Don't leave. Don't die.*

He sighed.

"What do you feel like for dinner?" she asked.

"I don't care. Want me to cook?"

"I don't mind."

"Neither do I," he said. "Go on, sit down, relax. You look tense."

She bristled. "I'm not." She picked up Spike and kissed the dog's head.

"Good." Conversation was clearly not their strong suit.

They were better at sex. At least, so far as he could recall. It had been a *bloody* long time. Fucking weeks. Or, more appropriately, not-fucking weeks.

The doorbell rang, causing Ratty to burst into a flurry of brain-hemorrhaging barks. *Yark! Yark! Yarkyarkyarkyark!* "I'll get it," Honor said, taking the dog with her.

Tom opened the refrigerator and surveyed his options. Living with Honor meant the larder was much better stocked than when he lived here himself, though he always tried to have some snacks on hand for Charlie. Now, though, they were swimming in food. Chicken, beef, lettuce, tomatoes, oranges, spinach, cottage cheese, Parmesan, yogurt, hummus. And lots of good wine, as well.

"Tom? Um, Pooky?"

He turned at the wretched nickname. Honor's face was blotchy, and her eyes were a little too wide. She stood in front of another woman. "This is Bethany Woods. She works for Custom and Immigration Services."

Bloody hell.

"Hallo there," Tom said, smiling. Bethany was somewhere in her forties, a stout, sturdy woman with tight black curls and severe glasses with rhinestoned corners. "Tom Barlow, lovely to meet you."

"Hi," she said. "This is an unscheduled visit courtesy of the U.S. government. Hope you don't mind."

"Not at all," Tom said. "To what do we owe this honor?"

Bethany gave a tight smile. "We've had a tip that you and Ms. Holland might be about to commit marital fraud."

Tom glanced at Honor, who looked like she was about to vomit. "Fraud? How so?" he asked. "Have a seat, Bethany, sorry. Would you like a glass of wine or a cup of tea?"

"No, thank you," she said, giving him a quick scan. The *Janice,* as he thought of it.

"Please sit, at any rate. Darling?" He held a chair for Honor, who hesitated, then sat stiffly.

"Dr. Barlow," Bethany said, "we've contacted the college where you work and discovered they have no plans to renew your green card."

"Right," Tom said. Honor was biting her lip. Another second, and there'd be blood. He took her hand under the table and gave it a warning squeeze. Ratty snarled, earning a significant look from Ms. Woods.

"Records show that your marriage license has been filed," she continued, "and a few days ago, someone called our office anonymously and said that you two barely know each other."

Now who in the bloody hell would do that? Honor's father, perhaps? The man had yet to look Tom in the eye. Droog, perhaps jealous that Honor hadn't chosen him instead of Tom? Probably not him; he was good bloke.

"Well, it was fast," Tom said. "I'll give you that. But we're getting married because we love each other. Right, darling?"

"We love each other," she parroted, her voice squeaking. He squeezed her hand again, and she gave him a panicky look.

"Glad to hear it," Bethany said briskly. Again, her eyes scanned him up and down. "Be that as it may, you're aware that marital fraud constitutes a fine of up to a quarter million dollars and a ten-year jail sentence."

Honor swallowed with a dry click, and her little dog whined, wagging her tail and scrabbling to get at Bethany. So far, the only person Ratty seemed to hate was Tom.

"Lots of times, the U.S. citizen will do it to help out a friend," the woman continued, extending a finger to Spike, which the dog promptly licked. "Are you a sweet baby? You are? Are you? You're so cute! Yes, you are! What's your name? Huh? What's your cute little name?"

"Spike," Honor breathed.

"Oh, I love that. Yes, I do! I love it! Anyway, Ms. Holland, helping out a friend doesn't make marital fraud any less illegal."

"This isn't one of those situations," Honor said. Her hand was clammy.

"Great. Then I'm sure you two won't mind if I separate you and ask you some questions."

"Of course not," Tom said. "Do we, Honor?"

"Nope," she squeaked.

Bethany smiled tightly. "Good. Mind if I see your upstairs before we get started?"

"Not at all." Tom stood up and smiled, offering his hand to the woman. She took it, her face coloring slightly.

"This is a cute house," she said.

"We like it," he said.

Thank God Honor had brought some things in, because the place was looking vastly improved from when Tom had been here alone. Pictures hung on the wall, the sofa had pillows, there were matching towels in the loo. It looked, in other words, like a real home, not just a temporary place to crash.

"How long have you two been together?" Bethany asked. "Spike, you said her name was? Spike, how long have Mommy and Daddy been together, huh, cute baby? Hmm?"

Dear God. "A couple of months," Tom said. "One of those instant-attraction situations."

"Right," Honor croaked.

"Spike! Is this your ball? Is this your ball? Go get it!" Bethany tossed the ball. It rolled under the chair. "I'll get it for you, babykins! Yes! I will!"

As the woman got down to retrieve Babykins's ball, Tom turned to Honor and gave her a quick kiss. "Get a grip," he whispered against her mouth.

"Okay," she whispered back, but her eyes were darting everywhere. He kissed her again, more slowly, cupping her head in his hands, her hair soft and feathery.

She smelled so clean and simple, so good. After a second, her hand went to his chest, and her mouth softened.

They might have to pretend to be madly in love, but he didn't have to pretend that kissing her was incredible. She had this way of melting into him, his brittle little bride, and seemed...helpless when he kissed her. Soft and sweet and a little surprised.

"And the upstairs?" Bethany asked. "Come on, Spikey! Upstairs!"

"Right this way," Tom said, stepping back from Honor. Spike barked once, in love with Bethany Woods.

Thank God Honor was a bit anal retentive about neatness, because the bed in Charlie's room was perfectly made, and not so much as a slipper or a pair of earrings gave away the fact that she slept in here every night. Smart girl. She'd anticipated this. He owed her one. More than one, that was certain.

"Who does model airplanes?" Bethany asked, surveying the half-finished Stearman on the bureau.

"My unofficial stepson," Tom said. "Um, I was engaged to his mum a few years ago, but she died. Her son and I are still close, though." Another lie.

"That's beautiful," Bethany said. "What a nice guy you are. Is he so nice, Spike? Huh? Hmm?" She picked up the little dog and kissed her.

"Thank you," he said, ignoring Honor's shallow panting. She really needed to calm down. So did Bethany, for that matter, he thought as Spike licked the woman's mouth. Disgusting.

Bethany walked into Tom's room and opened the closet. Again, well done, Honor. Her clothes made it seem like it was her room, too. "So when's the wedding?"

"Soon," Honor said.

"We thought about eloping," Tom said, "but her family want to be there, and she's got to get the poofy dress and all that. And I want her to be happy, of course." He looked at her. "You'll make a beautiful bride, darling."

"I love weddings," Bethany said.

"You're welcome to come to ours," he said. Honor gave a squeak, then covered it with a cough, and Bethany smiled and meandered into the bathroom. Opened the cupboard and nodded.

"You're laying it on a little thick," Honor breathed.

"She's eating it up," he whispered back. "Would it kill you to smile? We're supposed to be in love."

"I'm not good at faking."

"Yeah, that's obvious. Follow my lead. Darling."

"Honor," Bethany said briskly, back in business mode, "would you mind staying up here and answering these questions?" She opened her enormous purse and pulled out a sheaf of papers.

"No problem," Honor said. She started to go into Charlie's room, then did an about-face and went into his room instead.

Bethany's eyebrow raised.

Bollocks.

Back down the stairs they went, returning to the kitchen. "If you don't mind, we'll wait for Honor to come back down with her answers," Bethany said, scooping up Ratty.

"Not at all. Are you sure you don't want some water? Or that wine?" He smiled again. "I imagine we're your last stop of the day."

"When you put it that way, sure. Why not? White if you have it."

"We certainly do. Honor's family are winemakers. We've got all sorts of lovely choices. Gewürztraminer? Pinot gris? Chardonnay?"

"Chardonnay is great."

"Wonderful." He poured her a generous glass and handed it to her. "Do you mind if I start dinner?" he asked.

"Go right ahead," she answered.

Tom pulled off his sweater, revealing the Henley-style T-shirt he wore underneath. Ms. Woods flushed, staring at his Union Jack tattoo. "Can't forget where I'm from, can I?" he asked with a wink.

"And you have another one?" she asked, taking a sip of her wine and pointing to his other arm.

"I do, yes. Bit a youthful mistake." He pulled up his left sleeve and showed her the Celtic circle, which had absolutely no meaning to him but had seemed incredibly cool when he was seventeen. Was he whoring it up a bit for the sake of Ms. Woods?

Yes.

"What happened to your eye?" she murmured.

"Funny story," he said, and told her about the class and Honor's ring. "It's better now. The doctor did a nice job stitching it up, don't you think?" He leaned down so she could inspect it, then smiled.

"You poor thing," she said, her voice husky. Spike growled.

"How long have you worked for Immigration, Bethany?" he asked.

"Fourteen years," she answered. "You're right, this wine is wonderful."

"Great." He got out some chicken, grabbed a handful

of parsley and a few cloves of garlic and started chopping. "You must have quite a lot of stories," he added.

Cooking, he'd noted over the years, was a strangely intimate activity. Some of his best conversations with Charlie had been in the kitchen as he'd cooked, back in the day. With Melissa, too, who'd always appreciated not having to put dinner together after a workday.

It worked with Bethany, too. "We see all sorts of things," she said, taking another sip of wine. "These visits, we call them bed-checks. Make sure the couple is really living together and not just faking it. You know, is her stuff in the bathroom, or is it just his? Do they actually know each other, or are they complete strangers? You'd be surprised how many people think they can pull off this kind of thing."

"Really."

"There was this one time," she began, and with that, she started on a story about a green-card ring in which couples would try to make it appear they'd been together for months by Photoshopping pictures, pasting their heads onto other people's bodies. "So in one picture, she weighs maybe a hundred pounds. In the next, supposedly on the same skiing trip, she's double the size. Can you believe that? Can you, Spike?"

Tom smiled. "Funny," he said.

"It *is* funny," Bethany said. "Stupid, but funny. At least you two haven't lied about how long you've been together." She drained her wine. "How did you meet, anyway?"

"We met at O'Rourke's," he said, nudging the chicken. "The little bar in town here. I saw her, and I thought, 'That's her, Tommy, mate. That's your wife.'

Felt like I'd been hit in the head with a sledgehammer."
He grinned. "That sounds like a cheesy pickup line."

"No. Not at all. It sounds romantic, doesn't it, Spikey
baby?"

Honor came back into the kitchen, looking sweaty
and rumpled. "All done," she said, handing over the
papers.

"Right, right," Bethany said. "Boy, that smells good.
I'm starving."

"Would you like to stay?" Tom asked. Honor shot
him a murderous look.

"I'd love to!" Bethany answered instantly. Behind
her, Honor threw up her hands.

"Lovely. Darling, set the table, won't you?"

She did, rattling the plates and nearly dropping the
couscous. He gave her a warning look, but she seemed
incapable of relaxing.

"You're a great cook," Bethany said, falling upon
dinner like she'd just got back from forty days in the
desert. "This is fantastic. Can I give Spike a bite?"

At least Bethany was happy. Honor, on the other
hand, pushed her food around and remained silent until
he gave her a sharp look. She took a few bites. Was
not doing a great job convincing Bethany they were
madly in love.

"Okay!" Bethany announced, pushing back her plate.
"What I like to do here is ask you the same questions
Honor has already answered and see how well your
answers match."

"Fire away," he said. Kicked Honor under the table,
as she looked as if her dog had just been bulldozed in
the street. Speaking of, where was Ratty? Peeing in another of his shoes?

"What's Honor's favorite color?"

Shit. He had no bloody idea. Most of her clothes were… "Blue," he said.

"Specifically?"

"Dark blue."

"Navy. I'll give it to you." Bethany smiled at him with a little wink. "When is her birthday?"

"Oh, shit, this is where most husbands screw up, isn't it?" He gave Honor a grin. She didn't return it, her eyes open too wide. "January 4." *Thank you, Honor, for your anal-retentive dossier.*

"Good job!" Bethany leaned across for a high five, her eyes dropping again to his Union Jack. "Where does she fall in birth order in her family?"

And another shit. Let's see, there was the sex-addicted sister, who looked older but acted younger, the sister whose husband was the cop…younger, he thought, but what about the brother? "She acts like the oldest, don't you, sweetheart? Everyone goes to her with their problems. And she's quite bossy." He smiled. She still looked ready to puke. "She's in the middle."

"Correct," Bethany said, not noticing that he'd fudged the answer a bit. "Her favorite TV show?"

He grimaced. "Those dreadful medical dramas about tumors and the like. Horrible."

Bethany smiled at him. "I have to agree. Okay, next question. What would Honor say is your biggest vice?"

He cocked an eyebrow. Honor closed her eyes. "Drinking. Wait till she meets some of my mates back home."

"Drinking is correct, Tom." Bethany gave him another high five. "And what contraception do you use?"

He choked on his water. "Right." Took a second to

answer. "We're hoping to start a family very soon. So none."

"That's not what she said."

He looked at his bride-to-be. "Darling? I thought we'd talked about this."

"I, uh, yes. Just, you know." She was sweating, her forehead shiny with it.

He took her hand and tugged her onto his lap, where she sat like a brick. "I thought you wanted babies right away, sweetheart," he said, squeezing her knee to hopefully clue her in.

"Yeah, well, I don't...um. Definitely. Soon. But maybe we could be married for a few months before we toss the, um, pills."

"I can't wait," Tom said. He tried to pull her in for a kiss, but she was clenched. He leaned his head against her shoulder instead and smiled at Bethany. "Any other questions?"

"Nah," Bethany said. "I think you guys are really cute. Where's Spikey? Aren't they cute? They're cute!"

Thank the Christ child. In about five minutes, then, he was going to pour a very generous glass of whiskey. Just one, mind you, but generous.

He stood up, having to push Honor off his lap, then gripped her hand in his. "Well, this was lovely, meeting you. Thank you, Bethany."

"Thanks for dinner!" she said, pulling on her coat. "This was really nice. Most people can't wait for me to leave."

"Really?" Tom said. "Can't imagine why."

"Good luck to you both." Bethany shook their hands hard, smiling at them.

"Thanks," Honor said, letting out a massive breath.

He gave her a quick glare, then turned back to Bethany. Walked her to the door, dragging Honor behind him, and opened it.

Bugger.

A foot of snow had piled up.

"Oh, crud," Bethany said. "I don't know if I can drive home in this. My tires are completely bald, and it's an hour and a half to my house in good weather."

Tom closed his eyes for a second. "Not to worry," he said. "You can stay here for the night. Right, darling?"

HONOR FELT LIKE her head was about to explode. She stared at her reflection in the bathroom mirror. Her face looked wind-burned, she'd been blushing so long.

That woman had been here for *four hours*. Four hours of Tom kissing her ass, playing Devoted Fiancé, four hours of Honor trying to lie when all she could hear was *ten years in prison*. Which, yes, she already knew, but it had a different ring to it when said by a federal agent!

Finally, Bethany had yawned (hugely) and said a fond good-night to Tom, who looked like he was going to hug her.

"See you kids in the morning," she said. "Don't make too much noise, okay?" A gruesome wink that made Honor die a little inside.

And now she had to sleep with Tom.

Got to sleep with Tom.

Under normal circumstances—normal for them— the idea would have made her nervous enough, if rather thrilled. With a federal agent across the hall, she was close to losing control of her bowels.

How had Tom known her favorite color was navy

blue? And that thing about how she acted like the oldest...was he right?

"Is the bathroom free?" Bethany asked.

"Um, just a sec," Honor said. Too bad she didn't have sleeping pills. She could drug all three of them.

She opened the door, smiled at Bethany and went into Tom's room and closed the door.

"Do you think you could possibly act a little less like a piece of wood?" he whispered.

"What?"

"You sat there like a lump, Honor."

Four hours of stress had taken their toll. "It's better than stripping down to distract her," she hissed. "Think I didn't notice that? Were you going to do a little *Magic Mike* number if she kept asking questions?" The water turned on in the bathroom.

"One of us had to talk, Pooky."

"Do you think it's going to help our case if she says, 'Groom seems like a man-whore'?"

"I didn't strip. I took off my sweater. And since you seemed to be struck mute, someone had to keep her occupied."

"Look," she whispered. "I'm sorry I got hung up on the fact that there was a federal *agent* in my house who got invited to dinner and a sleepover!"

"Lower your voice, she's coming out."

"Good night!" Bethany called.

"Good night!" they chorused merrily back, then resumed glaring. Spike, at least, was comfortable; she jumped onto the bed and curled up on a pillow, yawned and closed her eyes.

The radiator ticked on. "Bedtime, darling," Tom said.

She was starting to hate that particular endearment,

as he had never once used it with sincerity. That being said, he had a point. "Sure." But she had to change into her pj's. "Um, can you close your eyes?" she whispered.

"I have seen you naked, you realize."

"Yeah, well, you're not going to tonight."

"Fine." He pulled his shirt over his head, all predatory male grace, tossed it in the corner, then unbuttoned his pants.

Right. She should probably turn around.

And she would. Soon. Anytime now. Definitely by tomorrow.

That was quite a beautiful male body. A boxer's body, arms curved with heavy muscle, broad chest lightly covered in hair, the hypnotic washboard abs. She remembered how it had felt to trail her fingers over that part of his anatomy, that night when she'd been a sex kitten, when she'd been so unlike herself.

Tom cocked an eyebrow, and she turned away, feeling her face ache with heat once more this night.

A second later, she heard the bedsprings creak. "Okay, close your eyes," she whispered.

"Done."

"Really?"

"Honor, for the love of God, would you just get into bed, please?"

She glanced back. He was sitting in bed, eyes closed, that beautiful, rippling torso begging for a thorough examination. His bruised eye and tattoos gave him an unbearably appealing bad-boy look, and his Saint Christopher medal somehow underscored his ridiculous sex appeal. Who would've thunk Honor Holland would have such a guy ordering her into bed, regardless of the circumstances?

She turned back and undressed, jacket, skirt and sweaty blouse going over the back of the chair. At least she wore nice underwear. Not that Tom would see, since he'd closed his eyes like a good boy. She unhooked her bra, pulling on her flannel pj's as fast as she could.

When she turned around, Tom's eyes were open, and he was looking steadily at her. No smile.

The air seemed to thicken, and Honor's heart banged against her ribs.

Would that she was closer and could read the expression in his eyes. Or just kiss him.

"Come on, then," he said, pulling back the covers.

She was never going to sleep tonight.

And she hadn't been sleeping well since she moved in here. But now, she was vibrating with nervousness, tingling with awareness, tightening with lust and utterly terrified of being sent to jail, all at the same time.

About that lust, the eggs said, adjusting their binoculars to get a better look at Tom.

She went to the unoccupied side of the bed and slid in. "Good night," she said, turning away from him.

Tom turned off the light and lay down on his back.

"We'll have to offer her breakfast," he murmured. "Think it'd kill you to be hospitable?"

Honor rolled over to face him, the light from the street allowing her to see his face in profile. "Tom," she whispered, "what if we get caught?"

"We won't, so long as you stop acting like a criminal, darling."

"I can't help it!"

"You said you knew all this before," he pointed out, his voice quiet. "You're the one who told me you were fine with the risks."

"I know, but—"

A knock came on the door, and Honor jolted closer to Tom. "Yes?" they called in unison, his arms going around her.

Bethany opened the door. "I didn't mean to interrupt," she said unconvincingly. "Oh, hi, Spikey-snooks! Are you all comfy there?"

Honor's face was right up against Tom's neck. It was a nice place to be. Or it would be, if she wasn't in ventricular tachycardia. Thank you, *Death in the E.R.*

"Do you need anything, Bethany?" Tom asked.

"Um, I just wondered if I could get a glass of water." For God's sake.

"Absolutely," Tom said, starting to get out of bed, but Honor pulled him back.

"Help yourself," she said. "Glasses are next to the sink."

Bethany paused, then sighed. "Great. Sleep well."

The door closed. "Water, my ass," Honor whispered. "She just wanted to see you without your shirt."

"At least someone does," he grumbled.

"What's that supposed to mean?"

"Maybe it wouldn't be so hard for you to fake a little affection if we were sleeping together."

It dawned on her that she was still pressed against Tom. Intimately. In fact, if she weren't swathed in flannel, the eggs would be quite happy, let's put it that way.

"I thought we were waiting till we got married," she whispered.

"I find that very hypocritical," he muttered. "Since you've already boffed me three times."

"One night. With three, um, sessions."

He didn't answer.

If he kissed her now, she'd offer no resistance. She was exhausted from stress, not to mention weak-willed and lustful. And the years were precious. Besides, the memory of his weight on top of her, the hard, thick slide of—

"Tell me about being mugged." His voice was quiet.

"What? Oh. Um, why?"

"Because I want to know."

She swallowed. "I already told you."

"Yes. But I was busy yelling." He pulled her closer, so that her head was on his hard and utterly wonderful shoulder. Her hand had nowhere to go other than his chest, and she felt his heart thudding, such a lovely, secret pleasure, that feeling, the marvel of the human body.

Bethany's footsteps sounded on the stairs. The door to the other room opened and closed.

"I was walking home from the library," Honor whispered. "My roomie and I had a little apartment about three blocks off campus, and it was only about ten, so I figured it was safe." Wrong on that count. How many times had her father fussed over the fact that she was in a big city? Warned her about walking home alone?

"All of a sudden, some guy had me by the arm, and he shoved me into this doorway and told me to give him my purse. He had a gun, and I remember looking at him and thinking I had to remember his face, but I couldn't. The details kept sliding away, like my brain couldn't quite grab on to what was happening." She paused, remembered fear making her knees tingle. "So he asked for my money, and I threw my purse over his head and ran. To a police station."

Tom's hand covered hers, and Honor's throat was

suddenly tight. "That was very clever," he said, his voice just a soft rumble.

"Thanks," she whispered.

"Why didn't you ever tell anyone?"

She hesitated. "I did. I meant I never told anyone in my family. It was over, and they would've just worried. But I told the police. And, um, a friend." She winced.

"Brogan?"

It was the first time Tom had gotten the name right. "Yes."

"And was he…what's that word you Americans like so much? Supportive?"

"Of course. He was very nice." She paused. "He's a nice man."

"I'm sure." Tom's voice was mild, but it suddenly felt awkward, lying this way. Her neck felt stiff, and the shoulder under her head seemed to have turned to granite.

"Did they ever catch the man who did it?"

"No."

"I'm sorry."

"Thanks. And thanks for asking about it."

"Right. I'm an engineer, after all. It didn't make sense, your hauling off and hitting me like that. I figured there was a cause and effect going on."

A car drove past on the street below.

She wanted to say something more, to address the stew of feelings that seemed to roil and change between them like a Midwestern storm. But maybe that was just her. Maybe Tom wasn't feeling much of anything, just an engineer who liked to understand how things worked.

"Sleep well, Honor," he said.

"You, too."

Honor turned on her side, away from Tom, and closed her eyes, but it was a long time before sleep wrapped her in its soft embrace.

CHAPTER EIGHTEEN

FROM HER OFFICE, Honor had a stellar view of the vineyard, the fields stretching down to the woods, Keuka
glittering a steel-blue this cold day. Weather was on
her mind. The cold hadn't let up, not that she expected
spring to actually begin on March 21; she'd lived here
all her life, after all. The snow had melted for the most
part, though there were still large swaths of white blank-
ing the fields. The temperature dropped to freezing each
night, only hitting forty-five or so during the warmest
part of the afternoon. Then again, she knew well that it
could hit seventy later this week. There was little rhyme
or reason to the weather of April, the cruelest month
for just that reason.

Tomorrow was supposed to be in the fifties, the
never-reliable forecasters had sworn. Honor was hoping
they were right this time; a little sun might be enough
to make more daffodils bloom in time for the Black and
White Ball this weekend. Last fall, Faith had planted
thousands of bulbs around the Barn, and the bravest had
already opened in the patches of ground where the snow
had melted, their yellow blooms so bright and hopeful.

The first of the spring weddings to be held at the
Barn was later in April. Faith had asked if she and
Tom would get married up there as well; Honor knew
it would mean a lot to her sister if they did. Then again,

the thought made her stomach hurt. Tom certainly had qualities that could make him a great husband—he was so devoted to Charlie, he loved his job and had a great sense of humor. Commitment. Stability. Sex appeal, heavens yes. But Honor would be promising to love, honor and cherish him all her life, and while she could definitely see herself doing just that, she was well aware that while he might feel some affection (and definitely gratitude) for her, and while he didn't find her unattractive, well…things weren't balanced.

She could love him at the drop of a hat.

If he felt the same way, he was hiding it well.

Speaking of weddings, Brogan and Dana's engagement had been in the paper this morning. It was still strange, the absence of those two as her constant companions. Especially Dana. Brogan was trying. Still sent her emails with links to articles or a funny cartoon, a postcard from L.A. last week. It was nice, really—he still cared enough to make an effort.

From Dana, there'd been nothing, and that was okay. Whatever loneliness Honor felt was mostly reflex by now. Besides, now she had other people. Faith and she were closer than they'd ever been, which was absolutely lovely. She had Jessica Dunn, who was proving to be a smart and steady employee for Blue Heron. Colleen and Connor, who'd always seemed off-limits as Faith's closest friends, felt more like Honor's friends, too, these days. Of course, there were Dad, Pru and Jack. And Honor still saw Mrs. J. every day at lunch. So she had friends.

And she had Tom.

Sort of.

Speaking of grooms, there was Dad, down in the

merlot vines with Pru. Honor smiled and waved, and made Spike wave as well, and they waved back in unison. Peas in a pod, those two, both wearing very similar plaid shirts. No coats. They were Yankees, after all. What was a little cold and wind to a farmer?

"Honor," Ned said, appearing in her doorway, "I'm gonna swing by some of the accounts. Press the flesh, maybe do a tasting here and there, since it's almost happy hour."

"Okay," she said. "Need anything from me?"

"Nope. I'm good." Her nephew smiled.

"Yes. You are," she said. It was true; unlike Dad, Pru or Jack, who preferred to be left alone to tend to their grapes and subsequent fermenting, Ned had the gift of schmooze. "You're a man now, Neddie dear. Which doesn't mean I've forgotten that you sucked your thumb until you were seven."

"Oh, I still do," he said with an easy grin. "Why give up a good thing? See you, Auntie."

Nice to have someone else from the family out there, representing Blue Heron. For twelve years, Honor had done it alone, dragging Dad along once in a while. But Ned *liked* doing it.

"Hey, Tom," she heard Jessica say. "How are you?"

"Jess, lovely to see you," Tom said.

Honor felt her cheeks fire up and couldn't stop herself from looking at her reflection in the computer monitor. There was just something about that accent that hit her right in the ovaries. *Preach it, sister,* the eggs agreed. *How about getting us a little action here?*

Sure, Honor knew sex was on the horizon. Very soon, in fact. She'd almost jumped him the other night when he kissed her hand. So they'd get it on, of course.

They had the marriage license, and this thing was happening. And once nooky commenced, Honor had the very strong suspicion that she'd be crazy in love, and a lot more vulnerable to heartbreak.

So what? Beats being celibate forever, the eggs pointed out. *Get a move on!*

"Yeah, yeah," Honor muttered. "Hang in there. We'll know when the time is right." She could just about imagine them pointing at their tiny watches in outrage.

Word. But Tom had this odd ability to be both wonderful and distant at the same time. Case in point—the discussion of the mugging the other night, as they lay in bed. Oddly intimate, until click, he shut off.

Last night over their mostly quiet dinner, Tom had asked about the Black and White Ball and what it was for, and Honor found herself inviting Tom to tramp around the property. Ellis Farm abutted the rear fields of Blue Heron, so they'd hike up past Rose Ridge and down onto the unused farmland, where soon, Honor hoped, they'd begin work to make the land more accessible. She'd been talking to a bike trail designer for six months now, and had a grant from the state to help offset some costs.

"Hallo, Honor," he said now, poking his head in her door. "How was your day?"

"Great," she said. "And yours?"

"It was good." He smelled like fresh air and coffee. "Brought you a treat." In his hand was a familiar bag—Lorelei's Sunrise Bakery.

"Thanks." She opened and peeked in, and Spike stuck her head right in. Sugar cookies. Very nice.

He wore faded jeans and hiking boots and a battered brown leather jacket. Effortlessly hot. And dang, he was watching her ogle him, a faint smile crinkling his eyes. "You don't dress like a math teacher," she said, clearing her throat.

"I'm not a math teacher." His smile widened, flashing that slightly crooked tooth, and hope flashed as fast and strong as lightning in her heart.

She could love this guy.

She slipped off her pumps (which Faith had deemed "tragically sensible" but were very comfy, unlike Faith's own complicated, painful and enviably slutty collection of footwear) and pulled on her muck boots. "Spike, want to go for a walk?" she said, smiling as her dog's shaggy little ears pricked up at the magic word, then clipped on the neon-pink leash she'd bought the past week. Already, it was frayed from where Spike had been chewing it. This would be the fourth leash since she got the wee terror.

Outside, the wind was sharp, the air growing colder by the minute. This would have to be a quick hike, or her ears would freeze. Even so, crocuses had pushed their way up through the lawn, and the maple trees were red-budded with the promise of spring. They headed up the hill toward the conservation property, birds calling to one another as they swooped and preened.

"This is lovely," Tom said, stopping at the family cemetery.

"Yes. Everyone from the ancestor who fought with Washington to my mom." She stopped, opening the little gate that enclosed the area, and put Spike down so the dog could capture leaves and make them her prisoners. Honor brushed a few leaves off her mom's headstone and adjusted the pot of pansies she'd left there yesterday.

For more than half of Honor's life, her mother had been gone. It didn't seem possible.

"You Hollands have a good bit of land, don't you?" Tom asked, breaking the silence as they continued up the hill.

"We do," she said.

"And here I am, a city kid who grew up in a three-room apartment, marrying into American royalty."

"Hardly that. American farmers."

Tom grinned. "Same thing in this country, isn't it?"

"I'll tell my dad you said that. Whatever misgivings he has will evaporate."

"Does he have misgivings?"

Honor picked Spike back up, as her teensy feet would be getting cold, and tucked the dog into her coat. "Well, sure. He's a father. You and I haven't known each other that long. If we were getting married a year from now, I'm sure he wouldn't worry."

"I imagine I'd feel the same, if I had a daughter."

A daughter. The thought made her heart swell with longing.

Faith's pickup truck was in the gravel lot at the top of the ridge. "My sister's working on the Barn," Honor said. "Want to go say hi?"

"Not really," he said, taking her hand. "You know you look a bit ridiculous with that dog's head poking out of your coat? In an adorable way, of course."

Oh. That was...that was *nice*.

His hand was much warmer than hers. Warm and firm and flippin' huge, and all of a sudden, Honor felt *incredibly* feminine and adorable...and randy. What— and when—to do about that was another question altogether.

She hadn't had any trouble figuring out what to do that night when she'd pulled open Tom Barlow's shirt and licked his neck and kissed him till he pushed her against the wall and held her hands over her head. No sir. No indeedy.

The eggs fluffed their hair and took off their bifocals.

"Ellis Farm Conservation Land," Tom read from the sign. "All right, Miss Holland. Give me your spiel."

"It's land. They don't make that anymore."

"Simple as that?"

"Yep. We'll put in a bike trail that will link up to the rail line. The 4-H club will use the barn for their cows, and we're going to put in a co-op vegetable garden. There'll be a picnic area, some hiking trails."

"Sounds lovely."

"And see that pond? In the winter, we'll flood it for skating." She paused. "Do you know how to skate?"

"No," he said.

"I'll teach you. I'm pretty good."

He smiled. "I bet you are."

She could see it very clearly—the skies gray and heavy, holding Tom's hand in the cold air, then going home to warm up. Naked.

"And your party this weekend, it funds the whole thing?"

"Excuse me? Oh, um, no. But the ball raises a lot of our budget. Private donors do the rest. Some of the local businesses."

"Including Blue Heron."

"You bet." Spike was wriggling to get loose, so she put the doggy down and let her wander as far as the leash would let her.

Tom was staring out over the hill. The snow had

mostly melted here, as the sun shone on the fields all day. The pond was still frozen.

When she was younger, Honor had skated there with the Ellis kids, when the pond had seemed like a foreign country filled with mysteries no one else had discovered, and only seven-year-olds on ice skates held the key. Then they'd troop back to the New House, and Mom would make cocoa and serve cookies, a Norman Rockwell scene if ever there was one.

And soon, that kind of thing would be available for all the kids in Manningsport. Kids like Jessica and Levi, who'd grown up in a trailer park, and kids like Charlie, who spent most of their days indoors, could have what the Hollands had been lucky enough to be born with. Land. Nature. Acres and acres of woods, water and forest. Birdsong and wildlife and hours of being outdoors.

Spike whined, meaning she had to pee. And to do so, she needed privacy, as the dog had a shy bladder. Tom was sitting on the fence that divided the Ellis land from Blue Heron and was just gazing out at the vista.

"Okay, Spike," she said, walking down the hill. "Let's find you a spot."

All of a sudden, Spike whimpered, trembling, then pulled at the leash. "Those are deer," Honor explained. "They're too big for you to take down, so stick with ants, okay?"

Spike didn't agree; she tugged again, and the frayed leash snapped. In a blur, the dog was off through the grass. "Spike, no," Honor said. "Come on. Come back here." There were coyotes around, after all, though it was still light. She started to run, clumsy in her boots. "Spike! Come!"

The dog didn't listen, charging forward at the deer,

barking with all her might, and the deer bolted into the woods on the far side of the pond.

Spike chased after them.

Oh, God. "No! No, Spike, no!"

Her dog was on the pond.

And the weather had been cold, but it hadn't been that cold. The pond was stream-fed, and Mr. Ellis had never let them skate there unless it had been below freezing for at least ten days straight. It was maybe twenty feet across, forty feet wide, and if Spike fell through—

"Spike! Spike!" she called, and she heard Tom yelling behind her, but the wind was in her ears.

Then Spike disappeared, blip, just like that, through about two-thirds of the way across. There, and then gone, swallowed into the black water where the current was too strong for ice to form unless it was freezing for ten days in a row, and Honor barely recognized her voice as she screamed her dog's name.

"Honor, no!" Tom yelled from behind her, but she was already on the ice. She could do it, she thought, her brain flashing with images of just how this would work. She was a skater. She knew this pond. She'd stay on the edge where the ice was thicker, and she'd head to the end of the pond, and the current would bring Spike there, and she could grab—

The ice broke, and the cold bit into her like knives, making the breath whoosh from her lungs. But it wasn't deep, Honor knew, maybe four feet, and if she could just get closer to where Spike had gone, she could find her dog. "I'm coming!" she yelled. "I'm coming, Spike!" Two steps. Four, the bottom slippery with icy mud that pulled at her boots.

Her foot slipped, coming completely free from the boot, and water closed over her head. Oh, God, it was so cold, the cold slicing right to her bones. She found footing again, barely able to feel the mud now because of the numbness. She slipped again, came up for air. This wasn't working. This was a bad idea, but Spike, her loyal, cuddly little friend, her only—

Honor tried to pull herself onto the ice again, but it broke under her numb hands, and her arms were too heavy, her legs weren't obeying. *The body's job is to preserve the heart and brain,* she could almost hear the narrator saying, because yes, chances were increasing that she'd become one of those stories on the *Back from the Dead* medical stories.

Hopefully.

Oh, Spike. A sob shuddered out of her. Her little dog had gone through so much. She didn't deserve a pointless death like this, alone in the dark water.

She slipped again, and this time, the water didn't hurt so much. And this time, her legs were even slower to kick.

Then she was being dragged upward, and held against Tom, and he was moving, he could walk, and the ice was breaking as he muscled his way through to the shore. She couldn't hear him, the blood was pounding in her ears so much, and it *hurt.* All of her hurt. Her sodden coat dragged at her, and water streamed from her hair.

The shore was steep here, and Tom heaved her out of the water. She landed with a tooth-jarring thud on the hard earth.

His mouth was moving, and my God, he looked so angry she was almost scared. "Spike," she said, shuddering with the cold, barely able to get the word out. "Please."

Fuck, he said. Well, his mouth made that shape, anyway. Honor was shaking so hard it was like one of her sister's epileptic seizures, and she tried to stand, to help Tom, because yes, he was going back into the water.

IF TOM HAD thought he was cold before he went in the pond, that had been a fucking walk on a tropical beach, hadn't it? Stupid, stupid Honor, going out on ice after the idiot dog. If it hadn't held a five-pound dog, how the hell was it going to hold a full-grown woman?

He could feel a slight current in the water, pulling at his clothes, and did a quick calculation in the water—weight, velocity, depth, momentum, resistance—and sloshed over to where he thought the idiot animal might be.

Chances were small to nil, let's be honest. His chest was tight, his skin screaming against the cold. If he had a heart attack right now, it would serve Honor right, because she'd scared the fucking blood out of his fucking veins.

He reached down, groping. Nothing.

This was not going to end well. He glanced back at Honor, huddled on the shore. Forget the dog. She needed to get warm.

Then his hand brushed something. He grabbed it. Ratty, all right, ice cold and limp, eyes open just a slit.

The dog was dead.

His eyes met Honor's and she let out a sound he never wanted to hear again.

"Fuck me," he said. Turned the horrible dog upside

down and pressed on its little belly. Water came out of its mouth. It still didn't move.

Honor was sobbing, crawling over to where he stood. Her hands were bloody.

Tom took the dog's tiny muzzle in his hand and blew into the dog's nose. This really took the cake. Mouth-to-mouth for a dog who hated him, bit him, destroyed his shoes, peed on his bath towel and was trying to eat his computer.

He puffed again. The dog's cheeks flapped, so Tom gripped her muzzle a little harder. Another puff. Two. Three.

Then there was a sharp pain in his lip. Tom jerked back, and Spike started gacking up water. It gave a watery bark, then shook itself, coughed again and barked once more. Alive, the little bugger. Good. Tom could kill it later.

He sloshed to Honor and handed her the evil creature.

"Spike! Spike, honey!" Honor gathered the dog against her chest, her hands shaking uncontrollably.

Without any finesse, as the cold was affecting him as well, he yanked Honor to her feet, grabbed the neckline of her coat and shoved the dog in against her skin. "Hold on to that little rat, because I'm not risking my life for her again," he said, then swung Honor up into his arms. One of her feet was bare.

By the time he reached the place where her sister was parked, Tom was breathing hard, had a cramp in his calf and was more angry than he could ever remember being in his life.

He tossed Honor in the front seat of Faith's truck. Good girl, she'd left the keys in. No time to ask for permission; he got in the driver's side and started it up, then threw it in gear and drove down the hill.

Honor was still shaking, shivering violently, hunched over, her arms folded around herself and the dog. Bloody idiot. Both of them.

"Thank you," she said.

"Don't say a word," he ground out.

Past her father's, past the grandparents' crooked house. The tires screeched as he pulled onto Lake Shore Road, and he gunned the engine, laying down rubber as he sped home. His breath made clouds of fury in the cold truck.

Onto their street, into the driveway. Tom barreled out of the truck in a flash. He yanked Honor's door open and pulled her into his arms again. He might've been a little rough, because she gave an *ooph* as he did, but bloody hell.

Into the house, his wet shoes squeaking on the floor. Up the stairs, into the bathroom. He set her down and threw on the taps, then started undressing her, as her hands were shaking too hard. Shaking and bloody and filthy.

From under her shirt, the dog moved. So it was still alive. Pity.

He yanked off her clothes. Her skin was nearly blue. Fuck.

He grabbed the dog and set the dog in the shower, where it barked. Then Tom lifted Honor in, following her, all his clothes still on.

He still couldn't look at her. Too bloody furious.

Or something.

Water streamed down Honor's body, her skin quickly turning pink. She had a bruise on her leg and several cuts, and her eyes looked too big. Tom picked up her dog and stuck it under the water with her, then lathered it up with shampoo, ignoring its little snarls. When he was assured the dog was as warm and mean as usual, he set it outside the tub, where it shook itself dry.

"Thank you," Honor said again.

Her shivering had stopped.

"You could've died for that little rodent," he said tightly. "Think about what that would've done to your family."

"I'm sorry I scared you, but—"

"No, Honor!" he yelled. his voice bouncing off the tile walls. "It was bloody stupid! A dog isn't worth what a person is. Look at you! You're all torn and bloody and you could've fucking died in that water! Christ Almighty."

"Why aren't you cold, too?" she ventured.

"Because I'm bloody furious!" he barked. "What would I do without you?"

He grabbed her weird pink scrunchy thing and doused it with her shower gel. "I mean, with Immigration," he muttered.

She didn't say anything, and after a minute, he glanced up from lathering her shoulders. Her eyes were wet.

"Don't you dare cry after what you just put me through. You took twenty fucking years off my life. Are you crying? Don't cry."

"I'm not crying," she said, and her voice only shook a little. "It's just the water."

He tossed down the scrunchy and kissed her. Hard. "You fucking terrified me," he muttered, and kissed her again, this time more gently.

She was alive. She was safe. She was wet and naked and warm.

Then, before he took her right here in the shower, he left, streaming water, sopping wet.

Because the last thing he wanted was to feel all this.

CHAPTER NINETEEN

THE PHONE WAS ringing when Honor got out of the shower. Tom's wet shoes were by his bed, and his car was not in the driveway.

She picked up the phone. "Hello?"

"Hey," said Faith. "I'm standing here in the kitchen at the New House. Did Tom steal my truck? Dad says he was driving like a bat out of hell. Is everything okay?"

Spike, her damp fur standing up in clumps, jumped up next to her and began gnawing on her thumb. Honor stroked her little tummy, and the dog's tail wagged. At least Spike was all right. Thanks to Tom.

Honor wiped her eyes. "Yes," she said. "I'm sorry. I had a little accident. Fell through some ice."

"My God! Are you okay?" Faith asked.

"Yeah. Just kind of cold."

"Is Tom all right?"

"He's fine. He's, um, he's not here right now," Honor said, and there was an embarrassing little tremble in her voice.

Faith was quiet for a second. "Dad will drive me to your place. I'll pick up dinner first, okay?"

Honor's eyes filled again, this time with gratitude. "That'd be great," she said.

An hour later, filled with chicken tikka masala from Taj's Indian and two glasses of pinot gris, Honor was sitting on the couch, wrapped in a fleece blanket, Spike snoring gently on her chest.

Dad and Mrs. J. had interrogated her about her rash actions. Mrs. J. brought a loaf of comforting blueberry bread and checked the larder to make sure she had enough food; Dad gave her a lecture about ice safety. After a half hour, Faith managed to kick them out. Then she tucked Honor in on the couch, fussing over her quite nicely. Blue cowered under the kitchen table, chewing his disgusting tennis ball, afraid to come within a thirty-foot radius of Spike.

"Tell me again how he tossed you onto shore," Faith said now.

"He just…did."

"It's kind of romantic. He's really strong, isn't he? Levi says he's got a right hook that could stop a tank."

"Well, he was furious."

"Sure. Which is pretty romantic, too."

"Is it?"

"Yes. Trust me. He was worried about you. He saved you. It's a good sign."

Honor finished her wine and set the glass on the coffee table, careful not to disturb Spike.

Faith was looking at her thoughtfully. "Honor, you don't have to marry him, you know. If you're not sure."

"Oh, I am. No. It's just…he's a little moody."

"He's a man. Of course he's moody."

"Imagine what they say about us."

"They don't talk about us. They're men." She paused. "I think you and Tom are really nice together."

"Do you?"

"Mmm-hmm."

Honor looked at her pretty sister. Faith had been in

love twice, once with Jeremy the Perfect, and then with Levi, whom she'd known forever. Could she tell something was off?

"Hey." The back door banged open, and Pru came in. "Heard you fell through the ice. That was stupid of you."

"Thanks for your sympathy, Pru," Honor said. "Faith brought me dinner, Mrs. J. brought dessert. What did you bring?"

"My good wishes," she said. "Is Tom in the shower? Can I check on him?"

"He had to run out," Honor said. Dad had also asked about Tom's whereabouts, and it was a little embarrassing that Honor didn't know where he was (and hadn't wanted to call, either).

"Damn." Prudence hurled herself into a chair. "Where's Dad? I thought he and Mrs. J. were here."

"They were," Faith answered. "We just got rid of them about half an hour ago. Honor and I were having a heart-to-heart."

"Cool! This place is cute, Honor. Nice work. It wouldn't kill you to invite me over, you know."

"Sorry." The place *was* pretty cute, Honor thought. Family pictures were scattered about, and a few prints hung on the wall. Honor had filled a shelf with paperbacks to go along with Tom's books on airplanes and bridges. Faith was curled in the leather club chair Honor had brought from her suite at the New House.

It was starting to feel like home, in other words.

"So when are you two making things permanent?" Pru asked, taking a piece of garlic naan and folding it into her mouth.

"Pretty soon," Honor said. Unless Tom came home and broke up with her, that was. "Maybe early June."

"Speaking of, are we getting matching dresses for Dad's wedding?" Pru asked. "Because I'd just as soon wear jeans."

"You're not wearing jeans," Honor said. "And don't wear jeans tomorrow night, either. You have to wear black or white."

"Don't get your panties in a twist. Faith made me buy a dress. You guys are so bossy. Okay, I gotta go. Just wanted to check on you, Honor." She bent down and planted a kiss on Honor's head. "See you tomorrow. Oh, hey! Guess what Carl and I did last night? Pumpkin pie has never been so sexy. Wanna hear about it?"

"Nope," said Honor.

"Never," Faith said at the same time.

"Fine, fine. No one ever wants to hear my stories." The front door opened, and there stood their brother. "Hey, Useless. What's up?"

"Hey, guys," Jack said, leaning down and hacking off a piece of blueberry bread. "Honor, I heard you were an idiot and went onto Ellises' pond."

"Yep," Honor said. "But I rescued your doggy niece, so show a little gratitude." She pointed to the sleeping Spike.

"You need to get a life."

Faith, Honor and Prudence all snorted at once. "What?" said Jack.

"Pot," Honor replied. "Kettle. Black. And I'm living with someone, soon to be married, so shut it."

"At least I don't wander out onto partially frozen ponds and then wonder why the ice breaks."

"Thank you, Jack."

Tom's voice made them all jerk around.

He wasn't smiling, and his eyes bounced off her and

went instead to her siblings. "This is very nice, all of you coming over to check on your sister, but I hope you won't mind if I ask you to leave."

"I personally wanna stay," said Pru. "Heard you were very heroic and manly, Tommy boy."

"Yes." He allowed a slight smile. "But you still have to go."

"I will if you'll take off your shirt," she said.

"Get out, Pru," Honor said.

"Oh, come on! I'm married to Carl. Throw me a bone." She eyed Tom appreciatively. "Faith got to see him when he was boxing with Levi. It's my turn."

"Let's go," Faith said. "Don't mind her, Tom, she's having a hot flash."

"I have been having a lot of those lately," Pru said thoughtfully. "I had to lie in a patch of snow today. Felt like simultaneously murdering someone and crying."

"Why do we always have to talk about female problems?" Jack asked.

"Shut up, you big baby," Prudence said, grabbing her coat. "Fine. See you, kids."

"Take care," Jack said, shaking Tom's hand. "Thanks for saving our idiot sister." Faith stood as well, and started to gather up the cartons of Indian food.

"I'll take care of that, Faith, but thank you," Tom said.

"Okay," she said, going over and smooching his cheek. "We'd be lost without her, you know." She hugged Honor for a few beats, her cheek soft and plump, her nice Faithie smell enveloping Honor. When she stood up, her eyes were wet. "See you tomorrow," she said. She kissed Spike on the head, then dragged Blue out from under the table and left.

The house seemed much bigger without them. Tom sat down in the chair opposite the couch and looked at her, his face blank. "How are you feeling?"

"Fine. Thank you." It was hard to look at him for some reason. Probably because he'd kissed the stuffing out of her in the shower. When she was naked. And then he'd left.

Faith was right. Men were not in touch with their emotions. "Why'd you kick out my family?"

"I wanted to apologize."

The words made her bones melt.

"I'm sorry I kissed you."

Oh, snap. Men were jerks. Even if this particular specimen had saved her doggy's life.

"Yeah, whatever," she said

"And I'm sorry I lost my temper."

We love this guy, said the eggs. "Shut up," Honor muttered.

"Excuse me?"

"Oh, um, nothing. Not you." She sat up a little straighter and adjusted Spike, who sighed and wrapped a tiny paw around Honor's thumb. "Don't apologize, Tom. You saved us both, and I really, really appreciate it."

"Yes." He paused. "I want you to promise me something."

"What's that?"

"You won't ever risk your life for an animal again. Even Ratty. It's not worth it, Honor."

Ratty's—er, Spike's fur was soft under Honor's hand, and she could feel the dog's fragile rib cage moving up and down with each breath.

"Promise?" he said.

"No."

He straightened. "Honor—"

"No. I'm sorry, but no. I can't."

"Don't be an idiot, Honor."

"Look, Tom, I'm sorry you had to come in to help me. I really am. I didn't start the day off thinking, 'You know what? If Spike ever goes through the ice, I'll definitely risk my life to save her.' I just…acted. I didn't plan it, and I'm sorry you had to be involved."

"You should be grateful I was! Since you would've died without me, don't forget!" He took a deep breath, and when he spoke again, his voice was calmer. "But you can't risk your life for a dog. She's not a child."

"I know that. But she means a lot to me."

"Too much, obviously."

Honor stroked the top of Spike's bony little head. "You know, I was like you. I always thought people were kind of dopey about their dogs. But I never had one before Spike. I mean, we had them growing up, but I never had a dog of my own."

Tom said nothing.

"I proposed to Brogan, did I tell you that? On my birthday. I figured what the hell, I was tired of waiting, so I just did it. You know what he said?"

"He turned you down."

"Yes. He said I was like an old baseball glove. Something you kept, but not something you needed every day."

"That's the worst metaphor I've ever heard."

"It's a simile, and thank you. But I wasted *years* on him. A decade of my adult life, waiting for him to really see me. He never did. If anyone had ever described that same relationship to me, I'd have said the woman was being deliberately blind to the fact that she was being used. But every time we were together, I thought, *This is the time he'll say what I've been waiting to hear,* that he'd finally realize he loves me and I'm special and perfect for him and he wants to spend his whole life with me."

The memory was still humiliating…all those years, all those other men she measured against a man who didn't really love her.

"He never said those things, obviously." She sighed. "So I was watching Faith and her dopey dog one day after he turned me down, and I called the vet and asked if they knew of any dogs who might need a home." Her throat tightened. "They were treating a dog who was maybe going to make it. Someone had poured gasoline on her. Her fur was mostly missing, and she was deaf in one ear and she was just getting over a broken leg."

Tom rubbed the back of his neck with one hand. "Honor, I—"

"When I got to take her home, they had to wrap her in gauze and put her in a special bag, because it hurt her too much to be lifted. And when I was walking to the parking lot, this firefighter came over, Gerard. And Gerard is six foot five and can probably pick up a car, and you know what Spike did? She growled at him. She was protecting me. Five pounds, all beat up and abused, wrapped in gauze, and she was defending me from a two-hundred-and-fifty-pound stranger. She loved me from the minute I saw her. No questions asked."

"I understand, but—"

"So when I saw her fall through the ice, I just went after her. Without thinking, because I couldn't bear the thought of her dying in there alone."

Spike chose that moment to sneeze, waking herself up, and Honor gave the dog a kiss. Spike licked her nose in return.

"Next time, you have to think," Tom said softly. "Please, Honor. You're someone's daughter, someone's sister, someone's aunt. And you'll be someone's mother someday. You can't just risk your life for a dog, no matter how much you love her."

He looked at her steadily, until she finally nodded. She couldn't imagine hearing that Faith had died trying to save Blue, or Jack saving that hideous, one-eared cat of his. Tom was right, no matter how wrong it felt.

She noticed he hadn't said *someone's wife.*

He stood up and bent over her. "Come on. Bedtime for you both."

"I can walk, you know."

"But isn't this more fun?" He gave her the smile she'd seen so much…the one that didn't quite make it to his eyes. Not that he was faking it; just that his happiness— and heart—seemed locked tightly away.

"Sure. Do your manly thing."

For the third time that day, he lifted her into his arms and carried her up the stairs, ignoring Spike as she wriggled and snarled, trying to bite his arm.

For a second, Honor thought Tom might put her in his own bed, and she wanted that so much her chest ached and her throat tightened, but no, he carried her into her own room. Set her down on the bed and pulled the covers up to her chin. "You need anything?" he asked.

You, she thought. "No," she whispered.

"Sleep well, then."

"You, too."

With that, he clicked off her light and went to the door. "Honor?"

Her heart rate sped up. "Yes?"

He ran a hand through his hair and sighed. "I'm very glad you and Ratty are all right."

Not what she was hoping for. The disappointment made her sink a little deeper into the mattress. "Thank you. For everything, Tom."

"See you in the morning."

And then he closed her door and went across the hall, leaving her alone in the dark with her dog.

CHAPTER TWENTY

TOM SPENT THE next morning at the airfield, first extracting a promise from his fiancée that she wouldn't overdo it getting ready for the fund-raising ball.

He hadn't slept the night before. Each time he started to drift off, the image of Honor going underwater would jerk him awake. Four times during the night, he'd checked on her, but she was dead to the world—poor choice of words, that. Ratty had growled at him, though. Ungrateful little rodent. Ridiculously adorable, though, he'd give it that, curled up on Honor's pillow as if watching over her. "You almost got her killed, Ratty," he whispered. "Do that again, and I'll put an end to you."

But sleep-deprived or not, he had work to do. His professor's salary was adequate, but only that. At university, he'd interned with a small airplane manufacturer. The company had a branch in New York, and a few times a year, Tom was hired to modify a plane for an owner. Those fees about tripled his annual income, and while he did love teaching (when his students were motivated, that was), it was nice to do some actual hands-on work.

Jacob Kearns had been as happy as a puppy when Tom had called him. This job was for an owner who wanted a bit more power for some stunt flying on his

Piper Cub. They needed to reconfigure the airfoil, as the bigger engine weighed more and threw off the lift. The rudders would need adjusting, as well.

Jacob was outgoing and cheerful and utterly enthusiastic about the work, doing calculations, listening astutely as Tom described how the airfoil created a vacuum that helped lift the plane. Funny to think the kid was a recovering drug addict.

For a panicky second, Tom wondered if that was what Charlie's problem was—drugs. That would account for his sullenness and withdrawal, wouldn't it? But first of all, Charlie had acted like that since his mother died. And secondly, Janice Kellogg had had him tested for that last year at his annual physical, and Charlie had been furious at the assumption that because he wore black eyeliner and listened to screeching noise that called itself music, he was an addict.

"So we can do all this work ourselves?" Jacob asked.

"Yes. It has to pass inspection before we fly it, but that shouldn't be a problem."

"Are you a pilot?"

"I have a license, yeah. You should try getting one."

"Maybe I will. Couldn't hurt with the cool factor."

Tom smiled. "Indeed."

They spent the next few hours working. Jacob ran out for sandwiches and brought Tom back the change and a receipt and asked questions about Tom's education and work experience, finding it quite hilarious that Tom had been an amateur boxing champion in Manchester.

"Dude, can you imagine if I told all those hot chicks in class?" the kid asked. "They'd go crazy."

"Don't you dare," Tom said. "They're terrifying enough as it is."

Around four, he packed up his tools. "All right, mate, let's finish up for the day," he said. "I've got an event tonight."

"What is it?" Jacob asked.

"It's a fund-raiser. Save the farmland." Except Tom rather hated the farmland after yesterday. Or maybe just the evil little pond.

"Sounds horrible," Jacob said. "Got some plans of my own. Hoping to bang that babe who sits next to me in your class."

"You probably shouldn't tell me that, even if you are both legal adults," Tom said. "Be a gentleman, use protection and all."

"Thanks, Mom." Jacob grinned. "And thanks for letting me help out, Dr. B." The kid shook his hand, then trotted out to his car.

Yes. It would be incredible if he could get one-tenth of the friendliness from Charlie that Jacob showed so effortlessly. Only at the self-defense class did Charlie seem to tolerate him, and only, perhaps, because Abby was around.

He should be used to it by now. Those ten months of having Charlie feel like his son were a long time ago.

On his way home, he stopped at a florist and, feeling a bit idiotic, asked for a corsage. "A corsage? How old is your date?" the florist asked, frowning.

"Thirty-five," he said.

"How about a wristlet instead?"

"What's that?"

"Goes around your wrist. Most women don't want to pin something on their dresses."

"All right. Whatever you say."

"What color is her dress?"

"I don't know. Black or white, I'm guessing."

"Are you British?" she asked, eyeing him.

"I am, yes," he said. "And engaged."

"Had to give it a shot," she answered with a smile. "Okay. Give me ten minutes."

While he was waiting, Tom's phone rang, a rare occurrence. Perhaps Honor needed him to stop and get something.

It was Janice Kellogg. "Tom," she sighed, "Walter and I need a break. Charlie has been up my ass lately." Lovely, especially coming from his grandmother. "Is there any chance you can come and get him? If I have to spend another second with him, I'm going to need a drink." There was a rattle of ice cubes. Why wait?

"Sure, Janice. I can get him."

"Oh, wait. You have plans, I bet. The Hollands are having their fancy party." Her voice oozed the sticky tones of martyrdom. "Don't worry. We'll be fine."

"No, Janice, I'd love to come around and pick him up. He can come with us."

Another rattle. "Well, Tom, I won't lie. That would be great. It's just endless, you know what I mean? Same old shitty attitude."

There was a hint of Melissa in that voice, those words. "I'd love to have him."

"Great. Bring him back around eleven tonight, okay? He has to go to church tomorrow. You know how important church is to us."

Yes. The better to revel in martyrdom. Janice and Walter Kellogg, doing their Christian duty and raising their no-good grandson. "Eleven, it is. I'll be there in fifteen minutes."

When Tom arrived, Charlie got into the car wordlessly, ignoring Tom in his customary manner. "Glad to see you, mate," Tom said into the void. "We've got an event tonight. Hope you don't mind."

Nothing.

"It's a ball. We can both suffer."

And still nothing.

"Charlie, is everything all right?" he asked.

"Yes," Charlie grunted.

Tom looked at him closely. "Are you being bullied?"

"No."

"If you are, you can come to me, you know."

"No, I can't."

"Yes," Tom said, his voice maybe a little too forceful. "Yes, you can. And you know things now. You can protect yourself."

"It's not like that!" Charlie said. "It's different."

"How? Tell me, mate."

Charlie just rolled his eyes.

They pulled up to the house, Charlie getting out before the car had come to a complete stop. "Careful," Tom said to his back, then rubbed his forehead, hard. If anything happened to that boy, it would kill him. And why he wouldn't tell Tom…ah, damn it all to hell.

He picked up the plastic box from the florist and followed the boy in.

Honor was there, wrapped in a bathrobe. "Hi," she said.

"Hi. How are you feeling?" The scrape on her right hand was still visible.

"I'm fine." Her tone was careful. "So Charlie's here."

"Yeah, Janice called me and asked if he could spend some time with us. I thought he could come to the ball, if that's all right."

She nodded. "Sure."

"If you'd rather not, we can stay here."

"I'd love for you both to come. That's great, in fact." Her gaze dropped to the box in his hands.

"Right," he said. "For you."

Her expression softened as she looked at it.

She was lovely. She had no idea, did she? Granted, he hadn't exactly been struck with lightning the first time he'd seen her (well, the second; the first time, she'd been quite impressive with that right hook). But hers were the type of looks that grew on a person. She had lovely skin and dimples when she smiled, which wasn't often enough, and her brown eyes were dark and kind.

That was a good face.

"Thank you," she said, looking up.

"It was nothing," he answered. "I hope it matches your dress."

"It's perfect."

"Good. What time do we need to be ready?"

"A little before seven."

"I'd better shower, then. You're sure it's all right if Charlie comes with us?"

"Sure," she said. "My niece will be there, so he'll have someone to hang out with."

"I'll tell him. Should make the evening less painful." And that came out wrong, as well. He started to explain, realized he had no idea what to say and went upstairs instead.

HONOR TRIED ON her dress for the fifth time.

It just wasn't happening. Yes, it was the obligatory black; white made her skin look like a piece of Wonder Bread left out in the rain. So black it was. But this dress was somewhat…nunnish.

She grabbed the phone and hit Faith's number. "Do you possibly have anything I can wear tonight? Something black?"

"Sure! I bet I do! Hang on, let me check my closet. You know what? Why don't you come over instead? I can help with your hair and stuff."

And so it was that ten minutes later, she was standing in Faith and Levi's bedroom, staring into her sister's closet. "How many black dresses do you have, anyway?" Honor asked.

"Um, six? No, seven. The problem is, half this stuff will be big on you, and a pox upon your house for that."

Right. Faith was curvalicious. Honor was not.

"This one? No. That's even big on me. How about this one? Nope, never mind, it's cotton. Not formal enough. This one? Um, nah. Too froofy for you. Oh, hang on! How about this one? I bought in a moment of self-delusion that, someday, I'd be a size smaller."

"You're perfect," said Levi from the doorway.

"Thanks, honey. You are definitely getting some tonight." Levi smiled, and Faith glanced at Honor. "Not that he's deprived, mind you."

"Glad to hear it," Honor said. "I'm really not, you guys are welcome to keep that to yourselves, but you're nothing compared to Prudence."

"I know. Did she tell you about make-your-own-sundae night? Honestly, she's ruined seven desserts for me. Okay. Levi, babe, get out. Honor, try this on."

The dress was long and sleeveless, high-necked but with a keyhole opening in the front. The black silk fell to the floor in a liquid rush, brushing against her skin.

"Perfection," Faith said. "I'm so good at this! Do you have shoes? Never mind. You don't. Here. Try these."

She handed Honor a pair of strappy black heels adorned with a sparkly decoration. "And let me do your makeup, what do you say? Tom's gonna die when he sees you."

"I hope not."

Faith dabbed foundation on Honor's cheek and started blending with a little sponge. "So Dad said something, and I'm not supposed to tell you, but here I go."

Honor frowned in the mirror. "What?"

Faith dabbed some more. "He's afraid you guys are rushing. He wants you to wait."

"I'm sure he does," Honor said, keeping her voice casual. "Maybe twenty years, like him and Mrs. J."

"Yeah, he'd probably prefer that." Faith laughed, then opened a peachy-colored eye shadow, held it next to Honor's left eye, then chose something else. "Don't take it personally. He didn't like Levi dating me, either. Close your eyes, hon. No, Dad just said that he wasn't…convinced."

Well, this sucked. Her family sensed the lie, apparently. "That's just Dad," she said weakly.

Faith paused. "Like I said, I think you guys are good together. And I do believe that, sometimes, love comes out of nowhere and hits you fast. But…you know, Dad does have a point. You just met the guy."

"I know," Honor said, her voice sharp. "But the years are precious, okay? I mean, I'm thirty-five, Faith."

"So?"

"So I'm not you," she snapped. "Men don't fall over

themselves for me. You know how many boyfriends I've had in the past five years? None, that's how many."

"I thought you were seeing someone last fall."

Ah, yes. In October, she'd told Faith there was a special man in her life. That was when she thought things were moving forward with Brogan. Honestly, how had she so misread the signs? "Well, I wasn't. So if Tom wants to marry me and if I'm gonna have a baby before I hit menopause, I have to get moving."

You tell her, sister, the eggs said.

"Easy, girl," Faith said, lifting an eyebrow. "I know what you're saying—"

"No, you don't, Faithie."

"—but it doesn't mean you have to settle."

"Settle for what? Tom is great!" she barked. "He carried me, okay? He carried me from Ellises' pond to your truck. He's great."

"He is," Faith said, putting her hand on Honor's. "And I really, really like him. But you don't have—"

"Look," Honor interrupted. "We can't all be like you and Levi. Tom and I are happy. We're...content. Okay? Please back off."

"Okay," her sister said. "I just felt like I should say something. I love you, Honor. Don't be mad at me."

The little sister shtick worked every time. Probably because it was sincere. Honor deflated. "I'm sorry. I know you're coming from a good place and all that."

"Any time you want to talk, I'm here, okay? Now, it's mascara time. This stuff is great. It takes days to get it off."

"And that's great?"

"Trust me. Your lashes will be amazing."

When Faith was done, Honor didn't look like herself.

She looked better. She looked kind of…gorgeous, really. Whatever Faith had in her magical basket of cosmetics gave Honor a luminous glow. Her cheeks were pink, her eyes smoky, lips with just a little shine.

"You're beautiful," Faith said. "You look just like Mom." She hugged Honor. "Now get out, because I have to get ready, and I think Levi and I might have a quickie—"

"What is wrong with my sisters?" Honor asked. "They don't keep anything to themselves."

"Hey, I was eavesdropping," Levi said, appearing in the bedroom doorway with Honor's coat and walking her to the door. "Sorry you have to go. See you at the party." He managed not to slam the door in her face.

Walking carefully in Faith's heels, Honor got into the car and drove home. It was time to get up to the Barn; she wanted to get there a little early to check on things, but not so early that Goggy and Pops, who'd doubtlessly been there since five, would pepper her with requests, such as *Can I have a small glass of water? Not too big, because I won't drink it all and don't want to waste any,* and *Why aren't you serving any raw herring?*

Tom and Charlie were waiting for her. "Hi," Charlie grunted.

"Hi, Charlie. You look very nice." He was wearing a navy blue sports coat—Tom's, no doubt, as it was big on the teenager. He'd washed off his eyeliner, and changed into black jeans that didn't look like they were meant for three people. His T-shirt showed a gravestone covered in thorns and a skeleton hand emerging from the soil.

But he'd tried—maybe because Abby would be there tonight, maybe because Tom made him. Either way, her heart tugged.

As for Tom, he looked…edible. He was checking his phone, so she had a moment of unadulterated ogling. Dark and dangerous and very European, in a black suit and black shirt open at the neck. No tie. He'd opted not to shave, and the two days' worth of stubble somehow made him look more sophisticated.

And he smelled so damn good, spicy and clean. Honor had a sudden, pulsating need to rub herself against him, like a cat.

But the air was thick with tension—he and Charlie must've had words, because Charlie was staring at the floor, looking almost literally bored to death. Tom was bristling with energy, and not the good kind. He glanced at her, then did a double take, but his expression didn't change. On the counter next to him was a glass of whiskey. His first (and last), she hoped. But no, he wouldn't drink too much with Charlie here. She was almost certain.

He picked up the florist box from the table. "For you, Miss Holland," he said, holding out her wristlet. He flashed that perfunctory smile, his fingers brushing the skin of her arm, and her knees turned to pudding, despite his blank expression.

"After you," Tom said, holding the door for her.

CHAPTER TWENTY-ONE

THE BLACK AND White Ball was raking in money. That was the good part. The reason for its existence, after all. On top of the ticket sales and raffles, an anonymous donor had given ten grand, which would put them over the top for their goal.

The rest of the night, however, was kind of sucky.

Honor's feet ached in the slutty heels, but she gamely ignored the throbbing as best she could, pressing the flesh of Marian White, the mayor, and the various members of the Conservation Trust, the big donors. Dad and Mrs. Johnson were out in their first appearance as a couple, Honor thought, and Mrs. J. looked quite lovely in a white dress. Dad cleaned up nicely, too.

The DJ was taking requests for twenty bucks a pop, all of which would go toward the cause. As a result, all sorts of romantic songs were rolling out as the DJ announced who'd dedicated which song to whom. "To Harley from Lana, 'Still the One'…to Victor from Lorena, 'Let's Get It On'…to Prudence from Carl, 'Love in an Elevator.'"

As for her own romantic state…who really knew?

Tom was wound tightly tonight, for reasons Honor didn't know. Every time she saw him, he seemed to be glaring at her, or watching Charlie, who was sitting at a table in the back, playing with his iPhone.

"I'm so bored," Abby said, taking a sip of her cranberry and seltzer.

"No, you're not," Honor said. "You're gorgeous, you're young, you have a new dress."

"I do look pretty incredible," her niece admitted.

"Abs, would you hang out with Charlie Kellogg?" she said. "He looks lonely."

"Sure!" Abby said. "He's a nice kid. Dork-tastic, know what I mean?"

"I do," Honor said, though her own experience with Charlie had been mostly silent. "Does he have friends at school?"

"Yeah. I think so. I'll go hang out with him. We can play Angry Birds."

Abby left, and Honor started off for a table so she could sit down and take some weight off her beleaguered feet. How Faith managed these shoes was a great mystery. "To Meghan from Steve, 'One More for Love,'" the DJ said. "Great song, guys."

"Honor! You look so gorgeous!" Jeremy Lyon gave her a kiss on the cheek, crazy handsome in his tux.

"Same to you," Honor said. "Hi, Patrick." Jer's significant other gave a small wave. He was adorably shy.

"So you're getting married," Jeremy said. "Will I be invited? Please? Pretty please?"

"Oh, sure," Honor said. "Of course."

Jeremy winked at her. "Let me know if there's anything I can do, okay?"

"Thanks, buddy. Now go dance, you two. Put these straight people to shame."

They obeyed.

"How you doing, boss?" Jessica asked.

"Good, good," Honor said.

"Anything need doing?"

"Nope. You look gorgeous, by the way."

"Thanks." Jessica wore a short white turtleneck dress that would look boring on anyone else. As it was, she looked like a Norwegian supermodel. Black shoes. No makeup. Simple and stunning, making Honor feel like she was trying way too hard.

"You're off the clock, Jess," Honor said. "Have fun, okay? Enjoy yourself, get a drink, eat."

"Will do. Hey, and you, too, okay?"

"Thanks. I will."

Nice to have someone looking out for her. Jessica went off to talk to Levi, her old friend. The woman had a way with men, that was undeniable. Maybe Honor should fix Jack and Jessica up. Then again, what did she know?

"Honor. You're beautiful."

Brogan. "Hey there," Honor said.

"To Paul from Liza, 'Someone Like You' by Adele!" the DJ boomed, and the song of perpetual misery and inability to move on wailed from the speakers.

"Looks like the night is a big success," Brogan said, an easy grin on his face.

"Yes, yes. We had an anonymous donation for ten thousand dollars," she said, glancing around for a sister. Nope. Never around when you needed one.

"Did you?" he asked, winking.

"Yes. Very—oh. It was you, wasn't it?"

"I believe it was anonymous," he said, his grin widening.

"Thank you." For some reason, Honor's heart felt thorny. Guilt money. Brogan was throwing money at her cause because he—

"Babe, there you are! Oh, hi, Honor. Don't you look nice."

"Dana. You, too." Dana wore a short, white lace dress that looked as bridal as could be. Her ring—the one Honor had so loved before she'd realized that antique was really more her style—flashed, and matching rocks winked from her ears.

"So where's this fiancé of yours?" Dana asked. "Did he come?"

"Oh, sure. He's here. Schmoozing, I think." Hopefully not drinking to excess or brooding in the back somewhere.

"How's his eye?" Brogan asked.

"It's good," Honor answered, her face prickling.

"Right! I heard you sent him to the E.R. Wow, Honor." Dana arched a silky eyebrow. "Impressive."

"She doesn't know her own strength, do you, darling? Here's your wine, by the way." Tom, thank God. He put a heavy arm around her shoulders, firmly back in the role of smitten fiancé.

Hey. She'd take it.

"So when is your wedding?" Dana asked.

"June 2, darling? Are we set on that date?" Tom asked.

"I think so," she said.

"Is that your ring?" Dana asked, seizing her hand. "Oh, wow! It's really cute. Brogan, isn't that sweet?"

"It's beautiful," he said. His eyes were...kind. Then he glanced at Dana, and his expression changed, and Honor recognized it immediately, having seen it on her own face for fifteen years, every time she was about to see Brogan.

Love. Slightly helpless, a touch confused, a dash

of vulnerable and a whole lotta happy. Brogan hadn't planned on falling for Dana, Honor could see it. It really had just happened…at least, for him.

"So we booked the Pierre," Dana was saying, "because Brogan knows the Steinbrenners, of course, and they do a lot of business there, so it should be pretty fab. But I have to admit, I'm a little nervous about meeting so many sports gods, right? I mean, like, Robbie Cano? At my wedding?"

"And who's that?" Tom asked. Honor felt like kissing him.

"He's the third baseman for the Yankees," Dana said.

"Second baseman," Honor and Brogan corrected at the same time.

Tom was looking at her. Flashed that adorable smile, though his eyes stayed somber.

"Heard you're quite a hero," came a voice.

"Colleen!" Tom said with genuine warmth. "My favorite bartender."

"My favorite Brit," Colleen returned. "Hey, guys. Everyone having fun?"

"Absolutely," Honor said.

"Who's your lucky date, Colleen?" Tom asked.

"My brother."

Tom laughed. "Ah. How uncomfortable for all of us."

Her laugh was big and hearty. "We're just friends, as the saying goes. So, Tom, there are no secrets in small towns, as you probably know by now. I heard you saved Honor from drowning. I won't lie. That's hot, Tommy boy."

"What?" Brogan barked. Dana's eyes narrowed.

"I wasn't drowning," she said. Tom raised an eyebrow. "But yes, he was very brave and heroic."

"Le sigh," Colleen murmured.

"Stop flirting," Connor said, joining their little knot. "He's taken."

"I know!" Colleen said. "I told you they'd be great together."

"Did you?" Connor said.

"Yes. I totally called that one. Don't you remember?"

"No." Connor gave Tom a long-suffering look. "I tend to ignore most of what she says."

"To your own detriment," Colleen said. "I know everything."

"What's eight times seven?" her brother asked.

"Everything except math." She grinned at Honor.

"What about us?" Dana said. "Did you call Brogan and me?"

An awkward silence fell like an undercooked cake. "No, Dana," Colleen said frostily. "Can't say that I did."

"I know. It took us totally by surprise, too." She smiled—too hard, Honor thought, and for a second, she felt a flash of pity. Dana was an outsider; here with Brogan, but without a…a gang, as it were. Drawing attention to herself, well, that was Dana's way of making sure she wasn't forgotten.

She was insecure. Funny. Honor had never noticed that before.

"I hope you guys will be really happy," she said, and Colleen sighed.

"Thank you," Brogan said gently.

"Yeah, thanks!" Dana chirped. "Babe, let's dance, what do you say?" With that, she pulled Brogan onto the dance floor and slid her arms around him.

"I hate her," Colleen said. "I need a drink. Conn,

come with me. I'm going to find you a date who's not your twin sister. See you later, guys."

Which left her standing alone with Tom. "Hi," she said.

"Hallo." He glanced around. "Shall we sit?" he asked, and her feet practically cried with gratitude.

He cared about her. She knew that. He may have even liked her.

But he didn't love her. All that shone from Brogan's eyes when he looked at Dana did not shine from Tom's. He was a tangled ball of emotions, Tom Barlow was, and whatever affection or attraction he felt for her was snarled in with disappointment and past heartbreak and possibly even some fear, then walled behind a six-foot cement barricade. The gentler, sweeter emotions were buried deep, flashing through only in times of duress, or loneliness.

Because Tom was a lonely man, and this acknowledgment made her feel a bit like crying.

"So," she began, but then Charlie was there, bounding up to Tom's side, his black hair flopping in his eyes.

"Tom, Abby said she might be interested in the boxing tournament," he said, and then those gray eyes did light up, and Honor's heart ached with the hope that flashed there, the helpless, hapless love he so obviously carried for this boy who was never his stepson.

Dang it.

She was in love.

"Listen," Abby said. "I *might* be interested, but probably not. I'm enough of a pariah with boys, okay?" She flopped down in the chair next to Honor.

"Yeah, right," Charlie said, blushing furiously.

"Charlie, you have no idea, because you're so nice,"

Abby said easily. "But seriously. My uncle is the police chief. My idiot brother shows my fat naked baby
pictures to anyone who comes through the door. Dad
glares at every boy in town, and no one can forget the
fact that my mother came to a school concert dressed
as a Hobbit."

"Then being a kick-ass boxer can only help," Tom
said, glancing at Charlie. "Right, mate?"

"Yeah! Totally!" Charlie said. He sat down next to
Tom, and Tom's eyes met Honor's.

This was why he was with her, Honor Holland, perpetual wallflower and old baseball glove. Because of
Charlie.

Here she was again, in love with a man who didn't
love her back.

"Another dedication, folks," said the DJ. "To Dana
from the man who can't wait to be your husband,
'You're Having My Baby' by Paul Anka."

"Oh, my *God*," Abby said. "Honor, aren't you friends
with that guy? Make him stop."

"Yes, darling, please do," Tom said.

It was tacky, sure. Or maybe it wasn't, Honor
thought, watching Dana and Brogan dance, looking
very much like a bride and groom. Maybe it was sweet.
Dana's face was red, and she was smiling…nervously,
maybe aware of how icky it was, having a guy announce
your pregnancy via an incredibly sappy song.

Brogan, though, looked as if they were the only two
people there.

Suddenly, the idea that Honor would be pregnant
one of these days, that she and Tom would be a happy
or even just contented couple seemed as far-fetched
as winning the Nobel Prize in physics. That being a

mother, a wife, having a family of her own, was just not going to happen. Her throat tightened.

When she glanced back at Tom and the kids, Tom wasn't there. Abby was showing Charlie something on her phone.

Dad and Mrs. J., however, were approaching, as well as Goggy and Pops. "How are you?" Dad asked, sitting down next to her. "Having a good time? You look so pretty, Petunia!"

"This party is wonderful," Mrs. Johnson said sternly. "You have done a magnificent job, Honor dear."

"I didn't care for the shrimp," Goggy said. "I prefer herring."

"Yet you ate seven of them," Pops observed, getting an elbow in the ribs from his bride.

"Where's Tom? I haven't seen you dancing together," Dad said, feigning a casual air. "Everything okay with you two?"

"Oh, you know how it is," Honor said. "I have to be in charge and all that." A lame excuse. Surreptitiously, she looked around for Tom, hoping he wasn't at the bar.

At that moment, the Paul Anka song ended (thank you, Jesus), and there was some anemic applause. "Another dedication, folks, this time for our chairperson tonight, Honor Holland—"

Uh-oh.

"—from her fiancé. Kind of a strange song choice, but he insisted it was her favorite. 'Paint It Black' by the Rolling Stones." The opening chords twanged, and Honor closed her mouth.

"I love this song!" Abby exclaimed. "Cool, Honor! I didn't know you liked the Stones!"

As Mick Jagger started bewailing the grim state of his soul, all eyes swiveled to Honor. "Uh…" she said.

"Why does he want to paint the door black?" Goggy asked, frowning. "Red is a much nicer color."

"Hallo, darling," Tom said. "Shall we dance?"

He was already singing along, already dancing there in front of her, and wow, he was bad. Looked a bit like Faith when she had an epileptic seizure, albeit a bit more energetic. "Come on, darling!"

He grabbed her hands and yanked her out of the chair, towing her onto the dance floor. Oh, dear God. She caught a glimpse of Faith laughing, and Colleen, too, and Levi shaking his head, grinning. Tom was jolting around her with complete abandon, singing with his countrymen at the top of his lungs, grinning so that his eyes crinkled, off-key and…and…completely adorable.

Then Abby grabbed Charlie's hand and pulled him out on the floor, and he began jumping up and down, Abby much more graceful. Tom grabbed Honor's hand and spun her around, and as Mick despaired that he'd ever be happy again, Tom wrapped his arms around her and kissed her soundly on the cheek.

Levi and Faith were on the dance floor now, and Pru and Carl, Connor and Colleen, and Tom stepped on Honor's foot and she didn't care one bit.

The night had just turned fun.

Tom was sweaty and ridiculous and utterly irresistible. His crooked smile made him go from knee-weakeningly hot to dorktastically goofy, and honestly, if he would smile at her like that every day, she'd never ask for another thing.

Except his love. And his baby.

Screw their arrangement. She wanted his heart.

Tom was almost sorry when the ball ended.

"This was fun," Charlie said as they pulled up in front of the Kelloggs' house. "See you, guys."

Tom almost choked in surprise. Two entire sentences, unprompted. Polite sentences at that.

"Great having you along, mate."

"Thanks for coming, Charlie," Honor added. "And thanks for dancing with Abby."

He smiled. Charlie Kellogg actually smiled. Crikey, it had been a *long* time since Tom had seen that.

They watched to make sure he got inside okay, and then Tom pulled away from the curb and drove the short distance to their place.

Now that they were alone, they didn't talk.

He'd made her smile. Laugh, even. Rather saved the day, in his own humble opinion, which was the least he could do, given that she'd worked so hard on this night. He'd bet that tomorrow morning, people would be talking more about Honor and her strange Brit than about Brogan and his viperous little fiancée and the bun in her oven.

He'd seen Honor's face when the other couple was dancing. He knew that face, that helpless, confused look. He'd seen it in the mirror often enough when he was with Melissa, after all. Perhaps he should've been jealous, but instead, without a lot of thought, he found himself doing something to change her mood.

He pulled up in front of their house. Odd, that—their house. Home. He got out and slid across the hood of the car so he could open her door before she did. Another smile, making him feel like he'd won the Irish sweepstakes.

"Miss Holland?" he said, offering his hand, and she

took it. Didn't let go, either. Then again, she was teetering a bit in those heels. Which were quite slutty and evocative. Wouldn't mind seeing her wearing those and nothing but, all pale skin and—

"Thank you," she said. "For the song."

"What's that? Oh. Sure, it was nothing." He let go of her hand and unlocked the door, causing Ratty to awake from her coma and begin hurling herself against the door.

"Honor," he began. "For what it's worth, I think Brogan's a right prat."

Her eyes flickered. "What exactly does that word mean, anyway?" she asked, fiddling with her bag.

"A wanker. An idiot. An idiot wanker."

She gave a small smile. "Oh. Gotcha. I appreciate that."

"You were the most beautiful woman there tonight." Bloody great. Next he'd be quoting Nicholas Sparks.

She gave him a dubious look. "Thanks."

"I mean it."

"Look, you don't have to—"

He was kissing her then, the cool night air wrapping around them, her dog thudding against the door from the inside. Her mouth was sweet and soft, and he pressed against her, because if he had to stop, it might ruin him. His mouth moved to her throat, his teeth scraping, crushing her against him, and he couldn't get enough; he'd do her on the porch if she—

"Tom?"

He pulled back, his breath uneven. Waited.

Her eyes were soft and huge. "I just…I don't want to do anything stupid."

He smoothed a wisp of hair behind her ear. "Does that rule me out, then?"

She gave a shaky laugh.

He was throbbing for her, every beat of his heart telling him to get her inside and naked and fast. "Come to bed with me, Honor."

Her breath shuddered, and her hands fisted in his shirt. She still didn't answer.

"Please," he added in a whisper.

That did it. She stood on her tiptoes and wrapped her arms around him, and then her mouth was on his, thank you, God. Without breaking the kiss, Tom fumbled with the door, and when they managed to get inside and Spike bit him on the ankle, he found that he didn't even care.

Up in the bedroom, they fell onto the bed, and Tom kissed her like his life depended on it, because that's how it felt. Then he unzipped her dress and pulled the silky fabric off her, following its path with his mouth.

He left the light on.

And her shoes.

CHAPTER TWENTY-TWO

EVERYTHING HAD CHANGED.

Okay, actually nothing had changed, except that she and Tom were sleeping together. As in doing it. Every. Night. And sometimes first thing in the morning, too.

Life was good. Life was meltingly, sweetly, achingly wonderful, in fact. She wasn't faking it anymore. This was the real thing.

For fifteen years (fine! seventeen years), Honor had been in love with Brogan Cain. There was no denying that fact. But with Brogan, she always had to work so hard, always putting forth her best face, never impatient or irritable or even just quiet. She turned herself inside out trying to match him, to be the most fascinating, smartest, funniest person she could possibly be, somewhat terrified that Brogan, who flew all over the world and photographed some of the most famous people on the planet, would realize she was not nearly as interesting as he was.

But Tom seemed to like her just as she was.

The other night, tired from a happy lack of sleep, she'd fallen asleep on the couch, waking up to find him looking at her from the other end, her feet in his lap, Spike curled on her shoulder. And his face, while not smiling, had been decidedly…interested. Then he'd crawled on top of her, setting her dog on the floor with only minimal hostility from Spike, unbuttoned her shirt and slid his hand under her skirt, like they were naughty teenagers necking on the couch.

And over coffee the other morning, when she told him about the new sales incentive program and the contest to name the latest vintage, he'd asked some questions, remembered what she said last week on the same subject and hadn't seemed bored at all. Seemed rather charmed, in fact. Then he kissed her and wished her luck and grinned as he left, taking her heart with him.

So yes, things were different.

As for his feelings, well, maybe it would take a little time for him to fall in love with her, for that locked-away part of him to hand over the key.

For now, she was happy. Happier than she'd ever been.

WEDNESDAY AFTERNOON, SHE stopped by the gym to see Tom's boxing club, which had morphed from a self-defense class into a boxing class for high schoolers who seemed to enjoy all sorts of medieval torture like push-ups and running stairs. Tom was sparring in the ring with a giant boy, both of them wearing helmets and gloves, but when he saw her, he came over, all testosterone-riddled, muscular, sweaty delicious alpha male.

"Don't you dare touch me, Rocky Balboa," she said, hoping like hell he'd disobey, and he did. Grabbed her and pulled her against him and kissed her full on the mouth, a hot, soft, killer kiss, until the kids had groaned and complained. A cheeky grin and he headed back into the ring, leaving her feeling like she'd gone a few rounds herself, rather dizzy and weak, Down Under clenching with lust.

"You're Tom's fiancée, aren't you?" a stocky woman asked. "I'm Dr. Didier, the principal at the high school."

"Oh, hi," Honor said. "I'm Abby Vanderbeek's aunt. We've met before."

"We have? Cool. So Charlie's doing great, isn't he? He's come a long way."

"Yes," Honor said. It seemed to be true. At dinner on Tuesday, he'd answered a few questions, hardly chatty but not quite so furious anymore. And he had quite a few good moves, Honor thought, watching him demonstrate a combination of hits and pivots on the heavy bag.

"All right," Tom called. "So for this tournament, which is in three short weeks, mates, I've got Abby, Charlie, Bethany, Michael and Jesse all signed up. Anyone else? Don't worry about your experience level, they take beginners far worse than you lot. Anyone else? Yes, Devin, good girl! Brilliant! I'll see you all on Friday, then, yeah? Now get out, your parents are waiting."

Tom bounded over to her again. "I've got to run Charlie home. Will you be around?"

"I have to go to my grandparents' house," she said. "Still trying to purge." A drop of sweat ran from his jaw down his neck, and she had to resist the urge to lick it. Huh. Imagine that. She was a nasty, dirty girl. *About time,* the eggs said.

"Tell me about it," she murmured.

"What's that, darling?"

"Oh, nothing. Hey, I forgot to mention it, but we have this thing tonight at Blue Heron. A family thing." She paused. "So I hope you can come. Charlie, too."

"Sounds fun. Though I did have plans to cook dinner for you tonight."

Oh, sigh. Not only could he shag like a friggin' Olympian, he cooked for her. "You can still cook for me." *If you take me to bed first, that is.*

He grinned as if reading her mind and went back to the kids, and Honor headed out of the gym and up the Hill.

Dad was at the Old House, listening as his parents gave closing arguments as to why they didn't need a downstairs shower.

"We didn't even have running water when I was a boy," Pops said. "We don't need a second bathroom!"

"I don't know why everyone's having a problem with me going up the stairs twenty times a day," Goggy added. "If this old fool would up and die, I could move into his room."

"You'd mourn me, woman," Pops said. "Your life would be an empty shell."

"Try me. Oh, Honor! Honey! How are you, sweetheart? You look exhausted."

Oh, I am, Goggy. Uh-huh. That's right. She cleared her throat. "How are you guys?"

"Your *father* thinks we need a downstairs shower."

"So do I," Honor said, kissing her grandmother's cheek.

"I have a perfectly good bathroom upstairs," the old lady said.

"She has a perfectly good bathroom upstairs," Pops echoed.

"You can't make us have a better bathroom," Goggy said.

"We hate better bathrooms," Pops added.

"Okay, you two," Honor said. "You're making Dad's life a living hell. He's getting married again, he doesn't want to have to come over here five times a day to see if either of you is lying in a pool of your own blood."

"So? Don't come over, then," Goggy said. "I'm just your mother. I didn't mean to be such a burden. I thought that three days in childbirth would've—"

"And I'm getting married, too," Honor interrupted. "And Jack is useless, as everyone knows. So let's talk about what we can do to keep you here safely, or maybe think about spending winters in Florida."

"Death's waiting room? Are you crazy?" Goggy sputtered.

"Do I look like I want to go to Disney World?" Pops said.

Honor looked at her grands. "Look," she said. "We love you. We don't want you to go anywhere. The best way to stay in this house is to make a few changes here and there."

"You think we're old," Goggy said.

"Mom," her father said, "you *are* old. Not decrepit, but old. I'm old. I'm sixty-eight."

"I *know,* John. Since I spent three days in childbirth with you."

Dad sighed and closed his eyes.

"Okay," Honor said. "I have a list—"

"Of course you do," Pops muttered.

"—of things that should be done. There are seventeen things on this list. How about if we pick five to get started?"

"Two," Pops said.

"None," Goggy said

An hour and twenty-three minutes later, after presenting an argument that would hold up in front of the Supreme Court, Honor had coerced her grandparents into agreeing to two of the seventeen changes. A stair-chair and a new furnace so they wouldn't die of carbon monoxide poisoning. "Fine," muttered Goggy. "But I won't use that silly chair. That's for old people."

"You *are* old, Elizabeth," Pops snapped.

"And you're older!"

Dad roused himself from where he'd been sitting with his head in his hands. "Okay, let's get going. We have the sowing ceremony tonight. Honor, sweetheart, walk with me to the New House. Mrs. J. and I haven't seen you much this week."

"You bet," she said. "See you up there, Goggy. Behave yourself, Pops."

She walked the short distance between houses with her father, the shrill, sweet sound of peepers rising from the pond. In another hour, it would be full dark.

"How are things with Tom?" he asked.

"Great, Daddy."

Her father looked at her thoughtfully. "I wasn't sure about him," he said. "Not at first, anyway. But he seems like a good guy."

"He is," she said.

"And you love him? Are you sure?"

Finally, she could look her father in the eye. "I'm sure."

Dad put his arm around her shoulders. "You look just like your mother when you smile," he said gruffly. "Now this doesn't mean I'm dying to give you away, you know. You can stay with Mrs. Johnson and me forever, so far as I'm concerned. You and Tom both, if you want."

"Oh, I don't think so, Daddy."

"You two kids should take the house, and Mrs. J. and I will stay in her apartment. It's perfect for two, and you and Tom will be having babies soon enough. Right? I'd love more grandchildren. Besides, the New House is where you belong.

She smiled. "I'll talk to him about it."

Because that image of her and Tom, and a kid or two…it was a lot easier to picture these days.

An hour later, as the sliver of the new moon rose on the horizon, every member of the Holland family, plus Tom and Charlie, gathered up near the cemetery.

The sowing ceremony took place on the rise of the first new moon of April. The origins of the ceremony were unclear, but tradition was tradition.

Tom came up next to Honor, smelling of soap from his shower, and kissed her on the cheek. Abby and Charlie were snickering, Levi was on the phone with his sister, growling to her about something, then passing the phone to Ned (and not looking too happy about it, either). Pru and Carl had their arms around each other, Goggy was fussing with the refreshments, which were laid out on a blanket in the back of Dad's red pickup truck. She tut-tutted as Mrs. Johnson tried to help, and Mrs. J. tut-tutted back. Dad and Jack were talking pH levels in the latest batch of Riesling, and Faith sat on the ground next to Mom's headstone, her face dreamy and sweet.

"So what's this about, then?" Tom asked.

"It's a blessing for the crops," Honor said. "We've done it for generations."

"Gather around, everyone," Pops said, and the family made a semicircle around the little cemetery. Pops stood a little straighter and took Goggy's hand. "All right, then," he said. "As father, grandfather and great-grandfather—

"And as mother, grandmother and great-grandmother," said Goggy. "We welcome you tonight."

"De liefde van God zij met u." the rest of them chorused.

"That means 'God's love be with you,'" Honor told Tom and Charlie.

"Tonight, we ask for God's blessing on the year to come. We pray that the rain will fall softly on the fields, that the sun will shine warmly, that the food we grow will provide for our family, this year and in all the years to come."

"Amen," they said.

Goggy handed the first bottle of wine to Pops.

"That's a wine we make only for the family," Honor explained as Pops wielded one of his many corkscrews. "We call it the blessing wine and only use it for weddings, christenings and the sowing ceremony."

Tom glanced at her, and she felt a prickle of heat in her cheeks. They'd be drinking the blessing wine again soon, both at Dad's wedding, and then again at theirs.

And maybe, in a year or so, at the christening of their baby.

"Cool," Charlie said, watching as Pops deftly uncorked that bottle, then two more.

"First we take a drink, then pour some on the ground," Honor explained as Pops took the first drink. "That way, we honor the family who came before us, and the soil that provides for us now."

"Lovely," Tom said. "I wish my dad could see this. He'd love it."

"Maybe next year," she said, and he flashed that grin.

Oh, yes, she loved him so much her heart hurt in a wonderfully sharp ache.

Faith passed the bottle to her, and Honor took a sip. Funny, all the ceremony over the opening and aeration of wine, assessing the bouquet and texture, the myriad flavors…but not tonight. Tonight, they chugged from the bottle, and it was the wine Honor loved most of all, sweet and smoky. One swallow, one slosh on the ground, a little prayer for the well-being of her family. And Tom. And Charlie.

She passed the bottle to the boy, who'd be her unofficial stepson, too, soon enough, whatever her real title might be. He gave Tom a questioning look; Tom nodded, and Charlie took a little sip, grimaced, then swallowed and poured some wine on the ground.

"Good job," she said. He smiled back at her, then passed the bottle to Tom, who did his part.

When everyone had had a sip, Pops took a box of matches from his shirt pocket and lit the fire Ned had laid earlier that day. As the wood began to crackle and the fire bathed all their faces in a warm glow, Tom took her hand. "I'm very glad I met you, Miss Holland," he said.

The words were ordinary; the feeling anything but.

"Tom, darling," Goggy said, "you have to do one thing for us. Since you're the newest member of the family."

"Wouldn't that be Charlie?" Abby said with a wicked grin.

"Well, Charlie *and* Tom, then," Goggy said. "Here you go, dears."

She passed them a plate. "What is that?" Charlie said. "Oh, man, you gotta be kidding me."

Honor grinned. "It's tradition, Charlie. Newest family members and all."

"What is this, love?" Tom asked, tilting his head to look at the traditional Dutch dish.

"It's raw herring and onions," Honor said. "Eat up, boys." Ah, the Dutch. Who else loved what was essentially cat food? She herself hated herring; just the sight of it made her stomach flip. Faith shared the sentiment and gave a subtle dry heave.

"You know, I'm not technically part of the family," Charlie said. "Tom's marrying you, but I'm kind of unofficial here."

"Not in our hearts," Abby said sternly. "Eat it."

"It's only horrible the first twenty years or so," Ned added.

"What are you talking about?" Goggy demanded. "It's wonderful."

"You first, mate," Tom said.

"Just take a little nibble, son," Dad said. "You don't have to eat the whole thing."

"Someone has to," Faith said. "Tom. Be a man."

Charlie held up the bony fish. "Oh, God," he said. Closed his eyes and took the smallest bite possible, just a scrape of the teeth, gagged and manfully forced it down his throat. "It's…good," he wheezed, tears coming to his eyes. "A little strong, maybe."

"Good job!" Pops said, clapping him on the back. "Tom? Go ahead. Finish it up, son."

Tom looked at Honor. She raised her eyebrows and

smiled. "For you, my love," he said, and, much to her horror, picked up the fish and bit it right in half, the bones crunching. His face contorted, and everyone laughed. He chewed, swallowed and then ate the other half. Dear Lord.

"Now *there* is a man," Mrs. Johnson said approvingly.

"Good job, babe," Honor said, taking the plate from him. Blick. The smell was wretched. Poor Tom. Time to get to the real food—the casseroles and ham and pies.

"Not so fast, darling." Tom jerked her back to him. "How's about a kiss?"

"No! Don't you dare!" She broke away from him and ran behind Levi. "Officer, help me. That man has fish breath."

"Far be it from me to come between a man and his wife," Levi said, stepping away.

"We're not married yet," Honor shrieked, dodging and laughing as Tom chased her. She bolted for the nearest row of grapes. "And we won't be if this keeps up. Daddy, help me!" Her traitorous father merely laughed.

"Go get her, Tom!" Pru called, and sure enough, he caught her arm and spun her around.

"Darling? Don't you love me anymore?" he said, his sweet, crooked smile flashing.

Then he kissed her, herring breath and all.

And you know, it really wasn't so bad. Her family gave a cheer, and Honor felt him smile. Then he kissed her again, and hugged her. "This is lovely," he said, his face growing more serious. He tucked some hair behind her ear. "Thank you for having us."

"Come get some real food, you two lovebirds," Goggy sang. "Did I mention that I always knew they'd be perfect together?"

CHAPTER TWENTY-THREE

On Saturday, Tom cornered Honor just after her shower. Little was more appealing than a woman wrapped in a towel, her skin damp and pink. Lose the towel, and life would be perfect.

But his unofficial stepson was waiting. "Want to come out with Charlie and me?" he asked.

"Sure," she said, and he watched as a flush spread into her cheeks. "Where are we going?"

"It's a surprise."

They stopped at Lorelei's and got sandwiches and iced tea from the sunny owner, then picked up the lad and headed north. Charlie was plugged into his phone, listening to music, but he wasn't sullen, Tom thought. Just a teenager. He had Spike in the back with him; the dog reserved her animosity for Tom and seemed quite content to sprawl on Charlie's leg in exchange for a belly rub.

The boy's face was changing, Tom thought as he glanced in the rearview mirror. He'd lost the softness of a little kid, and his bone structure was becoming more pronounced. His freckles had faded, and his eyes were more observant.

He looked a lot like Melissa.

Someday, he and Honor might have a baby in the

backseat there with Charlie and Spike. A car seat, a diaper bag, a knapsack, all that.

The image made his hands a little sweaty. But that was the deal, was it not?

Besides, he liked kids. He could handle a baby.

It was the family part that made him nervous. Perhaps not nervous in a bad way, though.

Speaking of family, he'd spoken to his father again this week. He should get Dad to move over here. Since he'd be staying and all.

"All right, darlings," Tom said, pulling off the highway. "Three guesses as to where we're going."

"Brigham Airfield?" Charlie asked as they passed the sign.

"Genius," Tom said. "Thought we'd take little project of mine out for a ride." He turned onto the airport road, and ten minutes later, they were standing in front of the Piper.

"So what did you do to it?" Charlie asked.

"We put in a bigger engine, modified the wings, adjusted the rudders. The owner wants to do some stunt flying."

"Cool."

The plane looked quite cheery. Tom walked around, explaining the preflight check, the different parts of the plane, and much to his surprise, Charlie seemed to be listening—no headphones, no sullen staring. When he was done, Tom opened the door. "Charlie, mate, up here. You're my copilot."

"You have your pilot's license?" Honor asked.

"I do. But I don't fly too much, so hang on tight." He winked at her, and she smiled, her dimples flashing.

In the cockpit, he showed Charlie which controls did

what, checked the switches, valves and the rest of it, then radioed the tower and started the engines.

It was a bumpy ascent, though not too bad. Everything felt worse in a little plane, of course, and Charlie was a bit pale. But once they'd gotten level, the kid was glued to the view.

"This is awesome," he said.

Below them spread the soft green hills of western New York, the lush fields and red barns, thick forests and the occasional white steeple. The sky was utterly clear today.

"What happens if a Canada goose flies into an engine?" Charlie asked.

"We pray," Tom said.

"Do you ever watch those airplane disaster movies?"

"As a matter of fact, no."

"There was this awesome flick last year," the kid said, then launched into a rather disturbing description of the plot. Tom glanced at Honor. She was smiling.

Something moved in Tom's chest.

"All right, Charles, you ready to fly this little darling?" Tom said. "All you have to do is keep a steady hand here, right? Nice and level, hands at ten and two, just like in a car."

"I don't drive," Charlie said, his voice a little panicky.

"I'm right here," Tom assured him. "You can do it, mate. And if you like it, we'll get you a pilot's license. You can fly before you can drive. Ready? The controls are yours."

Granted, he wasn't about to let Charlie do anything stupid or risky; the kid had a lot less control than he knew, but the expression on his face was priceless. Somber, focused, and then, miraculously, he flashed Tom a smile. "Am I doing okay?"

"You're brilliant, mate."

Tom took the controls back after ten minutes or so, then circled the plane out so they could see Lake Canandaigua, the nearest of the Finger Lakes. The water was cobalt blue this morning. "That's where we'll have a picnic," Tom said, pointing to a field below.

"Are we gonna land on the water?" Charlie asked.

"No, no. This isn't a water plane. The engine's too heavy. But they do have amphibious planes that land on both, right, Honor?"

"Absolutely," she said. "There's a fantastic water plane show in June on Keuka. We'll have to go."

A short time later, they were back on land, in the field Tom had shown them from the air. The lake shimmered, and birds wheeled and sang. They ate their picnic lunch, the sun warm.

If someone had told Tom two months ago that he'd be on a picnic with his fiancée and Charlie, and that Charlie would be speaking to him, Tom wouldn't have believed it. A night like the sowing ceremony, the solidarity of the Hollands, the history and closeness, the welcome for him and Charlie…Tom wondered what he'd done to deserve it.

Charlie was lying on his back, and Tom did the same. Honor, too. A few fat clouds drifted by; Honor murmured that there'd be rain by tonight, and she should know. There wasn't much she didn't.

He looked at her, her short blond hair ruffling in the breeze. She'd been quiet today, popping in with a comment here or there, but mostly watching the two of them, as if understanding that this was a momentous day.

Today, the old Charlie was back. Well, not really. There was no going back, Tom knew that. He knew that Melissa's death had changed her son irreversibly. But the boy Tom had always imagined he'd be—smart, friendly, focused, decent—that kid had shown up today, even without Abby to impress.

A lot of that had to do with Honor.

In all this time, she hadn't once complained about Charlie's manners, sullenness, stomping, refusal to eat, slamming of doors. She never rolled her eyes, never expressed anything other than pleasure when he came over, never sighed or muttered. She'd given him a family, a friend in Abby. She even seemed to like him.

Tom reached out and took Honor's hand. Kissed it, and watched as her eyes grew soft.

Two hours later, after one of the best days of Tom's life, he dropped Honor off, kissed her briefly on the mouth and said he'd be back in fifteen minutes or so.

"She's nice," Charlie said as they pulled away.

"Yes," Tom said. He glanced at the boy. "Feel like being my best man?"

"Seriously?"

"Yeah."

Charlie shrugged. "Okay."

It was enough. It was more than enough.

Tom pulled up to the Kelloggs' house.

A dark blue, vintage Mustang was out front, and for one second, he felt like he'd just been hit with a particularly brutal uppercut, right under the chin.

Charlie was out of the car in a blur. "Dad!" he yelled. "Hey, Dad!"

CHAPTER TWENTY-FOUR

MITCHELL DELUCA GOT out of his car in an unhurried manner, smiling as Charlie ran into his arms. Tousled the boy's hair and glanced at Tom.

Tom got out, his heart thudding sickly against his ribs. Stuffed his hands in his pockets and walked over. "Hello."

"Hey. Mitch DeLuca, Charlie's father. Nice to meet you." He offered his hand.

"We've met," Tom said.

"Oh, yeah?"

Nope, he was sincere. "I was engaged to Melissa."

Charlie looked between the two of them. "It's Tom, Dad. Tom Barlow."

"Right! Dude, sorry. Good to see you again." Mitchell gave Tom a baffled look—*So why exactly are you here?* Then he turned to his boy, and the resemblance between them was a little shocking. Yes, Charlie looked like his mum…but he looked a lot like his father, too.

"How are you, son? It's been a while, hasn't it? You're getting to be as tall as me."

Charlie smiled proudly, and Tom felt it like a knife to the chest. It had taken two entire years for Charlie to smile at him, but Mitchell…Mitchell got to see that right away. No resentment toward Mitchell, no indeed.

"What's new, pal?" Mitchell asked.

"Um, I'm may be getting my pilot's license. And I'm in this boxing club? There's a tournament in two weeks, and you should come!"

"Maybe. Let's get going, okay? Your grandmother isn't exactly thrilled to see me, know what I mean? Wanna grab something to eat, sport?"

"Sure! Yeah, of course!"

Mitchell glanced at Tom again. "Uh, listen, I'm gonna spend a little time with my son, okay?"

Tom nodded. "You do that." He looked at Charlie. "Talk to you soon, mate."

"Mate?" Mitchell smirked. "Yeah, that word has different connotations here, pal." He shot Charlie a look. "Am I right, buddy?"

For a half second, Charlie looked conflicted. Then he glanced at his father and smirked. "Yeah. I keep telling him that." He rolled his eyes. "It's kind of gay, Tom."

Ah.

"See you soon," Tom said, but Charlie was already talking to Mitchell, awash in happiness over seeing his father. Then Mitchell, the deadbeat, neglectful, selfish bastard, slung his arm around Charlie's shoulders and led him to the Mustang.

Charlie didn't look back.

It doesn't mean anything, Tom told himself.

Unfortunately, he knew better.

HONOR'S PHONE BUZZED with a text. Had to go to Wickham. See you sometime tonight.

That was...odd. Terse. Then again, texts were all too easy to misinterpret. She hit Call and waited. Tom's voice mail came on.

You've reached Tom Barlow. Leave a message, and I'll call you when I'm free. Cheers.

"Hi, Tom, it's Honor," she said, wincing. Hopefully, he knew her voice by now. "Just wanted to make sure everything was okay. I guess you're working? Um, let me know if you want dinner. Or we could go to O'Rourke's or something, if you were in the mood. Anyway, today was really great." She paused. "Have a good rest of the afternoon. Bye. See you later. Talk to you soon." *Hang up the damn phone,* the eggs said, peering over their reading glasses as they knit.

She hung up.

He's blowing you off, they observed with sympathetic certainty.

"No, he's not. There is no evidence of that," she said.

But by nine o'clock that night, the evidence was pretty strong.

What had happened? After a magically perfect ten days, when it had felt like something shifted, like that cement barrier had come down, the wall was suddenly back. No phone call. One text to say, Don't think I'll make it back for dinner.

She mentally reviewed the day. Four hours with Tom and Charlie. Had she said something? Was Charlie okay? Had Charlie said something like *Don't marry Honor, I hate her?* Because, quite frankly, she thought the kid might like her.

Screw it. She grabbed her phone, then put it down. Considered a text, typed a few words, deleted them.

Spike scrabbled against her calf, and Honor bent over and picked the little fluff ball up. "Any ideas?" she asked the doggy. Spike flopped on her back, offering her belly, and Honor idly rubbed it.

She watched TV for an hour—*The Mysterious World of Pork-Borne Illnesses*. Wondered idly if she had a tapeworm and, if so, could she eat unlimited amounts of Ben & Jerry's Cinnamon Bun. When her phone rang, she lunged for it, earning a bark of protest from Spike. "Hello?"

"Hey. It's Dana."

Honor jerked in surprise. "Hi."

"How are you?"

Spike yawned, already bored. "I'm fine. How are you?"

"You sound blue."

"Nope." The days of mood discussions had ended some time ago. "What can I do for you?"

Dana was quiet for a minute. "I don't know. I called on impulse."

Not every friendship was meant to last forever. Honor knew that. It didn't mean you couldn't miss the old times, even knowing those old times couldn't be repeated.

"How are things with you?" she asked.

"They're fine."

"You feeling okay?"

"Sure. Why?"

Honor paused. "Um, just because you're pregnant."

"Right. No, I feel the same. Normal. I mean, everything's normal." Dana paused. "So you and Tom were pretty funny at the Black and White Ball."

"I guess so."

"He seems…great." There was an odd note of yearning in Dana's voice.

"He is," Honor said. There was silence on the other end. "So why are you calling, Dana?"

"I don't know." She sighed. "You ever worry that Tom might find something out about you, and not like you anymore?"

Fungus. She didn't want to have a relationship talk with Dana. Dana, who pretended not to know how much Honor had loved Brogan. Who'd blindsided her and dismissed her feelings.

But maybe Dana had been right about those feelings. After all, Honor now firmly believed she was in love with Tom, her walled-off, funny, delicious Brit.

"Not really," Honor said hesitantly. "I don't know that there's anything to find out. That he doesn't know already, I mean."

"I probably shouldn't be calling you to talk about this stuff," Dana said, her voice small and sad.

"Yeah, it's a little weird."

"You were always a good friend."

The words brought an unexpected lump to Honor's throat. "Thanks."

"And I wasn't."

"Is that an apology?"

Dana sighed. "Yes."

"Accepted."

"So are we friends again?"

Honor smoothed the scraggly fur on top of Spike's head. "I don't know."

"You just said you accepted my apology." Already, there was a defensive note in Dana's voice.

"I really enjoyed our friendship," Honor said now, carefully. "But I'm not sure we can go back to that."

"But I just apologized! And I think you know that's not easy for me."

"Right. But…" She hesitated. "Dana, you have to realize—"

"Look, I'm going through some *stuff,* Honor, and people screw up, and I'm sorry! Are you going to hold this against me for my whole life?"

"No," Honor said. "I'm really over it. But I just don't—"

"You can forgive, you just can't forget that I dared to get the man you wanted. You know what? Forget it."

"Dana—" Nope. She'd hung up.

And that was just fine with Honor. Dana was demanding, selfish and always managed to give herself carte blanche when it came to her dealings with other people. She was always the wronged party, and never at fault.

While life had felt emptier without her friendship for a while, it also felt cleaner. Other people had filled the space Dana and Brogan had left.

She had Tom now. Didn't she?

The silence of the house was deafening.

Where was he? What happened today? Was she really going to have to call Levi and see if there'd been any accidents?

Spike yawned, then began gnawing on Honor's thumb.

The door opened, and Tom walked in. Unsteadily.

"Hey," Honor said, rising to her feet.

"Hallo, darling," he said. He put his wallet on the hall table and missed.

"Have you been drinking?"

"Yes."

"And driving?" she barked.

"No, darling. I'm not a bloody idiot, am I? No, I

drove stone-cold sober from the college to O'Rourke's and then had a drink. More than one. And then I walked home to our pleasant abode to find my affianced, adorably concerned."

"I *was* concerned. Why didn't you call me?"

"Sorry. I should have. Hindsight and all that. But here I am all the same." Spike jumped off the couch to growl. "Hallo, Ratty," Tom said. "Careful, I'd hate to step on you." Spike took the laces of Tom's shoes in her teeth and whipped her head back and forth.

The phone rang again. Honor answered it. "Hey, it's Colleen. Just wanted to make sure Tom got home okay. Connor took his keys."

"He's here and fine," Honor said. "Thanks, Coll. And thank Connor for me, too."

"No prob, hon. He's a sweetheart, your Tom. See you soon!"

She hung up the phone. "I thought you were going to cut back," she said.

"And I have," he said. "Three drinks is hardly pissed, my sweet little Puritanical nag. Nor is four."

"Connor O'Rourke had to take your keys."

"No, love. I gave him my keys on the minute possibility that I might have a fit of idiocy and decide to drive." He certainly sounded sober. "Now, I'm going to bed, darling. Care to join me?"

She didn't answer.

"Right. Good night, then."

With that, Tom gently shook Spike free and went upstairs, leaving Honor standing in the middle of the living room, surrounded by the quiet once more.

CHAPTER TWENTY-FIVE

It HAD BEEN five days since the return of Mitchell De-
Luca, and Tom was losing hope.

Mitchell was staying in a motel down near the Laun-
dromat. Aside from four lunches in three years, Charlie hadn't seen his father at all since Melissa died. Two
trips to McDonald's, one to Pizza Hut and one to Wen-
dy's. And now, for some reason Tom did not trust at all,
Mitchell was here, all parental interest after fourteen
years of essentially ignoring the boy.

It was bloody awful. Honor knew something was off.
If he could've talked about it, he would have, but the
words stayed jammed in his throat. Admitting that he'd
lost Charlie, now, after all this time...well, shit. It felt
like those words would crack him in half. He wanted to
hold her, take her to bed, bury himself inside her, but
instead, he was brittle and jolly and fucking exhausted.

Charlie hadn't wanted to see him on Tuesday, their
usual night together. That was understandable, Tom told
himself. The kid only got to see his idiot father once
every year or so—or less—and naturally, he'd want to
spend whatever time he could with Mitchell.

"Is Charlie coming over?" Honor asked.

"His dad is visiting," he answered, turning a page in
his magazine. Which magazine, he couldn't quite say.

"Really." She frowned. "How are you doing with that?"

Such an American question. And she didn't want to know. "It's fine." Such a British answer.

She didn't ask any more questions.

On Thursday, the boxing club met, and by the time it rolled around, Tom was climbing the walls. He had to go up to Blue Heron after this and take a look at the bottling system; John Holland had asked him to check it out, being an engineer and all. And Tom recognized it was a way of Honor's dad showing his approval, which he'd instantly revoke if he knew just why Tom was marrying his daughter.

But, of course, he'd said sure. He imagined taking Charlie up, maybe having a nice family dinner chez Holland with his future in-laws, give Charlie the chance to remember that he was part of that clan, as well.

But Charlie wasn't at boxing club. Apparently, he hadn't been in school, according to the other kids. "All right," he said. "Start running laps. I've got to make a call. Ten times around, mates."

He went over by the heavy bags and called Janice. Yes, Charlie had taken a day off from school to go to a car race with Mitchell.

"Do you think it's a good idea, Janice?" Tom asked. "Letting him spend so much time with his father?"

"Of course it's a good idea," Janice snapped. "How could it not be?"

"Because Mitchell has a habit of disappearing on the kid, that's why."

"So? This time, maybe it's different." There was the telltale rattle of ice cubes. "Charlie's older now and not such a pain. Maybe he'll want to go live with Mitchell."

Jesus. He clenched the phone a little harder. "Janice, you can't be serious."

"Why? We already raised our child, Tom. We never signed up to do it again."

"I *asked* you if I could take custody of Charlie, and you said—"

"And you're not his father, are you? You're just some guy my daughter slept with for a few months."

A solid body blow, right in the lungs. "Thank you, Janice."

"You know what I mean. Listen, I have to go. Talk to you soon, Tom."

The remainder of class seemed to take hours.

When Tom was packing up his gloves, his phone buzzed with a text. Charlie.

Can't do the tournament next week. Sorry.

Tom hit the call button. Thank God, the boy answered. "Charlie, it's Tom."

"Yeah. I know. Your name comes up on the screen." The too-familiar tinge of disgust lay heavily over the words.

"Listen, mate, don't drop out."

There was a long pause. "Yeah, well, the thing is, it's not my thing. Boxing and whatever."

"I thought you liked it." There was a hateful pleading note in his voice.

"Not really."

There was music in the background, and a lot of voices, too. "Where are you?"

"With my dad."

"Can I see you? Talk to you in person?"

"Why?"

"Because, Charlie, you've put a lot of time into this. And the rest of the club will miss you."

"Whatever. I'm still quitting."

Tom rubbed the back of his neck. "Can I talk to your dad?"

An exhausted sigh was his answer. "It's Tom," Charlie said, and there was a muffled laugh in the background.

A second later, Mitchell's voice came on the line. "Mitch DeLuca here."

"Mitchell, listen, um…I've been coaching Charlie on boxing, and he's really—"

"Yeah, he says he's kind of bored with that, and I don't believe in making kids do something they don't want to."

Oh, so he had a child-rearing philosophy now, did he? "He wanted to very much until you came to visit. I'm sure that if you encouraged him—"

"He's a teenager, not a baby. He can make up his own mind."

Tom scrubbed the back of his neck with his hand. "Look, I think it's great that you're visiting, and I know how much Charlie loves you."

"This is sounding very gay."

"Mitchell, he's been really struggling since Melissa—"

"Dude, I don't need some stranger telling me how my son is doing, all right? I don't get to see him as much as I'd like, but we have an unbreakable bond. Right, bud?"

"Sure, Dad." Tom could hear Charlie in the background, could practically see the hope on the boy's face.

"And why *don't* you get to see him that much?" Tom asked, his voice hardening. "I've always wondered."

"Not that it's any of your business, dude, but things may be changing."

Ice knifed through Tom's stomach. "Mitchell, if you're going to be a part of his—"

"Like I said, not your problem. Hanging up now. Bye. Mate."

And that was that.

"Hey." Tom looked up from the phone. Levi Cooper stood in front of him. "Everything okay?"

Tom shoved the phone into his bag. "Everything's brilliant."

"You up for a few rounds?"

"I am indeed," Tom said, and, climbing into the ring, proceeded to put a beating on the town's police chief.

Six rounds later, Levi held up his gloves. "Enough. You're gonna kill me if I keep going. And if you kill me, my wife will kill you."

The rage still broiled in Tom. But shit, he hadn't meant to go quite so hard on Levi, who seemed like a decent guy. "Sorry."

"No, it's fine." He gave him a long look, and Tom looked away. "You wanna grab a beer?"

"No. But thank you."

"All right. If you change your mind, give me a call."

"Thanks, Levi."

In the locker room, Tom took a long, steaming shower, his rib cage sore. Levi might've thought Tom was going to kill him, but that hadn't stopped the cop from landing a few significant blows himself.

He got out of the shower and pulled on clean clothes.

Six o'clock. The day was endless, as if the hours were swimming through sludge.

His phone rang. *Janice,* the screen said. He answered it fast.

"Oh, Tom. Hi. Listen, I know you'll be upset to hear this, but Charlie just got home and guess what? He's moving to Philadelphia to live with Mitchell, and Walter and I are thrilled. I think it's for the best, don't you? What's that, Walter? Oh, Tom, I have to go. Talk to you later, I guess."

She hung up.

He could follow, of course. He had before.

But that was before Mitchell had decided he was interested in his only child. It was one thing to get Janice and Walter to let him spend time with Charlie. Mitchell wouldn't. While it seemed that Charlie had been miserable with the Kelloggs, he certainly wasn't when he was with his father.

No. Tom couldn't pretend that Charlie wanted him around. For a few short weeks, maybe it had seemed like he had. Boxing club, the Hollands…Tom himself— none of that compared with a father's love, apparently.

He should be glad for the kid. After all, Tom knew what it was like to have an absentee parent. It was just that he fucking hated Mitchell DeLuca, and not because of what had happened with Melissa. Well, sure, that was partly the reason. But more than that was the fact that Mitchell had broken Charlie's heart, had walked away from that little boy whose mother had just died, because it hadn't been convenient. Left him in a pit of tarry black grief, and only now that Charlie was finally a little bit happy, did Mitchell want to swoop in and have some quality time.

But Charlie didn't see it that way, and it was probably time for Tom to acknowledge that he'd lost the war.

Charlie was leaving.

Tom's heart sat like a chunk of dirty ice in his chest. He'd done what he could do for Charlie Kellogg. Tried to do right by the son of the difficult woman he'd loved. Maybe it had been worthwhile, despite how it seemed, but one fact seemed starkly, coldly true.

He was no longer required.

Tom bent to tie his shoes. Didn't quite make it and found himself sitting with his head in his hands, the silence in the locker room underscoring the hollow in his chest.

Mitchell was going to crush Charlie. Again. Or he wouldn't. He'd take the kid away to a transient life of car racing and bars and school truancy and tattoos in questionably hygienic places. Charlie would never eat a vegetable again in his life. He wouldn't go to college. He wouldn't be forced to take hikes and participate in after-school clubs. He'd play Soldier of Fortune and Call of Duty and become fat and careless, and he'd barely remember some guy his mother had slept with.

Tom wasn't Charlie's father. He wasn't even Charlie's stepfather. He was an idiot who didn't know when to quit, who didn't know his place, who rented a house and taught at a fourth-rate college, lived an ocean away from home and was about to commit fraud, just to be near a kid who wasn't even his.

And what *was* his, exactly?

Nothing.

The bass from the music in the gym thudded through the walls.

Nothing.

But maybe—perhaps—someone.

Someone with gentle brown eyes and a way of listening and not passing judgment. Someone who was waiting for him to see what was right in front of his face.

With that thought, Tom grabbed his bag and strode out of the building.

CHAPTER TWENTY-SIX

"IT'S SO TRAGIC here," Goggy pronounced loudly, causing a herd of scowls to stampede over the elderly faces at Watch and Whine. "All these people, like sore-covered dogs dropped off at the pound."

"It's beautiful here. I wish they'd lower the age restriction so I could move in," Honor said, pouring wine into the last glass.

"We'd love to have you," Mr. Tibbetts said to her boobs. And hey, God bless him. She could use a little ego boost, given that she'd apparently taken on old baseball glove status with Tom this past week.

"Okay, people, our movie's about to start," she said, forcing some good cheer into her voice. "Help yourself to some merlot, please note the bloodred color and sit back and enjoy Alfred Hitchcock's masterpiece, *Psycho.*"

Sue her. She'd run out of wine-themed movies. Also, this little flick suited her mood. The patrons of Rushing Creek didn't seem to mind; this movie had come out in their day, after all.

Spike was dozing on the ample bosom of Emily Gianfredo and looked too comfortable to be removed. Honor sat down and tried to watch the flick.

"It's the son," Mildred announced as Janet Leigh

drove toward Bates Motel. "He killed his own mother and kept her body. He dresses up in her clothes."

"Thanks for ruining it," grumbled her husband.

"You've seen this! You just forgot. We saw it with the Merrills when it first came out. You remember, at the theater before it burned down?"

"I'd rather have someone stab me than live here," Goggy said, sniffing.

More wine? asked the eggs. *Thanks, I'd love some,* Honor mentally answered, and poured herself a second glass. The day called for it.

Once again, she was in love with someone who didn't love her back. Once again, she'd managed to tell herself a pretty little story with butterflies and Lindt chocolate truffles and a devastatingly wonderful man who adored her but just didn't quite know it.

And, she sensed, once again she was about to be dumped.

Something had happened with Charlie, that she knew.

That ten days (ten and a half) after the ball had been…everything. Tom had brought her flowers one day (and yes, pathetic female that she was, she saved a rose petal, because dang it!—no man had ever brought her flowers before, if you ruled out Dad). He pressed her against the wall and kissed her till her knees wobbled, and they did it on the kitchen table. The kitchen table, people! Come on!

The sowing ceremony with her family…had she ever even pictured being the woman chased by her honey so he could steal a kiss? No. She hadn't. Then, the day of the plane ride, the culmination of everything. For a little while, it had felt so perfect that the air itself shimmered. They'd been a family, a couple and their teenage son, biology be damned. And when Tom had kissed her hand and smiled at her, there'd been something in his gray eyes she hadn't seen yet.

Peace.

And maybe a little love, as well.

I believe that's called wishful thinking, said the eggs, their eyes glued to Anthony Perkins as he peered through the knothole. *Is there any popcorn?*

"Oh, no, she's getting in the shower," Mildred observed. "Honey, don't do it! He's about to kill you!" Honestly. It was like watching a movie with Faith.

"I can't see," Margie Bowman said. "Juanita, why did you get that perm? Your head is too big now. Sit in the back next time."

So far as Honor could tell, there were two possible scenarios for the future. One, she'd marry Tom and live in pathetic hope that he'd come around. Have a baby if she was lucky. Yearn for Tom to love her. Gradually adjust to the fact that he didn't, or couldn't. Work out a divorce when the time came. Move back in with Dad and Mrs. Johnson and raise her child, always a little melancholy to see those pieces of Tom Barlow in him or her, always blue when Tom came to pick up the kid for Wednesday night dinners and every other weekend. She'd come to Rushing Creek and do Watch and Whine and gradually add her own aching knees and lactose intolerance to the list of complaints. Send her child off to college and move in here and talk to her shriveled ovaries, the eggs long since committed suicide.

Two, see above, minus the kid.

"Anthony Perkins would've made an attractive

woman," Frank Peters said as Norman Bates killed the detective. "He has nice eyes."

"My mother had that same dress," murmured Louise Daly.

When the movie ended, Honor turned up the lights, wincing at the sight of Victor Iskin and Lorena Creech making out in the back row. Emily handed Spike back. "She's an angel," she said.

"Thanks, Mrs. Gianfredo," Honor said. "It's true," she murmured to her dog. "Hey, where's everyone going? We still have the discussion." Pathetic, that she'd rather stay here than head home to face the tension there.

"Sweetheart, the Girl Scouts made grape pies for their baking badges, and we don't want to miss out," Goggy said.

"We? Are you eating here? What about the food poisoning?"

"That's different," Goggy said. "This is the Girl Scouts. They'd never poison me. Your grandfather is meeting me here, so you go along. Tell that handsome Tom I said hello."

"Okay," Honor said. She waved as the Watch and Whine audience tried not to trample one another in their rush to get to dinner.

With a sigh that she couldn't suppress, she put Spike in her bag, stood up and started packing the movie projector.

"Honor?"

She startled, banging into the cart, and Spike barked, then whimpered. "Brogan!" Honor said, clearing her throat. "Hey. How are you?"

"I'm okay," he said. "I called your office. Ned told me you were here."

"Yes. *Psycho*. Part of the movie club."

He gave a ghost of a smile. "Do you have a second?"

His face was drawn, jaw tight. She glanced around; the auditorium was empty even of Victor and Lorena now. "Sure. What's going on?"

Brogan ran a hand through his thick hair. Bent down to pet Spike, who really only resented Tom, come to think of it, then straightened up again. "I'm really sorry to do this to you, On. It's just…" His voice broke. "It's just that you're my best friend, I think." He swallowed.

The wine and cheese had yet to be cleaned up. "Um, want a glass of merlot? It's really nice. Velvety texture, currant and blackberry jam overtones, dark chocolate and tobacco in the finish."

He smiled, more genuinely this time. "Thanks, On. You're the best."

That was true. She got him a glass and sat down, glancing at her watch. Six o'clock. Tom would be done with the boxing club. She wondered if things would be easier at home tonight. Kind of doubted it.

"So what's up?" she asked. Her dog had already curled up on Brogan's shoe.

"I did call you," he said. "Your cell phone was off."

"Yeah. The movie and all. I'm old-school."

He looked at her with those brilliant blue eyes. Much to her surprise, they were filled with tears. "Dana's not pregnant."

Without thinking, she reached out and gripped his hand. "Oh, Brogan, I'm so sorry."

Poor Dana! A miscarriage, just when—

"She never was."

Honor's mouth opened. "What?"

Brogan covered his eyes with one hand. "She lied, Honor. This morning, she told me she thought she might've had a miscarriage, and so I rushed her into Jeremy's office, and she was being all weird and resistant and stuff, and then she didn't want me in the exam room, and I was freaking out, you know? I wanted to take her to the hospital, but then Jeremy asked me to come into the room, and she told me. She never was pregnant."

"But…did she think she was?"

"No."

"Why would she lie about that?"

Brogan shook his head. "She said I put all this pressure on her and she maybe thought for one day that she *was* pregnant, and then she kind of ran with it because I was so happy. So we had this huge fight, and I just don't know what to think."

"Wow," Honor breathed. "I'm really sorry." She paused. "Where did you leave things?"

"I don't even know," he said, his voice shaking. "I mean, can I marry someone who'd lie like this? Should I? And, On, the thing is, I really wanted to be a dad."

She squeezed his hand. "I know how you feel." She paused. "I really want kids, too."

"I hope you and Tom have a bunch," he said, trying to smile at her.

Oh, poor Brogan!

"I guess you need to talk things over. Maybe cool down a little," she said.

He nodded. Then, abruptly, he covered her hand with his and held it hard. "You know what I wish, On?" he said. "I wish I'd fallen in love with you. I wish it so much."

"Gosh. Thanks."

"No, I mean it." His eyes were brimming. "You and I, we're perfect for each other. I don't know what was missing. We like the same things, we can talk for hours, and with Dana, maybe it's just sex. Just a primal, physical reaction. All we do is screw—"

"Okay, that's probably too much information, big guy. Listen, I'm really sorry about all this, but I think you should be talking to Dana."

"I've always loved you, On."

She took a breath. "I seem to remember being compared to Derek Jeter's old glove. Anyway, you're upset, and—"

"Maybe I just didn't appreciate you."

"Yes, that came through loud and clear."

"But I would now. Especially after being with Dana. I can't believe she lied to me! I told everyone I knew, Honor! Everyone! You'd never do something like that!"

Honor sighed and extracted her hands. Patted Brogan's knee. "Look, Brogan, you've had a big shock, and I'm really sorry. But you have things to work out, and I should go."

"I love you. I really do. We've stayed friends for a reason, after all. Maybe we should give it a chance."

"This is so uncomfortable. And you don't mean it."

"I think I do." With that, he leaned forward, hesitated and kissed her.

She could've stopped him. Maybe she just wanted to see if he still had any hold over her. Maybe it was just years of reflex, accepting whatever affection Brogan had seen fit to bestow. Maybe her brain was just too slow to react. Whatever the case, she kept her mouth firmly closed, and didn't feel anything at all. Well, no, that wasn't true. When she'd been in seventh grade, she'd practice-kissed the cement pole in the church basement. It felt rather like that, a cold nothingness.

Brogan pulled back. "See?" he said.

"Hallo, darling."

And then she did feel something, oh, yes indeedy.

Tom's face was dangerously calm. That face, which could convey more in the quirk of an eyebrow and the slightest smile, had nothing on it now, and Honor felt ice wrap around her heart. "Hi," she said. "Um, how are you?" Great question.

"Didn't mean to interrupt. Your phone was off." His eyes were as cold as the lake in December.

"Listen, man, I'm sorry you had to see that," Brogan began.

"Not at all. It was quite educational." He looked at her for another beat, but his eyes were blank. "Right." With that, he turned to leave.

"Tom," Honor blurted, "it's not what you think." Her heart was jangling in her chest, panicked and cold. "Tom, I—"

But he was gone, the door closing quietly behind him.

"I'm sorry, On," Brogan said. "I'm all messed up. I didn't mean to make trouble for you. Well, I guess I did, maybe. I don't know. I mean, I do care about you. Maybe it's for the—"

"Oh, shut up." She grabbed her purse and hurtled up the aisle toward the doors.

"On, what do you think I should do about Dana?" Brogan called.

"Figure it out yourself, Brogan! I have problems of my own."

But by the time she reached the parking lot, Tom was already gone.

CHAPTER TWENTY-SEVEN

TOM WASN'T HOME. Honor threw some food in a bowl for Spike and dashed back out, then ran back in, wrote a note that said "Please call me ASAP" and taped it to the front door. Called his cell. He didn't answer. She didn't blame him.

Should she go to Wickham? Better yet, maybe she could call before driving all the way up there.

"Dees ees Dr. Dragul speaking," came the voice. "How may I help you dees evening?"

"Oh, Droog, hi, it's Honor Holland. I'm looking for Tom. Is he there, by any chance?"

"Ah, Honor, how nice to hear your voice! No, I em afraid that Tom is not here, but I veel tell him you called eef I see him. I must talk to him myself, as a metter of fact, but I heff date tonight. A luffly young woman named Clarissa, and I feel very—"

"Good luck," she said, cutting him off. "Gotta run. Sorry, Droog. See you soon."

She bit her lip.

Okay, this was all very juvenile—she hadn't *really* been kissing Brogan—but her heart was pounding so hard she thought she might levitate. Tom would understand once she explained things to him.

She just had to find him, that was all.

Just then, her phone rang, making her jump so much

she dropped it, causing Spike to pounce on it. "Give that back," she said, pulling it free of her dog's tiny mouth.

"Hello? Tom?"

"Hey, it's Pru. When's your wedding again?"

"Um, I'll call you back."

"Fine. I'll just ask Tom. I meant to, but I was distracted when he took off his shirt. Those tats *do* something to me. I wonder if Carl would get one."

"Okay, I'll— What? When? Where did you see him?"

Prudence paused. "You okay? You sound weird."

"Where's Tom, Pru?"

"He's in the bottling room, fixing something for Dad."

"Talk later. Bye."

A few minutes later, Honor pulled into the parking lot of the vineyard. Tom's car was there.

Maybe he wasn't mad, after all. He was here, being a good almost-son-in-law. He probably understood. How mad could he be?

Very, apparently.

He was lying on the floor in jeans and a T-shirt, and Pru was right. It made a very nice picture indeed, her college professor gone all handyman on her. "Hi," she said.

He didn't look up. Twisted a wrench, undid a coupling, then sat up in one neat movement.

"I should explain what you walked in on," she said as he brushed past her. He didn't pause, just went down the stairs into the cask room, where some of the wiring from the bottling machines ran. Honor followed, twisting her hands.

She wasn't used to men being jealous. It was a freakishly new sensation, and not one hundred percent bad, if she was being honest. Seventy-five percent bad, sure. Twenty-five percent thrilling, in a guilty sort of way.

The cask room was dim, as always, even with the lights on, the hulking barrels standing guard on one side, the stone walls giving off their pleasant, limestone smell. Tom was already reaching up for a wire that laced under the floor of the bottling room and into the cask room's ceiling. He took a knife out of his pocket and stripped away the rubber sheath.

"Okay, here's the deal," Honor said, figuring he could at least listen. "Um, it's not what you think."

"Yes. So you said earlier. Funny, that phrase. Everyone uses it when trying to excuse their bad behavior."

She pressed her lips together. "I didn't do anything that can be construed as bad, Tom."

"Darling, just because you and I have a business arrangement doesn't mean I like it when you go off snogging your old boyfriends."

"We weren't—"

"Your mouth was on his, Honor. Looked like snogging to me."

A hot blast of irritation surged unexpectedly through her. "I'm not the type, Tom. I've never flirted with another woman's boyfriend. I've never littered, never broke the speed limit and I certainly never even entertained the idea of cheating on you."

"Really. So kissing the great love of your life—"

"I have to say, I'm a little surprised you noticed. Since you've been ignoring me this past week."

"Is that grounds for cheating?"

"I didn't cheat on you! I would never do that."

"It looked rather convincing to me."

"Maybe you could just listen."

"Why?" he snapped, yanking a wire down from the ceiling. "So I can hear how you accidentally kissed him? This is what you wanted, isn't it? Your best friend stole your man, and now you've got him back."

"No! That's not it at all. I don't want him back. I never had him to begin with, and honestly, he's very upset about something—"

"Poor lamb."

"And he kissed me! There's a difference."

"You sound bloody ridiculous." He yanked down some more wire and practically attacked it.

She took a breath. "You don't understand, Tom. I've been friends with him since I was nine years old, and I can't just—"

"I know the whole story, darling, and I certainly don't want to hear it again." His voice was cold and calm now, and he still wouldn't look at her.

"So you haven't talked to me in eight days, and now you won't listen."

"I believe I spoke to you this very morning."

"To ask if I wanted coffee. You know what I'm talking about. Something happened with Charlie, and you won't tell me anything. What kind of a relationship is that?"

"A business relationship. Remember?"

Irritation unfolded and grew. "You know what your problem is, Tom?"

"I love when women start a sentence that way. Please, go on, tell me."

"You've got this huge part of yourself locked away, and every once in a while, something shows through, and then you race to lock it away again, and I have no idea who you really are. And I think that's much more of a problem than stupid Brogan stupidly kissing me because he was upset with stupid Dana!"

Tom tossed down the wrench with a very satisfying clang. "And I happen to think it's a problem that every fucking turn of our relationship has come about because of something your Brogan has done."

"What?"

"You only met with me that first time because you were desperate to get over him. The first time you slept with me was when he told you Dana was pregnant. You agreed to marry me to show him you weren't mooning over him, and the night of that ridiculous ball, you slept with me again because you were heartbroken seeing them dance. And now the first chance you get, you let him kiss you. So yeah, I've got a problem. This is not what I signed up for."

"Oh, I'm well aware of that. A single U.S. female citizen willing to commit marital fraud was what you signed up for. We don't have an audience, Tom, so save the jealousy act, okay?"

Tom strode across the room, heading for the stairs.

No. Not for the stairs.

For her.

He grabbed her by the shoulders and kissed her, her breath leaving in a squeak of surprise. He pushed her against a giant barrel, his mouth hard and hungry and demanding, yes, yes, finally. His arms pulled her against him, his body hard as oak, and all the pent-up frustration of the past week burst out, and she kissed him back just as hard. Her mouth opened under his, taking as much as she was giving. He was hers, damn it. They belonged together.

His hands drifted down to her ass and lifted her against him, one hand groping under her skirt, and holy porno, it was hot and tawdry and wonderful. She wrapped her legs around his waist and buried her hands in his short hair, wanting him in an overwhelming throb, right here, right now.

It was hard and urgent and so, so good, his breath rasping out of him, the muscles in his shoulders bunching as he lifted her, and yes, she was so definitely that type.

When they were done, he stayed against her, which was good, given that her legs were water and Honor was positive she'd collapse if he let go.

Sex in the cask room.

Who knew she was that kind of slutty person?

We were hoping, the eggs said smugly.

Her legs, wrapped around his waist, were shaking. She pressed a kiss onto the side of Tom's sweaty neck, and it seemed to bring him out of his fog.

He stood up, smoothed her hair away from her face, his eyes on her mouth, rather than her eyes. Then he stepped back a little and pulled down her skirt, then buttoned his jeans. "Sorry," he said.

She sure as hell wasn't. "No apology necessary," she murmured, swallowing. A repeat performance, however, would be most welcome.

He turned away, rubbing the back of his neck. "No, I'm sorry, Honor. You deserve better."

"I don't think better exists."

He wasn't smiling. "I don't love you."

The words were like a slap, and yes, that did take some of the sheen off the moment. Tears stung at her eyes, and she swallowed.

"I wish I could. I'm sorry." He started to say something else—once, twice—but then closed his mouth. "I'm sorry," he said again, and with that, he went back upstairs and resumed fixing the bottling machine.

TOM WAITED TILL he heard Honor's car pull out of the parking lot. She'd been crying. *Nice, Tom,* he thought viciously. *Very fucking nice.*

He wanted to tell her what she needed to hear, but he couldn't. The truth was, not everyone gets saved. Not everyone becomes a better person. His mother didn't. She never came back, never made an effort once he turned eight. Melissa wasn't saved, didn't become a loving wife, didn't lose her restlessness. She left him, too, to take up with Mitchell.

It didn't seem that Charlie would be saved, either. The fact was, Tom wasn't going to get to find out.

And Tom's name could be added to that list, as well.

He knew what Honor wanted. He just didn't have it.

He'd failed with his mother, failed to win her attention and devotion, failed in somewhat the same way with Melissa, failed with Charlie after three long years of trying.

If he failed with Honor, what then?

This was not what he signed up for. Honor was supposed to be easy, a low-maintenance, pleasant companion. He wasn't supposed to want to beat the living shit out of her ex-boyfriend, wasn't supposed to lose control and take her against a rough wooden barrel, wasn't supposed to feel like kissing her feet out of gratitude for letting him. He wasn't supposed to have to worry that she might leave him for the wanker who rejected her, worry that she was settling for him, because of *course* she was settling for him. That was the whole fucking point.

Everything was wrong. It was just wrong. He didn't love her. Not yet.

And even if he did, he'd been shown again and again that his love wasn't quite enough.

What if she left him? What if she had his kid and left him, and instead of just Charlie, there'd be another child out there in the world that he loved and failed? What if Honor Grace Holland, who was everything her name implied, decided she wanted something different? He'd be ruined, even worse than he already was.

Two hours later, Tom was sitting in his classroom at Wickham. In his in-box was an email from Jacob Kearns, asking for a recommendation to the University of Chicago, where he was hoping to transfer for the fall semester.

The one good student Tom had. It probably didn't matter. Tom would be back in England, anyway, now that his reason for staying was moving to Philadelphia.

The door opened. "Ah! Tom! Vat are you doing, sitting here all alone! I thought you vould be home with dee luffly Honor! She called for you, did you know?"

"Droog. How are you?" Tom dragged his eyes off his computer screen to the head of his department.

"I am well, thank you, Tom! I think I have met Dee One, as you say. She is so…beautiful."

"That's great, mate. I'm glad for you."

"And I heff good news, Tom! Again and again, I petitioned dee board of dee college, and yes! You vill heff your vork visa after all!"

Ah, irony, always good for a brisk slap. A green card right at the exact moment when he no longer needed it.

HONOR WAS STILL awake when he got home, Ratty sprawled on her back on the cushion next to her.

"Hi," she said, lurching to her feet. On the telly was an X-ray of a woman with a metal hook in her eye, so it must be *World's Best Impalements,* one of those nasty shows she loved. He'd almost miss those. "Listen, Tom, I'd like to say something."

"I've some news," he said.

"Oh. Okay."

He took the remote and turned off the show. "The college has renewed my work visa."

"That's great!" Then his words seemed to register, because her face changed. "Oh."

"Right. Also, Charlie's moving to Pennsylvania with his father." The words, jammed in his chest for so long, came out in a surprisingly smooth rush. He looked at her dog. "So I don't…require you to commit fraud any longer." He paused, forcing himself to look back at her. "And I will always be tremendously grateful that you were willing to do so."

Her face was pale. "Are you breaking up with me?" she whispered.

"Yes. I'm sorry."

She swallowed, her throat working. "Tom, I— Look, I know what you said. That you don't love me, and I believe you. But I think you could, maybe. And I already lo—"

"Don't say it, darling."

She paused and pressed her lips together. "But I do. I love you. You're right, what you said before. We were getting married for other people and other reasons, but that's not true, not anymore, not for me. I'd still marry you, Tom. I'd take good care of you."

The words hit his dead heart and seemed to bounce right back off. "I'm sure you would, sweetheart," he said as gently as he could. "I'm not sure the reverse is true of me, however."

"I think it is," she whispered. "I think I'd be lucky to be married to you."

He went to her, and pressed a kiss on her forehead. "The fact is," he said in a whisper, "I'm all used up inside, love."

Two tears slid down her cheeks. "That's not how I see you at all."

"Which says more about you than it does about me, darling. I'm sorry."

He was.

And after that, there was nothing left to say.

CHAPTER TWENTY-EIGHT

Honor was living in the New House once again.

Oddly enough, her family had been stunned by the breakup. Even Mrs. J. and Goggy, who knew the truth, seemed stricken. Dad wanted to put off his own wedding, which Honor wouldn't hear of. Faith and Pru had come over to console her, but Honor was oddly calm, saying only that things hadn't quite worked out, and no, she didn't have hopes for a reconciliation. Jack offered to beat Tom up (not that Jack could, but it was a sweet thought, anyway), then stayed to watch *Emergency Amputations* with her.

The house was quiet with Dad and Mrs. J. in the apartment, where they intended to stay, despite the fact that there was roughly ten times more room in the New House. For the first time ever, Honor was living alone, at the ripe old age of thirty-five. In college and grad school, she'd always had a roomie. But now she found the solitude comforting.

This would be where she'd live forever, more than likely, Honor thought one night as she drifted from room to room. Faith and Levi wanted to stay in the Village. Pru and Carl had a great house on the other side of town, and Jack lived in a house he built a few years ago.

It was strange being back, surrounded by her parents' things. She'd lived with Tom for five weeks, and yet it had been hard to leave the little house. She waited till he'd been at work, and she went into his room once more, breathed in the smell of him and left her lovely engagement ring, so different from the one she thought she wanted, on the bureau.

Back to the New House, which had an air of abandonment about it, even if Mrs. J. still vacuumed twice a week religiously.

So if it was hers, it was time to make it truly so. After checking with Dad, Honor told her siblings to come over and raid whatever their father and Mrs. J. didn't want. Ned had an apartment in the Opera House apartment building where Faith and Levi used to live, so he took a good bit of furniture, and Abby claimed a few things for the future, as she'd be headed off to college next year. Pru and Carl had finished the basement and took a queen-size bed for reasons best kept (but not actually kept) private.

Then Honor broke out the paint, starting with her bedroom. What had once been pale blue became fire-engine red. Her sedate quilt was replaced with a fluffy white comforter that looked like a cloud, and an array of various-size pillows, which were instantly claimed by Spike. Had a chair reupholstered in big blue polka dots and put it by the window overlooking the big maple. A fluffy white rug, a dark mahogany cedar chest and, best of all, a mobile she found at the gift shop in town—little paper birds in a riot of color. She went to the used book store and bought two shopping bags full of romance novels and horror stories and fully intended to read them all.

No longer was this the bedroom of a spinster workaholic. This was the room of a woman who was, finally, comfortable with herself. Who could relax. Who appreciated some creature comforts. Who wouldn't mind shagging in that big mahogany bed.

The thought of shagging someone other than Tom, however, held no appeal.

But things would change. She wouldn't be alone forever.

Just for now. For a little while, and then she'd register on those dating websites again and find someone nice. Or she'd check out the sperm bank again. Or call an adoption agency. She wouldn't mind an older kid, even someone with an attitude. If she could win over Charlie, she could probably win over anyone.

Except for Tom, that was.

The eggs remained silent.

It was May, the month of apple blossoms and lilacs, and tourism season was perking up. The seaplane show on Keuka was coming, and there'd be a tasting on the green that weekend, too. Dad and Mrs. Johnson's wedding was next weekend, and after that, Honor had a sales trip to the city planned. In the meantime, tour buses pulled into Blue Heron's lot daily, and Honor and Ned led two tours a day each. Every time they came to the cask room, her heart would thud.

And though she tried so hard to be practical, she missed Tom so much she ached. Missed his crooked smile, his sudden laugh, his mouth, his soft gray eyes, his endless patience with Charlie, even the way he called Spike Ratty. She missed his accent, the way he called her *darling,* missed his big hands and irreverent sense of humor. Missed sleeping with him, not just for the sex (though yes, there was definitely that). But she also missed the sound of his breathing, the warmth of his skin, the way it felt to wake up with his heavy arm around her, the slight crinkling of his eyes when he was about to make a joke. Spike's little snores and propensity for hogging the pillow just weren't enough anymore.

Charlie was gone. Abby said she'd gotten a text saying goodbye. That was all.

On the fifteenth night of staying home, Honor was climbing the walls. Should she reorganize the bookcases in the living room? Cook? Bake? Eat? Watch *Plastic Surgeries Gone Wrong,* which was having a marathon tonight?

What would Mom advise?

These past weeks, when her heart felt bruised and weak, Honor missed her mother almost unbearably. Mom would've been brisk and sympathetic both, finding things for Honor to do, kicking Dad out of the room and sitting down with some pithy words of wisdom. She summoned her mom's memory as best she could, the smooth curve of her neck, the smell of her hair, her pretty, capable hands.

"What should I do, Mom?" she asked her mother's picture.

Get out and let the wind blow the stink off. It was one of her mom's favorite sayings, and the woman had a point.

Time to go to O'Rourke's. No more catfight talk; now she could answer the question of *What happened, honey?* with the line she had prepared—*We just weren't suited for each other in the end.*

Right up there in truthfulness with *I'm too busy for a relationship right now.*

Because Tom had felt pretty perfect to her. Not every day, no, and not at first. But now, she couldn't imagine loving someone as much as she loved Tom Barlow. She'd loved Brogan for years, sure, but that had been a childish love, one-sided and unrealistic. She'd idolized Brogan.

Tom, she knew. Flaws and qualities both. He was real. He was home, he was hers.

Or he had been. Almost.

Great. She was crying. With a sigh, she wiped her eyes and gave herself a mental slap.

"Spike, I'm leaving. If you eat my shoes, it will come out of your allowance, okay? Love you, sweetie." Spike wagged, then leaped up on the couch and burrowed under the throw pillow, her tiny head sticking out as if begging to be the cover shot on a calendar of Ridiculously Cute Dogs. Honor kissed her, scratched her little bitty chin and headed into town.

She opened the door to O'Rourke's, and there he was.

He was sitting at the bar, talking to Colleen, and he was smiling, though his eyes were somber. Didn't anyone else see that, how sad his eyes could be, even when he was smiling? Didn't they see that he was lonely? That his heart had been yanked out of his chest when Charlie moved?

Then he looked up and saw her, and his smile dropped a notch. She gave a small wave, and he nodded back.

The bar was noisy tonight, and Honor was grateful. The Yankees game was on and apparently was a good one, judging from the cheers from the patrons on that side of the bar. In addition, the fire department was having one of its famous meetings, which seemed to involve such grave activities as Jessica Dunn flipping quarters off her elbow. Brogan wasn't there, at least, though she'd seen his car at the firehouse the other day. Gerard Chartier whispered into Jessica's ear, and she rolled her eyes and slapped him fondly on the head before waving to Honor. Now there was a woman who didn't mind being single. See? It could be done.

Welp. Time to say hello to her ex-fiancé.

She took a breath and went over, her heart stuttering. "Hi, Tom."

"Hallo, Honor."

Oh, fungus. Would she ever get over the way he said her name, his voice low and rich as hot fudge? *Probably not,* the eggs said, rubbing Ben-Gay into their knees.

"How are you?" she asked, and by some grace, her voice was steady.

"Quite well. And yourself?"

"Just fine, thanks."

How's Charlie? Have you heard from him? How's your dad? Are you staying in town? Please don't move without saying goodbye. I think about you all the time.

"It's good to see you," she said, and this time her voice was husky.

This was a mistake. She shouldn't have come, because it seemed like she was about to cry.

"Hey, Honor."

She jerked her eyes off Tom to see who was speaking. "Oh, Dana. Hi."

Dana glanced between her and Tom. "Um, want to have a drink?"

Honor waited…for what, she wasn't sure. For Tom to say, *Actually, darling, I want to talk to you,* and then tell her he'd made a horrible mistake.

"Good night, then," he said, turning back to his beer.

"Take care, Honor." Maybe there was something in his voice, too, but his eyes were on the Yankees game.

"You, too." She followed Dana to a table and sat down with her back to Tom.

"I heard you guys broke up," Dana said, sitting down across from her.

"Yes."

"I'm really sorry."

The words sounded sincere. "Thank you."

Hannah O'Rourke brought over a martini. "On the house," she said, "courtesy of the owners of our fine establishment."

"Thanks, Hannah." Honor turned back to Dana. "So how are you? Um, Brogan and I talked a couple weeks ago." Brogan had emailed her a couple of times since the dreadful kiss, apologizing profusely, telling her about his confusion over Dana, yadda yadda.

He was a good guy. But Honor was a little tired of him these days.

"I guess everyone knows," Dana said tightly. "I faked being pregnant."

"So he said."

"Aren't you gonna ask why?"

"Why?"

Dana sighed. "I don't know."

"Sure you do."

Her perfectly waxed eyebrows rose. "Yeah, okay, so I do." She shrugged and took a sip of her white zinfandel (the very thought of which made Honor shudder). "Here's the thing, Honor," she said. "Men want what they want."

"Do they want women to lie about being pregnant?"

"Okay, fine, I guess I deserve a little bitchiness from

you. Brogan and I are still apart. Probably forever. As you probably know." She shrugged, the misery on her face belying her tone. "Maybe you have a chance with him, after all."

"I'll pass."

"Why? Isn't that why you and Tom broke up?"

"No." She didn't want to talk about Tom with Dana, that was for sure. "Did you ever love Brogan, or was this just…whimsy?"

Dana looked at the table. "I loved him. Who wouldn't?"

"Then why did you lie to him?" Dana shrugged, and all of a sudden, Honor was tired. "How about if I tell you what I think, hmm? From my point of view, there's only one reason why a woman would pretend to be pregnant, and that's because she wasn't sure the guy would stay with her otherwise."

A tear slid off Dana's face onto the table. "You're right. Congratulations. As usual, Honor, you know everything."

"What do you want, Dana?"

Dana's face crumpled. "It was so stupid," she whispered, still not looking up. "You ever feel…I don't know. Like you're on the outside, looking in?"

"Everyone feels like that sometimes."

"Well, me, too. Ever since I met you, you and Brogan were a thing. You had a special relationship, and he was so awesome and all that. And you had this big fun family, and such a cool job. And I was jealous. I mean, there it is. I was." She swallowed. "And I really did like him. I always did. But I wasn't about to make a move when you guys were together, even if it was kind of a fucked-up relationship."

"Gosh. Thanks."

"But then you broke up, and you were done with him. So yeah, I made a move. I mean, single men don't exactly grow on trees around here. And imagine my surprise when it seemed to work." Another tear plopped onto the table. "Men like to sleep with me, Honor. But men *love* you."

Honor snorted.

"Look at Tom. Right? He comes to town and boom. He falls for you."

"It's not exactly working out for us," she murmured.

"Whatever. There's not a guy here who doesn't respect you and like you and think you're smart. That doesn't happen with me. Brogan was one of the few who seemed to want more than sex. But you're right. I was afraid that the more time he spent with me, the less he'd like me, because that seems to be the way it goes. So I made up a baby, figured I'd get pregnant fast. I didn't think beyond that."

"I thought you didn't want kids."

"With him I did. Never thought I'd say those words." She wiped her eyes discreetly.

All of a sudden, Honor wanted to be truly done. For way too long, Brogan had been a huge part of her life, bigger than even he knew. And for the past few months, Dana had been, too.

It was time to end that.

"Listen, Dana," she said. "It *was* the wrong move, obviously. So own it, take responsibility for it and see where that gets you. I think Brogan really loves you. I don't know why, but he seems to. If you tell him what you just told me, I think you might have a shot."

Dana looked up, her green eyes watery. "Really?"

"Yeah. I'm gonna go now, okay? *Top Ten Tumors* is on."

Dana gave a snort of laughter, then grabbed her hand. "I'm sorry, Honor. I really am."

"It's really okay. Don't think about it anymore. And good luck with Brogan."

Strange, that she meant it.

"Honor?" Dana said. "Listen...I called Immigration on you. A while ago. I just wondered if you were marrying Tom because of a green card thing, and...well. I hope it didn't screw things up."

Ah. Mystery solved. "No. It wasn't that."

As she fished her keys out of her purse, she looked over to where Tom had been, but he was gone.

ON SATURDAY, HONOR decided to take a bike ride, because that's what people who had weekends did.

May was so beautiful, the fruit trees blossoming in the small orchard the family still kept. There was Goggy, hanging out wash, waving as Honor rode past the Old House. Tomorrow, hopefully, she'd sneak some crap to the dump—Pops's newspaper horde was taking on terrifying proportion, but that was tomorrow. Today was all about exercise and fresh air.

"We will be cheerful," she told Spike, who was nestled in the handlebar basket on a fleece blanket. "We are cheerful people, Ratty." Spike yipped in agreement. She loved bike rides.

Dogwood and crabapple trees were in full glory as she pedaled up Lake View Road to where the hill flattened out. She passed Bobby McIntosh mowing his lawn, and the smell of cut grass made her smile. Life was good. It wasn't entirely complete, but it was a happy life. This beautiful town, the job she loved, her family, her faithful little doggy…it was enough. For now, it was enough. More would come in its own time.

After a few miles, she pulled into a shallow parking area at the foot of the Keuka hiking trail, pushed down the kickstand and clipped Spike's leash on. "Come on, baby, let's take a walk."

Birds hopped and twittered in the trees, and Honor could hear the rush of water from a nearby stream. The sun was warm, the breeze gusted.

There was a bench up ahead, and a lovely view of the Crooked Lake. A familiar figure was sitting there, clad all in black. Spike went crazy, pulling on the leash, barking away.

"Charlie?"

The boy turned, then jerked his gaze back to the view.

"Hi. How's it going?" she asked, sitting next to him. Spike jumped up on the bench and wagged.

Charlie said nothing, but he extended his hand so Spike could sniff it, making the little dog whine in joy.

"Are you back for a visit?" she asked, wondering if Tom knew. God, it would mean the world to him if Charlie had come to see him.

"I'm back for good," Charlie mumbled. He picked at a hole in his jeans.

Oh, crap. She'd never met Charlie's father, but she had the sudden urge to throttle him. "I'm sorry," she said.

"Why? So my dad couldn't make it work. Big deal. It doesn't mean anything. What's it to you?"

"Does Tom know you're back?" she asked carefully.

He shrugged.

"Have you called him?"

"No, okay? Jeesh! Leave me alone."

"You should call him, Charlie. He cares a lot about you."

"I don't care! I don't care about Tom, okay?" Spike barked madly. "He's not my father. I never asked him for anything! I didn't want to learn how to box! I never *asked* him for that. He treats me like an idiot baby with those stupid model airplanes and presents, like he can buy me! Like I can't tell that he hates me!"

Yark! Yark! Yark! "Spike, be quiet," Honor ordered, scooping up the dog. The dog obeyed. She looked at Charlie and squinted. Teenagers. Attitude. Yawn. "So you're not a baby?" she said.

"No," he snapped.

"Then stop acting like one." Huh. Hadn't planned on saying that.

"What do you know about anything?" He kicked his shoe in the sand.

"A lot more than you, apparently. Tom has spent three years trying to stay in your life."

"I never asked him—"

"Shush. Now I know it must be incredibly hard to have had your mom die. My mom died when I was young, too."

"My mom didn't just *die*," he said. "She…left."

Honor softened. "I know, honey."

"And what if she wasn't coming back?"

"I bet she was."

"Yeah, well, you don't know that."

What was it about teenagers, that they loved thinking of themselves as the single most tormented individual on the face of God's earth? "From what I've heard, she loved you, and even if she went away for the weekend, I imagine she was coming back." Charlie said nothing, and Honor sighed. "Mothers do die sometimes, and it does suck, and you never quite get over it. I'm sorry it happened to you."

"Wow. Thanks, lady."

Oh, the attitude. "And I'm sorry your father is such a shit."

"He's not! He's not at all!" Spike barked again. "My dad is great."

"You want to be treated like an adult? Then you need to grow up. Open your eyes, Charlie. Your father breezes in and out of your life when he feels like it, then dumps you off at your grandparents' when he's got other plans."

"It's not like that."

"It's exactly like that, and pretending it's otherwise doesn't help you one bit."

Charlie opened his mouth to protest, then shut it, his eyes filling. He stuffed his hands in his pockets, looked at the ground. A tear fell on his black jeans. She put her arm around his skinny shoulders. "I hate you," he said.

"I'm sure you do. But, Charlie, Tom…Tom loves you. His whole life has been about you since the day you first met, and he was willing to marry a stranger just to stay near you."

Oops. Maybe shouldn't have mentioned that. Charlie gave her a sidelong glance. "What are you talking about?"

She ran a hand through her hair and sighed. "Wickham College wasn't going to renew his work visa, and to stay in this country—to stay near *you,* Charlie—he had to find someone to marry to get a green card. Me."

"I don't believe you."

"Fine. You don't have to. You can spend your time being bitter and hateful because your mother went away and died and your father is an ass, or you can acknowledge that there's a person who's loved you since the day he met you and moved heaven and earth and was willing to risk being sent to jail for fraud to be near you. Your choice."

He didn't answer.

She'd tried. Maybe she shouldn't have said what she did, but it was a little late for that.

Taking Spike's leash, she stood up to leave, then paused. "Do you need a ride home? I rode my bike here, but I can call my dad."

Charlie didn't look at her. "I'll walk home."

"I'll call your grandmother in an hour and make sure you got there."

He rolled his eyes. But he didn't protest, either, and after another beat, Honor left.

CHAPTER TWENTY-NINE

WHEN JANICE KELLOGG called, telling him in a whisper that Mitchell Kellogg had returned Charlie, Tom's fist clenched so hard around his coffee mug that it broke, and the red haze colored his vision.

"Can you take him for a few hours? He's killing us," Janice said. "Honestly, how did we get into this?"

"Of course," Tom said.

"We'll drop him off in ten minutes."

"Brilliant."

Tom's heart was roaring in his ears. A shard of coffee mug was sticking out of his palm, and without feeling it, he pulled it out.

That fucking Mitchell. Did he have really so little heart that he'd return his son, his boy, back to the Kelloggs like a dog who hadn't quite worked out being brought back to the pound? No, that wasn't fair. The pound had standards. They wouldn't let a person like Mitchell DeLuca take a vicious pit bull, let alone a lovely boy like Charlie. He'd been lovely once, at any rate. He was probably ruined now. How much could a child take, after all?

He cleaned up the broken mug and spilled coffee and bandaged his hand. Then the front door opened, and Charlie walked in.

"Hello, mate," Tom said as gently as he knew how.

The kid didn't even pause, just shuffled past, his horrible jeans dragging on the floor, the chain from his belt clinking, and went upstairs, ninety pounds of hate and misery. After a second, Tom followed.

Charlie stood in his room, looking around as if he'd never seen it before.

"I'm sorry about your dad," Tom said.

The boy turned and looked at him, his expression incredulous. Then he turned to the bureau, where the Stearman PT-17 waited, still unfinished, seized it in both hands and hurled it to the floor. It exploded, pieces flying everywhere, and Charlie picked up his foot and stomped on it, again and again and again, obliterating it, the crunching sound sickening, his screaming far worse. Then he ripped down the Manchester United poster, then flew to the nighttable, to the photo of Charlie and Melissa, and hurled it against the wall.

He tore the comforter from the bed, kicked the nighttable over and then, having run out of things to destroy, collapsed to his knees, the sounds coming from him soul-shredding, and then Tom was kneeling there among the shards of airplane, wrapping his arms around the boy.

"Get off me! I hate you! I hate you!" Charlie struggled against him, but Tom didn't let go.

"I'm sorry," he whispered. "I'm sorry, mate. I'm so sorry."

Charlie punched him, tried to wrench away, but Tom was bigger and stronger, and for once, it mattered. Charlie punched him again. "I hate you! I hate you! I hate you," he said, but the last one was just a sob.

He went limp, hoarse sobs shuddering out of him,

racking his whole body, and Tom closed his eyes and held him tighter.

"Why do you still love me?" Charlie choked out, and the words cracked Tom's heart.

"I don't know," Tom whispered, kissing the boy's hair. "I just do. I always will."

"He doesn't want me," Charlie said with a sob, and Tom's heart broke entirely.

"It's his loss." God, he wished he could do better, find the words that would heal this boy's heart. "I'm so sorry, Charlie, but I'm more sorry for him."

The boy cried and cried, and Tom didn't dare move, for fear that Charlie would lock himself in his room, or run away and never be found. He held him tight and shushed him and wished he could think of something more to do. But eventually, the sobbing tapered off.

"Don't you hate my mother?" Charlie asked, his face still hidden against Tom's shoulder. "She left you for someone else, and you got stuck with the kid she didn't want."

Tom pulled back to look at Charlie's face. The kid looked heartbreakingly young. "I think she really did love your dad, Charlie. She wanted to work things out so the three of you could be a proper family. I don't hate her. I loved her. And yeah, she hurt me and the whole bit, but that's life, mate."

"She was so stupid, texting when she was crossing the street. She didn't have to die."

"I know. But she didn't leave you, Charlie. She left me."

"She did, though. She and my father went off without me."

"For a weekend. She never would have left you for good. You were her best thing."

"Do you know that, or are you just saying that to make me feel better?"

"I know it." He looked into Charlie's eyes, ringed with smeared eyeliner. "I think the reason she stayed with me for as long as she did was because she thought I might be good for you."

Something flickered through Charlie's eyes. "Were you really gonna marry Honor so you could stay near me?"

"Who told you that?"

"She did."

Something squeezed his chest. "Yes."

Charlie mulled that over, then used his sleeve to wipe his eyes (and nose; honestly, boys were disgusting... he'd been the same way).

The boy was quiet for a long minute before he spoke again. "Tom?"

"Yes, mate?"

Charlie rubbed his eyes. "You know how you call me your stepson?"

"Yeah."

"I hate that."

"Right. I just don't know what else to call you. I won't do it anymore."

"Maybe you could just..." Charlie's voice broke. "Maybe you could drop the *step*."

Tom bent his head, the feeling so overwhelming it would've brought him to his knees if he hadn't already been there. He pulled Charlie into a hug, and the boy let him, and if it wasn't completely returned, it would be. Someday in the not-too-distant future, it would be, and Tom could wait.

From the floor, Melissa's face smiled up at him from its broken frame.

All this time, Tom realized in the ruins of the room, he thought he was staying so he could save Charlie.

It was the other way around. Charlie had given him a family, a purpose, a place.

In fact, it was Charlie who had saved *him*.

CHAPTER THIRTY

ON A BEAUTIFUL spring day, in front of the old maple tree where the swing still hung, Dad and Mrs. Johnson got married, and Mrs. J. became Mrs. H.

Jack was Honor's date for the event. "That makes me feel really gross," Jack said. "Like I'm Connor O'Rourke or something."

"I know. And we're not even twins, so we have no excuse," Honor said.

The reception was right there in the yard, as neither bride nor groom had wanted a fuss. Goggy wept loudly through the whole thing and repeated again and again that Mrs. Johnson was like a daughter to her (despite their two-decade rivalry over who made the better turkey on Thanksgiving, but it was a nice thought). Pops forgot about the wedding and had to be fetched from where he was crooning to the grapes. Faith twined some flowers in Mrs. J.'s hair, and Abby played the wedding march on her saxophone.

The ceremony was brief and beautiful.

As they sat down to the picnic lunch, Pru, as eldest, made the toast. "Dad, Mrs. J.— Hey, what should we call you, by the way? Anyway, I hope you're happy and have a great time discovering each other, you know what I'm saying, and, oh, gosh, I don't know, I guess we can't hope for more siblings, because that would be gross, and how old are you, anyway, Mrs. J.? It doesn't matter. Long life, happy times and great sex, you two."

"Wow, Mom," Abby said, pointing to her eyes. "Tears."

"So? Not everyone is great at public speaking," Prudence said, chugging some wine.

"Are you saying you're not great?" Ned asked.

"Honor, say something nicer than I did," Pru ordered. "These panty hose are riding where no man has gone before, can I say that?"

"Dear God," Levi murmured as Faith wheezed with laughter.

"Just fifteen months till I go to college," Abby said. "But who's counting?"

Honor stood and looked at her father, who was quite dapper in his suit, and Mrs. Johnson in her beautiful, elegant dress. "You two," she began, feeling a smile start in her heart. "Look at you. All these years, Mrs. Johnson, you've taken care of us. Cleaned for us, cooked for us, yelled at us. I can't remember a school concert or graduation you missed. And all these years, you watched Dad by himself, doing his best to be happy. But some people just aren't whole unless they have someone to love, and I think Dad's one of them." Dad wiped his eyes and kissed Mrs. J. "And, Dad, what a brave guy you are, daring to kiss Mrs. J. that first time when it must've seemed like she was going to bean you with a pot!"

"I was brave," Dad said. "Thanks for noticing."

Honor grinned. "So thank you, Dad, for picking such a great woman, and thank you, Mrs. J., for loving our father, and for being our second mother all these years."

"Hear, hear," said Jack, and Mrs. Johnson bustled

over and gave Honor a watery kiss. Then Abby put on her iPod, and Etta James's voice came over the speaker. "At Last." Indeed.

Cars drove by and honked their horns, as news of the wedding had been broadcast. Dad and Mrs. J. started dancing. Faith and Levi, Pru and Carl, Ned and Abby, Goggy and Pops, joined in, and when Jack sighed and stood up, extending his hand to Honor, she took it.

"I hate weddings," he said, stepping on her foot.

"Ouch. Are you sad because you can't be Mrs. Johnson's favorite anymore?"

"Why wouldn't I be her favorite anymore?"

"Um, because Dad is?"

"Oh, please. Mrs. J., am I still your favorite?" he called.

"Of course, Jackie, my darling boy!"

"See?" he said smugly, going to cut in on Dad.

Dad stepped in to dance with Honor. "How's my girl?" he said, putting his cheek next to hers, humming.

For a second, she remembered what it was like to be little, when her father would come home from the fields and pick her up to dance, how high she'd felt, how small her hand had seemed against his neck. How adored and safe she always felt. "I love you, Daddy."

"I love you, too, Petunia. My beautiful girl." He leaned back to look at her, his blue eyes kind. "How are you really?"

As in *Are you sobbing inside?*

"I'm fine," she said.

"I loved your toast," he murmured. "You might take your own advice, of course. Half of a whole and all that."

"I just ordered a husband on eBay," she said.

"I saw Tom the other day. I was under the impression he'd moved."

"Not that I know of."

"Any chance you might get back together?"

She stumbled a little. "Sorry. I don't know. I don't think so."

I don't love you.

"Whatever happens," Dad said, almost reading her thoughts, "you're the heart of this family, Honor."

The words were a gift, and Honor's eyes filled. She leaned her cheek against her father's shoulder and hugged him tight.

LATER, WHEN DAD and Mrs. J. had left for a night in the city before they'd go on to Jamaica for their honeymoon, when everyone else had gone home and the yard was tidied and the dishes were all done, Honor went to bed, and while she'd expected to be tormented with thoughts of Tom, she surprised herself by falling fast asleep.

She woke up abruptly. Glancing at the clock, she saw it was 2:41 a.m. But it seemed more like six, because the sun was rising in an orange glow. Maybe the power had flickered and the clock was wrong.

But then she heard it. A low roar, and before her brain had processed the sound, she was on her feet and at the window.

Three hundred yards away, the Old House was on fire.

Jeans. A heavy sweatshirt, shoes, a blanket. She'd already dialed 9-1-1 before she was conscious of reaching for her phone. "A house fire," she told the dispatcher as she ran down the stairs. "The Hollands' on Lake View Road."

Every stride, every footfall, was so clear. The sound of her breath rushing in and out of her lungs as she ran, the wool blanket wadded up under one arm like a football. The cool spring air.

The fire was a living creature, roaring, cracking, keening. The old saltbox, built in 1781, was a tinderbox, how many times had they said that? Why had Honor allowed her grandparents to stay there? This was bound to happen.

Pops was in the side yard, twenty feet from the kitchen door, on his knees, coughing, rocking back and forth as he tried to suck in air. Smoke inhalation, but he was alive. "Pops! Where's Goggy?" she said.

He pointed, tears streaming down his face, unable to speak.

She looked. Assessed. *You're the heart of this family.*

She could do it. She was calm, cool and collected, wasn't she? She got things done.

"Stay here. The fire department is on its way. I'll get her, Pops. I promise." She tossed him her phone, then ran, ignoring his choked cry for her to stop.

There were four entrances to the Old House: the kitchen door, most used and now engulfed in flame; the front door, which Pops had nailed shut last winter; the cellar door bulkhead; and the side door into the dining room. She headed for that last one, mentally calculating what she'd do.

Ladders? No. Jack had them up at his place; she saw them there just two nights ago when they were watching *Dermatological Nightmares*. Ladders were not an option.

She turned on the spigot for the hose, check. *Remember that intern who stitched up Tom?* her brain mused.

She said check, too. Oh, look, the tulips are blooming. Despite the thoughts that were tumbling through her head, she felt completely efficient and oddly calm. She doused the blanket with water and wrapped it around herself.

She looked up to the window and saw movement.

Her grandmother was still alive. And she was not going to die in a fire.

Not on Honor's watch.

In the distance, she could hear the sirens of the Manningsport Fire Department. Because they were a volunteer department, they'd have to go to the firehouse first to get to the trucks. Sure, some guys would come in their pickups, but they wouldn't have a hose or ladders. She'd seen it a bunch of times, the guys in their turnout gear, waiting for the engines.

Levi would be on his way as chief of police. Ned, too. Jessica Dunn, Kelly Matthews. Gerard Chartier, the big guy, would be the optimal person to save Goggy, a paramedic and firefighter with years of experience. But even as these thoughts were coming to her in laserlike clarity, Honor was inside the narrow side door.

She couldn't afford to wait.

She'd never been in a burning building before. Pausing for a microsecond, she looked at it. The fire, beautiful and terrifying, devoured the kitchen walls, thick smoke making the room seem far away. The sound was shocking, the whooshing roar of the fire's hunger, the cracks and pops.

Hurry, Honor.

It was her mother's voice.

Through the dining room toward the front hall, where hopefully the fire hadn't reached the stairs. The taste of smoke was acrid and oily. So much to fuel the fire—Pops's wine magazines, Goggy's boxes of patterns, Great-Gran's sideboard. Into the living room, and her clothes were hot, God, it really was like an oven, just like people always said. The smoke was thick, cutting visibility to almost nothing, and Honor crashed into the side of the couch, coughing, then hit the wall. The photo of Dad and Mom's wedding. The six-year-old calendar of the Greek Isles, too beautiful to take down, Goggy said.

The fire roared, and Honor couldn't help feeling awed.

Like so many colonials, the Old House had a door to every room, so that drafts could be contained. Honor groped for the door that led to the stairs, found it. The knob was already warm.

Close the door behind you.

Good advice. She obeyed, going up the stairs, her breath short, throat burning from smoke, eyes streaming. Steam rose from the blanket as she ran charged up, and why did Goggy have to live upstairs, huh? But no need to panic, hadn't Kate Winslet saved an old lady, too? If she could do it, so could Honor. Then again, that woman had weighed maybe a hundred pounds. Goggy was sturdier stock. But this was her grandmother. She was not going to burn to death. Nuh-uh.

Honor went through the door at the top of the stairs, pulling it closed behind her. Her throat was tight and dry and hot. "Goggy!" she called. The croak in her voice was not reassuring.

The upstairs bedrooms were connected by doors, rather than a hallway. Honor went into the first room, the lilac room where she used to sleep with Faith on those rare occasions when Mom and Dad went out of town. Goggy's bedroom was in the back, over the dining room where Honor had come in, across from the back stairs that led to the kitchen.

The kitchen, which was already engulfed. And if Honor had seen the fire in the kitchen from the dining room, that meant the door hadn't been closed. And the dining room was where their exit was.

Not good.

She felt the door that connected the two rooms. It was warm, but maybe not hot. "Goggy!" She choked and coughed, unable to get anything but smoke in her lungs. Tried the doorknob.

It was locked.

It occurred to her for the first time that she could die here. In fact, there was an excellent possibility of it. Her father would never get over it. She'd never see Faith as a mother; she wouldn't see Abby graduate or Ned get married. Jack would be devastated and Pru would never be the same.

She crouched down. The air was a bit better here.

You have about a minute.

"Goggy! I'm here!"

Oh, please, God. Please, Mom.

Then the door opened, and there was her grandmother, coughing, her hair wild.

"Come on," Honor said. She threw the blanket over Goggy's head and shoulders. Goggy's face was wet with tears, and she was choking without stop. "We're getting out," Honor wheezed. "We're not dying this way." Grabbing Goggy's hand, she pulled her back through the lilac room.

There was a crash somewhere very near. The kitchen

ceiling was collapsing. Almost like a movie playing in her head, Honor could picture it. The seconds had slowed to hours, and her mind was strangely clear.

She opened the door to the front staircase. "Hold on to me," she told her grandmother.

Close the door, honey.

Honor did. The front staircase was clearer than the lilac room, and breathing was slightly easier. Goggy was still coughing, hard. Down the front stairs they went, Goggy's hands on Honor's shoulders as the fire taunted them with its high-pitched, crackling laugh.

If the front door hadn't been nailed shut, they'd be out right now, running across the lawn, sucking in the sweet, clean spring air.

But it was. She tried it just in case, banged on it, yanked it, kicked it, but it opened inward, and Pops had done a good job of making sure it wouldn't blow open again. Another kick. Another. The door didn't budge.

Her phone was with Pops.

"Help us!" she yelled, doubting that anyone could hear her over the roar of the fire.

"Okay, we have to make a run for it," she said to Goggy. Maybe the fire department would be there to help them. Please. Maybe she could break a window if they couldn't get to the dining room door, though the twelve-over-twelve panes would make that hard. "Keep the blanket over your head and hold my hand."

"Go without me," Goggy said, coughing. "Go, honey."

Honor looked into her eyes. "No. We can make it. We're Holland women. Okay? I'm not leaving you. Now are you ready?"

Goggy gripped her hand. "Yes."

Honor opened the door.

A wall of smoke and flame greeted her, and she yanked it shut again, shoving Goggy back onto the stairs.

That's when the roof fell in.

CHAPTER THIRTY-ONE

TOM COULD NOT sleep.

His entire body hummed with adrenaline.

Charlie would be all right. Charlie was going to be just fine, in fact. Tom had brought him back to the Kelloggs' house after dinner. "I'll see you soon," he said.

"Yeah," Charlie said. "That'd be good." He hesitated, then leaned over and hugged Tom. "Thanks," he whispered, then ran into the house.

Tom sat there another minute and had to wipe his eyes. Maybe Charlie could come live with him. Or maybe there were some good things about him living with Melissa's parents. Maybe seeing Tom a few times a week would be enough.

He'd wait and see. For now, he'd be content.

Charlie would be fine. That wasn't why Tom was awake.

Honor was the reason for that.

The fire siren went off three blocks over. Lonely sound, that.

And yes, he was lonely. Oh, he had friends enough here in this little town, Colleen and Connor, Droog. He had the kids in the boxing club, Dr. Didier, who now used him regularly to spot her, and even Levi Cooper, who'd bought him a beer the other night, despite the fact that Levi was Honor's brother-in-law.

But he missed *her*. Her gentle voice, her way of thinking before speaking, the feel of her mouth, her hands, her hair.

God, he had it bad.

It had been twenty-two days since he broke her heart. Eight since he'd seen her at O'Rourke's. Roughly one hundred and eighty-six hours since he'd seen her, five hundred and twenty-eight since he'd kissed her in that soul-wrenching encounter in the cask room, since he told her he didn't love her.

Idiot.

Liar.

Without further thought, he rolled out of bed and pulled on some clothes. Her father would probably strangle him on sight, and more power to him; he'd do the same thing if he had a daughter who was jerked around by some prat foreigner.

Nevertheless.

But perhaps a phone call was in order.

Her voice mail picked up. It was 2:50 a.m., after all.

"It's Tom," he said. "I miss you. I love you. I'm on my way to see you right now, so if your father has a gun, please talk him down, and tell Ratty not to attack me. I love you, did I mention that?" He paused. "And I'm sorry, Honor."

Then he went downstairs, grabbed his keys and headed for the car.

He didn't think much of it when the first pickup truck passed him, the flashing blue light indicating one of Manningsport's volunteer firefighters.

But when a second, and then a third, vehicle flew by him, all heading in the same direction he was, up the Hill, cold dread suddenly sat in the passenger seat next to him, certain and unwavering.

Honor was in trouble.

He floored it.

The glow told him what waited ahead. Flashing red lights against an evil orange flicker, a herd of vehicles on the lawn of the grandparents' house, people milling around, water arcing onto the roof of what appeared to be a massive ball of flame, once the Old House.

Please, God, the grands made it out.

An old man with a fire police vest was waving him over, but Tom veered around him, ignoring his shouts. Into the driveway, onto the lawn, behind the other cars and trucks, a police cruiser.

Only two fire trucks. Shit.

Levi Cooper was there, yelling into the radio. There was Honor's grandfather. Faith was on her knees, sobbing.

Then part of the roof collapsed in a great cloud of smoke and sparks.

Tom wasn't aware he was running until someone grabbed him.

Brogan Cain, dressed in firefighting gear.

"Where is she?" Tom asked.

"I'm so sorry," he said, his eyes wet.

"Why aren't you in there?"

"It's too dangerous. The fire chief called us back."

"Is Honor inside?"

Brogan face crumpled in answer. Tom ran, but Brogan grabbed him, pulling him back. "You can't, Tom! It's too dangerous. And it's too late."

Then Brogan's head jerked back and he fell, and Tom's hand was vaguely stinging. Shouts followed him across the lawn, and the heat slammed into him as he got close to the house.

Fire twisted and leaped out of all the front windows, roaring with glee. The back of the house was gone, a pile of burning rubble. Tom could see the refrigerator.

Jesus.

His skin drew tight from the heat, and the air in his throat was ground glass, too hot to breathe.

He grabbed the front door handle and tried it, smelling something odd. The latch clicked down, but the door didn't budge. He took a step back, kicked the door, once, twice. There was a tremendous crash from above. From the corner of his eye, he saw a firefighter running toward him, to pull him away, no doubt.

Tom noticed that his clothes were smoking.

The third kick did it.

DEATH BY SMOKE inhalation or fire…very low on Honor's list of ways to go. Freezing to death had always sounded peaceful. She imagined a coma would be okay, too, so long as the incident that preceded it wasn't too violent.

But not this.

The smoke would kill them soon…if the flames didn't.

It was hotter now, and Goggy was fading. "Goggy?" she said. "Stay with me, okay? I'm scared. I need you." *Stay with us, Mommy.*

Goggy squeezed her hand.

Dad. Faith, Pru, Jack, Abby and Ned. Mrs. J.

Tom.

Her heart gave an enormous throb, and she was so glad, then, that she'd been in love, had known what it was like to truly love someone, to have had that small time when it seemed like they'd work out. What a gift it had been, to love Tom, to feel loved in return.

And then the door exploded inward, and she and Goggy jumped, and he was there. Tom stood there, then reached for them, and his hand was sticky. He pulled them up and out, and the air, it was so cool and sweet, and maybe she had just died, and this was heaven, but if so, where was Mom?

You made it, honey.

Then she was crying and choking, and firefighters swarmed around them, people were yelling, and then Pops was there, and he pulled Goggy into his arms; he was sobbing, and Levi, and Faith! Oh, Faithie was crying, too, grabbing on to her, and Levi guided both of them to an ambulance, and there was Jessica Dunn, looking beautiful even in fire gear as she smiled and wiped her eyes.

Kelly Matthews put an oxygen mask to her face, and Honor inhaled gratefully, choked and inhaled some more, her chest burning. Pops gripped her hand, kissed it. "Thank you," he said, still crying. "Thank you, my angel."

"You get to go to the hospital," Kelly said with a smile. "You kick-ass woman, you."

The rest was a blur—a gurney, Gerard, sooty and smiling. Ned, her sweet, beautiful nephew, eyes wet, a grin on his face. The ambulance ride—her first. Lordy, she was tired! Jack was waiting at the E.R., and so was Jeremy Lyon, bless his heart, who kissed her cheek and held her hand. The doctors, fire chief and Levi alternately lectured her about foolishly running into a burning building and praised her for bravely running into a burning building.

Goggy was doing fine; also being treated for smoke inhalation. Pops, too, refusing to leave his wife's side.

"Where's Tom?" Honor asked. Her voice didn't sound like her own.

"He's here," Faith said, still hiccuping with sobs. "He came in someone's truck." Then she held up her phone. "It's Dad. I called him five minutes ago, and they're on their way home. Say hi. He doesn't believe you're okay."

"I'm okay, Daddy," Honor said, and her father burst into tears.

"My brave, brave girl," he wept.

All Honor really wanted was a nap.

And Tom.

But the doctors wouldn't leave her alone, and she had to have tests and oxygen and then she was asleep.

When she woke up, it was much quieter. She was in a regular hospital room, not the E.R., wearing a johnny coat. Light spilled in from the hall.

And Tom was there, sitting in a chair by her bedside. "Hallo," he said, and her eyes filled with tears.

"Thank you for saving my life," she whispered. "Again."

"Thank you for taking twenty years off mine," he said. "Again. I'll be dead in a month if this keeps up." He reached down and picked something up. Spike. "Say hallo, Ratty."

Spike wriggled onto the bed, whimpering in joy, and climbed up Honor's chest to lick her face. Her tears, specifically. She gave a watery smile, then frowned. "What happened to your hands?" she asked Tom. They were both bandaged.

"I burned them on the door handle."

She winced. "Sorry."

"Oh, for Christ's sake. It was worth it. Now move over." He lowered the side rail of her bed and climbed in with her, the mattress creaking under his weight. "And put this back on, and don't take it off again."

He slid her engagement ring onto her finger.

"Tom," she began.

"Shush," he said, and much to her astonishment, his eyes filled with tears. "You're marrying me. That's the end of it."

The words made her heart ache in a bittersweet swell. "That's very sweet," she whispered. "And I'm sure I scared the life out of you, but you don't have to—"

"Check your phone messages. I was way ahead of your dramatics."

"What do you mean?"

He smoothed her hair back with one bandaged hand. "It means I didn't need to almost lose you to realize that I love you, Honor."

Ratty—er, Spike—licked some more tears, as they seemed to be flowing out of her, then turned to bite Tom's hand.

He smiled, that goofy, crooked, sweet smile that made her heart stutter with love, and she found that she was smiling back. "Say yes, miss."

"What was the question again?"

His smile grew. "Will you marry me? For no reason this time, other than the fact that I can't live without you and will probably die of misery if you don't."

"In that case, I guess I have no choice."

He leaned in and kissed her. "I'll take that as a yes."

EPILOGUE

Eighteen months later

THE AUDITORIUM WAS extremely crowded, loud and didn't smell so great. Then again, it didn't smell so bad, either. Honor was pretty used to it by now.

"Do you need anything, darling? All set? Hungry?"

"I'm fine, Tom. Sit down. You're making me nervous."

"Yeah. Good idea." He didn't sit down. He did bend down and give her a kiss, however, then resumed pacing.

"I'm afraid to sit down," Goggy said, sitting down, anyway. "The germs in here! Do they clean it every day, do you think?"

"I don't know, Goggy."

"They should've held this at the activity center at Rushing Creek," the old lady said. "Much cleaner." Not that the activity center was big enough, but yes, Goggy and Pops had moved into the "asylum," a month after the Old House fire, and they loved it there. Pops flirted with "those trashy sixtysomethings," according to Goggy, and still showed up to check the vines every day. Goggy took up swimming in the Olympic-size pool and had yet to drown, and no one got food poisoning, though Goggy came up to the New House at least twice a week to cook and fight with Mrs. Johnson (who was still called just that, despite her marital status).

Today, the entire Holland clan had come out for the big event, front row seats, of course. Even Abby had come home from NYU, looking incredibly glamorous with her new bangs and leather jacket. Ned was flirting with Sarah Cooper, Levi's little sister, much to Levi's chagrin. Faith and Levi held hands and smooched occasionally, their toddler son asleep in the stroller. Even the Kelloggs had come, too, and while Janice still stared at Tom like she wanted to smear him with butter, well, it was nice for Charlie.

"Drink this," Mrs. Johnson said, handing her a thermos and patting Spike's head. "You need to stay hydrated. It's cucumber water. Very healthful and delicious."

"How's my grandchild?" Dad asked, rubbing Honor's tummy. "Hello in there! Grandpa can't wait to meet you!"

Yep, she was pregnant. Four and a half months, and already totally in love with the little thumper inside of her, and dying to find out if it was a boy or a girl. But they wanted to wait to find out. Old-school.

Six months after the wedding, Charlie had asked Tom if he could come live with them at the New House. The Kelloggs put up a little resistance at first (what would their friends think?), but it was only a token. Everyone, including Charlie, knew that Janice and Walter really didn't want the responsibility of raising him the rest of the way.

Tom did. So did Honor.

Mitchell DeLuca was more problematic, hanging up when Tom had called him, putting a heavy guilt trip on

Charlie via text. Tom's plan had been to drive to Philly and beat the snot out of him, but Honor invited Mitchell to the New House for dinner instead. Made Goggy's ham and salt potatoes and Mrs. Johnson's pineapple upside-down cake, and wrung a promise out of Tom that he'd stay cool and let her handle things. She told Mitchell simply that, while no one could ever take his place in Charlie's life, she and Tom both loved Charlie, could give him stability and an extended family, and that Mitchell was welcome to visit or have Charlie visit any time he liked. Then she stared him down, waiting until he said yes.

Which he did. She was good at that sort of thing.

And when Mitchell left, Tom held her tight and said that he loved her more than he knew it was possible to love anyone, and thank God they were married, because he'd be lost without her.

So it was that five years almost to the day after his mother met Tom Barlow, Charlie came to live in the New House. He was quiet and horribly sloppy, his grades were mediocre, his taste in music hadn't improved. And clearly, he loved Tom. And her, even if he never said the actual words.

And now, a baby. She couldn't wait to see her child's face. Couldn't wait to see Tom's when he held their little one for the first time, couldn't wait to see Charlie as a big brother.

"They're starting," Tom said, sitting down next to her. She took his hand, which was damp with sweat.

"He'll be great," she said.

Tom gave her a rueful smile, then rubbed the back of his neck. "I might be having a heart attack," he said.

"Me, too."

"Which one is Charlie?" Goggy asked, squinting.

"Why won't you get glasses?" Pops asked.

"I don't need them. You're the one who's blind as a bat."

Dad leaned forward and gave Tom's shoulder a squeeze. "Good luck," he said.

The bell rang. "Go, Charlie!" Abby bellowed. "You can do it, buddy!"

The rules of the Western New York Regional Junior Golden Gloves Competition stated that Charlie would have to go three rounds, each lasting ninety seconds. He'd won the first two fights—this was the championship match. Unfortunately, his opponent looked like Oscar de la Hoya and the Incredible Hulk rolled into one, seeming to outweigh Charlie by fifty pounds. Tom said that wasn't possible, but it sure looked that way to Honor.

The longest two hundred and seventy seconds of her life, Honor bet, gnawing on her thumbnail. She almost couldn't watch.

But, of course, she did, flinching every time the other kid landed a hit. Tom was on his feet yelling encouragement, "Come on, Charlie, that's it, mate, get out of there, move away, almost there, bring it home, lad!"

Honor, too, jolted to her feet. "Hands up," she yelled. "Get in there, Charlie!"

The entire Holland clan was screaming by the end, and when the referee held up Charlie's arm, proclaiming him the winner, they just went wild.

Then Charlie, who was staggering with fatigue, went to the ropes and waved for Tom to join him.

Tom froze for a second, then turned to Honor. "I love you," he said. It was something he told her at least five times a day, something that still made her heart squeeze. It always would, she knew. He bent down and kissed her stomach. "And I love you, baby," he said.

Then he was off, into the ring to join their son.

* * * * *

ACKNOWLEDGMENTS

At Maria Carvainis Agency, Inc., thanks to the Boss, Chelsea Gilmore, Martha Guzman and Elizabeth Copps. How lucky I am to have you all in my corner!

At Harlequin, thanks so much to everyone who works so hard on my behalf, especially Margaret O'Neill Marbury, Susan Swinwood, Kate Dresser, Tara Parsons, Michelle Renaud and Leonore Waldrip.

Kim Castillo at Author's Best Friend and Sarah Burningham at Little Bird Publicity help me in so many ways, it would be impossible to enumerate them all, and in addition to that, they're both the loveliest people imaginable.

Thanks to Kyle Bennett, aka Cute Boxing Trainer, for whipping my butt into shape while teaching me about the elegant sport of boxing. I appreciate the pain and suffering! Thanks also to Jennifer from United States Citizenship and Immigration Services (who is nothing like Bethany in the book). Any mistakes or exaggerations are all mine. To Hank Robinson, my second father, thanks for advising me on aeronautics and engineering. Love you! To my brother Mike Higgins, owner of Litchfield Hills Wine Market, thanks for help with all things vine-related. To my mom, who proofreads my stuff and laughed so hard over Droog Dragul, thanks, Mommy!

In the Finger Lakes region of New York, thanks to the helpful, wonderful people at Finger Lakes Wine Country and Steuben County Conference & Visitors Bureau, and especially to Sayre Fulkerson and John Iszard at Fulkerson Winery and Kitty Oliver at Heron Hill Vineyard.

In the world of writers, I am blessed with many friends, as that world seems populated with the nicest and most generous people imaginable. Thanks especially to Jill Shalvis, Robyn Carr, Susan Andersen, Huntley Fitzpatrick, Shaunee Cole, Karen Pinco, Jennifer Iszkiewicz and Kelly Matthews for their love, laughter and support.

Thanks to the love of my life, Terence Keenan, and our two beautiful children, who bring me endless joy, happiness and laughs…well, heck. I love you more than I can say.

And thank you, readers, for the privilege of spending some time with my book. That honor never fades.

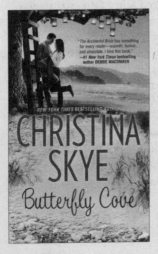

New York Times bestselling author

KRISTAN HIGGINS

Lucy Lang isn't looking for fireworks...

She's looking for a nice, decent man. Someone who'll mow the lawn, flip chicken on the barbecue, teach their future children to play soccer. But most important: someone who won't inspire the slightest stirring in her heart…or anywhere else. A young widow, Lucy can't risk that kind of loss again. But sharing her life with a cat named Fat Mikey and the Black Widows at the family bakery isn't enough either. So it's goodbye to Ethan, her hot but entirely inappropriate "friend with privileges," and hello to a man she can marry.

Too bad Ethan Mirabelli isn't going anywhere. As far as he's concerned, what she needs might be right under her nose. But can he convince her that the next best thing can really be forever?

Available wherever books are sold!

Be sure to connect with us at:
Harlequin.com/Newsletters
Facebook.com/HarlequinBooks
Twitter.com/HarlequinBooks

HARLEQUIN® HQN™
™ www.Harlequin.com

PHKH734

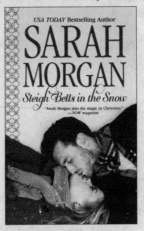

There's nowhere better to spend the holidays than with *New York Times* bestselling author

SUSAN MALLERY

in the town of Fool's Gold, where love is always waiting to be unwrapped...

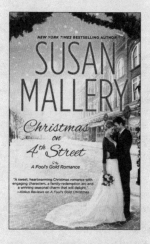

Available now wherever books are sold!

"Susan Mallery is one of my favorites."
—#1 *New York Times* bestselling author Debbie Macomber

www.SusanMallery.com

REQUEST YOUR FREE BOOKS!

2 FREE NOVELS
FROM THE ROMANCE COLLECTION
PLUS 2 FREE GIFTS!

YES! Please send me 2 FREE novels from the Romance Collection and my 2 FREE gifts (gifts are worth about $10). After receiving them, if I don't wish to receive any more books, I can return the shipping statement marked "cancel." If I don't cancel, I will receive 4 brand-new novels every month and be billed just $6.24 per book in the U.S. or $6.74 per book in Canada. That's a savings of at least 22% off the cover price. It's quite a bargain! Shipping and handling is just 50¢ per book in the U.S. and 75¢ per book in Canada.* I understand that accepting the 2 free books and gifts places me under no obligation to buy anything. I can always return a shipment and cancel at any time. Even if I never buy another book, the two free books and gifts are mine to keep forever.

194/394 MDN F4XY

Name _____ (PLEASE PRINT) _____

Address _____ Apt. # _____

City _____ State/Prov. _____ Zip/Postal Code _____

Signature (if under 18, a parent or guardian must sign)

Mail to the Harlequin® Reader Service:
IN U.S.A.: P.O. Box 1867, Buffalo, NY 14240-1867
IN CANADA: P.O. Box 609, Fort Erie, Ontario L2A 5X3

Want to try two free books from another line?
Call 1-800-873-8635 or visit www.ReaderService.com.

* Terms and prices subject to change without notice. Prices do not include applicable taxes. Sales tax applicable in N.Y. Canadian residents will be charged applicable taxes. Offer not valid in Quebec. This offer is limited to one order per household. Not valid for current subscribers to the Romance Collection or the Romance/Suspense Collection. All orders subject to credit approval. Credit or debit balances in a customer's account(s) may be offset by any other outstanding balance owed by or to the customer. Please allow 4 to 6 weeks for delivery. Offer available while quantities last.

Your Privacy—The Harlequin® Reader Service is committed to protecting your privacy. Our Privacy Policy is available online at www.ReaderService.com or upon request from the Harlequin Reader Service.

We make a portion of our mailing list available to reputable third parties that offer products we believe may interest you. If you prefer that we not exchange your name with third parties, or if you wish to clarify or modify your communication preferences, please visit us at www.ReaderService.com/consumerschoice or write to us at Harlequin Reader Service Preference Service, P.O. Box 9062, Buffalo, NY 14269. Include your complete name and address.

ROM13R

HIGGINS   Higgins, Kristan,
           author.

           The perfect match.

$7.99

DATE			